THE PILGRIM'S RULES
OF ETIQUETTE

Also by Taghi Modarressi

THE BOOK OF ABSENT PEOPLE

THE

Pilgrim's Rules

OF

Etiquette

TAGHI MODARRESSI

Doubleday

NEW YORK LONDON TORONTO SYDNEY AUCKLAND

PUBLISHED BY DOUBLEDAY
a division of Bantam Doubleday Dell Publishing Group, Inc.
666 Fifth Avenue, New York, New York 10103

DOUBLEDAY and the portrayal of an anchor with a dolphin
are trademarks of Doubleday, a division of
Bantam Doubleday Dell Publishing Group, Inc.

Library of Congress Cataloging-in-Publication Data

Modarressi, Taghi.
The Pilgrim's rules of etiquette / by Taghi Modarressi.—1st ed.
p. cm.
ISBN 0-385-23879-7
I. Title.
PS3563.O26P55 1989
813.54—dc20 89-31497
CIP

All Rights Reserved
Printed in the United States of America
August 1989
Designed by Ann Gold
First Edition
BG

My thanks to Alma Troccolie
for helping me prepare the
English version of this novel.

THE PILGRIM'S RULES OF ETIQUETTE

O N E

This time Hadi Besharat would write the letter on onionskin paper. He would put it in one of those special airmail envelopes that have an aboveboard appearance. Maybe then the officials wouldn't be suspicious. Maybe the letter would reach Professor Humphrey and he would answer. Surely they were censoring Hadi Besharat's mail or even throwing it away. It couldn't take more than two weeks for a featherweight letter to reach America.

Oh, Lord, how many years had it been since their last meeting? His arithmetic wasn't up to that! The months and years were beyond him. A black, endless void had fallen between them and somehow transformed time itself. He grew dizzy just thinking about it. In the mirror of his mind, in the bottom of the tunnel of years past, Professor Humphrey's face kept repeating itself and backing away.

He couldn't remember now exactly what year he had gone to America. As best he could recall, he'd returned to Iran from his first trip around Christmas of 1969. Or maybe he was mistaken. Maybe that was his second trip. In those days the newspapers were reporting extensively on the Vietnam War; yet Woolfy Humphrey's letters still reached his father regularly from Khe Sanh.

Whenever it was, Hadi Besharat remembered that the night

before his departure Professor Humphrey had taken him home for dinner and given him the antique magic lantern as a Christmas present. The moment they entered the study Hadi Besharat's eyes had fallen on the four brass angels grouped around the lantern. The angels lifted their faces to the sky and prepared to blow their trumpets. With extraordinary care, Professor Humphrey bent forward and lit the candle beneath each angel. Then he stepped back and a nervous smile stretched his face—a smile like that of a surgeon behind a mask, or a thief behind a nylon stocking. Perhaps he didn't know quite what to do with Hadi Besharat, who had drawn himself up to his full five feet five inches and was gazing at Professor Humphrey with his black, shining eyes like a cat in a trance.

At first slowly and hesitantly, then quickly and gleefully, the angels started chasing each other and their shadows fluttered on the wall. Professor Humphrey burst into laughter and took Hadi Besharat's arm. They went into the dining room to eat supper.

Professor Humphrey's wife was away for the evening, so they were free to discuss their favorite subjects to their hearts' content. Professor Humphrey wanted to hear who had been the most influential people in Hadi Besharat's education. Hadi Besharat mentioned his high school history and geography teacher, Fakhr Zanjani. He didn't know where to begin or what to say that would give Professor Humphrey the best example of Fakhr Zanjani's manner. He thought of his teacher's huge, bony body and the clumsy way he walked, dwarfing everybody around him like Frankenstein's monster. There was something unkempt and yet delicate about him. He wore a green tie that looked as though he kept it on even when sleeping. His crumpled dusty suit seemed never to have been pressed.

He remembered the afternoon that he and his classmate, Hushang Gharib, went with Fakhr Zanjani to the Tehran Theater to borrow costumes for their play about the prophet Mani. It was raining so hard that even inside the theater office water kept running down their faces. Fakhr Zanjani sat on a chair like a drowned mouse, the rain dripping from his big, loose galoshes onto the threadbare rug, while he sharpened his Alligator brand pencil with a pocketknife.

But the moment Fakhr Zanjani stepped into the theater's storage room his mood changed. First he closed the door in the theater attendant's face. As soon as he heard the attendant's retreating footsteps, he opened the door and shouted into the corridor, "Many thanks! Much honor to you! May your kindness last forever!" Then he closed the door again. With his hands clasped behind his back, he walked among the costumes from different historical periods. He passed his hand over the statue of Alexander the Macedonian. He stuck his head out of a window in Haroun El Rashid's castle. On the banks of the Tigris the famous ode, "Lo, you learning heart . . ." flowed across his tongue. He tried on Churchill's frock coat. He put Napoleon III's cocked hat on his head. He continued this aimless fidgeting until he grew tired. Finally he sat down on Louis XVI's couch and ordered Hadi Besharat and Hushang Gharib to leave the storage room. For three quarters of an hour they waited in fear until Fakhr Zanjani emerged and showed them Bahram I's hand-warming stone. With a trembling finger he pointed to the royal seal on the stone. "This design dates from a period before the Sassanid Empire. It dates from the Dylmon Empire period. Perhaps Mani brought it from Babylon or Lagash or Sippar as a gift for Bahram I."

"Fakhr Zanjani could estimate the stone's age just by touching it," Hadi Besharat told Professor Humphrey. "When we asked him how, he recited this poem by Rumi:

" 'With the next fit, I'll die from being human.
I'll grow angel wings and feathers.
Once again, I'll soar above the angels
And I'll become that which is beyond imagining. . . .' "

The Pilgrim's Rules of Etiquette

"Are you saying that Mani held this stone while he traveled to the world of light?" Professor Humphrey asked.

Hadi Besharat touched his napkin to his lips and said, "When you held the stone for a little while, a window would open in your mind and you'd be connected to a world that was centuries away."

"I understand. That is a Gnostic belief. Because we're only travelers in this world, we've lost our origins and we have to return to the world of light."

"We have to return to the world of counterparts—a world of people and events exactly like ours. The mirror image of our world, except that this world is not here; it's somewhere else. That is what the late Fakhr Zanjani believed."

Hadi Besharat put down his knife and fork. He glanced around the dining room. The curved bay window faced the orchard, and the winter snow lay on the pine trees like sugar crystals. The walls met overhead at a sharp angle, making the dining room resemble an upended sailboat. He felt he hadn't given an adequate description of Fakhr Zanjani. Waiting for the right words, he turned his head and paused. Then he said, "Fakhr Zanjani believed that if you held that stone in your hand and touched its smooth, polished surface a window would open in your mind because your palm is a mirror. As soon as you touched the stone, it would light the world of counterparts for you."

Professor Humphrey stared at him for a moment. Then he changed the subject and talked about the last moments of Mani's life and his hanging. He wanted to prove that Mani's hour of death had occurred at around sunset on the Monday that corresponds to the first of February in the Roman calendar. However, the scrolls in the Parthian language that are found in Turfan refer to this Monday as the fourth of Shahrivar in the Persian calendar.

They finished their dinner and in the cold of winter they went to the orchard for a walk. Hadi Besharat felt as if they were in a monastery chapel listening to the hum of the votive candles' teardrops. They walked through the orchard's corridors like two medieval monks. Outside the dining room's bay window they looked in at the roses arching over the table in an innocent, proud gesture. The dingdong of the cathedral's astronomical clock caressed their thoughts. They admired the moon and the stars rotating across the clock's face. It was late. They returned to the study and now they had to say their good-byes. The magic lantern's candles had burned to the roots and the shadows were no longer circling the walls. Hadi Besharat felt he had disappeared. He felt he had shaken his sleeves free of both worlds. Under these circumstances, it wasn't appropriate to say goodbye. They shook hands and bowed to each other. That was all.

Where was Professor Humphrey now? How was he occupying his mind? What Manichaean text was he studying and what branch of Gnostic theology? Hadi Besharat had no idea.

What a strange land, America! Skyscrapers that stretched their heads upward to Capella. Each street passing between the buildings like a telephone cable. When Hadi Besharat wanted to look at the top of a building, he had to hold tight to his beret so it wouldn't fall off. In that unfamiliar city his heart felt clouded and the memory of his homeland drove him mad. Late at night he sat by the window to catch the fresh breeze and stare at the naked pavement. The First National Bank Building shone on the horizon like a new car, and its reflection fell upon St. Peter Street. Tired buses and sleepy people moved slowly like distant memories. Steam twisted into the air from the manholes. A police car cruised the back alleys with its red light spinning like someone delirious.

After three trips he still hadn't figured out how to live in America. How to come to terms with life. Continuously he shifted his legs, took baths, changed clothes, and every day wrote a silly, pointless letter to his wife Farangu and Khosro, his son. Professor Humphrey teased him about his foreignness. He asked, "In a strange country where you don't know the language well, what would you say if you didn't understand what someone said to you?"

Hadi Besharat smiled condescendingly and asked, "What would *you* say?"

Professor Humphrey shrugged. He pursed his lips and then answered, "I would say, 'Is that true? Really?'"

"I would say, 'How nice. How right you are.'"

"There you have the difference between the Westerner and the Easterner."

Professor Humphrey had urged him to stay in America for good. Initially Hadi Besharat was evasive, and then finally he said his staying would be like the quince-orange tree and the mule. Professor Humphrey chuckled, "No one is as funny as the Iranians!" He lifted his gold-rimmed glasses over his tear-filled eyes and blond eyebrows. He kicked up his feet in a manner unsuitable to his high forehead and ironed hair. He took a fresh breath and said in his American accent, "Hadi, Hadi, what quince-orange tree? What mule?"

He laughed again, but this time in a more dignified way. His face was so closely shaved that it looked powdered. Hadi Besharat didn't understand his strange behavior. Nevertheless, he answered with utmost seriousness. "To be sure, there are common features between the Easterner and the Westerner, and in certain respects each can benefit the other. But in the end their encounters remain barren. It's like the quince-orange tree, which is a graft between a quince and an orange, or the mule, which is the result of horse-and-donkey copulation. Of course each has some use. But they themselves are barren and fruitless."

Professor Humphrey drew his head back in another short burst of laughter, but meanwhile, through the window, he followed the traffic with a watchful eye.

Despite all that had happened, Hadi Besharat missed Professor Humphrey very much. He should practice his Syriac more. If someday he chanced to pass through Whitehurst College again, he could recite some hymns in Syriac for Professor Humphrey.

Day by day reduces
The number of souls below
As they are distilled and piled up. . . .

At Whitehurst College he would work on the translation of the *Book of Giants,* the introduction to *Masbuta,* and the article on the Nahashbat Angel. He would pay a visit to the W. B. Henning Study Hall, which was named in honor of the late professor. What a high ceiling it had! In the center of the ceiling was some interesting plasterwork which differed from the plasterwork in Iran. Instead of flowers, plants, and arabesques, it showed a naked man and woman with their heads lowered, running in some direction. The center aisle of the library stretched between two rows of chalk columns. The ceiling arched over the columns like eagles' wings, sweeping down on both sides with a solemnity that forced Hadi Besharat into silence, or at least made him speak very quietly. Round and round the ceiling's border, a thick jungle of entangled paintings showed a new pattern with every glance. Among the plaster branches and leaves was painted a row of Mani's writings. The Manichaean believers in their fezlike white hats, like the figures on a deck of cards, sat ear to ear. Each of them held a pen and wrote on a scroll. Hadi Besharat felt elated just looking at them.

The bird of his imagination grew wings and he remembered the photograph of the basilica at Porta Maggiore that Professor Humphrey had taken on his trip to Italy. The professor used to say that he had come across important historical evidence on the origins of the basilica and he planned to write an article very soon. Except he kept procrastinating, kept rubbing his hands, and then the state of affairs changed drastically and no news came from him any longer. Not a single piece of news, not a single trace. The earth had opened its mouth and swallowed Professor Humphrey whole.

That afternoon Hadi Besharat was busy in his study translating *The Death of a Great Savior.* He told himself again that he must write another letter to his old friend. Perhaps this time it would reach him and he would answer. But the February cold was merciless. He had to light the little heater, and while he waited for the room to warm up he stood in front of the window. The sun passed through the curtains that his wife Farangu had hung, turning the checkered pattern to orange. An orange glow spread over the antique objects, the photographs on the walls, and the books on the desk. He felt so alone that life's breath seemed about to leave him. After all, every human being needs someone who will listen to his words and take them to heart. But Hadi Besharat's specialty was distant, obscure historical events, and who wanted to listen to those?

Who had the patience to sit for hours while he told the story of Mani, for example—an Iranian prophet who wandered the world seventeen centuries ago converting people to his strange and complicated religion? Eventually Mani was hanged from the city gates in Jundishapur by order of the Sassanid king, Bahram I. For centuries he was forgotten. Nothing remained of his theories of good and evil, or his propositions about the worlds of light and darkness. Sweet is his memory! Except for Professor Humphrey, no one else to Hadi Besharat's knowledge had read all the ancient Manichaean and Mandaean texts. The professor alone could speak those dead languages like a native without referring to rare encyclopedias and the reference books of the Library of Congress. He and Hadi Besharat used to go to City Park, find a pleasant, shady corner, and talk for hours without stopping. Hadi Besharat explained to Professor Humphrey that the human being is an extra fruit in the basket of this world, constantly struggling to clear a space for himself. The only thing that prevents him from slipping and falling is others' need of his compassion. In this forlorn life a man should be a source of hope for others.

During Hadi Besharat's lectures the students' eyes grew wide with wonder. While they were listening to his stories they totally forgot him. Then he felt he was not among them. He grew lightweight with his lack of presence and he felt they couldn't see him. The details of the Marathon and Salamis battles were clearly visible, but Hadi Besharat was not. He was transformed from a corporeal being into pure knowledge. He pulled events from the depths of forgotten centuries and held them in front of his students' hungry eyes. A sheet of rapture and drunkenness enclosed him. He imagined that he had been called by name and that a force drew him out of the classroom—a feeling that came over him often these days.

These days Hadi Besharat was very involved in his translation, but Farangu had nothing to do now that the religious authorities had banned actresses from the stage. Early every evening she swallowed her headache pill, stretched out on the living-room couch, and went to sleep. In the solitude Hadi Besharat's imagination would take over. He would listen to the vague sounds of the house and to the movements of the night, and doubt would strike at his heart.

The heater wasn't working right and the room was growing colder. He went to the bedroom door and said, "Farangu, the heater's broken. It smells of gas and it's not giving off any warmth."

His wife sat at her mirror and smoothed the pouches beneath her eyes. But she couldn't smooth away the swelling of her face, the cushions of her comfort-loving cheeks. "What junk this makeup is!" she moaned. "My precious face is being ruined. When I put on this powder, my skin sticks to the powder puff leaf by leaf."

There was a shortage of cosmetics and Farangu didn't know how to cope. Hadi Besharat's old classmate, Engineer Gharib, was supposed to bring her some shampoo samples, scented soap, toothpaste, and a special lotion that he had made in his laboratory, but two hours had passed and still there was no word from him.

Hadi Besharat said, "I don't know why this heater's not working. Something's obstructing its air flow. Let's go buy a new one."

"By the time Engineer Gharib comes, it will be warm."

"Dear heart, it's no use. In ten minutes it should have warmed the whole room."

"Well, put on a sweater. Get yourself a blanket."

The Pilgrim's Rules of Etiquette

Irritably, Farangu pulled down the shades, swallowed her headache pill with some water, and stretched out on the couch. She slowly closed her eyes, and grew as motionless as the marble statue on the tomb of Queen Elizabeth I. The wax mask of sleep melted over her face. The up-and-down of her chest reminded Hadi Besharat of the circular movement of epochs, the eternal rotation of years and centuries, the repetition of the seasons, the ceaseless journey of the moon and stars.

In his introduction to *Death and Destiny*, the book that had made him so widely respected as a professor of history, he wrote:

> Some historical events provide us with a concentrated pattern which not only reflects the mysteries of the past but alludes to the future as well.

Earlier in the day, in the district park, he had read this same piece for General Ghovanlu and the general was very pleased. In front of Engineer Gharib and Mr. Bayat, the general confessed that he hadn't seen a piece of such beauty, form, and power in all of the French books he had studied. He lamented that foreigners couldn't read Farsi and discover what sort of treasures are buried in this ancient land. He complained, "Agha, why is it that the instant our young people's feet reach the shores of America and Europe they roll up two pieces of toilet paper, tuck them under their arms like diplomas, and descend on the homeland? No sooner have they returned, the sweat of travel not yet dry on their bodies, than they go to the podium and, without a smidgen of knowledge of the cultural treasures of this land, let words bigger than themselves come out of their mouths and affect everyone."

Hadi Besharat had grown angry. He had addressed an invisible audience of young people and shouted, "Gentlemen, are you the philosophers of the world? What about the rest of us? Don't you count us even among the nobodies? Strange! What a generation, really."

Now, hours later, he decided to go buy airmail envelopes. He

tiptoed out of the house so as not to wake Farangu. In contrast
to his usual manner, he kept his head lowered and walked
quickly, hoping no one would recognize him. Of course he was
fooling himself. People had no problem recognizing that short,
slight figure, that bony head and walrus mustache. He passed
people in the street, meanwhile gazing at the world with dark,
deep, curious eyes like two worry beads. A few strands of hair
sprang out of his navy-blue beret, giving him the look of a
shedding bird. Not only in that district but in the world at large,
Hadi Besharat was unique. He knew this himself, but he didn't
wish to bring it to anyone else's attention.

Lifting his head, he saw that he was far from home. White
arrows curved on the pavement, guiding traffic toward the
depths of the city. Here and there a few stores were still open.
He realized he had passed the Shahin Bookstore without buying
the envelopes he needed. However, a few peddlers squatted on
the sidewalk with their eyes tracking possible customers. Batter-
ies and pocket radios and screwdrivers were piled on their trays.
He asked the first peddler, "Agha, do you have airmail envelopes?"

The peddler called to his friend, "Asghar, this gentleman
wants airmail envelopes. Got any?"

The second peddler swallowed his food hastily and said, "Got
some. How many, Agha?"

Hadi Besharat ran his fingers over the envelopes from the
second peddler's tray. They were very thick and of no use to
him. He asked, "Agha, where were these made?"

"Where do you want them to be made? Obviously they're the
product of our own country."

"Why, what sort of a country is it where even the paper mills
aren't working? Our economy grows worse day by day. This is
Hell Valley."

As he returned the envelopes, the peddler asked, "Agha, what
do we have to do with that?"

Hadi Besharat shrugged angrily. He looked up and down the

street and said, "You call this a country? With all these new street names, how do you find your way home?"

The peddler's eyes narrowed and he asked, "Where is it you want to go?"

"My home is near Martyr Taher Nabavi High School. If you show me which direction that is, I know the rest of the way."

"Agha, are you lost?"

"Me, at my age? Lost? You just tell me the direction of the high school."

The peddler asked his neighbor, "Abbas, do you know where Martyr—" He turned back to Hadi Besharat. "Martyr who?"

"Taher Nabavi."

"Tell me its old name, then."

"Do you remember Mirza Isa the Minister High School? I myself, maybe twenty years ago, taught history and geography there. You could have been one of my students. I am Professor Besharat, former teacher at Mirza Isa the Minister High School."

"Oh! Agha, you're not lost, you're in your own district. Pass the first traffic light, at the second light turn left, pass the circle where the hourly cabs park. Mirza Isa the Minister High School is next to the mosque."

Hadi Besharat started walking again. On several corners they had erected bridal chambers for the war martyrs in memory of St. Ghasem—the saint who was martyred in Karbala just before his wedding fourteen centuries ago. Hadi Besharat was puzzled by this new tradition, which had begun when the casualties started mounting in the Iran-Iraq War. He couldn't understand the connection between these little huts no higher than his waist and the slaughter on the battlefields.

It was hard to make out the names of the stores in the dark. He felt he really had lost his way. As he approached the second light he nervously searched for a cab and walked faster.

Farangu would scold him for going out of the house like this and walking in the street. Recently she had changed so much. She kept finding fault with him and nagging him. But how long could he sit home and listen to her heartaches? There was a limit to his tolerance. If it weren't for young Mehrdad Razi's inordinate love of the ancient texts, Hadi Besharat would have gone insane by now and ended up in the asylum.

After his compulsory retirement from the university he didn't have anyone to teach anymore. Only Mehrdad Razi took private lessons from him. Hadi Besharat had been amazed by the passion that young man had expressed for dead cultures and languages. Initially he had thought it might have something to do with the execution of Mehrdad's poor father. Perhaps Mehrdad had merely wanted to push the disturbing thoughts away. But gradually he saw that Mehrdad was very serious. He had even decided to enlist and go to the front just so he could see Mesopotamia with his own eyes. After his departure Hadi Besharat was left empty. Every day around ten o'clock he went to the district park and visited with the neighbors a few hours, frittering away his time with a lot of silly words, trying to fill the void.

A verse of the Mandaean hymn, "Manda d'Hayye," came to his mind and he whispered it to himself. Each word turned into a sigh and the sighs started whistling like wind in his ears. How strange that he could call back the memories of Khezrabad! But after the recent avalanche no cars went to Khezrabad anymore and the roads were closed. Hadi Besharat felt the avalanche was just an excuse. He had to get to his own village somehow, even if it meant going there on foot. To go! To go! To be enchanted by the majesty of the mountains! He had to think of a way.

The memory of August 1941, the Allied invasion, and the closing of the roads grew vivid in his mind. The memory of his father standing by the river and burning the life-sized photograph of Reza Shah, the king who abdicated after the Allied invasion. Around sunset the girls and boys on vacation from Tehran gathered one by one on the landlord's veranda. They put their arms around each other and danced a tango, "La Comparsita." Like a band of angels, they spun in ecstasy so that Hadi Besharat grew dizzy. From afar he could see a black-eyed girl who was dancing in front of the bus station to the accompaniment of Naser Lotfi's fiddle. It was the gypsy girl known as Huri.

The Pilgrim's Rules of Etiquette

Those magic eyes pulled him toward her so he feared he would leave his body. He murmured to himself:

> *"Of the soul's departure from the body*
> *They tell many stories. . . ."*

He imagined now that he heard the poem like a song from the mouth of the gypsy girl. Over a distance of forty-some years, that faraway, caressing song drew him into sadness and rubbed its nose against the borders of his memory. The scent of pennyroyal twisted in the air, a cradle rocked in the depths of his mind, and a black-garbed mother sang a lullaby for a traveling beloved. A tiger moaned halfway up the mountain and the finger of time leafed through the book of years—the fleeting years, the fickle years.

As soon as he tried to focus on these memories they evaporated, leaving a deep vacuum. His heart brimmed with apprehension. He heard a sound from deep inside, growling like a wild animal trying to escape his throat: the voice of the material world, the screaming of the archons from Mani's heavenly kingdom, the roaring of the inhabitants of darkness who attack by night. He must remain alert, examine his surroundings as carefully as a medieval alchemist, tie a mirror to his back to guard against the monster of time. In the solitude of the highlands an animal lurks and ambushes from the rear. Hadi Besharat could see the Allies' warning leaflets falling from the tail of a biplane, fluttering over the potato fields.

Now he had to take to his heels and finish the hymn on the hanging of Mani. Before the recent avalanche, he had traveled to Khezrabad to visit his mother-jon's grave. During one of his early morning walks he had been inspired to name the hymn "On the Hanging of Mani." But now it seemed to him that so simple a title failed to reflect the complicated character of Mani. It reduced the dignity of the moment of his martyrdom. Instead he would call the hymn "A Porturne for a Hanged Man." Of course, the invented word "porturne" was an imitation of "nocturne"—

"port" meaning gate, combined with suffix "turne." The word hinted at Mani's hanging from the city gate, and at the same time it gave the hymn an ancient, poetic feeling. He ought always to write in this sumptuous and heavy style. His next letter to Professor Humphrey would begin like this:

> Oh, my friend! Now we are standing in the passage of history in such a way that our numb cheeks are flushed with the flow of events and no one is able to speak with us.

He imagined himself at the edge of a battlefield, witnessing a horrible event in absolute silence. The many thousands in the Iranian army, multitude after multitude marching to Rome. The terrifying stillness of a nightmare making everything appear to be in motion. Mani tells Bahram I, "Remember this well, it is possibilities that govern people, not people that govern possibilities."

Surely after seventeen centuries the Euphrates is silent under the sunset. The wet fingers of winter pass through the grassy land and the cold sky shimmers on the silvery waters like the naked body of a young girl. On the purple shore, there is no trace of sailboats. Only the barefoot ghost of Mani wanders the banks of the Euphrates, constantly repeating a question: "Do you have the courage to cry?"

Finally Hadi Besharat arrived in his own neighborhood. How he had accomplished that he didn't know. He passed the circle where the hourly cabs stood. Then he saw the row of shops. Saadat's Candy Store was lit like a jar of honey and even the dark vegetables in the greengrocer's looked wet and alive. He passed the Sina Pharmacy. He noticed some commotion in the street. Lately he'd grown accustomed to sudden, crushing news and he wouldn't allow anxious thoughts to rush to his mind. He passed the Head and Foot Restaurant. Arriving at the three-way intersection, he turned toward his house. Every building was silent, prepared and expectant like a hospital. The facades of the mosque and Martyr Taher Nabavi High School laced the sky like an epitaph on a tomb. In front of the mosque, lines of people curled and no one uttered a word. The silhouettes of a few Revolutionary Guards clung to the Komité Building's window frames. What a dirty district. What a bad smell. Nobody collected the garbage anymore. It was scandalous.

Compared to the newly built houses of General Ghovanlu and Mr. Bayat, his own seemed worn and undistinguished. Instead of limestone, the walls were brick and cement. They were powdery as sawdust and crumbled at a touch. The water pipes were leaking and the kitchen drain was stopped up. With the staggering price of construction materials, neither Hadi Besharat nor anyone else could afford to repair and repaint. Farangu checked the kitchen drain constantly and fretted, "And what if the roof collapses on our heads? What then?" Hadi Besharat explained that the house's foundation was firm and they had to watch their expenses. He showed her how quickly their savings had shrunk in their bankbook. Farangu fell silent, but it was a heavy, closed silence that secretly blamed him. Later she stood in front of the full-length mirror and asked in a monotonous, nearly inaudible voice, "Besharat, do you hear that dripping?"

Hadi Besharat pricked up his ears. The house was as quiet as a cemetery. He answered, "I don't hear it, dear. It's your imagination."

"I can't take care of everything all by myself. I have to get out. My heart is about to die from being trapped in this house."

Hadi Besharat wished he could discover a pharaoh's tomb. He could even feel the rush of the tomb's stale air on his face. The air that was trapped in the dark for thousands of years. The ancient tomb would make him conscious of the moldy smell of centuries and the halting of time. There every broken bowl and pitcher, every dusty, rusty color was a sign of interrupted events, of the human imprint on the flow of happenings, of a truth more real than the news in newspapers and the funeral announcements. There, the incarnate essence of Izrail, the angel of death, asserted itself. That stiller of movement, that separator of souls would raise the believers to the highest, wrapped in musk-scented white silk. He would throw the corrupters to the depths of hell in a bucket of tar.

The year Hadi Besharat lectured at Whitehurst College on the comparison of Jewish, Christian, and Islamic angels and their heavenly classifications, he had told the students repeatedly, "Gentlemen, the ancient scholars and philosophers thought almost like contemporary scholars and philosophers."

The electricity was cut off as usual. For a few seconds he stood in doubt at the head of the street. There was some disturbance in front of Mrs. Razi's house. Like a handful of shadows, people came and went and mingled with one another. Lord, what was going on? What had happened?

Why all of a sudden were thoughts of his old teacher Fakhr Zanjani entering his head? Why were his internal questions phrased in Fakhr Zanjani's style? With the same emphasis, the same drawling of words? The only difference between the two men was that Hadi Besharat didn't place such stress on discipline. Although that permissive attitude of his had eventually caused his students to grow more daring. In his classes they said behind his back that nobody chopped any chives for him, that his voice carried no weight. But they had to admit that when he decided on something he took a stand like a mountain, and not even an elephant could move him.

Now he could see Engineer Gharib and Farangu. They were standing at the front door and their heads were drawn close together as they spoke. As soon as he approached, Farangu ran up asking, "Besharat, where were you for so long?"

"I went looking for airmail envelopes. Why? What's happened?"

Farangu suggested they go inside. She took on the resigned expression an actress assumes when faced with the inevitable— an expression she had often worn during her stage career. Not a word came from anyone till they were in the front hall with the door closed tightly behind them. Engineer Gharib motioned Hadi Besharat toward a chair. Doubtful and worried, he sat down and didn't take his eyes from them. Under his breath he repeated, "What's happened?"

Farangu glanced at Engineer Gharib, evidently hoping he would explain. But the engineer wasn't ready. His dull face contrasted with his usual carefree, humorous attitude. He stood under the weak kerosene lamp and had difficulty speaking. Hadi Besharat lost his patience. He asked, "Is it news from America? Did something happen to Khosro?"

He looked over at Farangu. Instead of answering, Farangu wrapped the hem of her black veil around her arms and gazed slackly at the ceiling. Finally Engineer Gharib said, "Early this evening they brought news from the front. Mehrdad Razi was shot and he has a broken foot. They're bringing him back tonight."

Hadi Besharat jumped up from his seat and asked, "Was he killed?" He grew pale and blinked rapidly. "You're telling me lies. A person who's only wounded doesn't come back from the front."

Farangu said, "Besharat, I'll bring your Agilax powder." She hurried out to the kitchen.

Hadi Besharat asked, "What about his poor mother? Does Mrs. Razi know anything?"

Without waiting for an answer, he dropped his head into his hands and collapsed on the chair.

Engineer Gharib sat in the opposite chair, crossing his legs, and said with a frown, "We went to see her earlier, but she wasn't home."

From the kitchen Farangu called, "They came from the mosque to offer her congratulations and condolences, but the engineer turned them away. Well, he was right. After the execution of her poor husband, God forgive his soul, the woman won't be able to bear the death of her precious son. I wish I could die, oh, dear God."

Hadi Besharat threw his hands in the air. "Dust be on their heads, all of them. Let the washer of the dead take their congratulations and condolences! This very thing is our nation's problem. Somehow we always want to slur over the truth. Let's go. I'll tell her myself."

But Engineer Gharib said, "Professor, what's it to you? Are you the guardian of this nation?"

Sighing deeply, Hadi Besharat rested his elbows on his knees. He lowered his head and clenched his hands together. "Do you remember the first bell on Tuesday mornings? The late Fakhr Zanjani used to tell us in his lectures, 'People die, but history doesn't know death. History is a mask of death.' We couldn't understand it."

"Oh, baba, how you remember the past."

"Almost forty years have gone by since the death of the late Fakhr. But I still remember."

"Oh, no, baba! Do you really mean it? Forty years?"

"Time passes just like that. He used to say, 'Dying is for ordinary people.' Can you believe it? Two weeks ago, when that poor Mehrdad was home on leave, he too talked of dying. As though he sensed something."

Farangu returned bearing a tray with a glass of water and the jar of Agilax powder. She set the tray on the table and said, "Oh, baba, think of something to help Mrs. Razi. I wish I could die for her. When she hears the news she'll die a sorrow's death."

Hadi Besharat stood up. "Let's get going. Let's go to Mrs. Razi. I'll talk to her myself."

Engineer Gharib started to protest, but then evidently he changed his mind.

The three of them set off for Mrs. Razi's house. Of course she needed help and encouragement—a woman alone whose husband had been executed and whose eldest son, Nurdad, lived in America. Now that Mehrdad was dead she would sit in her house every night looking at the walls and doors and listening to the birds coo—that empty house where only the pigeons returned at sunset to sleep.

Even though the electricity was off, a few people were coming out of the mosque. Each held a candle and followed the others slowly. The dark of night gave life to the flames so that a flock of bats seemed to be going through seizures against the walls. The scene reminded Hadi Besharat of the children's chorus that always seemed to float in space in the cathedral at Whitehurst College. Or the dizzy spell that tugged a cord in his heart whenever his plane was landing. Or the vacuum he felt in his chest whenever he stood at the edge of a cliff.

What a lengthy discussion he and Mehrdad had had about death two weeks ago! Hadi Besharat had bought a bag of fruit at the head of the street, and he was on his way home when the poor boy appeared on the corner. Lately Mehrdad's attitude toward Hadi Besharat had changed. He had behaved more casually and more warmly. He had told jokes and imitated the courtiers of the Ghajar Dynasty. Strange! Hadi Besharat could still hear the boy's voice in his ears. What a pity. How easily that precious young man had flown away. When he and Mehrdad reached his house, Mehrdad had said, "Professor Besharat, what would Nasreddin Shah the Ghajar king say when he wanted to annoy his jester, Karim the opium addict?"

"What would he say, dear man?"

Mehrdad put on the expression of an executioner and said, in majestic tones, "Son of hell, shall I order my guards to push a stick through your sleeves so you can't use your hands? Then flood you with a strong laxative and keep you for hours till it starts working?"

Then he became Karim the opium addict, giving the king a raspberry, and he burst into laughter. When he stopped, he turned away. He always turned away like that, with that look of disappointment. Basically, there was some constant restlessness in that young man.

When Mehrdad walked away, Hadi Besharat couldn't hear his footsteps. He heard only the jingling of coins in his pockets. Instead of wearing his jacket, Mehrdad draped it over his shoulders. He was always buying excellent navy-blue suits and shiny black shoes from Barak's Department Store. But around the time he was preparing to go to the front he switched to military fatigues or blue jeans.

Before the Revolution, Mehrdad often visited the Shahin Bookstore early in the evening. Then he went to sit in Termeh's Bar with a vodka and Coca-Cola on his table. Late at night he wandered the streets, heading homeward. Sometimes on the way he would stop by Hadi Besharat's and ring the bell. Hadi Besharat would open the door with a welcoming expression. Mehrdad would come in and stand in the hall, rest his elbow on the banister, loosen the white silk scarf around his neck, and talk.

Hadi Besharat didn't have to force it; forgetfulness would come on its own. The sort of forgetfulness that altered the distance of time, stretching each second to the length of a century and squeezing centuries into a second. Only two weeks ago the poor boy had asked, "Professor Besharat, is it true that the end-of-time story and the Noah's flood story are remnants of the Akkadians' funeral rites?"

Hadi Besharat had wondered why Mehrdad was talking about funerals. He had said, "Dear man, you're so young. Why are you thinking of death?"

Mehrdad laughed, and the twinkle in his eyes gave him a bashful look. Letting out a trapped breath, he lifted his hand from the banister and said, "I come alive only with thoughts of dying, and that's how I keep going."

Then he grew silent and thoughtful. Something was bothering him. Hadi Besharat had wondered if he were thinking of his father's execution. That was why Hadi Besharat stayed silent too, not wanting to bring up anything unpleasant. Oh, how sorry he was now that he hadn't said something to ease Mehrdad's pain!

He heard Farangu's voice: "Besharat, let's don't go. Mrs. Razi will hear about it tomorrow. Giving her bad news this late at night will ruin her nerves."

"You just want to forget. Don't you remember? Don't you see his face in your mind?"

"Why, of course I do. How well I do! Two weeks ago when his leave was up, didn't we go to the bus station to see him off?

How many boxes of pistachios and candy and baklava you bought for him! Everyone was surprised. General Ghovanlu's wife needled you: 'On the battlefield, how can that young boy carry a truckload of nuts and sweets in boxes?' I stood up to her and said, 'He who bought the boxes knows what he's doing.' I wish I could have died for that young boy. You can't believe it."

Engineer Gharib whispered, "We went to the bus station for nothing."

"I wish we hadn't gone. Especially in that rain. That downpour . . ."

What a rain! The volunteers were still tying the "St. Abelfazl, Help Me" bands around their heads as they boarded the bus. Mrs. Razi looked pleased at all the attention. She turned her head like a peacock and said, "Oh, baba, is there no end to this rain?"

Because of the rain, the rusty drainpipes shone like pomegranate skins. Nili, Mr. Bayat's eighteen-year-old daughter, hugged a rolled army blanket in her arms. Despite her youth, she was always getting mixed up with the grownups, always trying to be the bean in every soup. When that poor boy stuck his head out of the window to find her in the crowd, Nili jumped up and down in hopes that he would see her arms weren't empty after all. Mrs. Razi seemed happy and smiled at everyone who had come.

The crowd of people, each carrying a candle, walked behind Farangu and Engineer Gharib. Hadi Besharat led the way. Farangu clamped her long veil between her teeth while her shuffling slippers hurried to catch up with him. She said, "Besharat, Besharat, wait for us! This haste is unbecoming. Is it your child who is lost? This isn't good, Besharat!"

He couldn't make her see the importance. He raised his voice: "A little patience, Farangu. Do you think you understand everything? In this country we're in the habit of thinking we're all-knowing. But as soon as something happens, as soon as the knife cuts to the bone, we try to hide it. We pretend we haven't noticed, we convince ourselves that nothing is wrong, that the waters weren't disturbed. Not at all. No such thing. But there's a limit to self-delusion. Bah!"

He lifted his fist to knock at Mrs. Razi's, but the door was unlatched and it opened by itself. He hadn't expected that. The blood rushed to his face. All at once the old doubts returned, and he wasn't sure whether this visit was a result of wise deliberation or sudden raw impulse. He glanced across the courtyard. A portable lamp burned on the veranda. The windows were dark as needle eyes. On the second floor that poor boy's room was lit and somebody's shadow moved on the window shade.

Engineer Gharib said, "Professor, are you sure we won't upset Mrs. Razi?"

"Engineer, no one can foretell the future. But humans must prepare themselves for life's hardships. Without fear in their hearts, they must meet events."

Farangu said, "Besharat, somehow I sense that Mrs. Razi is hiding in the dining room and doesn't want to see anyone."

"Then who is that walking upstairs?"

"Nili, Mr. Bayat's daughter. Why is she everywhere? Why is she the first to see Mrs. Razi? You would think she'd received a personal invitation and it was all her responsibility."

Hadi Besharat didn't want to delay any longer. He crossed the courtyard and went toward the dining room. A few in the crowd followed. When they reached the entrance hall they realized that Mrs. Razi was standing behind the closed doors waiting for them. Hadi Besharat wanted to remain as clearheaded as possible. But this was no simple matter! A twenty-five-year-old man at the height of his youth goes to the front and perishes without knowing what hit him. It took a strong heart to put the news of such a horrible event into his mother's palm. Especially for Hadi Besharat, who always spoke plainly and frankly. He couldn't say that the poor boy had had an accident or was sent to America on an important mission. He could only tell the truth.

Silent and determined, he opened the dining-room doors. Mrs. Razi stood in the darkness. Her dyed brows and her eyeliner gave her moonlit face a dead look, like a photographic negative. Her dead face gazed at this world from another world. She took off her glasses, examined a crack in the left lens, and then turned her face upward. She looked at everyone with frightened, unsure eyes, not taking even one step forward. Perhaps she was afraid she couldn't see her way in the dark and would stumble on her high-heeled Italian shoes. She smiled meekly and apologetically —an off-focus smile like a lunatic's. She waited for Hadi Besharat to speak. He said simply, "Ma'am, I hope you won't feel bad because of what I have to say. As you know yourself, this world is just a caravanserai. We're brought into it by force and we're taken away by force. Of course, Mehrdad was a source of pride for all of us . . ."

Farangu started wailing in the entrance hall. Mrs. Razi's glasses trembled between her fingers. The lines in her face drew together and she fell to her knees on the floor. Clenching a fist, she dug her nails into the carpet as though she wanted to uproot a weed. Then she straightened and her veil slid from her head to her shoulders. She pulled it up angrily and rose to her feet. There was a hush in her voice. "I apologize for this clutter, this untidy house," she said. "You've kindly taken the trouble to visit and I'm indebted. God willing, I hope you won't be offended but without standing on ceremony, at present I have no patience left. I beg you, I would be grateful if you'll all leave."

Hadi Besharat said, "Ma'am, the death of the apple of your eye is not an easy thing. But as a Manichaean elegy would have it, the apple of your eye hasn't really left you. He's here right now." He pounded his chest two or three times with his fist. "He's in our hearts and he's speaking to us all. He has joined infinity. Infinity is here. Here is infinity. If Einstein says there's no infinity in the world, he's dead wrong. Don't accept it. Because it exists. Seven hundred years ago our own great mystic, Sohrvadi, proved it and I can prove it too. Imagine a circle and draw three diagonals from its center . . ."

He drew a circle in the air. "We draw these diagonals in such a way that they form sixty-degree angles. What does it turn out to be? An equilateral triangle whose angles are one hundred and eighty degrees altogether. Now let us extend the circle's radius to infinity . . ."

Mrs. Razi looked dazed.

From behind, someone tugged Hadi Besharat's arm. He turned and protested. "Why are you pulling me?"

It was Engineer Gharib. Hadi Besharat asked, "What is this? I just want to say two words. What I'm telling her isn't that complicated. I just want to give her the image of a triangle. A triangle! See?" He planted his feet wide apart. "Look at this!" he told Mrs. Razi. "What do you see between my legs?"

Engineer Gharib said, "That's enough, that's enough."

"But it's simple! It's a triangle. One leg here, one leg here, and the ground forms the base."

Engineer Gharib said quietly, "Professor, it's better to leave now."

Hadi Besharat looked around at the others. He could tell from their faces that they felt the same way. In their company he retreated slowly from the dining room. When they reached the courtyard his eyes rose to the second-floor window. Nili stood watching their departure, clutching a few pieces of the poor boy's clothing.

Once in the street, the neighbors returned to their homes with bowed heads, tacitly agreeing not to discuss the incident. Farangu opened their front door. But Hadi Besharat said, "You go ahead. I'll be back in a minute. I want to speak with Engineer Gharib."

He followed Engineer Gharib and walked shoulder to shoulder with him till they came to the engineer's laboratory. Each was sunk in his own thoughts. Perhaps Engineer Gharib too was thinking of Mehrdad at various moments of his life, from the time he was a little boy until two weeks ago when he returned for a few days' leave. During that last visit he had come to Hadi Besharat's study wearing military fatigues and carrying a knapsack. Gone were his navy-blue suit, shiny shoes, and white scarf. The scrubbed and youthful freshness of his face made him look unfamiliar, like a movie star. He stood in the doorway and said,

"Professor Besharat, the road is open to the Tigris. You can see the ruins of Babylon. Some say nothing is visible on the horizon —only the dust of the Iraqis' tanks and the volleys of their bullets. But you can see those broken walls. After so many centuries, they're still standing. Don't tell me going to the Tigris is insanity. In our next attack I'll figure out how to reach the ruins of Babylon."

It hadn't occurred to Hadi Besharat that Mehrdad would get himself killed. He had stood up and taken a copy of *Death and Destiny* from the bookshelves to give the poor boy as a present. Turning to the first page, he wrote a couple of verses beneath the photo of himself as a college student:

> *In contrast to me, you remain eternal.*
> *Oh, my counterpart,*
> *You remain a testimony of me*
> *In my youth.*

Then and there he had decided to start a cardboard file as a gift for Mehrdad's return from the front. He would fill it with notes about Mani's last journey and the connection between Mani and the Mandaeans, who still lived on the Iran-Iraq border and performed their ancient rituals. Now that this had happened, to whom could he present that file?

Engineer Gharib had installed a special generator in his laboratory so that when the electricity failed the refrigerator would keep running. He turned on a lamp and the white walls swelled with light. Hadi Besharat found a stool and sat down. Everything affected his nerves—the walls' nakedness, the white of the tiles, the smell of alcohol and nail polish, the twisted plastic hose in the sink, the rust around the drain, the refrigerator purring like a kitten.

A sense of loneliness, a sense of time's skeleton and his own separateness, reminded him of that poor boy. He saw a row of white plastic jars filled with colored pastes. Different colors: emerald green, jujube red, indigo blue. The colors Engineer Gharib used to make eye shadow, rouge, nail polish, and God knew what else. There was a sharp scent of perfume in the air, the concentrated smell of face powder, and a chemical odor that reminded him of Sina Pharmacy and doctors' waiting rooms. A smell that evoked the memory of sleepless nights in the hospital. He rubbed his hands together and said, "Engineer, what an impact death has on us. All of a sudden, everything loses its importance." His hands drew apart, as if stretching a piece of chewing gum. "You are occupied with your lab work, so retirement hasn't changed your life much. And I keep busy too. But when you deal with death, nothing seems important anymore."

Engineer Gharib brought out a gallon of homemade vodka and set it on the counter. "Do you remember you talked this way when the news came of Fakhr Zanjani's death?"

"When I heard he had died, all I could think of was the way he used to shake hands. Those huge, bony hands with rough palms. Only that."

"Remember the last year Fakhr Zanjani taught at Mirza Isa the Minister High School? He screamed at the principal, 'Shaygun, you illiterate, you cart driver, don't you know that it's not St. Abolfazl, it's St. Abelfazl? If you want to swear by someone, the least you can do is swear correctly.' "

They both burst into laughter. The principal had put a banana peel in Fakhr Zanjani's path and kept a dossier on him until Fakhr Zanjani was transferred to the hot city of Zahedan. Poor Fakhr. Innocent Fakhr. He always quarreled with life and expected the worst of everyone. In less than a year he was wiped out by tuberculosis in Zahedan. Why? Because of the intrigues of a tattletale like Mr. Shaygun.

It was planned that Fakhr Zanjani would ride to Zahedan in a battered limousine. Hadi Besharat went to see him off with the rest of the students. They piled the roof of the limousine with bundles of mattresses, worn-out suitcases, and other belongings. Under such a load, the car sank like an old shoe. After much struggling, poor Fakhr pushed the other passengers aside and waved out the window at his students. They tried to present him with a bunch of dahlias, but he couldn't reach it. One of the passengers felt sorry for him and rolled the window down farther. Fakhr Zanjani wet his lips and asked the students, "Do you understand why they're sending me to Zahedan?"

Engineer Gharib poured some vodka for Hadi Besharat and himself. "Besharat, drink this. Let yourself get a little light-headed. Everything else is a game."

Hadi Besharat took a sip and nodded. "I can't forget. To forget you have to have a memory in the first place. But whatever happens is still alive for me. Right now Mehrdad's face is in front of my eyes. It's on that wall."

Engineer Gharib glanced at the white wall. Then he turned and said with a smile, "Like Fakhr Zanjani, you have your own particular character. You walk in circles, waiting for someone to come out of nowhere and work a miracle."

Engineer Gharib was mistaken. If Hadi Besharat occasionally imitated Fakhr Zanjani, it was only because he wished to lessen that distance of almost forty years. It was difficult to remember a man like Fakhr Zanjani because he had always had such an indirect, slanted manner. If he wanted to scold one of the students, he wouldn't look into the student's eyes. Instead he would go after the student's notebook. He would hold a pencil between his bony fingers and search fiercely for mistakes and omissions. This behavior made Hadi Besharat feel both pity and disapproval. In spite of Fakhr Zanjani's intelligence, his lamps burning late at night, and his labor over other people's children, he didn't possess any more than a sigh. Why? What was it all for? The students would become ministers, deputies, or heads of organizations, leaving him to struggle on alone with a bunch of rough drafts and unreadable notebooks. The old man pretended not to mind this. Only on occasion, when correcting examination papers, he would read out some of their nonsense in a loud voice: " '. . . on the north, Alaska borders with the North Pole. On the south, it borders with America and on the west with the United States. . . .' Light on the graves of those parents who present society with such ass-heads. Aren't you the descendants of the physician Raze, the theologian Farabi, the philosopher Avecina? I hope you break your writing hands. You're making a mess of this country's culture."

In front of the students' terror-stricken eyes, he would rip the examination papers to pieces and never once look at his victims' faces.

After swallowing his vodka, Hadi Besharat said, "Engineer, during the time of mourning, people gather around each other so they don't feel alone in the presence of death. Death shows its presence like a mask. Like the makeup on the face of a clown. A mask is the sign of death." He took a pinch from the jar of red paste and rubbed it between his fingers. He stared at Engineer Gharib with wide eyes, forcing him to pay attention. "When people are ashamed of themselves, they always put on a mask. They cover their faces with another face. But a mask is the sign of Death's presence."

He caught sight of his own reflection in the mirror. He brought his face closer and inspected it carefully. He drew a fingertip down the bridge of his nose, leaving a thin red line. He turned back to Engineer Gharib.

Engineer Gharib shrugged. "You're still imitating Fakhr Zanjani. He liked to act dramatic too."

Hadi Besharat picked up the towel next to the sink and erased the red line. Looking through the window, he saw that the street was empty. General Ghovanlu's shadow moved up and down behind the curtains of his house. No doubt the Ghovanlus had guests and a card game was in progress.

Oh, how tired he was! What a strange day! A day when he got lost in the streets of his own district, a day when he heard the news of that poor boy's death. He stood up and searched for his umbrella, which, of course, was not there. In the middle of his search he paused and said, "Engineer, somehow we have to look after Mrs. Razi. I am obsessed with the idea of going to her house. That young man kept a lot of notes. I'm sure that if we look among his papers we can find something. Maybe he's left us a message."

Again Engineer Gharib shrugged. "Well, what's the use? It won't bring Mehrdad back to life."

Hadi Besharat nodded, raised two fingers in farewell, and stepped out of the laboratory.

Before the Revolution the neighbors would greet each other only from a distance. Only from a distance did they keep track of who had departed from this world, who was behind in his mortgage, and who had illness in the house. But now they all seemed to have retired and they had lots of time to socialize. They were getting up in age. They didn't excite themselves with absurd and hollow matters as did the young, unprincipled people of this generation. They wouldn't throw themselves into fire and water for just anything. They understood who held the strings, who played the game, who baited the hook for people.

And each of them possessed some particular skill. Hadi Besharat himself knew a few things about historical subjects. His poetry wasn't bad either—weaving a few silly words together and calling it modern verse. Engineer Gharib, his old friend and high school classmate, manufactured cosmetics and brewed illegal vodka in his laboratory. He also photographed the neighbors and sold their portraits to them. Mr. Bayat, although he was old and alcoholic, knew something about herbal medicine and carpet weaving. Even General Ghovanlu, who had never committed himself to anything, was learning Arabic from Mr. Bayat. The lessons satisfied Mr. Bayat's need for incessant talking. After his last stroke, in the middle of a conversation he would start talking about St. Hosein's passion. He would repeat the memories of the war years like a broken record; he would go on and on about the Americans' donated silo bread and his visit to Mashad. He complained to heaven about the illegal trip he had made to Pakistan in the company of his eldest son, Mojtaba, and General Ghovanlu's wife. He and General Ghovanlu's wife formed a chorus together: "The trains in Pakistan are so dirty and crowded. The people in Pakistan are nothing like us. They have no grasp of the civilities. Like a herd of cows, all they know how to do is mill around and drop babies from their behinds like turds. Can you call these humans?"

Arriving in his own courtyard, Hadi Besharat sensed from the silence in the entrance hall that Farangu had taken her sleeping pill and gone to bed. The electricity was still off and she had placed a lantern at the foot of the stairs so he could see his way. When he reached his study he lit the lantern there. The accursed thing was almost out of kerosene, and its chimney was chipped and the wick wasn't burning right. It made the room stink so that he had to blow it out.

He thought of the magic lantern and how in the Middle Ages it was lit to please the souls of the departed. Of course this custom dated back to the Phoenicians and their tradition of putting a burning torch on the door of a house in mourning. Perhaps setting a lamp on a grave was another souvenir of this tradition. He struck a match and lit the candles one by one, and the angels began to move.

He started work on his translation of *The Death of a Great Savior.* By now he had reached Chapter Three. Professor Humphrey was giving an account of Mani's last visit, quoting from the fifth Parthian scroll:

> The noble prince (meaning Mani) kept his word and addressed us. "For your sake, I shall wait for you in the sky's sea-chariot (meaning the Moon, which according to some sources is his place of rest till the end of time) and shall always send you help."
>
> Fifth Parthian Text, MM III, pp. 863–65

According to the notes of the two disciples who stayed with Mani till his last moment, the Living Paraclete's demise occurred around the eleventh hour of the Monday corresponding to the eighth of Amshir in the new Coptic calendar (apparently the translation of the eighth of Shabath in the Syriac calendar). But actually it must have been the first of February, A.D. 277.

Hadi Besharat opened his study door and stuck his head into

the corridor. Except for the ticktock of the clock on the wall, he heard no sound. The lantern was still burning at the foot of the stairs. The doors to Khosro's room and the sewing room were left open. Darkness hollowed the spaces. Hadi Besharat went downstairs, picked up the kerosene lamp, and returned to place it in front of Khosro's door. The weak glow lit Khosro's room and Hadi Besharat felt relieved. He rubbed his palms together, checking to see that he hadn't forgotten anything. Everything was in its place and the house was breathing calmly. Hadi Besharat was tired. He wanted to sleep.

T W O

Tossing and turning in his bed, he couldn't stop thinking about poor Mehrdad. It was two o'clock in the morning and General Ghovanlu's party was still going on. From a distance he could hear the whispery sounds of the guests gambling and drinking and laughing. Then the wind started up and he felt a cold draft. He rose to get another blanket, and as he passed the window he looked toward Mrs. Razi's courtyard. It was three o'clock now; yet a light still burned on the veranda. No doubt she was waiting behind the courtyard door for that poor boy to return from the front. Whenever Mehrdad used to step out of the house into the scuffles of the Revolution, Mrs. Razi had stood behind the court-yard door and without pausing for breath recited the Prayer for Protection, blowing it toward the passing cars on the avenue. Maybe that would keep them from running him over. Perhaps, if she dedicated seven hundred Prayers of Praise to St. Mus-ibn-Jafaar, she could bring Mehrdad back alive. Or perhaps it would be better to donate fifty tumans to a deserving descendant of the Prophet, so that even if Mehrdad were shot the bullet would miss his vital organs and he wouldn't perish.

During the uprising of September 1979, Mrs. Razi went crazy. Anyone who came her way, she asked about her boy. What kind of hell was he lost in? She didn't know that he was close by, drinking beer and eating pistachios and talking to a bunch of strange young men in Termeh's Bar. Around nine o'clock in the evening he came out of the bar. He stood shifting his feet in front of the Shahin Bookstore so he wouldn't run into Nili. It was unsuitable the way Nili loitered alone in the streets. At the time she was only fourteen and she should have had someone looking after her. But everyone in the Bayat household was busy with other matters and they paid her no attention.

As soon as Nili's mother had sensed that the country was growing less stable she had packed her belongings and fled to America. The day of her departure she was seen in the street, holding a handkerchief to her red eyes. She sobbed loudly, saying to the neighbors, "Good or bad, whatever I've done, please forgive me. I must go live in America with Mojtaba."

Mojtaba, her eldest son, had married an American and he worked in the Iranian Embassy. He'd returned only once, just recently, and that was because he wanted to take his father back to America for treatment. Her second son, Ahmad, was involved in the Revolution and nobody saw him for months on end. And Heli, her eldest daughter, passed her time shopping for strangely fashioned clothes. In those days Heli still had her sight, and she invited her friends over every evening to play records and dance till all hours on the rooftop. But Nili loitered in the streets. She would appear out of thin air wherever poor Mehrdad appeared. She was there that night, behaving as though she had no particular plans and was merely picking up her father's prescription at the Sina Pharmacy.

Mehrdad, oblivious to everything, walked along with his hands in his trouser pockets. He looked bored when he entered his courtyard. As soon as he stepped in, Mrs. Razi slapped him hard in the face and screeched, "You dead body, in what grave have you been? What have you done with that innocent Nili? It's because of a useless rascal like you that the neighbors gossip about her."

She clamped her dentures tightly between her gums. She lisped and it sounded as if she had a pebble under her tongue. Mehrdad didn't defend himself. Instead of insulting her, he sweetened her up with adoring words. He put a bottle of perfume in her hand and said, "I bought this for you with my own money."

Mrs. Razi melted like wax. Happily, she turned around and smiled at the general's wife, who had come out to her balcony to see what all the noise was about. "What do you do with a boy like this? Everything he does is like a movie star."

Then she took him to the kitchen and made him a vegetable omelet and a tomato sandwich. But later Mrs. Ghovanlu told all the neighbors what had happened after that. Suddenly Mrs. Razi had started thinking. Where did Mehrdad get the money to buy that perfume? No doubt he'd taken it from her purse. She set her paring knife on the table, stared at Mehrdad, and asked, "Where did you find the money for that perfume?"

Mehrdad answered absent-mindedly, "Oh, somewhere. Don't worry about it."

His offhand, drawling tone of voice made her even more suspicious. She asked, "How much did you pay?"

"A hundred and forty tumans."

"In what grave did you find a hundred and forty tumans?"

"Why all the fuss? If you don't like the perfume I'll take it back."

"What do I want with that sickening perfume? Do I go to cafés, or out dancing? Has anyone invited me to a Seven-States Ball that I need to wear perfume? I'm sure you bought this garbage with the money for your English class. Where's the receipt for your English-class tuition?"

When Mehrdad didn't answer she grew even louder. "You heartless person! You know how your poor mother is scrimping and saving so that contemptible you, ungrateful you, can take your dead body to America. Now just wait till your father comes home. Just see what I'm going to do. I'll tell him all about you. He'll settle your account."

The young man bowed his head and went up to the roof. Leaning against the railing, he smoked a cigarette. The smoke twisted from his half-parted lips and rose into the air. Meanwhile

Mrs. Razi stood on the veranda, pressing one fist into her side and rapidly puffing on a cigarette of her own. Over on the Bayats' roof, Heli and her friends had put a record on and were practicing new dances. The Ghovanlus and the Gharibs came out to gaze up at them. They saw Mehrdad cross over to the Bayats' and spin Heli around. He and she waved to the people down below and smiled with feverish eyes and sweaty faces. Hadi Besharat had thought of Khezrabad, of the young Tehranians who danced with each other on the veranda of the landlord's mansion. The tune of "La Comparsita" passed over the river and wandered above the village, spreading into the distilled atmosphere of the evening.

> Bum-bum, baa, bum-bum,
> Bum-bum, bum-bum, bum-bum, baa, bum-bum . . .

To Hadi Besharat there was no real difference between the young people and their elders. They all spun each other around at the command of that eternal draftsman's compass, imagining they were in perpetual motion. But why did the young people find it necessary to wear such strange outfits? To return to the seventeenth and eighteenth centuries? Outfits with slit boots and feathered hats like Louis XIV's chevaliers', with shoulder belts and aiguillettes like the Russian courtiers', with white open-collared shirts like the French revolutionaries'. They viewed the landscape as a mirage that turned the local scenes into something distant and romantic. What was wrong with the scenes as they were? Scenes like the sun rising on the whitewashed walls of the Martyr Taher Nabavi High School. Like the peddler wandering from street to street selling kettles and Japanese rice-makers. Like the dragging voice of Mr. Abolhassan Hashiyeh dictating to his students from the ancient animal stories of *Kelileh and Demneh.* "It is narrated that a monkey . . . that a monkey . . . saw a carpenter . . . saw . . . a carpenter . . ."

Finally Hadi Besharat slept. When he awoke everything was back where it belonged. The sheet stretched away to the tips of his toes. Old newspapers and magazines were piled in a corner. His spectacles lay on a table with the lenses gazing upward like the eyes of a plastic doll. The ice in his drinking glass had melted. All the paintings and photographs were in their places.

He put on his slippers and went downstairs. Farangu lay wrapped in her veil in front of the dining-room door. He could tell from the smoothness of her veil that she was sleeping calmly and her migraine wasn't bothering her. The dawn spread through the air like a sheet of nylon and the wall clock sliced equal distances in the entrance hall. As drops of water fell on the tiles in the bathroom, a cat stopped licking the leftovers from supper and listened to the silence. The ghost of the darkness faded into the folds of light. Little by little the sun rose behind the red clouds. The sky assumed the dusty color of turmeric, highlighting the framed photos of the ruins of Babylon and the monument on Lord Nelson's tomb and Canova's statue of Pope Clement XIV. Pope Clement stood on his pedestal with one hand raised like a hero and issued a command—a triumphant command that contrasted sharply with the expression of the figure of Meekness at his feet. Meekness was a woman sitting next to a lamb, absorbed in sad thought. Her maternal softness and sorrow evoked a feeling in Hadi Besharat that he couldn't describe. A feeling of time leafing through the days, of the world growing undependable. A feeling that he was a stranger to everyone, that he had been left behind. He imagined that at any moment someone would ring the bell and come into the entrance hall. In his mind he could hear the words Fakhr Zanjani had repeated so many times in his history class: "Gentlemen, time is a product of the human mind. Time is only the mental distance between eternity's two dark holes which have temporarily opened a crack for us. Cicero says, 'History is a witness to the passage of time.' I say, 'Time is a witness to the passage of history.' "

But what was the use? Why struggle with a bunch of capricious students who changed their minds like clothing styles? In these chaotic days, where was a listening ear? Retirement was a blessing in disguise. It protected people from having to deal with foolishness. As the blessed Koran says, "And many a thing you dislike is beneficial to you. And many a thing you like is harmful for you."

Maybe Mehrdad Razi was not dead after all. Maybe at this very moment he was watching the Masbuta ceremonies of baptism on the banks of the Tigris and reciting the Manichaean hymn of ascendance in the Coptic language. From the depths of his heart Hadi Besharat heard a voice like a hungry animal moaning: "Hadi-jon, wait awhile! Don't be deceived by appearances!"

Just then Farangu stirred and turned over. She raised her pale face and sat up cross-legged on the floor. She tucked a lock of hair behind her ear and said, "Besharat, I'll put your grape juice in the kitchen. First have some Agilax powder to soothe your stomach. Then drink your grape juice."

Hadi Besharat walked toward the kitchen. "I'd better take my vitamins too."

"Leave those for tomorrow," Farangu said, following him. "Those vitamin pills are too strong. They make your skin itch."

"What a long sleep you had!"

Farangu tucked her hair back again. "It wasn't a real sleep. It seemed as if someone had drugged me. Sometimes it was so light that I could hear voices. I wanted to say something, but as soon as I opened my eyes I grew dizzy and fell away again. Around daybreak I passed out and I didn't feel another thing."

Hadi Besharat drank his grape juice to the last drop and asked, "What are your plans for today? Are you going over to Mrs. Razi's to find out how she's doing?"

"Let me take care of my chores first. Later, we'll see. There are plans to set up the poor boy's bridal chamber. Besharat, what's happening in the street?"

"How would I know? You're the one who's out all the time."

Farangu got up. Hadi Besharat supposed she would put on her veil and pay her Mama Aliyeh a visit. Mama Aliyeh would comfort her, show her the straight and narrow and point out all the pitfalls. Then Farangu would go window-shopping, looking at the new fashions. In her mind she would draw up copies, and later she'd sew dresses for herself that didn't differ by a hair from foreign-made. When she got tired of prowling the streets alone she would visit Mrs. Razi and take her shopping in places Mrs. Razi hadn't been before.

Hadi Besharat ought to go see Mrs. Razi himself. He imagined sitting in her drawing room, placing his palms together, and talking without pause. He would explain to her that the death of such a young man was not to be misused. They shouldn't let the boy's identity be changed by processions of breast-beaters, their mourning and memorial gatherings, or renaming the street "Martyr Mehrdad Razi Street." Hadi Besharat would not allow it, and he meant to stop these theatrics. That young man had possessed an interior world that other people couldn't understand. Just to look at him, they could never appreciate his intelligence and curiosity.

Was it possible that Mehrdad had heard the same beautiful interior music that Hadi Besharat heard? Had he heard that melody, that bird song fluttering in the middle of a desert like a solitary candle flame?

Hadi Besharat had heard that music even as a child. He had heard it that time he and Farangu went mountain climbing in Khezrabad. This was when he'd just started teaching history and geography at Mirza Isa the Minister High School. He'd been married barely a year. Farangu was running here and there looking for a new play and she had finally won the role of Desdemona in *Othello*. The Friday before the opening they went with a group of actors to mountain-climb in Khezrabad. The higher they went, the thinner the air grew and the harder it was to breathe. Hadi Besharat was excited by the height and by the closeness of the sky. He wished he could open his arms like wings and let the wind take over. He looked at Farangu and she gave him a pleased and ironic smile. A lovely, bashful smile that tugged beautifully at the corners of her lips and brightened her eyes with pride—those virginal eyes.

Passionately he took Farangu's arm and drew her close. The hail-cold air of the highlands made it hard for him to speak loudly enough. He formed a cluster with his fingers and asked, "Do you know why I came hiking with you?"

Farangu shook her head. "Why?"

"For me, breathing the mountain air is like making a connection with the earth. It's like returning to my origins. I do everything in reverse, exactly the way the ancient Iranians did. When I want to touch the earth I climb closer to the sky."

Farangu started laughing and Hadi Besharat felt brim full of a feeling that he had been awaiting for a long time. In his mind his private symphony had grown clamorous. The trumpets blared and the cymbals clashed. But he pretended not to notice. He frowned and said, "Why are you laughing like that?"

Farangu covered her mouth with her hand to hide her laughter. "Because I'm pregnant," she said. "I'm two months pregnant."

A stone slipped under Hadi Besharat's feet. Fortunately Farangu was standing next to him. As he started to slide she grabbed his arm and shouted into the hissing wind, "Besharat, what's wrong with you? Watch your step! Keep your eyes on the top of the mountain. Don't look down."

Hadi Besharat shut his eyes tight and spoke quietly, out of fear. "What's happening? Am I falling? Is there anything under my feet?"

"Don't be afraid, Besharat. I have hold of your hand and the ground is under your feet. Maybe it was hearing about the baby that made you dizzy."

He pulled himself up. He brushed the dirt from his hiking clothes. "I'm not dizzy because of that. I'm very happy."

Surprised and grave, Farangu asked, "You mean it doesn't bother you to have a child?"

He threw his hands in the air and said, "We're all inhabitants of the planet Earth. A person's child is not his private property. A child belongs to the world. If you believe the theory of creation, then we're all the children of Adam. If you believe in Darwin, it's the same. We're all the result of a sexual mishap, a mistake."

His excitement subsided and he returned to his usual mood.

Now he looked at Farangu. Thirty years later, she seemed tired. She started climbing the stairs, loose and sleepy-headed. Hadi Besharat called after her, "Don't you want to visit Mrs. Razi?"

Farangu shook her head. "Besharat, you can't force your way into people's houses. Mrs. Razi doesn't want to see anybody. Why should I lower myself?"

"Because you two are friends," he said, following her up the stairs. "Why don't you go downtown together? Go on, go ahead. She'll let you in. You're different from the others. That poor boy was like our own son."

Farangu sat down at the mirror and began putting on her makeup. Listlessly she applied dark lipstick. "I couldn't believe it," she said. "We went to buy fabric and Mrs. Razi found fault with everything."

She was referring to last week's excursion, when she'd taken Mrs. Razi shopping. They had walked for hours in an unfamiliar district with whitewashed, slanted walls and a narrow stream of water that passed through the little bazaar like mouse piss. Mrs. Razi had demanded, "Miss Farangu, how did you find a place like this?"

"Dear lady, the seeker is the finder."

In the Ghar Gate district Farangu had come across an instant-photo studio that charged only eight tumans for four passport photos. She had struck up a friendship with a bird seller who sold partridges and sparrows and also owned a yogurt shop. The bird seller had told her that sparrow extract did wonders for anemia and stomach spasms. They bought yarn at another store and put it in their bags. Farangu took Mrs. Razi by the arm and led her to the slaughterhouse so they could watch the slaughtering of cows and sheep. Mrs. Razi had felt ill and insisted that they take a cab and return to their own district immediately. But Farangu had begged, "A little while longer, Mrs. Razi."

"A little while longer to do what?"

"To go eat some sheep's head and leg of lamb. Aren't you hungry? It's an hour past noon."

"Miss Farangu, I fail to understand you. First you bring us to watch these bleating souls being slaughtered. Then you want us to eat their heads and legs. How can the meat of these tongue-tied creatures slip down your throat?"

But she had finally agreed. After lunch they'd taken a cab back to their district. As soon as Farangu reached home she had flung off her coat and thrown it on a chair. "What a hard person to please that Mrs. Razi is! Whatever you do for her, it's still not enough. Well, it's my own fault. I've spoiled her."

Now Hadi Besharat couldn't restrain himself any longer. He said, "You have to make Mrs. Razi understand that she shouldn't consent to the funeral arrangements and the burial in Behesht Zahra Cemetery. If that poor boy were here he wouldn't appreciate this pretentiousness. He didn't go to the front for the sake of martyrdom. He just wanted to see an ancient land."

Farangu said, "He had other reasons as well. If nothing else, he lost a father to the firing squad."

"Are you going to visit his mother?"

Farangu sighed. "All right, Besharat."

She put her black dress on and set off to visit Mrs. Razi. After she had left, Hadi Besharat went into his study. The clean, broken sunlight passed through the seams of the blinds and fell strip by strip across the daybed. Farangu had laid out his black socks and white shirt so that everything would be ready for his walk to the district park. He chewed a corner of his mustache as he looked in the mirror. He erased an invisible spot on his front teeth. He sat down at his desk and started his letter this way:

Dear Friend, Your Excellency Professor Humphrey,
  Now with quill in hand, expressing the secrets of my

wounded soul, I am compelled to sail on the boat of imagination toward these Arabic verses:

> *There is a split in every man's heart*
> *Which is the seat of his secrets*
> *And nobody knows anything about it.*
> *He wanders the cities and his secrets*
> *Are just a stone fragment, the cracking of which*
> *Will cripple him. . . .*

The noises in the street distracted him. He set down his pen and got up to look out the window. The sunlight had risen about two meters on Engineer Gharib's laboratory wall. Way up at the top of the street a few neighbors moved around poor Mehrdad's bridal chamber. Farther down the avenue, someone was shouting slogans into a megaphone. Ahmad Bayat, Mr. Bayat's second son, was walking around the bridal chamber. Farangu was just leaving Mrs. Razi's, her veil slipping off her head to reveal a flustered expression. Apparently she had not been allowed inside.

In a couple of minutes Hadi Besharat heard Farangu enter the house. He went downstairs and found her sitting on the couch, rocking like a pendulum. Without waiting to catch her breath, she asked, "Why is Nili acting so cold and uncaring? Why did she slam the door in my face?"

Her bleak mood made her face look opaque and indistinct, like the pictures printed in newspapers. She stretched out on the couch, set the back of a hand to her forehead, and complained, "Why has she made herself Mrs. Razi's gatekeeper? Why won't she let anyone talk to the bereaved? Where have old-time friendships and affections gone? Why does everyone complain of the cruel, pitiless world, when they behave the same way themselves?"

She told Hadi Besharat how Nili had opened the door for her. "Why, dear God, she's only eighteen and she looks older than

Mrs. Razi!" It was understandable that Nili wore black, but Farangu had been horrified by the paleness of her face.

She had pressed Nili to her chest as she offered her condolences. Still, Nili didn't let her in. She claimed that Mrs. Razi didn't feel up to seeing anyone. To Hadi Besharat it was plain that Farangu didn't understand what Mrs. Razi must be going through. He told her, "Death, or more correctly martyrdom, is first and foremost a hint of life's evolution and the changing of its direction."

But while he was speaking he wondered why it was that he thought so much about death. Perhaps he was afraid of dying a natural, ordinary death himself. He had always imagined that he would be wounded on the battlefield and the blood would turn his uniform red. Then he would look up at the sky and fall from his steed. Senior commanders would carry him off on their shoulders, wrapped in a blue satin sheet. They would unbutton the brass buttons of his uniform and place a hand on his heart. He would take a few short breaths and say his last words. In ancient death scenes, at least the dying man was allowed to observe his own death, and give his last testament, and ask for forgiveness. Ancient death scenes, unlike today's, were not instantaneous. It was only in modern times that a plump, healthy person could be walking in the street or standing in line for bread, meat, and eggs when suddenly a bullet hit him in the forehead and he was gone forever from this world.

Hadi Besharat decided to go over to Mrs. Razi's house, to enter by force if necessary, and talk with her. He changed his clothes and patted his face and hair in the mirror. Then he tiptoed downstairs so as not to disturb Farangu, and he went out through the courtyard.

Because of the leaky pipes the outside wall of their house was wet. The wetness had seeped in all directions and formed a stain like a map. It made him dizzy just thinking of the cost of the plumbing repairs. There wasn't much money left in his bank account, and he was afraid that with his meager monthly pension they were going to run into debt.

That poor boy's bridal chamber stood at the head of the street, its candles still burning in the light of day. Hadi Besharat held a hand in front of his chest and a hand in front of his crotch and walked quickly, as if stepping out of a bath. He had to think up an excuse for visiting Mrs. Razi. Perhaps he would knock on the door and say he was a trash collector come for her garbage. Perhaps he could find a Revolutionary Guard or a ranking officer and they could enter the house together under the pretext of offering their congratulations and condolences.

He didn't see many people in the street, only the district religious patrol, Mrs. Kobra, who stood holding her baby and chatting with someone in front of the poor boy's bridal chamber. Hadi Besharat scurried along the wall to Mrs. Razi's house. As soon as he pressed the doorbell a frowning Nili Bayat, big as life, appeared behind him. He decided to pay no attention and continued pressing the bell. Nili angrily removed his finger from the button and shouted, "What is this? Don't people have the right to sleep peacefully in their own homes?"

That domineering expression didn't become her young face. In a fatherly tone Hadi Besharat said, "Of course they do, Miss Nili. But I have to see Mrs. Razi. It's important."

With tight lips she said, "Absolutely not."

"That's it?"

"That's it."

"What business is this of yours? Mrs. Razi is not a child in need of a guardian."

"But she has the right to look after her own pain, doesn't she, Professor Besharat?"

Hadi Besharat blinked rapidly. "After all, we're neighbors."

"Even so, she doesn't want to see anyone just now. Please don't bother her."

Nili wore a black taffeta dress and her short, freshly shampooed hair was combed back with care. Every word she pronounced carved soft, clear lines around her lips and nostrils like a circling compass. She had come to look exactly like Mrs. Razi. In the same angry manner she pulled a key from her pocket, opened the door, and entered, closing the door firmly in Hadi Besharat's face. He stood dumfounded in the middle of the street, not knowing what to do next. He tried to figure out where Mrs. Razi was. Maybe she had gone shopping at the crack of dawn. According to Mrs. Kobra, she was visiting the shrine in Ghum for a few days. But nobody was certain and they continued to wait for her.

Suddenly three men ran from the avenue toward the bridal chamber. Hadi Besharat asked Mr. Abolhassan Hashiyeh, "Mr. Hashiyeh, what's going on?"

Mr. Hashiyeh stood next to the wall, holding a folded newspaper under his arm. He jabbed a thumb toward the crowd and said, "Mrs. Razi is reaching the intersection. They say she's returning from the bazaar with a sack. Professor Besharat, the Akkadians had interesting views about death, did they not?"

"Yes, the ancient Akkadians believed that death is a journey to a future life. They couldn't communicate verbally with the dead, so instead they sent them alms."

Mr. Hashiyeh spread his arms in feigned surprise, drew back his head, and said, "Professor, a few years back I was fortunate enough to read your article in—by the way, what was the name of the magazine that published your article? I think it was *Sokhan* magazine. I may be wrong. If you give me a minute it will come to me. Was it *Armaghan* magazine? Yes, it was *Armaghan*."

"It was *Ancient Times* magazine."

"Oh, yes, yes. Only a few issues of it were printed. What a nice magazine. What deep and heavy articles they published. I remember the title of your own article very well indeed: 'The Hidden Faces of Death.' Did I get that right?"

Hadi Besharat kept his eyes on the crowd. Mr. Hashiyeh went on talking. "I myself have done some studies in this field. Of course not at your level. Frequently I've visited important cemeteries like Behesht Zahra, Ibn Bavay, St. Abdollah, and Mesgarabad."

Now at the head of the street Mrs. Razi was approaching the

bridal chamber. She held a shopping bag in her hand and passed absentmindedly through the morning's curtain of light. By Islamic standards, no fault could be found with her appearance. A black veil covered her head and she wore a long black coat. Only her tight, narrow, delicate, high-heeled Italian shoes were inappropriate. They looked almost garish. She seemed to be walking on two stilts like a circus clown. Hadi Besharat worried that she might fall down in the middle of the street in front of everyone. And from the way she wore her veil it was apparent that she wasn't skillful at it. She didn't have the casual walk of a woman accustomed to veils. She moved quickly and with a rebellious demeanor. As she reached the poor boy's bridal chamber, she paused, the tip of her nose in the air. Lowering her eyelids, she glanced at it and, without a word, continued toward her house.

Ahmad Bayat blocked her way and said, "In this neighborhood you are our crown and our pride. The people of this district have given me the honor of standing in your presence and offering you our congratulations and condolences for the martyrdom of that lion in the forest of bravery, that fighter for the path of God and His prophet. The word 'martyrdom' was constantly on his tongue. He waged war with the Iraqi aggressors. He conversed with martyrdom, always burning in the flame of longing. Longing for that moment of arrival, that moment of ferment, that moment of blood birth . . ."

Mrs. Razi glanced again at the bridal chamber. She thought for a minute. Then she bit down on her dentures and said with a lisp, "Thank you very much."

She started to walk away. But Ahmad Bayat continued, "Lady, I swear by the pure saints and the martyrs of the righteous path that the people of this district say only one thing. They say that we must learn courage from you. In this calamity you don't even raise an eyebrow. You don't complain of the world even to a single soul. Instead you shake the warm hands of your kind son's martyrdom. What a lady!" He turned to Hadi Besharat and Mr. Hashiyeh. "I'm proud of this woman. In courage, she's the equal of a man. This is not a woman. This woman is more man than any man."

Mrs. Razi rose up on those narrow, high-heeled Italian shoes and peered at them from behind her cracked spectacles. Then she pulled her veil forward on her head. "Ahmad Agha, dying is a right," she said.

Inside the mosque the lamenters began to sing in mournful, elastic voices:

> "My distressed Ghasem,
> Fare thee well,
> Fare thee well . . ."

Suddenly Mrs. Razi turned and hurried toward her house. In the blink of an eye she disappeared into her courtyard. Then the Revolutionary Guards and the members of the Komité came out of the mosque, bearing the casket of some new martyr on their shoulders and marched down the middle of the avenue, which grew crowded. The black-garbed women etched parallel lines on the horizon like calligraphy. The casket was uncovered and the shroud looked whiter than new snow. White as an iceberg, floating on the North Pole's silvery waters. Cold as the snowy Russian steppes on which the frostbitten army of Napoleon passed. Among Stalingrad's ruins the skeleton of a truck burned upside down in the flames. A scene from World War I stretched to the horizon. General von Schlieffen sent a message to his commanders from his deathbed: "Don't forget. Keep the right wing of the German army strong."

The new commander general, General von Moltke, is afraid of France's Seventeenth Plan. He rubs his hands together: what if the French attack? He fears they will pierce the heart of the German army from Alsace and Lorraine. But in those navy-blue uniforms the French soldiers could be beautiful targets for the German artillery. The Germans aren't dumb or blind. They can easily punch the French soldiers' chests full of a thousand holes, like sieves. At night General von Moltke dreams of General von

Schlieffen repeating the same instruction over and over: "Don't build garrisons and shelters. Build railroads."

The German army must be mobile. You can't crush an army of iron and steel with élan alone. To confront the Tsar's Russians, he must dispatch a fresh force from the right wing. In our time the army has no use for sentiment. Only mobility! Only speed!

Hadi Besharat snapped his chin upward and told Mr. Hashiyeh, "No, Agha, nothing cures these people. They always insist on making an epic out of sudden death."

Mr. Hashiyeh drew the newspaper from beneath his arm. He said, "God willing, I hope there will be more opportunities to enjoy your company."

"God willing."

Hadi Besharat had to find another way to visit Mrs. Razi. He returned home. Without looking for Farangu, he climbed the stairs to his study and shut himself inside. The constant, empty silence oppressed him. He didn't have the spirit to continue his letter to Professor Humphrey, and so he sat at his desk and held his head between his hands. Like an astronaut, he was floating in space. He was swimming in a dry river, fixing his eyes on a nearby shore that he was unable to reach.

He wondered what Farangu was doing. She used to watch over him silently and from a distance. She used to be a voiceless ghost who tiptoed around him in his study. With a damp cloth she would dust the book covers, the antique objects, and the desk. She would put a white handkerchief in his pocket and pour tea into his glass, disappearing afterward into the dark of the passageway. He had known she was there only from the sound of her bare feet. Her breathing was like the monotonous rustle of a broom dusting the house's solitude. But this was before her recent change of attitude, before she started snapping at him all the time. Where was she now?

He opened the door and saw her below, sleeping on the rug in the entrance hall. He went downstairs and called her in a low voice. "Farangu!"

She raised her head and glanced blurrily at the wall clock. "What time is it? It's getting on toward noon and I haven't started lunch yet."

"Wake up! See how the neighbors have gathered around the poor boy's bridal chamber. They're tying wish-cloths to it, and beating their breasts, and singing passion songs as though a saint has risen. That is what we're waiting for: someone to come out of the dust on the road and perform a miracle for us."

"How about Mrs. Razi? Has anyone seen her?"

"Only for a second. She still keeps her door closed and Nili won't let anyone talk to her."

Hadi Besharat drifted out to the kitchen, leaving Farangu in the hall. Over his shoulder he said, "Farangu, what if that poor boy is not dead after all? Nobody's come from the front and we haven't heard of any eyewitness. There've been a lot of casualties lately. Maybe the officials made a mistake."

"No, Engineer Gharib has taken a picture of the poor boy's body. They've put it in his bridal chamber."

"Does it look like him?"

"A body that's lain three days under the merciless sun of the Khozestan desert, what do you expect? It swells up and the face changes."

"Why was it necessary to take a picture of that? Mrs. Razi has a thousand different photos of the boy. They might not be as good as those the reporters take. But at our own level they're presentable. Why didn't they choose one of them for his bridal chamber? Personally, I don't believe Mehrdad is dead. Maybe he's crossed the border. Maybe he's been captured. I feel sorry for these people. They look at that picture and think they're looking at a martyr's face."

With barely controlled anger Farangu said, "Was Engineer Gharib wrong in wanting to do a bereaved mother a favor?"

"No, no. Never mind me. We're just a nit-picking nation."

Hadi Besharat stood in the middle of the kitchen with his hands at his back. The sky was visible above the iron grate in the ceiling and the tangled branches of the wisteria vine crisscrossed it. He thought he heard the chirping of a bird. Doubtfully he asked, "Did you hear a bird?"

"What bird?"

"Have you noticed this year there are fewer birds around? We don't see any green finches or starlings. Do you remember how the courtyard used to be full of starlings? They covered everything so completely, you couldn't see the ground."

"Oh, my God, I'm getting tired of listening to you. It's winter. You expect birds to cover the ground in winter?"

Hadi Besharat returned to the hall. Squatting next to Farangu, he said, "Why do I think of dying all the time?"

"How should I know? Maybe you're losing your mind."

"If I die, do you promise to stand in the same doorway every Friday night and remember me?"

The veil slipped down on Farangu's shoulders. The wandering light dallied in the hall and glowed like crystal on her skin, on her soft face and her hazel eyes. Hadi Besharat took hold of her arm and whispered in her ear, "Do you promise to remember me Friday evenings?"

"Remember you how?"

"Sing me the Mandaean evening prayer."

Farangu shrugged and said, "I don't know it."

Hadi Besharat held her hands and whispered, " 'You come from the house of life . . .' "

" 'You come from the house of life . . .' "

Hadi Besharat recited:

> *"You come, what did you bring for us?*
> *I brought you the news that you shall never die*
> *And your souls' ascension to heaven shall not be prevented.*
> *For the day of your death, I brought you life*
> *And for the day of your sorrow, I brought you joy. . . ."*

A silence flowed between them. Farangu lifted her veil from her shoulders and stood up. She raised her chin and said, "Besharat, let's sell our house, cash in everything we own, and go to America. To hell with a few miserable pennies of pension money! Khosro is running a good business, God bless him. The car wash will bring a nice income once he finds a partner to pay his debts, and he'll soon be getting his business degree. Then he can live comfortably. In America there are all kinds of opportunities. We'll rent a tiny apartment and buy a little car with good gas mileage. You can teach and I'll keep busy sewing. What's wrong with that?"

Hadi Besharat was thoughtful. He didn't want to discourage her, and yet he didn't agree with her. "Let's talk to him. Let's see what he says."

Farangu seized her advantage. Immediately she threw aside her veil, sat next to the telephone stand, and dialed Khosro's number. She pressed the receiver to her ear, looking excited and smiling at Hadi Besharat out of the corner of her eye. The prolonged ringing at the other end of the line bridged the distance between continents, the oceans, and the geographic boundaries.

Hadi Besharat asked, "What if he's asleep? What time is it now in America?"

Farangu shook her head impatiently. A smile brightened her face and she said, "Here he is, Besharat. Here he is!" Now she was talking to Khosro. "Khosro, Khosro-jon! Did we wake you up?"

Hadi Besharat said, "Ask him what time it is there."

"Dear, your father asks what time it is there."

Khosro said something, and Farangu said, "We thought it must be midnight in America. . . . Really? Is it raining?" She covered the receiver and told Hadi Besharat, "It's raining there. He has a cold. Doesn't feel good. . . ." Again she spoke to Khosro: "Well, why didn't you write? We would have sent you some aspirin, dear. The aspirin is much better here. Did you get the pictures? . . . That's the trouble with growing old. Pillows under my eyes. Do you want to talk to your father?"

She held the receiver out to Hadi Besharat and he sat down next to her and put it gently to his ear. Distant noises and other people's conversations made a long tunnel inside the receiver. At the end of it, Khosro was waiting. His waiting pressed heavily against Hadi Besharat's eardrum. Hadi Besharat began to cough and he said with difficulty, "Khosro-jon, what's the matter with you? Are you sick?"

"Papa-jon, nothing's wrong with me."

"Your mother's worried, son."

"Do you have some extra money? If I don't get hold of twenty thousand dollars within two weeks I'll be bankrupt."

"Dollars? At sixty tumans per dollar? Where do you think I would find twenty thousand dollars?"

"In three months I can send it back to you with ten percent interest."

"But I thought your car wash was doing so well."

"I can't find a partner and I'm going bankrupt."

"It would've been better to buy an uninhabited island in the Atlantic instead."

"In the Atlantic Ocean?"

"There are a lot of uninhabited islands in the Atlantic and nobody wants them. You could have bought one. Then you'd be king of the island and your own boss."

"What could an uninhabited island do for me?"

"Well, nowadays, you know, there are a lot of terrorists who constantly hijack jet airplanes. No country gives them permission to land, but you could."

"Well, suppose I did and they landed on my island. What would I get out of it?"

"In return, you take their airplanes. Do you know how many millions a jet plane is worth? You can junk it and sell it for spare parts to our own government. They need those."

"You're joking."

Farangu tugged Hadi Besharat's sleeve and said quietly, "Besharat, that's enough now. How you talk! Tell him we want to go to America."

"Khosro, think about it."

"Besharat!"

"Look, your mother wants to speak to you. She wants to go to America. What do you think?"

"This call is getting expensive. I'll phone you in a few days and we'll talk about it. Would it be possible for you to go to Mr. Bayat and ask him to send me that two thousand dollars he owes me? Make sure you say that I don't mean to pressure him. It's just that I need the money."

"I'll have to think about it."

"Here I delivered all those girders to him, and I didn't expect any favors, either. Tell him now I'm stuck. I have to pay wages, electricity, water and phone bills . . ."

Farangu put her lips to the receiver and said, "Oh, baba, that's enough. We're getting ready to come there. Send us an official invitation. We need a letter of invitation."

Khosro said hastily, "I have to hang up."

Farangu said, "Good-bye, dear. Don't forget to take your tonic."

Hadi Besharat replaced the receiver.

Farangu squeezed his arm and wiped her tears on a corner of her sweater. Hadi Besharat pressed his hands to his knees and stood up with a heavy sigh, mumbling, "How can you make these young people understand logic?"

"Besharat, I want to go to America."

"Why is it so cold? I'm shivering. What's today's date? Is it March yet?"

"I don't know."

"We've lost count of the days."

He went up the stairs slowly, sat at his desk, and began to write the rest of Professor Humphrey's letter. But this time he wrote in a notebook, in English. Since high school he had always kept a notebook close by for jotting down sudden ideas.

Dear Professor Humphrey,

Because I read and write my subjects of interest in English, it is better that I not write this letter in Farsi. You have to understand that my questions are purely for the purpose of clarifying scientific issues and are not related to any personal problems.

After this preamble, you have no doubt recognized this letter's importance. It is a questionnaire about this century's high ideas and our much-disturbed time. Because we believe that the evolution of time leaves no imprint on the human being's fixed and eternal ideas.

My request is this. Please express your opinion on the following issues:

1. Is the soul superior to the body?
2. Is the existence of the supernatural possible?
3. Is the human's capacity limited or can we be optimistic that he will find acceptable answers to his philosophical problems?
4. How can conclusions be drawn from life's experiences? What possibility is there for a deeper appreciation of life?
5. Is there any hope for the annihilation of war?

Please allow me to introduce another question which is totally different from those above. I want to take this opportunity to ask a question about yourself. There is no doubt that you are a learned, serious, logical, and just human being. But why don't you feel more responsibility for your fellow humans? Why don't you answer people's letters? Why does the destiny of man, this two-legged and sinful animal, not frighten you? What has happened to us? Are we going backward?

I want an answer!

> Your friend of many years,
> Professor Hadi Besharat

He put his pen down. His eyes fell on the framed photograph that he'd taken during his first trip to America. Every Easter, Professor Humphrey used to invite a group of Orientalists to something he called Ali Baba's Picnic. He'd asked Hadi Besharat to join them. Hadi Besharat had arrived before anyone else. Half an hour later the whole bunch of mad-looking, self-satisfied specialists appeared. They brought their antique carpets, spread them out side by side on Whitehurst College's green lawn, and began impressing each other with their expertise.

One said, "This is a Gashgai rug that was captured by the Russians in the war of Turkoman Chai, early nineteenth century."

Another said, "There are plenty of those rugs all over and they aren't worth more than three thousand dollars apiece."

An old woman shielded her eyes from the sun. She asked Hadi Besharat, "Who are you?"

Hadi Besharat answered politely, "I am Professor Besharat."

"Where are you from?"

"I'm from Iran. I'm a lecturer on heavenly angels."

"You've come from Iran to lecture on heavenly angels? I can't believe it!"

"Why not? Listen carefully; you can hear the angels sing. That whispering at dawn is the sound of Gabriel's fluttering wings. The lowered head of the daffodil is an angel bowing in prayer. Every day they sing songs for us—the songs of the heroes in the world of counterparts, the songs of the silent battlefields."

The old woman shook her head in bafflement and walked away. Hadi Besharat felt like a foreigner. Deep in thought, he sat down on a swing in the middle of the lawn. All of a sudden a hand pushed him from behind and he started swinging. He turned and saw a small child. The child's corn-tassel hair cascaded over his forehead, and he looked at Hadi Besharat with blue eyes. Hadi Besharat braced his feet on the ground and asked, "Do you enjoy swinging people?"

The child bit a fingertip, clutching a doll to his chest. Hadi Besharat thought of his own son, Khosro. He said, "What's your doll's name?"

"This is a lion."

"It doesn't look like a lion."

The child hugged the doll to his chest. Hadi Besharat tried to ease the boy's disappointment. "Well, it's your doll and you can call it whatever you want."

The child put the doll in front of Hadi Besharat's face and imitated a lion growling, showing his fangs and claws. Hadi Besharat couldn't help laughing. The boy said angrily, "It's a lion. You have to believe it."

"Why should I believe that?"

"Really, you have to believe it."

An idea occurred to him that might please the boy. He turned his head and began to talk to an invisible person. The boy asked, "Who are you talking to?"

"Whenever I have a problem I consult with an imaginary friend of mine."

The boy grew curious and asked, "Well, what does your friend say?" He held up his doll and said, "Does he believe that this is a lion?"

"My friend says, 'It's not important that I believe you. It's important that you believe yourself.'"

The boy put his hand to Hadi Besharat's back and pushed him harder. "You shouldn't believe what your friend says either."

Hadi Besharat threw his head back, laughing loudly as he swung.

He wasn't sure what year it was that an American astronaut first orbited earth. That was when Farangu made a space suit for Khosro. He wore the suit whenever they went to a party. He used to pretend he was an astronaut flying to the moon. Anyone who saw him in his space suit said, "Goodness! Dear Lord!"

Hadi Besharat used to take Khosro by the hand and they would go buy ice cream cones or fruit juice. When they passed the window of the Sina Pharmacy he would show Khosro the glass jars containing human fetuses, snakes, scorpions, and tarantulas. He said, "See how alive they look."

He wanted Khosro to understand that human beings are always struggling against death, fighting for immortality. But Khosro was too young to fathom it. He would only stare at his father and recite something he had learned in school like, "Two times three equals six."

The child was learning the four mathematical operations and he kept trying to make Hadi Besharat happy with his quick mind. Of course Hadi Besharat didn't object to this, and he smiled approvingly. But Khosro's attention would wander and he would press a small fingertip to the pharmacy window, drawing a few short lines which came to resemble a swastika. What can you do? You can't force children. They don't want to hear. Then they grow up, get their diplomas, and go to America. From year to year they don't write or call or send news of themselves. Only when they hit an impasse in their lives or need money do they remember their parents once again, and night after night they phone to ask why no one comes to their rescue.

Well, let it be. Just knowing that Khosro was healthy and doing well in his studies was enough for Hadi Besharat. Every father hopes that his children won't get bogged down in life. Khosro had become a man now and he was running his own business so as not to be dependent on his parents. It wouldn't be a bad idea to send him some more of those photos that Engineer Gharib had taken of Farangu, to make him remember home while he was in a foreign country.

Once again Hadi Besharat recalled Khosro in that space suit. How really cute he had looked. He felt his heart weaken just thinking about it.

T H R E E

Hadi Besharat listened to the ticktock of the clock. The constant dripping of the pipes made him feel that a secret crisis was developing in the corridor. A crisis that took a breath after each pause, waiting for the next pause, keeping him in a state of apprehension. The moments unwound and the flow of events ceased.

He began translating Chapter Three of *The Death of a Great Savior.* He had arrived at Professor Humphrey's introductory discussion of Mani's final journey from Maysan to Pargalia. At Pargalia, Mani reads parts of his epitome on repentance and confession, and his companions weep upon hearing the legend of the Babylonian angels: Gabriel, the angel who watches over young people's deaths; Kafziel, the angel who watches over kings' deaths; Mashadber, the angel who watches over children's deaths; and Hemah, the angel who watches over domestic animals' deaths.

The courtyard door slammed and shuffling footsteps broke the silence in the corridor. He heard Farangu speaking to Nili. "Nili-jon, you look so much like both your papa-jon and your mama-jon."

He was surprised. After all her complaints, why was Farangu acting so friendly toward Nili? The rhythmic dripping sound didn't interfere with the flow of her words. It only gave them a special order which made it easier not to hear them—like the whispering of a prayer repeated minute by minute, or the sound of her sewing machine stopping and starting at intervals.

Nili answered, "I can see your point about my mama-jon, but where's the resemblance to my papa-jon?"

"You look like your eldest brother, too."

"You mean Agha Mojtaba? No!"

"I swear to God. The corners of your eyes, the curves around your lips. You resemble each other very closely. It's been a long time since we've heard from him. How is he doing?"

"After he was fired from the embassy he enrolled in agricultural school. Now he wants to remarry his wife in an Islamic wedding. Not like our own Islamic weddings, though. There's a gentleman in America who performs weddings with poems by Hafez and Shakespeare."

"Hmm, with poems by Hafez and Shakespeare? Mojtaba told you this himself?"

"He calls us up and talks for hours. He has a list of telephone numbers and he calls everyone. I would say three times a week . . . four times a week."

"What will you have? There's fruit, sherbet, and nonalcoholic beer."

"No, plain water's fine. Pour me some water. I'll drink that."

Farangu must have gone out to the kitchen, for her voice grew fainter. "When is Mrs. Razi coming back? Behesht Zahra Cemetery isn't that far."

"She hasn't gone to Behesht Zahra. She's gone to Shabdolazim. Did I tell you that Engineer Gharib and I went to the morgue and claimed the poor boy's body?"

"Yes, you told me. I wish I could die. How could you bring yourself to do that?"

"Because we didn't want Mrs. Razi to do it. Everyone said she ought to go to the morgue herself. But I said, 'Why should she? She's the mother. She should be left alone with her misery.'"

"Hmm, what is your involvement in all this?"

"It's something I can do in Mehrdad's memory. I can take

care of his mother for him." Nili paused for a moment. "Well, where's Professor Besharat?"

"How should I know? No doubt he's in his study, keeping himself busy with his work. Besharat! Besharat!"

He laid down his pen and listened without answering. Now that Farangu was calling his name, he felt awkward about eavesdropping.

Farangu went on talking. "Usually he stays up late at night. Then he sleeps half the next day. You can't leave him alone for a minute; he suddenly gets up and goes for a walk and gets lost in the streets. Then he takes a cab to come home and forgets the address." Her voice grew louder as she returned to the drawing room. ". . . he doesn't pay attention to anything. What if someone entered our house and took all we own? Do you remember a few months back? They broke into Mr. Lajevardi's house in the middle of the night, put a pillow over his mouth, and told him, 'Give us whatever you have, Agha.' "

"No, they said, 'We're not thieves, Agha. We're freedom fighters. We attend the university. We're getting our diplomas.' "

Hadi Besharat said to himself, "When a thief comes with a lamp, he takes better-quality goods."

Nili continued speaking. "Miss Farangu, why do you keep the light on in front of Khosro's room? It's daytime now."

"I don't know. We're used to it. Since he went to America, we keep his light on all the time."

"Do you want me to go turn it off?"

"No, dear. Let it be."

"Can I see Khosro's room?"

"No, dear. I haven't swept it in quite a while. It needs dusting. You can see it some other time."

Farangu and Nili must have run into each other in the street and been unable to avoid greeting each other. Perhaps General Ghovanlu's wife had acted as go-between, seeing to it that they kissed and made up. Well, this would keep Farangu occupied, at least. But Hadi Besharat was obsessed now with the idea of escaping. He looked out the window at that poor boy's bridal chamber. Two women had wrapped their fingers in the corners of their veils and were pressing them to their lips. They were exchanging pleasantries and preparing to separate. The wind blew the black and green banners and moved the tip of St. Abbas's metal hand where it pointed skyward above the bridal chamber. Focusing on these details pained Hadi Besharat, but it also cleansed his heart like a sorrow endured in solitude.

He took off his gray shoes, the ones with the zippers instead of shoelaces. Holding them against his chest, he tiptoed downstairs so that Farangu and Nili wouldn't waylay him. Once in the street, he put his shoes on again and started walking.

He saw the mourners' flags and the amulets hanging from the bridal-chamber roof—the protective eyes and five-fingered tin hands twisting around each other in the wind. In his mind he heard a song repeating itself. He had heard that song in the corridors of Whitehurst College's cathedral. The chorusing of a group of boys not fully grown circulated in the hollow, covered spaces of the cathedral, ascending to the arches of the ceiling as though the angels were growing wings and floating soundlessly in the sky. He knew he was searching for something, but the description of what he wanted was beyond him. A view, a sound, a smell almost within his grasp, bringing him intense excitement and a feeling of tenderness. He stretched his hand passionately in every direction but he couldn't reach it.

He quickened his pace. On the avenue he passed the Komité Building and the Head and Foot Restaurant. Ramezan the ice seller was just getting ready to eat his lunch; Hadi Besharat glimpsed him through the restaurant window. Ramezan had shaved his head like a newly mown lawn, and he wore a white shirt and a shabby suit. When Hadi Besharat stepped inside to greet him, Ramezan plucked the handkerchief from his lap and laboriously raised his heavy body to a standing position. "God's blessing." He put a hand on his chest and bowed his head. "We are devoted. We are at your service."

These were the greetings exchanged by street Arabs. Hadi

Besharat put two fingers to his beret and saluted him. "Our eyes are brightened."

Ramezan bowed again. "Excellency, you are kind to favor us. Please sit down. There's a little bread and lamb. It's not worthy of you."

Hadi Besharat waved a refusal and said, "Thank you. I'm not hungry. How are your wife and children?"

"With your kindness, they all kiss your hand."

In 1941, newly arrived from Khezrabad for his studies, Hadi Besharat had rented a small room from Ramezan just behind the old icehouse. Early every evening Ramezan's flunkies would bring Ramezan a tray containing a bottle of Arak 55, a bowl of marjoram beans, and salt and pepper. Ramezan wouldn't touch the food immediately. He would pull out a Gorgan cigarette, put it in his cigarette holder, and puff steadily while he surveyed his men.

Now Hadi Besharat asked him, "What are you doing in this district?"

"We've been summoned by the Komité. They've been interrogating us since early morning. We didn't get a chance to have our lunch till now. Please excuse me . . ."

A plate of lamb, a bowl of pickles, pita bread, a tomato, and a bottle of mineral water sat in front of him. Ramezan took his time and cut the tomato into four wedges, removing the yellow seeds one by one with the tip of his knife. Then he pressed the meat into the pocket of the bread and offered it to Hadi Besharat. "Please. It's not worthy of you."

"Thank you very much. I don't have any appetite." Turning to look out at the poor boy's bridal chamber, Hadi Besharat asked, "Why did the Komité summon you?"

Ramezan chewed his food and wiped his mouth with his handkerchief. "They want to hand us down an unjust sentence. I swear to St. Hosein, they've broken our horns. They say we're running games of chance and opium houses." Flapping one arm despairingly, he continued, "Aah, that was ten years ago. Today our worldly goods are a few odds and ends that don't amount to a penny."

"Don't worry. A man with a clean heart is afraid of nothing. You drink the water from your own heart."

Ramezan the ice seller held his food between his fingers and stared at him. He was waiting for Hadi Besharat to add some explanation. Hadi Besharat touched his beret in a farewell gesture and went back out to the street.

Now he saw Ahmad Bayat running toward him with a hand pressed to his heart. When he came close he stopped, panting, and said, "Professor Besharat, how are you? Why don't you come jog with me a little?"

"We are only holding onto our hat so no one can snatch it off," Hadi Besharat told him.

Ahmad Bayat rolled up his sleeves and looked around impatiently. He started running in place. He asked, "When will you come out of your little hole?"

Hadi Besharat pulled his handkerchief from his pocket and dabbed his nose, shaking his head regretfully. Then he started toward the bridal chamber. It wasn't something he'd planned. Very naturally and almost without choice, he was propelled in that direction. It was a task he'd been postponing all this time. Whenever he thought of the bridal chamber an eerie feeling came over him, warning him not to go there and yet urging him secretly onward.

He saw an old woman coming toward the bridal chamber, struggling with her tremors. She mumbled a few admiring words to Mehrdad and whispered the prayer for the dead. Two young women passed by, less attentive. They covered their faces tightly with their veils and walked rapidly.

Hadi Besharat himself, having made all those studies of death and martyrdom, could not remain indifferent. He took off his beret and felt the way he had in Paris, when he stood at attention in front of the Tomb of the Unknown Soldier and listened to the funeral march. An insistent thought bothered him. The thought that in the meanderings of history he'd been given the role of mere observer and couldn't change the course of events. He wasn't allowed to bring the mistakes of great world conquerors to their attention and say to them, "Oh, Napoleon, Darius, Genghis, with all your genius and your passion for conquest, why can't you see two feet in front of your noses?"

He put his beret back on and prepared to leave. As he walked past the bridal chamber his gaze skimmed the tulip lamps and five-fingered hands and tin eyes hanging from the edge of the roof. Inside, the chamber was decorated like a bridal tray. If it had been up to Farangu she would certainly have placed a mattress and pillow and quilt there. Not life-sized, but a little smaller. Like a doll's bed. If she were in the mood, perhaps she would have made a bride doll and a bridegroom doll, each the size of her hand, and put them in the little bed so it would look more natural. Hadi Besharat ducked his head through the lace curtains and smelled dried mint leaves. Everything inside was arranged in a very orderly manner. He saw an icon of a handsome oppressed saint, holding a sword the size of a fishbone. The sword had passed through the head of an accursed monster, descending to the level of its belly button and splitting its body in two like an overripe squash. No doubt it was Nili who had put Mani's psalm book and the roses and the plate of halvah there as a memorial offering. An inexperienced, emotional girl who got mixed up in people's lives for no good reason, never listening to anyone. No doubt she had put these candles in the bridal chamber. The teardrops of the half-burned candles fell into a saucer filled with flour. Like an invisible finger, the melted wax broke the flour's surface and left a hole behind. The weak light from the flames fluttered on the glass that covered the poor boy's picture, showing his face in a way that disturbed Hadi Besharat.

What a strange photo Engineer Gharib had taken of him! It wasn't very different from a living person's photo. But the width of the face pressed the borders of the frame, and the nose was flattened and the lips swollen as if Mehrdad were squashing his face against a windowpane. He wore a black shirt, and its tight collar squeezed his neck. Hadi Besharat was reminded of a wax statue that sits in a museum and holds an empty wineglass. An example of Japanese elegance, keeping the hidden violence under control. The elegance of a glazed bowl's flower and bird designs, the delicacy of a newly sprouted branch, the curve of a rosebud petal.

And what a large face! With those closed eyes and puffed cheeks, he appeared to be holding his breath. As though he were surfacing from underwater and the wet strands of hair were sticking to his forehead. Strands of hair like the branches of a tree that had lost their leaves after some explosion. Medusa's hair, tangled like a stag's horns. Like snakes stiffened by a flash of lightning, recoiling after striking at the sky.

Hadi Besharat withdrew his head from the bridal chamber. He could find almost no resemblance between that photo and Mehrdad. The poor boy's living face came to his mind. He had always had a slight smile on his lips, but not a sarcastic smile. It had only shrugged off momentary defeats and awaited further events. As if saying, "Wait a bit. I'll show you."

Hadi Besharat looked toward his own house. From this distance he could see that two thirds of the outside wall was completely soaked. The wet spot was spreading like a giant galaxy. As the damp reached the brick foundation it widened. He had to talk to Farangu about getting that leak fixed.

He passed by Mrs. Razi's house. The windowpanes had been smeared with liquid chalk so he couldn't see through them. There was no trace of anyone around. He tried the door. It was locked and resisted the pressure of his fingers. He peered through the keyhole to find out what was going on. The courtyard was silent and the winter wind barely rippled the water in the pool. He grumbled, "What is this?"

He was no longer certain that discussing Mehrdad with Mrs. Razi was such a wise idea. Better that he limit himself to a simple, casual visit. He could sit in front of her in silence and just stare at her. Then he could find his way home again.

When he arrived at his house Farangu was standing at the top of the stairs gazing into the full-length mirror. She wore a green satin dress that dated from the time she'd played Tosca, many years ago. It had been her costume in that scene where the police commissioner whispers in her ear, trying to tempt her with promises. She lifted her ringlets off the back of her neck. From her tilted face, it was obvious that her mind was drawn to the police commissioner's temptations. But at the same time she was enjoying her reflection in the mirror.

She walked the corridor from end to end and when she turned back her eyes fell on Hadi Besharat. She thrust her hair behind her ears and said, "Besharat, look. After twenty years, it's still not too tight. See how nicely it hangs. Don't you like it?"

"How silly you're acting!" Hadi Besharat said. "Why was Nili here?"

"You don't appreciate beautiful dresses, Besharat. Nili just came to visit awhile. She's lonely and she wants me to teach her to sew so she can keep herself busy."

"And what is this photo that Engineer Gharib has taken of that poor boy? It doesn't look like him at all."

"Enough of your talk about death! You're giving me a headache. Besharat, you have to think of some way to get that leak fixed. Our house is being ruined."

"Tomorrow we'll call the plumber."

Farangu turned her back to him. She said, "Do you think Khosro will ever come home and start a business here?"

"What's wrong with where he is now? You want him to be caught in this mess like us?"

"If he decides to stay there we have to pack up and go to America. I can't stand it here anymore."

"Life in America isn't easy. You put a parrot and a crow together in a cage, can they get along? Some people are like water. They flow wherever you want them to. Some people are like sesame paste. You can spread them on anything. Some people are solid as lead, like myself. I'll remain the same no matter where you put me. In a foreign country you have to get along with its people. When I wanted to leave America in 1969, Professor Humphrey told me that giving up such a good position was insane. Well, he's American, he doesn't know much about our culture. I said, 'I should stay in America for what? My expertise has no technological value. I only know how to say a few things about Jewish, Christian, and Islamic angels.' "

Farangu fell to her knees, held her head between her hands, and swung right and left like a pendulum. Hadi Besharat thought she was excited about what he was saying. "Moreover, I am getting up in years. Fifty-seven years is no joke. I told Professor Humphrey, 'Oh, baba, I am not the Angel Barya'il to enjoy five-hundred-year journeys. I am Dumah, the Angel of Silence and Stillness. I am Cassiel, the Angel of Solitude and Tears . . .' "

Farangu shouted, "My head is bursting!" She pressed her temples with her fingers. Whenever the accursed migraine hit her she isolated herself this way. Nausea would make the world heavy and indigestible for her.

Hadi Besharat lifted her chin with a fingertip and said, "Your left eye is red. Do you think that's from your migraine? Why are you wearing this flashy dress?"

"Leave me alone. Just leave me alone. Besharat, I want to go visit my Mama Aliyeh tomorrow."

"What for? Do you miss her pointless conversation?"

"She won't come to our house anymore because you've offended her."

Hadi Besharat made a face and pretended to be Mama Aliyeh: " 'What did I say? When did I ever meddle in your life?' "

"You have to call her and get it out of her heart."

Hadi Besharat threw his hands up. "Pah! I don't have the time. I don't care for nosy people who try to interfere in other people's business."

Farangu rose and started down the stairs, with Hadi Besharat close behind. She went into the kitchen and took her headache pills from the cabinet. "Do whatever you like," she said, swallowing a pill. "There's no point arguing with you. When do you want your supper?"

"I'm not hungry."

"Well, eat what you can and leave the rest, then. Put it in the refrigerator for tomorrow's lunch, when I'm at Mama Aliyeh's and there's nobody here to cook for you."

Farangu angrily slammed the plate on the table. Hadi Besharat sat down in silence and began to toy with a cutlet. He ate very little, so that he wouldn't get gas and have trouble sleeping. His stomach felt heavy. He mixed some Agilax powder into a glass of water and forced himself to drink it down. "God bless the Agilax powder. When I swallow a spoonful after a meal, I can sleep soundly till morning."

Whenever he took his Agilax, it lubricated his bowels beautifully and got them moving by the crack of dawn. Dr. Nezali, a former student who lived in Germany now, sent him a huge package of the powder every year. How well those Germans made medicines! Without the Germans' tablets, drops, and syrups, he would lose his spirit completely. He would be forced to scowl and walk around the flower beds instead of working on his translation and his studies. He would look anxiously at the tops of the pine trees. On those occasions Hadi Besharat was unbearably aware of his own bodily existence.

That night, for the first time in quite a while, he slept deeply. When he opened his eyes in the morning the vague sounds of the house came alive again—the murmur of the old foundation, the creaking of a door in need of paint and repairs. He listened for the sounds of Farangu moving about the kitchen. But then he remembered that she'd gone to visit her Mama Aliyeh and left him alone in the house. In the entrance hall the clock struck eleven. How late he was sleeping these days! It was almost noon and he hadn't yet shaved or changed. Pale bands of winter sunlight had already reached the foot of the daybed. He had to get up quickly and start work on his translation.

While he was changing clothes he heard the doorbell ring. First he thought it was his imagination, but then he heard it again. He zipped his trousers in a hurry and ran downstairs to open the door to the courtyard. There stood Nili Bayat, holding her blind sister's hand and trying to peer up into his study window. As soon as she saw him she asked in surprise, "Professor Besharat, were you still in bed?"

"Why, Miss Nili?"

"We rang the bell three times and nobody answered. We thought you might be asleep."

"What sleep? Sleep is not so easy for me. Did you want something?"

Quickly and smartly, she showed him a pack of airmail envelopes. She held them out as if presenting him with a bunch of flowers. She said, "Before going to visit her Mama Aliyeh, Miss Farangu told us you needed these. She gave me the money and asked me to buy them for you."

He took the envelopes and looked at them in a daze. "Thank you very much. You shouldn't have bothered. I was planning to go shopping today in the little bazaar." He opened the door a bit wider. "Please come in. I was just going to pour myself some tea. Would you like . . ."

He couldn't figure out why, but he felt as if Nili were passing him a concealed message. On the surface, though, she was pleasant enough—natural and almost childlike, as though nothing in the district had changed. Hadi Besharat turned his eyes to Heli. She was smiling. She knew something but she wasn't giving it away.

A little over a year ago acid had been thrown in Heli's face because she wasn't properly veiled according to the new Islamic rules. She had spent a few months in the hospital while the burns healed. Now the skin on her cheeks and the blurred lines around her eyes and lips were unnaturally flattened. The healed scars had troweled her face and leveled it like the palm of a hand. Instead of eyelids, a soft, shining membrane covered her eyes. Hadi Besharat could hardly bear to look at her. Sometimes he would accidentally catch a glimpse of her face and he would feel sick. Then he didn't know what to say. He wanted to pretend that things were still the same and so he would talk hurriedly of other matters, referring to the days when she and Mehrdad used to throw their arms around each other and spin like pinwheels on Mr. Bayat's rooftop.

Nili tugged Heli's hand and the two of them entered the front hall. Barefoot and with uncombed hair, Hadi Besharat walked in front of them, leading the way to the drawing room. "I don't know where Farangu keeps the fruit and cookies."

Nili gently guided her sister to the couch. After she had seated her, she helped her arrange the knitting that Heli had been carrying under her arm. Then she began wandering around the room, curiously sizing it up. She said, "Professor Besharat, the light's still on at the top of the stairs. Do you want me to turn it off?"

"No, thank you. Leave it on. You sit here next to Miss Heli. I'll go bring the tea."

"I can do that for you."

Hadi Besharat was growing annoyed, but he forced a smile. "There's no need to trouble yourself."

"Whatever you want I'll bring you."

Hadi Besharat paused, thinking of how to block her. Heli said, "Let her do it. She gets bored just sitting. Meanwhile you and I can have a little talk."

Hadi Besharat yielded. "You embarrass me with your kindness."

After Nili had left the room Heli started fiddling with something. The glaring light from the window behind her made it hard for Hadi Besharat to see her. It was only from her elbow movements and the clicking of her needles that he sensed she'd begun knitting. Facing her made him feel ashamed and neglectful. He spoke to her cautiously. "Well, how are you feeling?"

"Fine, thank God."

"I haven't heard any news of your father for some time. Is he all right?"

"Thank God, he's getting better. His speech has improved a lot since he returned from America."

"It wasn't a good idea for him to come back. He should have stayed there. This is not the place to live."

"How do you know? A man his age can't forget seventy years and go live in a foreign country. What about you? Aren't you planning a trip to America?"

Hadi Besharat became nervous and answered, "No, not at all."

The sun turned the room a solid white, blurring the details of the front wall and the borders of the antique objects. He felt he might have just moved here from their old house in the Salsabil district. He heard Khosro's cradle rocking. Beside the cradle Farangu sat curled like a comma, her bare feet stretched to one side on the rug and her date-colored hair hanging over her face. He asked Heli, "When Miss Nili brings the tea, is there some special place I should put your cup so you can find it without difficulty?"

Heli laughed like a little girl and said, "Professor Besharat, it's true I can't see, but I can still sense where everything is. For example, I sense you're standing in the middle of the room, feeling uneasy and not yet sure where you want to sit."

"Strange! You can tell that?"

"In my mind I always make a pattern of things."

"Are you making a pattern of me?"

"Everything in life is like knitted clothing now. I make a stitch for everything."

Her hand passed through a curtain of light and groped for the teacup on the side table. Hadi Besharat grew anxious and said, "Wait a minute. Miss Nili will be bringing the tea soon." He called, "Miss Nili, Miss Nili . . ."

He cocked his head toward the kitchen but Nili didn't answer. Hadi Besharat wondered where she was. It didn't take that long to pour three cups of tea. What a nosy girl. Wherever she went, she acted as if she were in her own house and had the right to search the drawers and bookshelves.

Heli said, "Professor Besharat, would you like me to knit you a sweater?"

He hadn't expected this. He answered, "I don't want you to

go to any trouble. With so many responsibilities, you shouldn't bother yourself for my sake."

"Not at all. Knitting a sweater is no trouble. It keeps my mind busy. It keeps me interested. You know why?"

"Why?"

"Because when I hold these knitting needles, somehow everything falls into place. I can feel the house better, and in my imagination I see the movements of my hands. I can sense minute by minute that the sweater is growing on my lap. These things give me hope for life. I tell myself that life is like some kind of knitting. It grows all the time. It continues all the time."

Hadi Besharat's eyes fell on Heli's knitted blouse, light brown with buttons down the front. The buttons shone like yellow candies. He asked, "Miss Heli, that blouse you're wearing, is it the work of your own hands?"

Heli took a corner of the blouse between her fingers and said, "You mean this?"

"Yes."

"Yes, it's my own work. Do you like it?"

"Wonderful. How beautifully you knit."

"Don't embarrass me, Professor Besharat. I've made a very poor job of it. Look how tight the armholes are. The first time, it turned out so badly that I had to undo it and start all over again. I felt discouraged. But what choice do you have? You're forced to undo it to the last stitch. In the end, all that's left are the buttons. Then I say that these buttons are the eyes of my blouse. I warn you, don't laugh. Don't think I'm out of my head. Believe me, it's the truth."

She patted the row of buttons on her blouse and turned her veiled eyes to the ceiling. Hadi Besharat said, "Miss, excuse me. Why would I laugh?"

For a moment Heli kept her face tilted, listening with a smile. Then she said, "I sense you feel a little uncomfortable. Why don't you sit down next to me and rest awhile?"

"Because I don't know what's keeping Miss Nili. It shouldn't take so long to pour three cups of tea."

Heli raised her eyebrows and smoothed the length of knitting in her lap. "Nili is still a child. She can't sit listening to our conversation all the time. If you ask me, her problem is she feels homeless. She's always looking for a home somewhere."

"No, Miss Heli, I think she's looking for trouble."

Heli threw her head back in a burst of laughter and said, "Professor Besharat, you have to judge her more kindly than that. She's been left without her mother and she's looking for a place she can call home."

Hadi Besharat was not convinced. In fact he grew even edgier and he said, "I have to go find out what she's doing. I'll be right back."

He rushed into the kitchen. Nili was nowhere in sight. He heard a sound which was unclear, like the ringing of a spoon against a plate. It was the water in the kitchen drain.

It seemed very likely that Nili had gone to his study. No doubt she wanted to find that poor boy's notes and read them. In dismay, he climbed the stairs. He was angry with Farangu for leaving him at the mercy of this flighty young girl. He paused before entering the study. The corridor extended before him like a private conversation.

In the study Nili was stretched out on the daybed with her sneakered feet hanging over the end. She rested her chin on her palm and turned the pages of *The Death of a Great Savior*. Her hair was unruly, her clothes were rumpled, and she wasn't fazed by his presence. She concentrated on the book, muttering the words beneath her breath. Hadi Besharat stood in the doorway waiting. Nili ran her fingers through her hair. She seemed to have reached a suspenseful moment in the story.

Hadi Besharat moved forward and asked, "Miss Nili, what are you doing here?"

Instead of growing flustered, Nili set the book on the side table. She stood up and arranged her skirt and said calmly, "Professor Besharat, one time poor Mehrdad described your study for me, but I didn't know what he was talking about. What a room you've put together for yourself! I would love to come here now and then to see your antiques. Would you allow it?"

Her effrontery left a bitter taste in his mouth. But he held back and merely said, "We were waiting downstairs for the tea. What keeps you busy up here?"

"Such a strange room. Professor Besharat, would you be willing to teach me too?"

"What is this? Why have you come into my study without permission?"

Nili rolled her eyes and looked at the painting of the Phoenicians dragging a broken boat to shore. She said, "I want to take lessons from you."

"Lessons in what?"

"I don't know. History, English. Whatever's possible. I can even make copies of your works, like Mehrdad did. Would you let me?"

"Please, let's go downstairs. Your sister's all alone. We have to bring her some tea."

Nili found a thread on the front of her dress and began to twist it slowly around her finger. "When you go to America you need to know English. My English isn't that good. You can't learn English from books."

Hadi Besharat said, "Tell me the truth. What was your real purpose in coming to this room?"

"Would you let me ask you a question?"

"Please, go ahead."

"When a person is martyred, does he know it himself? I mean in the final moments, when his eyes spin dizzily, what does he think about? Does he know it's his last glance at life, that in a second it will all be dark?"

"I haven't been to the other world to answer your question. What are you referring to? Are you talking about that poor boy?"

"Yes, I want to know what was on his mind in his final moments. Who was the last person who appeared before his eyes. Did he remember how we walked in the street only three weeks ago and he recited the hymn of 'Manda d'Hayye'?"

The Pilgrim's Rules of Etiquette

Nili had herself in control, but it was obvious these questions concerned her passionately. Hadi Besharat said, "I don't know how to answer you. No one has ever come back from the other world. No one knows what our fate is after we pass away."

"I realize that, but I want to hear what you think."

"I think that at the time of death we review our whole life in every detail. All of our life minute by minute. I mean that all life's events occur all together in the blink of an eye."

Nili said, "Will you agree to teach me?"

Hadi Besharat asked, "Why don't you go to your own school?"

Nili began to unwind the thread from her finger. "Because of my papa-jon's illness I have responsibilities at home."

"Nevertheless you have to go to school, no matter what."

"Mehrdad's face is always in front of my eyes. I walk in the street, I go to the Sina Pharmacy for a prescription, Mehrdad is standing in front of me. An hour ago I was looking at the wall of your house where the water has stained it. In the middle of the stain I saw a pattern like . . . like Mehrdad's face, if you look at it closely."

Hadi Besharat held the study door open and said irritably, "Please, go down. Your sister's waiting for her tea."

"You don't believe me. Come see for yourself. I'll show you."

"Miss, please. This isn't a joke."

"I'm not joking. Let me show you."

She headed toward the stairs, motioning for him to follow. Hadi Besharat raised his hands. "I don't have my shoes on. I can't go out this way."

"Put them on, then. I'll wait for you."

As she descended the stairs Hadi Besharat stood debating. It seemed to him this girl was making a fool of him. Nevertheless he went back into the study for his shoes.

When he arrived downstairs the drawing room was empty. The front door was wide open and a cold draft blew through the entrance hall. Hadi Besharat stepped outside cautiously. Nili and Heli were standing by the wall. Nili beckoned him over. "Professor Besharat, come here. I'll show you. Come see with your own eyes."

Hadi Besharat approached. He narrowed his gaze and focused upon the twisting pattern on the wall. He couldn't see anything. Putting on his glasses, he bent over and examined the stain more closely. Still he saw nothing. He said, "I don't see anything whatsoever. Show me."

Nili outlined the stain with her finger and said, "Do you see this circle, his eyes and eyebrows? That shadow under the lip? The edge of his chin? And pay attention to this: here's a halo around his head."

Hadi Besharat said, "I can't see it."

"Look carefully. I mean this shadow that's like a flying saucer."

Hadi Besharat lifted a palm in bafflement. "That doesn't look like a flying saucer. I believe it's a turban. What do you say, General?" He turned to General Ghovanlu, who was making his way toward the district park. "Do you think this stain looks like that poor boy?"

General Ghovanlu paused. He eyed the stain. "How much water has been seeping through your wall, Professor? This isn't good for your house. It might cause serious problems. Send for a plumber to come fix the leak."

Hadi Besharat asked again, "General, do you see anything in this stain?"

The general bent forward and frowned. "What do you mean?"

"I don't know for sure. I myself see nothing at all."

Heli started laughing. "Professor, the price of your house will go sky high. People will gather around and tie wish-cloths to your door."

Here and there the stain was more concentrated, especially at the center. Efflorescent, spiral lines circled the center like a whirlwind, spinning outward to the edges of the wall. It was a scene that he had observed only in disturbed dreams. The scene of a cat night-walking on a ledge, a sun setting in a black pond, broken moonlight glowing on a window frame. Nili's hand dropped from the wall. Abruptly she turned and started walking away, saying, "All right, don't believe it!"

Her pace quickened and she headed toward Mrs. Razi's house. Hadi Besharat hurried after her. "Miss Nili, Miss Nili, listen to me."

Nili didn't turn around. "Maybe not everything I said is correct," she called back, "but some of it is. At least some of it."

"Miss, I can't keep up with you. Slow down!"

Nili entered Mrs. Razi's courtyard door like a flash of lightning. Just before she slammed it shut Hadi Besharat told her, "From now on, ask my permission before going into my study."

He was short of breath. He stood in the middle of the street and collected himself. The air felt heavy despite the cold. Wide bands of sunlight carved the afternoon shadows from the pillars. Except for the cry of Mrs. Kobra's newborn baby, he heard no sounds. A thought started nagging him. He wanted to examine the stain on the wall more closely. Perhaps it was only anger that kept him from believing in the existence of a face. In certain respects, such a phenomenon was not so farfetched.

As he approached, Heli was groping for her own door. She was about to enter when Hadi Besharat called, "Miss Heli, did you see anything on the wall?"

Heli turned her head, smiled, and closed the door behind her.

He wished Farangu was here so he could talk to her. He had to phone her and urge her to come home as soon as possible. He sat down next to General Ghovanlu on the stone bench in front of the Martyr Taher Nabavi High School. For years he had passed by this same stone bench and all the students had greeted him. He used to take it for granted. But now everything struck him as unstable. He turned to General Ghovanlu and asked, "Where is Engineer Gharib? We three could go to the district park and walk a bit."

General Ghovanlu brought his meaty face close and pointed to a spot on the ground. "I'll tell you that Engineer Gharib was standing right there just before you arrived." Then he jabbed his finger toward the poor boy's bridal chamber. "He went that way to see what all the talk was about. They say a group from Mashad is coming around sunset or maybe early tomorrow. The gypsies will be here too."

"What for?"

"To see the picture on your wall."

"What picture? There's nothing on our wall. You saw for yourself."

The general rubbed his chin pensively. "Someone says something and the others believe it. I'm afraid of things like that. People look at each other's mouths to find out what to believe."

"Has anyone seen that poor boy's body to make sure he's really been killed?"

"Engineer Gharib has seen it. Mr. Bayat's daughters have seen it. You know the desert in Khozestan Province is as flat as the palm of your hand. However you try to hide yourself, you can easily be spotted by the Iraqis. That poor boy was too young. The heat of battle drove him crazy. No matter how they begged him, he threw himself at the Iraqis' machine guns, imagining that heaven's gates were opening for him, that he was looking at the angels and the fourteen innocents."

Hadi Besharat slammed his hands down on his knees and stood up. "General, I have to go."

As he walked toward his house he could hear General Ghovanlu's voice behind him. "Professor Besharat, don't take it so hard."

It was true. Life was changing and taking a strange turn. It seemed to Hadi Besharat that they had arrived at an unrecognizable epoch. As if in the blink of an eye the moon would split and a newborn infant would begin to talk.

He listened to the Condition Red siren and the ambulances carrying the dead and wounded to hospitals. There wasn't a thing he could do. Everything was in the hands of those stupid field commanders who were totally ignorant about the historical battles. They thought war had been invented in modern times and educated professionals such as Hadi Besharat didn't know a thing about it. In fact, if they took him to the battlefield he could easily teach them some subtle mysteries, some ancient tricks of warfare. He would warn them never to take a position in an isolated place. The movement of branches is the sign of an advancing army and the sudden flight of a flock of birds is the sign of a night attack. As soon as frightened animals appear on the field the commanders should prepare for assault. Dust rising into the sky means approaching foot soldiers. But if the dust is shifting position it means the soldiers are setting up their tents on dusty ground. Peaceful proposals not accompanied by a signed agreement are nothing but a ruse. Birds fly over only those fields where the enemy has already packed up and left, escaping in the dark of night. Soldiers who are hungry and have no food lean against their rifles in front of their tents. If they don't put their pots on the stove and if they give their food to their animals instead, they don't plan to return to their tents and they've decided to fight to the last drop of blood.

But how could he believe the story of that poor boy's death? Perhaps they were envious of him. Jealous of his intelligence, talent, and daring. How eager he was to study "The Song of Gabriel's Wing" and "The Red Wisdom" by Sohrvardi, the thirteenth-century mystic whose bold ideas caused him to be suffocated in jail at the youthful age of thirty-eight. How eager to study Tertullian and Mani's *Book of Giants.* How many hours they had spent talking about the moments when a nation's future hung by a thread, the moments when a nation's victory depended upon a commander's intellect and courage. How many times Mehrdad had asked Hadi Besharat to draw maps of the important historical battles on a piece of yellow paper and to criticize modern strategies and tactics, the transportation of ammunition and the speed of ground forces.

Hadi Besharat took refuge in the permanent silence of the house. He stood in the doorway with his hands clasped behind him and looked at the white walls of the empty rooms. He'd had nothing to eat all morning. He didn't think he was hungry, but he knew he ought to take a few bites of something so he wouldn't get weak and catch cold.

The idea that a picture had appeared on their wall was completely unacceptable. This style of thinking belonged only to the youths of today who made an epic out of death and bloodshed. How strange that there was a finality to such a death. A death that became more rebellious every day and asked for more blood. It seemed to Hadi Besharat that, in the East, death is not separate from life. In the East death is like a mother with a newborn infant in her arms, unaware of the passage of time, expectant and enduring, patient and resigned.

In the kitchen he placed last night's leftover cutlets, some yogurt, and a piece of bread on a plate and sat down to eat. No news from Farangu. Perhaps she would stay overnight at her Mama Aliyeh's, a mistake as far as Hadi Besharat was concerned.

He felt lethargic, sluggish. Maybe Ahmad Bayat was right. He ought to exercise a little and run around the Komité Building early every morning. Rising from the table, he stood in the middle of the kitchen and stretched his arms out and took a deep breath. He jumped up and down to get the blood flowing in his lazy arteries. If he fell asleep and the stopped-up drain caused the sink to overflow, who would wake him up? Maybe he should lay a naked electrical wire on the tiles and connect it to the doorbell. As soon as the water touched the wire, the doorbell would ring and rouse him. Were his calculations correct? Was such an invention possible?

He went to his study, sat down at his desk, and continued translating the story of Mani's death and his final journey. In Jundishapur, burdened by an iron collar and chains, Mani walked the dark streets. His disciples and his nuns in their mantles and white buglelike hats walked behind him. Their mouths moved with the singing of a hymn and their words were blown away in the night air.

Hadi Besharat went to the closet and took out a gallon jug of vodka that Engineer Gharib had presented to him as a sample of his laboratory products. He poured a little into a tumbler and drank it in a gulp. The vodka slid down the lining of his throat, and its burning passage defined the anatomy of his stomach.

The Pilgrim's Rules of Etiquette

He imagined he heard Fakhr Zanjani delivering his lecture at the first bell on Tuesday morning:

"Read your country's proud and epoch-making history. Many a time this nation has gone to the edges of the pit of destruction. Each time by God's will an invisible hand has saved us from the abyss of death. Don't forget that the ancient conquerors were interested in more than the capture of foreign lands and bodies. Their basic intention was to capture the human soul. Bahram, the Sassanid king, wanted to stuff not just the body of the Living Paraclete with straw but his mind as well."

Fakhr Zanjani gathered his books and notes in a hurry and left the classroom. But Hadi Besharat didn't move. He sat on his bench and heard those words resonating in his mind as if he were still listening to the story of Mani's journey from Maysan to Pargalia. Under the grapevine, beneath the autumn moonlight, Mani lectured his students about the end of time and sang them the hymn of "Manda d'Hayye."

> *"Manda d'Hayye will come to me,*
> *He will call me and*
> *He will tell me: 'Little Enosh,*
> *Why are you afraid?*
> *Why are you trembling?*
> *I have come to make you aware.*
> *Don't be afraid of the evil forces in this world.' "*

Hadi Besharat poured himself another vodka and thought again of that wintry day, the first class on Tuesday, the way the slanted sunlight came through the window and spread across the floor. He put a hand beneath his chin, as entranced as a child watching a magic show. He smiled at the world and believed in what he could not see.

FOUR

Late that afternoon he sat in the drawing room reading a newspaper from 1943. His eyes glided over the photos, the advertisements, the war news. A yellowed column of sympathy messages attracted his attention and he felt, suddenly, as though he was sitting in a funeral gathering where speaking would disturb the other mourners. He crossed his legs and listened to the workers repairing the pipe in the bathroom.

In one respect Nili was right. Perhaps she did draw strength from seeing Mehrdad's image on the wall. Perhaps it eased the cold feeling of detachment caused by her confrontation with death. Such a thing was possible only when one witnessed a miracle or an act of magic—like the story of Daniel and the writing on the wall, like the rising of the magic moon Nakhshab from the depths of a well in Turkestan seven hundred years ago.

But for Hadi Besharat the real images of mourning remained internal and he could commune with them only in silence. Those images kept walking in the dark and showing him that poor boy in different scenes. Here he is standing beside a Turkoman horse and munching on a head of lettuce. There he is going to Termeh's Bar with his jacket draped over his shoulders and his white satin scarf flung around his neck. In these scenes a city atmosphere pervaded everything—the unhealthy atmosphere of a room in which a St. Abbas tablecloth is spread for the recovery of a dying patient, with those wide spaces between the plates of halvah and the bowls of saffron rice pudding and the stale flat-bread. The food always stayed cold and untouched on that table-cloth that blinded the appetite with its solid whiteness.

It was the winter of 1950, a Friday, and he was visiting his father-jon's grave. The snow came to his ankles, making it difficult to climb the hill as fast as he wished. Many years had passed since his father-jon's death scene, but he had not once recalled it. Even walking toward the cemetery, he didn't recall it. Instead he made plans for a comparative study of rural and urban funeral rites, and he worried about Farangu, who had still not agreed to marry him. She said she wasn't ready and she wanted to postpone their wedding for another two years. She preferred to go on acting and mingling with the other actors. This troubled Hadi Besharat's heart and he imagined that a page was turning in his life and a bleak fate was awaiting him. He complained to Engineer Gharib, "In the game of life, when we're dealt a bad hand we're showered with all kinds of mishaps and calamities. If just one bird is flying in the sky, its droppings will fall straight down and land on our heads."

He reached the wrought-iron gate of the cemetery, and all at once the face of his father-jon appeared before him. It looked exactly as it had seven years earlier, that cloudy day when he brought Hadi Besharat from Khezrabad for his second year of study and left him in the care of his old friend, Fakhr Zanjani.

That day Hadi Besharat had risen very early in the morning. His mother-jon was busy in the back room, wrapping his clothes, books, and notebooks in a travel bundle. Then she took a toasted flatbread from the clay oven on the veranda and placed it next to a glass of hot milk on a leather mat for his breakfast. The field next to their house was foggy and the air was filled with the smell of the dried manure that was burning in the oven. His mother-jon went to the storage room and returned with a tray of walnuts, roasted wheat and marijuana seeds, sheets of dried plums, pieces of dried cream, and three milk- and honey-covered breads. She dumped these on a big cloth and tied the corners of the cloth and set it at the top of the steps. Hadi Besharat greeted her and she murmured an answer. Then she took another toasted bread from the oven with her poker and tossed it on the leather mat. The silence persisted—the silence of the moist, cool, early morning and the fog moving toward the house.

His mother-jon wanted him to bring back some butter when he went to wash up. Hadi Besharat nodded and set out for the spring. His father-jon was riding a horse, trotting around an oval track in the field. He sat loosely in the saddle, his chin repeatedly hitting his chest and his riding stick coming down at his side. *Tarap, tarap . . . tarap, tarap . . .*

Hadi Besharat stood for some time watching his father-jon, as the fog closed in on the field, and the straw scattered beneath the horse's hoofs. Then he followed the footpath to the spring. He passed the mosque, which was merely a one-room hut made of straw and clay mixed together, its walls not whitewashed. Tavus the fixer and magician lay on the mosque's porch. He had covered his head with his robe and he was sound asleep in front of the tools of his two trades.

Hadi Besharat sank down by the spring and couldn't bring himself to move. There was a sickly feeling in his heart as if he were mourning a death. But no one had passed away. Somehow he managed to perform his ablutions before entering the mosque to recite the morning prayer. The mosque was completely empty. Only a lithographed Koran and a kerosene lamp stood in a niche in the wall. That was all.

He stood in prayer, holding his palms in front of his face and reciting the verses. No matter how hard he tried, he couldn't bring a presence to his heart. He heard only the sound of his father-jon's horse trotting: *Tarap, tarap . . . tarap, tarap . . .*

When he came out of the mosque he saw his father-jon putting his head to the horse's ear as he gently slapped the animal's rump, encouraging it to gallop. Hadi Besharat felt apprehensive. Apprehensive about going to the city? About neglecting his duties at home? Abandoning his responsibilities?

He heard the honking of the bus to the city. Passengers had to be at the station in thirty minutes. Hadi Besharat forgot about the butter and returned immediately to the house. His mother-jon had put his bundles on the edge of the veranda and his father-jon was fitting his billfold into his rear pocket. As Hadi Besharat and his mother-jon kissed good-bye his father-jon bent to snip a few plant leaves which he kept in his fist. He began to walk toward the bus station. Hadi Besharat was forced to follow.

Once they were seated in the bus his father-jon reached for his billfold and took out some banknotes which he laid one by one in Hadi Besharat's palm. Hadi Besharat counted them in a monotone. "Five tumans, fifteen tumans, twenty-five tumans."

His father-jon said, "You count very well. Now, can you figure out how much your daily expenses should be?"

Hadi Besharat said, "Twenty-five divided by thirty . . ." He mumbled the figures in his mind. ". . . equals point zero eight rials, and three and three and three to infinity. . . ."

His father-jon nodded. "You learned this in school?"

"It's easy to learn that. Then you can divide anything you want."

"Like what?"

"Like if you want to know whether you have enough hay for the winter. You have to divide the total amount of your hay by the heads of your livestock."

"Really?"

"If you want to know how much seed you can sow per acre you have to divide the total amount of your seed by the number of acres."

His father-jon said nothing, and Hadi Besharat continued. "If you want to know how many people live in each household you divide the number of the total population by the number of the houses in the community . . ."

His father-jon opened his fist and showed Hadi Besharat the leaves he was holding. "Do you see these? These are the leaves of the khatmi plant. Stuff them up any big talker like an enema and they should take care of his problem."

Hadi Besharat nodded his head in disagreement. "Modern

medicine doesn't believe in things like that. You have to prove that it works."

"I'm illiterate and I never went to school. You want to go to the university. *You* prove it."

His father-jon remained silent for the rest of their trip.

When they entered Fakhr Zanjani's small living quarters his father-jon sat down on a chair, holding himself erect. He tilted his head at a stiff right angle as if he had indigestion and might belch. Slowly, he asked Fakhr Zanjani to look after Hadi Besharat's education. Fakhr Zanjani threw a glance at Hadi Besharat and said, "How does it feel to be back in Tehran?"

"It feels very different from Khezrabad."

"These differences are superficial. Basically, people are the same no matter where you go.

> *"The war between nations is but an excuse.*
> *They couldn't find the truth, they went after fairy tales."*

Hadi Besharat was grateful for these words and wanted to tell him so, but suddenly his father-jon's face started to twist. Fakhr Zanjani showed no reaction. He took out his pocketknife and sharpened his pencil. Then Hadi Besharat's father-jon collected himself. He breathed deeply and told Fakhr Zanjani, "I'm think-ing of buying Hadi-jon a house in the Salsabil district. When you don't own a house it's difficult to find a wife in Tehran."

Then his head fell sideways and it was all over. This happened in the blink of an eye. Gradually his face became pale. A cold and oily sweat filmed the corners of his mouth and the skin around his nostrils. After that the signs of death's eternal silence began to parade through the room. The window had been left open and the wind blew in, lifting the hem of the curtain. The air moved across Hadi Besharat's face as gently as spring water. His father-jon's head lay on the arm of the chair, twisted toward him in a yawning expression.

Fakhr Zanjani had not cared much for sentiment, but he had tried to say something to comfort Hadi Besharat. He talked like a teacher. "We cannot fathom creation's preordained plan. We know only this much, that everyone has a destiny and destinies are of different kinds."

Hadi Besharat was moved. With just a few simple words Fakhr Zanjani had built a bridge for him between city and village, helping him to feel more at home. Those dry words rescued him from the maze of city life. In the city he kept stumbling in the street and bumping into strangers. If he moved to lift a tumbler of tea from a table he would hit a glass of water with his elbow and the water would be all over the table.

He stood in the doorway, afraid to touch anything. He was thinking of just seconds before when his father-jon had been lecturing him. "Hadi-jon, from now on you have to find a job and earn your own pocket money. You behave as if the world is spinning in a magician's hand. Hadi-jon, why don't you understand that every effect has a cause? When you need money, why don't you balance your account? Do you think money grows like pasture grass, do you think it comes from an invisible treasury?"

Again and again he heard the private code words: "Hadi-jon, Hadi-jon . . ." Only his father-jon called him "Hadi-jon."

In 1950, dejected and hopeless, chilled by a cold wind, he had returned to his room from the cemetery. He had stood alone at the window, staring at the falling snow. Under the tired snow the empty streets slowly lost their breath. Like an ancient sage, Hadi Besharat seemed to have had enough of this world at the tender age of twenty-five. He decided to commit suicide. He drank as much vodka as he could. Then he picked up Hafez's collected poems and tried to get an answer from the poet. There was an answer for him:

> *Don't go to India, but get along with your own God.*
> *Wherever you go, the sky is the same color.*

He wasn't satisfied with that. Sitting cross-legged on the rug, he picked up the Koran. He patted the cover with a beseeching hand and tried to forget about himself. Maybe he would be granted presence of heart, liberating him from the world and beyond. He felt that in his short life he'd been walking an endless path. Confused and bewildered, he was getting nowhere. He slid a finger through the pages of the Koran. Strange! From afar he heard that trotting sound of his father-jon's horse again: *Tarap, tarap . . . tarap, tarap . . .*

He paid no attention. When he opened the Koran his glance fell on the chapter, "Time."

> *In the name of Time!*
> *Man is a sustainer of loss*
> *Except those who believe and benefit others*
> *And those who take refuge in righteousness and patience.*

Tears began to spill from his eyes. He threw himself down and put his forehead on the rug. He didn't deserve such favor. Now his existence was purified by the blessings of sincerity and virtue. On the wings of that rapture his soul soared. He felt the clarity and brilliance of ordinary words. Like a mirror, he was radiant and empty of any resistance. He had consulted the Koran with presence of heart and now it was easier for him to let everything go than drinking a glass of water. He would sell the house he had inherited from his father-jon, pack up, and leave to pursue his studies of art and science. He would seek understanding and knowledge. He would attend Whitehurst College and travel around the globe, just as the great sages had done in the past. With a knapsack on his back and a cane in his hand, he would hit the mountains and the fields. He would see other skies and other peoples. Ah, what joy! Now he was released from any needs, shaking his sleeve free of both worlds and giving up on the earth and its inhabitants.

At the time he didn't know that Farangu would eventually consent to marry him, after many ups and downs. Nor did he know that he would agree to let her go on acting and that all his life he would hear the horse's hoofs warning him: Hadi-jon, prepare yourself for a long walk and the hardships of the journey!

The Pilgrim's Rules of Etiquette

A human being is only a pilgrim pursuing a destination! He must be thoroughly familiar with the pilgrim's rules of etiquette!

The workers had finished fixing the pipe and they were ready to leave. He paid their wages and saw them out. After he'd closed the door behind them he listened curiously to the silence. The house felt strange without the dripping sound, as if someone were asleep, breathing at the top of the stairs, or a thief were searching for jewelry and valuables in Khosro's room.

Why hadn't he heard from Farangu yet? He wanted to phone her but he wasn't in the mood to argue with Mama Aliyeh. She would start her eternal complaints. He could hear her now: "Just because I say a couple of words about Khosro doesn't mean I bear a grudge of some kind. . . . Didn't I tell you he shouldn't deliver all those girders to Mr. Bayat without asking for a receipt? Mr. Bayat may not remember, but Khosro paid for those girders out of his own pocket. . . . Khosro was too young to head a construction company. He understood no more than a sheep does. . . . Truckload after truckload, he sent all those girders to Mr. Bayat on an empty promise. . . . Thank God he went to America. God be praised that he's established a car wash there and his business is booming."

Hadi Besharat picked up the receiver and dialed Mama Aliyeh's number. He felt disappointed when Farangu answered, because he'd expected to hear that she was on her way and would be home soon. At the other end of the line music was playing so loudly that he couldn't make out what she was saying.

> *"Never again will my pain*
> *Be cured by drunkenness.*
> *Until you come to me*
> *This frown on my face won't go away . . ."*

He lost control and shouted angrily, "Farangu, Farangu! Lady, where are you?"

The rhythmic beat of a man's singing mingled with people's clapping.

> *"Is this a hip?*
> *No, it is a beautifully coiled spring.*
> *Give me your lips,*
> *Give them to me . . ."*

Hadi Besharat raised his voice even further. "Farangu, do you hear me?"

Farangu was laughing. "Besharat, you don't know how cute and funny Sayid-jon is."

"Have you given any thought to your home and family? When do you plan to return? It's already twilight. You won't be able to find a cab."

"Even after all those years that Sayid-jon's been in America getting his Ph.D., he still knows a lot of Rashti jokes. He makes you laugh so hard you want to pass out. A man from Rasht marries a chubby woman. They get in their car to drive to Chalus for their honeymoon. In the car the Rashti man puts his hand on his wife's leg. His wife says, 'Dear, now that we're married, you can go farther than that.' The Rashti man changes gears and drives to Tehran instead of Chalus . . . ha, ha . . ."

"What is this charade? You get up right now and come home."

"Do you know what's written on a traffic sign outside of Rasht? It reads, MAXIMUM SPEED, SLOW . . . ha, ha, ha . . ."

Hadi Besharat slammed down the phone. He went back to work but the phone started ringing. He didn't want to answer it. Nevertheless he reached over and picked up the receiver. It was Farangu. "Why were we cut off? Did you do it on purpose? Besharat, you don't know what kind of magic acts Sayid-jon can perform. He can do card tricks. He can raise the skin of his forehead and move his ears any way he wants. He can pull a boiled egg from an empty handkerchief."

"Get moving right now. I'm waiting for you."

He slammed down the receiver again. Just hearing the name of Farangu's cousin was enough to bring back the old fury. That good-for-nothing clown who had caused him so much embarrassment. It was June of 1963 when Hadi Besharat had finally finished work on his book, *Death and Destiny*. Then as soon as it was out Sayid-jon had called him from America, waking him in the dead of night to congratulate him on writing such a fine book. He told Hadi Besharat that it had been translated into English and important publishers in America were fighting over the rights. Hadi Besharat was forced to give permission for its publication, but he insisted that Sayid-jon first send the galleys for his inspection. For a few months he heard nothing further from Sayid-jon. Then in the middle of September the phone rang again. This time Sayid-jon said that his book had been received extremely well in America and the members of the Nobel Academy had decided to award him the prize in the historical philosophy category. Hadi Besharat grew pale upon hearing this. He would have to prepare his Nobel address, which was not an easy task. Helplessly, he said, "Sayid-jon, you're a marvel. I'm not ready."

"Not ready for what?"

"I have to write an acceptance speech."

"Writing is easy for you."

"Writing in English may be easy for me. But what do I do for the Swedish version?"

Three weeks before the announcement of the Nobel Prizes he wrote the English text after much consultation with the faculty at the university. Then he prepared the Swedish version with the help of the Swedish Embassy. He also wrote a version in the Middle Parthian language so as to give a sample of the book's original prose. Then that good-for-nothing clown revealed the truth. He confessed that it was all a joke and he had only wanted to tease him, never dreaming it might cause Hadi Besharat embarrassment. For a long time Hadi Besharat was ashamed to face his colleagues at the university.

Despite his empty stomach he poured himself a little vodka

from the gallon jar. He was about to swallow it when he heard the sounds of a quarrel. Mrs. Razi was screeching in her courtyard. "Why don't you go away? How many times must I tell you? If you say another word about a picture on that wall or any other stupid things like that, I'll close your mouth with mud."

Hadi Besharat jumped up from his chair. Setting down his glass, he opened the window and craned his head out. Mrs. Razi was just kicking her courtyard door open and shoving Nili into the street. With her head unveiled and her hair all disheveled, Nili stumbled forward a few steps and landed just across from Hadi Besharat's window. She smoothed her hair, a sulky expression on her face. Her movements were sluggish, like those of a person who'd been beaten. At the same time she seemed to be trying not to show weakness. She stayed where she was, refusing to go any farther. Then Mrs. Razi came out after her. Her bony, delicate body trembled as if connected to an electrical current. She pointed a thin finger at Nili. "Give me that sack and those fatigues."

Nili drew a limp hand from behind her back and threw the poor boy's belongings at Mrs. Razi's feet. The older woman picked them up and examined them for dust. Then her screeching began all over again. "It may be true I'm in mourning, but I still watch everything very closely. I take care of this house very well. Do you imagine this house doesn't have an owner, that you can come here all the time and do whatever mischief you wish? Who gave you permission to visit whenever you like and search the room of that unfulfilled son of mine? Who said you could go through his clothes and handle his books? Who said his face has appeared on Besharat's wall? A wall is not a roll of film. What is this nonsense? If our ordinary superstitious neighbors get wind of it, they'll gather around our houses and not let us eat or sleep."

She searched over her shoulder for the hem of her veil. Failing to find it, she returned in fury to her courtyard. Nili glanced at Hadi Besharat out of the corner of her eye. She pulled down the corners of her mouth and said sarcastically, "Is it a movie you're watching?"

"Miss Nili, what happened? Why is Mrs. Razi doing this?" Hadi Besharat asked in a compassionate tone.

Nili smoothed the collar of her dress. "Don't you want to go visit her?"

"Of course, Miss Nili. She's a grieving mother and deserves our consideration. But what's all the fuss about? What's going on?"

"Very well. See the house? See the door? Be my guest! I'm not there anymore to stop you. Anyone who wants can visit."

Hadi Besharat took heart. "Really? I can go see her?"

Paying him no further attention, Nili walked toward her own house with a determined step. Hadi Besharat craned his neck again and peered over the wall of Mrs. Razi's courtyard. Maybe he really could go see her. Maybe he really could.

Kyumars Gharib was practicing his clarinet in his room and its solitary moan trailed through the silence. When it reached the end of the street it died like a sigh against the windowpanes. Hadi Besharat saw Engineer Gharib and General Ghovanlu coming his way from the avenue. He cupped a hand to his mouth and called, "Did you hear that? Did you hear the fight?"

Engineer Gharib asked in surprise, "What fight?"

"Mrs. Razi had a fight with Nili and threw her out just a minute ago."

General Ghovanlu frowned. "Well, she was right. Nili is making up strange and unbelievable stories. This business about Mehrdad Razi's face appearing on the wall. Poppycock! If the news reaches the mosque, then you'll have to bring an ass to carry all the rumors. People will be pouring in and giving us headaches with their breast-beating and their demonstrations."

"She ought to get married," Engineer Gharib said. "Whatever Nili does, it's because she's not married."

"Do you understand what this means?" Hadi Besharat asked, "Now we can go and visit Mrs. Razi. Nili said we could."

General Ghovanlu grunted, "You have to ignore Nili. Then she'll behave like a human being. Mrs. Ghovanlu doesn't let her in our house at all. Everyone else should do the same."

Hadi Besharat sighed regretfully. "According to Heli, Nili is a homeless person and she's just searching for a home of her own. Everything she does is because of that."

He was about to close the window when General Ghovanlu looked at his watch and said, "Professor, there's a rumor that the Iraqis will be bombing tonight. We're planning to go in a group to Lashgarak. Why don't you join us?"

"I can't, General. Farangu is visiting her Mama Aliyeh. I have to wait for her at home."

After he'd closed the window he returned to the side table and gulped down the rest of his vodka. The room was almost dark now, but when he tried to switch on a light nothing happened. He imagined that the electricity must have been cut off again, because of the Condition Red indicating an imminent bombing attack.

He thought awhile. Then he put on his coat, wrapped a woolen scarf around his neck, and prepared to go to Mrs. Razi's. To protect himself even further, he oiled his nose and eyelids with Vicks ointment. He then placed the kerosene lamp on the floor in front of Khosro's room and dropped a few eucalyptus leaves in the bowl of water steaming on the stove. Then he left the house.

It was hard to find his way without streetlights. The solitary moaning of Kyumars Gharib's clarinet floated past, giving life to the hushed murmurs of early evening. There was a smell in the air of steamed rice, lima beans, and roasted lamb. The Ghovanlus and Gharibs were rushing about behind their windows, packing their dinner pails for the trip to Lashgarak. Hadi Besharat pushed Mrs. Razi's door open and entered the courtyard. He surveyed the house cautiously in all directions, up and down, right and left. The front portion of the veranda was lit by a lone kerosene lamp that burned on an iron table. Its cold, static light made a halo in the darkness.

Hadi Besharat's heart always felt clouded by the Razis' house. As long as Colonel Razi was alive, God forgive his soul, he had stuffed the rooms with linens and priceless rugs and velvet mattresses and cushions. He was crazy about electronic gadgets, too.

Whatever he had he spent on radios, televisions, and video recorders. Whenever Hadi Besharat went to visit, he felt he was stepping into a scene from World War II.

A portable stove stood in the middle of the corridor and the aromas of coffee and cardamom trailed across the courtyard. A heavy funeral coffeepot sat on a gas burner. At the far end of the corridor he could see the dining room, lit by camphor candles. Their flames flickered over a large photograph of Mehrdad and highlighted the black mourning bands draped across one corner of the frame. The candles burned softly, as if they were counting the passing seconds in memory of the boy. As if the souls of the departed were gathering in the dining room, placing a shrouded body on the floor with his feet toward Mecca. That slow passage of Time! Indifferent and enduring Time!

A white tablecloth covered the long table in the middle of the dining room. On both sides earthenware dishes of halvah, saffron rice pudding, and flatbread kept equal distance from each other. The Koran reciter sat on the floor next to another, lower table. He was reading in a hushed whisper from a bound chapter of the Koran. A piece of white cloth was wrapped around his head, its tail end crossing his shoulder to his chest. He lifted his eyes and saw Hadi Besharat. He closed the chapter and put a finger to his lips. "Ssh. The lady is kneeling in prayer. Your Excellency?"

Hadi Besharat knew he should keep very quiet so her prayer could continue unbroken. He too talked in a whisper. "Professor Hadi Besharat is here. I'm a very close friend."

The Koran reciter nodded, bracing a hand on the rug so that he could rise. His slippers sat next to each other at the edge of the rug. He went over and slid his feet into them. Then he straightened and looked at Hadi Besharat expectantly. His white shirt hung over his black pants, which came down to his bare ankles like two stovepipes. He sighed and talked in the same hushed voice. "This is life, Agha. It is fickle. It is mindless. I have recited the Koran for twenty years. Have seen a thousand funerals for the old and young alike. They say you get used to it. But each time it happens it's like the first time."

They could hear Mrs. Razi reciting her prayers through her loose dentures, saying her last glorias loudly. "God is great!"

Hadi Besharat said, "Let me go see if she's finished."

"Wait a bit. She'll be done soon."

The Koran reciter walked out to the corridor and bent forward to lower the flame of the gas burner. Mrs. Razi must have heard him, for she raised her voice angrily. "God is great!"

The Koran reciter pulled back his hand in embarrassment and said, "Miss, should I lower the flame a little?" He still spoke in a whisper. Something seemed to be wrong with his throat.

Mrs. Razi screamed, "God is great! God is great!" Unable to tolerate it any longer, she broke off her prayer. "Haj Ghadam, haven't I told you a hundred times not to call me in the middle of my prayers? What are you doing with that burner?"

"It's burning too high. I thought I would lower it."

"If that girl Nili Bayat comes back, don't let her in. Tell her that the lady's not home, she's gone to the lowest depths of the lowest hell. Kick her out."

"I'll be obliged, miss."

"What balderdash! The face of a human being never appears on a wall."

Hadi Besharat entered the drawing room quietly. In the middle of the room Mrs. Razi had spread her prayer rug. She had her back to him and she was kneeling with her hands on the floor. A flashlight stood beside her, its beam aimed at the ceiling. Upon hearing Hadi Besharat enter she raised her head from the prayer stone, picked up the flashlight and turned it in his direction. Recognizing him, she set the flashlight down again. She loosened the knot that held her long veil over her face. Then she proceeded to end her prayer, throwing her hands above her head a few times. After this she said, "Professor Besharat, at first I thought you were Nili coming back to make a nuisance of herself. She never leaves me alone, always sticking to me like a hair in my nose. Agha, these days we're not safe from anyone. That girl keeps going to my poor boy's room, picking up whatever she can get her hands on, and hiding it somewhere. By the pure Fatima, I lost my patience today and threw her out of the house. Stealing is stealing, whatever fancy name you give it. She's like any other thief. They break in and cut people's throats from ear to ear. There's already been one burglary in this district."

She meant the incident with Mr. Lajevardi, a hardworking civil servant for the past twenty years. A month ago he had awakened in the middle of the night to go to the bathroom and heard a few noises in the courtyard. Carrying his flashlight, he went to the servant's room and called her. "Sedigheh, Sedigheh." All of a sudden they jumped him, smothering him to death with a pillow held over his face.

Mrs. Razi said, "For my peace of mind, always let me know you're coming. There's so much crime nowadays. These mangy Afghanis and Koreans can't find anything to eat. They come to our country to steal and commit murder."

"There's no resemblance between me and those foreigners. Why should you be afraid of me?"

"You always misinterpret things and take offense."

She rose from her prayer rug and moved the coffee table back where it belonged. Then, with a frown on her face, she sat silently on the couch, crossing her ankles. She put her palms together with her fingers interlaced. "Professor Besharat, there's a lot of food in the dining room. Please have some."

"I'm not hungry. I can't."

"The neighbors keep bringing food. They leave it in the dining room and nobody touches it. It's going to waste and I'll have to throw it out."

Hadi Besharat sat down in a chair opposite her. He said, "Miss, I don't want to bother you. I know that, with your grief, you're in no mood for visits, but I've thought of a few things and I have to tell them to you straight."

"Professor, by God or whoever else you worship, please don't trouble me. If you want to talk about that picture on the wall, I have no time for it. You're an intelligent man. You shouldn't pay attention to a lot of garbage coming from a crazy girl. Ignore her till she behaves like a human being."

"I just want to talk about the plans for the funeral ceremony. I don't mean to add to your pain. I just want to offer my advice."

"Why should I need your advice? Praise God, my eldest son, Nurdad, God grant him a long life, is still alive. Nurdad is in America. He'll be happy to take care of me."

"America's far away, miss. What are you going to do here?"

"It's all the same. Leave me to myself, Agha. Let me die with my own pain. I don't expect anything from anyone. Did you lock the outside door when you came in? You can't be sure. They'll come and steal whatever we own."

"The door is locked."

"Neighbors keep coming all the time and asking all kinds of strange questions. By God, I have no nerves left. I'm only a human being. Sometimes I snap. Sometimes I open my mouth and say something."

"I agree with you that these rumors about the poor boy are baseless. There's no picture on my wall."

"People look at the sky and see all kinds of saints and saints' descendants. Professor, you're an educated man, you shouldn't be deceived by superstitions."

"Yes, they fan these rumors to mislead people."

"I have just one wish. I wish they would leave me alone. I want to close the door of this house and find some peace. Why won't they let us lick our wounds in privacy? We haven't done anything wrong. Whenever possible, we've even tried our best to look after those humbled masses. Then they come, arrest my poor husband, put him in front of a firing squad, and execute him for no reason. Again, we don't say a word. We don't show a thing on our blessed face. We just try to spread our deathbed in a corner, sleep on it, and eat our hearts out without a sound. By God, sometimes I think maybe they're right. But the poor colonel couldn't hurt a fly. If he saw a drop of blood he passed out. Now they say he tortured people, pulled out their fingernails. Well, let it be. Maybe they're telling the truth. We don't have any knowledge about what we didn't see for ourselves. But can you tell this uneducated woman why they're putting on all these theatrics for my precious son? You knew that poor boy. Was he the type who wanted martyrdom? Oh, baba, he didn't want to go to the front. He had a plan to smuggle himself to America via Turkey and live with his brother Nurdad."

"Miss, in this life you have to be patient. A life without patience is hell."

"God is my witness that I have a lot of patience. But I can't forget the death of my son. For me, dying is simply dying. It makes no difference if my child is run over by a car or they put him in front of a machine gun or they use him for cannon fodder. The distance between life and death is the batting of an eye, Agha."

Hadi Besharat spoke in measured tones. "The truth is that death is part of life. You have to accept it."

"What do you mean, part of life? If that's so, I don't want either death or life. I'll sell whatever I have left. With the money I'll buy dollars at sixty tumans per buck and I'll go to Los Angeles. I'll go to Nurdad. God protect him. He's built a fine, presentable house for himself. I'll go there so I can draw an easy breath in my last years."

"Basically, life is like traveling to a foreign country. It requires a passport, a visa, and a green card no matter where you go. Even if it's the home of your own Nurdad, even if he wears you on his head like a crown, still life will take its toll. Our history teacher, God rest his soul, always used to say that living in this world does not come free. To enter this world or to leave it will cost you."

"Maybe living in this world will cost me. But when I draw my last breath I won't need anything anymore. You're free to do whatever you wish with my body. The person who draws his last breath is released from sorrow. Admission to heaven or hell in the other world is free of charge."

She brushed imaginary dust from her lap. Hadi Besharat sat back in his seat. A feeling of defeat came over him, making it hard to continue the conversation.

Then Mrs. Razi stood up and beckoned. "Come with me. I want to show you something."

He rose and followed her out to the corridor. With one hand she picked up the kerosene lamp and with the other she raised the hem of her veil so it wouldn't trip her. She went upstairs slowly. Climbing behind her, Hadi Besharat felt sad. What would poor Mehrdad say if he were here now? Surely he would open the door of his room for them. He would lift the kerosene lamp above his head to keep them from stumbling and falling. All this made Hadi Besharat remember the boy's intelligence and his quick wit. His Coptic was as good as his Hebrew. He pronounced Soghdian words with the tip of his tongue in a cute and interesting way. After Hadi Besharat had taught him to use an astrolabe, he had gone on to master the even more difficult Mojeyb astrolabe as well—an ancient astronomical instrument with two end bars that spin on a brass plate.

Now Hadi Besharat could hear Mrs. Razi breathing as she searched for her key ring. "I knotted my keys in my veil so Nili wouldn't find them. These days we're not safe in our own homes."

As they entered the room, Mrs. Razi put the kerosene lamp on the mantel, then went over to the poor boy's stereo, looking for something. The lamplight was weak and Hadi Besharat couldn't make out the color of the couch in the middle of the room. He saw only the white zigzag pattern of its spread, which jumped out at him like the warning symbol on an electrical plant. A potted palm arched over a low table. A few inlaid photo frames and ornamental boxes sat on the table. The window curtains came straight down to the floor in a motionless stream. The bookshelves and the prints of medieval pictures hung in rows on the walls.

He noticed that Mrs. Razi was dragging a big bundle from one corner. She seemed out of breath. Her face was as slack and distracted as a seventy-year-old woman's. Hadi Besharat insisted, "Miss, let me give you a hand."

Mrs. Razi gestured for him to stay put. "No, Agha. Don't

trouble yourself." She straightened, rubbing her back with her fingertips. "Everyone has some sort of private hell. My own hell is what I'm doing now. At my age I have to take care of everything myself. I look around and see how they've done the colonel in. That poor boy is now a martyr. Nurdad has his head in his own feed bin in America. I ask myself who will hold my hand, who'll look after me in this situation. But don't think I can't manage. On the contrary, I've been active all my life and never could sit still for a minute. The late colonel used to say, 'Zari-jon, we don't need money. I want you to resign from the Ministry of Education and stay home and rest.' But I wouldn't listen. In the modern world, a woman must be active."

She knelt on the floor and opened the bundle. Inside were all kinds of clothes. She held up a flannel jacket and said, "Look at this. How much do you think that mindless son of mine paid for it?"

Hadi Besharat rubbed the fabric between a thumb and forefinger. "Really. It's not bad. Looks like it's foreign-made."

"Do you remember how he used to wear it, parading in the street so the girls would take notice?"

Hadi Besharat was overtaken by a sense of sadness. "How high-minded, how disinterested he was. What a heart. Clear and pure like a mirror. I remember I was heading home one day with a sack of fruit. He stopped me on my way. Strange! Right now his face is before my eyes. I hear his voice in my ears. When you ran into him in the street he came close with open arms, took hold of you, and asked about you warmly."

Mrs. Razi crumpled a corner of her veil to her face, sobbing loudly. Hadi Besharat sat down on a chair and continued. "He asked me, 'Professor Besharat, by what sort of sign can one recognize the ruins of Babylon?' He was planning to get himself to the ruins of Babylon and discover the pit of the fallen angels, Harut and Marut. The angels who are confined in a pit head down and are supposed to teach mortals the art of government. He believed that the legend of Harut and Marut had some historical truth. Other young people go to the front in hopes of seeing heaven and the spring of eternal life. But that poor boy's only aim was to pursue his historical studies. I explained to him that there are always sulphurous gases and flames coming out of Harut's and Marut's pit. I warned him to stay away. He could mistake the dust of the Iraqis' tanks for the smoke from that pit. Do you know what he answered? He quoted a sentence from the animal book, *Kelileh and Demneh,* and it stunned me. He said, 'He who avoids danger will not attain greatness.' Miss, you have the right to cry. They have taken a young man from you who was head and shoulders above the rest. I know all too well how your heart is grieving. Cry, miss, cry for all of us. Cry for that blossom in the garden of youth who has perished."

Mrs. Razi raised her head and stared at him. Wiping her nose on the corner of her veil, she said, "Professor Besharat, he was my own child. Now that he's beyond the reach of this world, God have mercy on him, I shouldn't speak ill of him, but he was the type who took people at their word. When anyone said anything he believed it. In thoughtlessness and carelessness he went to extremes. I opened an account for him at the Export Bank and deposited a few pennies I'd gathered from selling some belongings. But in a month's time he went through all the money, spending it on fancy clothes and his trip to Gorgan. Well, we have to give credit where it's due. His taste in clothes was excellent. Look at these clothes and see the sort of material he selected. If you searched the world you couldn't find anything like this. I won't stand on ceremony with you. I'm willing to give you the lot for half the original price. Send it all to America for your Khosro-jon."

She paused for a moment, examining his face. Hadi Besharat couldn't believe what he was hearing. He just looked at her.

"If I weren't in need of cash," she said, "I wouldn't do this. I can't go to Nurdad empty-handed. The late colonel was an honest man. He wasn't stealing like the rest of the military. Otherwise I wouldn't be pressed today for a couple of miserable pennies. God grants luck to those who wheel and deal. Those men used to go home to their villas every evening and their butlers brought them whiskey on a silver platter. Now those same people are living in America, enjoying themselves on their seventuman-per-dollar money and free of worry."

Hadi Besharat said, "I don't have any information about the condition of former military personnel in America. It's been a long time since I've received a letter from Professor Humphrey. But I hear they're not doing so well. Rumor has it they're washing cars and selling sandwiches so they can support themselves."

"Well, that's none of our business. Let them live any way they wish. It's their own concern. My main problem is these clothes. Can I give you the lot for ten thousand tumans?"

Hadi Besharat was not only embarrassed but astonished. Mrs. Razi didn't notice his reaction. She insisted more vigorously. "Khosro-jon's measurements match the poor boy's exactly—not that I want to compare them. But Khosro-jon used to borrow my boy's clothes to wear to parties."

Hadi Besharat sat straighter in his chair and said, "I swear, miss, our financial situation is not that good. With these dizzying prices, how can one stretch a monthly pension of a few tumans? But if there's anything else I can do, you'll hear no argument from me. I'll be glad to help out."

Before he had finished, Mrs. Razi began rewrapping the clothes. She tied the bundle in a knot, then rose and threw it back into the corner. "If you don't have any money, what else can I ask for? Was it for this kind of trickery that you pulled the door off its hinges to visit me? No! I don't need you. I've stood on my own two feet from the start and I don't need anyone. I know how to take care of my problems myself."

She placed her hands on her hips and screeched, "Don't think you're talking to a crippled woman with four clawed limbs. General Ghovanlu always says, 'No one in the world has been able to hoodwink Miss Zari.' He says, 'You have to learn child rearing from Miss Zari.' You know my relationship with the colonel wasn't perfect. God have mercy on him, all his life he moaned about his backache loudly enough to raise the dead. But I still loved him. He was a good man. He was the father of my children. Whenever he got sick I nursed him myself. I sat by his bed all night and put the bedpan under him. The night they executed him, tears welled up in his eyes as soon as he saw me. He reached through the prison bars, grabbed my wrist, and said, 'My little chicken, whatever I have done is not worth an execution. They're wasting their bullets.' I comforted him and he felt a little better. He said, 'My little chicken, thank you. Look after the children. Whatever harm I've done, forgive me. . . .' "

With shaky hands she opened her cigarette case and lit a cigarette. She took deep puffs and spoke rapidly. "You think you're talking to a helpless, incompetent woman. I have led a hundred American-educated doctors and professors to the well and returned them still thirsty. Well, Agha, what did you hope to get out of corrupting my witless son? Why did you take advantage of his youth and inexperience and lead him astray? I'm asking you. Why did you send my child to Bibi Shahr Banu Shrine and Ab-eh Ali Spring? What were those useless books that you made my silly son study? Why did you encourage him to go to the front and throw himself in front of the tanks of those Iraqi crocodile eaters? Only to see the Tower of Babylon? Or whatever other snake poison you call it? If you think you can get out of this so easily, you're sadly mistaken. If God doesn't take revenge, I will. Do you think you're talking to a cleaning woman?"

Utterly stunned, Hadi Besharat sat in the middle of the room not knowing how to answer. The blood began to rush to his head. He gathered himself up and said, "God forbid, have you lost your mind to talk like this? A bereaved mother shouldn't utter such bitter words. Never send for me again or ask about me. I won't allow it."

Mrs. Razi waved him away with the backs of her hands. "Shoo, shoo! What are you waiting for? All of you crowd around me, congratulating me, expecting me to be happy, to snap my fingers and sway my hips in a dance for you. No! I'll kick you in the butt and heave the lot of you out of this house."

Hadi Besharat was shaking with anger. "You killed that boy

yourself. You caused him to rebel and throw himself in front of the Iraqi tanks. Do you remember how you screamed at him? How you slapped him the night he came home from Termeh's Bar? How could you bring yourself to slap a twenty-year-old boy? It's because of mothers like you that the country's in this condition. When are you going to wake up from your three-thousand-year nap?"

"Little man, watch what you say. You're not talking to your servant. From your trips to America, from reading and writing a bunch of nonsense, all you've learned is how to dump your emotions on the head of a bereaved mother. So much for your education and scholarship! Get out, leave me alone."

"It's your own doing. Why blame me?"

"You know what I wish for in life? My one wish is to come back to my house after running in the streets like a dog. Finishing my evening prayers, I pour myself a cup of tea and wrap myself in my veil. Then I curl up on the couch and smoke a cigarette." She raised both arms wide and looked at the ceiling with a thankful smile. "All of a sudden the weariness of life is lifted from my shoulders—the weariness of searching for an illegal travel agent, buying a forged passport, and depositing a handful of money in the bank. No, Professor. Let me go to Nurdad. Let me go to Los Angeles so that I can do business with the proper people."

Hadi Besharat grew a little calmer. He even felt some compassion for her. More gently, he said, "Well, go ahead and leave."

"Don't worry, I will! In America people understand and care about you. There I have a son who'll look after me. On holidays he'll take me to Los Angeles's kebab houses. Our own kebab houses are not worth the little fingers of those in Los Angeles. What a kebab! Not like our own dry kebabs where you don't even know what kind of animal is used. Each kebab is as wide as your palm. General Ghovanlu says, 'Miss Zari, you always have someone to look after you.' I answer him, 'No, General! I don't need anyone in my life to hold my hand and help me.' He says, 'Miss Zari, you are a lucky person. No matter what you step into, you cause something good to happen. They should call you Lucky-Step Lady.' "

Hadi Besharat stood up. "I will leave and bother you no more."

Mrs. Razi grew nervous and said, "Why, Professor? Why so soon?"

"I must go. I've heard enough for seven generations before me."

"Let me show you the letter that came from America yesterday for my poor boy."

"A letter from America for Mehrdad?"

"Yes, Professor Humphrey finally answered him. I can't understand English. I gave it to Nili to read to me. I wish I hadn't done that. She doesn't know English either and she asks her father's inheritance for each line she reads."

"The boy wrote a letter in English?"

"Did you expect him to write it in pig Latin? Don't you remember he used to study English at the Shokufeh Institute?"

"Of all people, why did he write my old friend? Is there a scarcity of human beings in America?"

"All the young people in the district write Professor Humphrey every day. Why couldn't my own child? Did you expect him to fold his hands and look at the wall?"

"How about my reputation? No doubt Professor Humphrey thinks I've opened my own travel agency, applying to American colleges for everyone and getting them passports and green cards. Now I know why he hasn't answered my letters."

He didn't wait for Mrs. Razi's response. He slammed out of the room and went downstairs. When he reached the corridor a cold wind hit his face. The camphor candles were still burning in the dining room and the moonlight spread over the courtyard. The trees were tall and black around the courtyard pool, their outlines clearly delineated by the moonlight. Their branches rose like the standards that the breast-beaters carry. Geometric patterns of moonlight were scattered across the ground.

He regretted losing his temper. Why had he lowered himself

in front of Mrs. Razi? You couldn't expect anything from such an ordinary woman. She had no interest whatsoever in listening to him. In the midst of her misery she'd wanted only to sell the poor boy's clothes to someone. Only to get a visa for her trip to America. She had even insulted Nili, who had endured her outbursts all this time.

He pulled his coat collar over his ears and left the courtyard. In front of the mosque he met people who had arrived here from the provinces. They had come from those faraway lost villages and small townships where the night's silence is broken only by the barking of dogs in the desert. Their skies turn purple at every sunset from the smoke of the clay ovens. The newly ripened girls swing their little baskets of charcoal on the rooftops, leaving sparkling traces in the air. How far they had traveled. How much dust they had gathered on their clothes. They must have ridden the whole way on the backs of trucks. The cold wind made their eyes look greedy and their faces cross. Hadi Besharat sat down on the stone bench in front of Martyr Taher Nabavi High School, wrapped himself in his coat, and watched the crowd from a distance.

Suddenly antiaircraft volleys started and the Condition Red siren blared. There was an uproar as people ran in every direction. The neighbors rushed up and down their stairways and the light from the kerosene lamps melted in the darkness. Mrs. Razi appeared on her rooftop and gazed at the sky. She must not have been able to see the Iraqi bombers themselves. But from the sound of the explosions it was obvious they were striking somewhere in the northern suburbs. From the other end of the street, Nili appeared pushing Mr. Bayat toward their house and shouting, "Mrs. Razi, what are you doing up there? A bomb's going to fall on your head and destroy you."

Mrs. Razi shouted back, "I'm not a child. Those little firecrackers aren't dangerous. They're not bugabears to scare me." Then she changed the subject. "Engineer Gharib, weren't you supposed to go to Lashgarak?"

"The roads turned out to be closed. We couldn't go. Now

we're planning to have dinner at General Ghovanlu's instead and play some cards."

"Come up here and look at the city. It's very interesting. I haven't seen anything like this in all my life. How well you can see everything from here! The Iraqi bombers are heading toward Maghsudbak. Now they've just hit Maghsudbak. Oh, Lord of the Faithful, please help. When a bomb falls, it explodes in flames and lights up everything."

The doors and windowpanes began to rattle. A strong wind hit Hadi Besharat's face and left an acrid taste in his mouth, as if anesthesia had numbed the roots of his teeth, his tongue and gums. A hand rose in the tumult of darkness, swung a little, and submerged again. The wife of Engineer Gharib shouted, "Oh, dear God! Please listen to the screams of innocent children. Oh, dear God, please listen to the screams of all the patients in Martyrs' Hospital. Oh, dear God, who will listen to the screams of the crippled and the handicapped?"

The roaring of the Iraqi bombers and the antiaircraft volleys gradually died down. Mrs. Razi was still talking to the neighbors from her rooftop. "General, how are you? How much Arabic have you learned from Mr. Bayat so far? Do you listen to the Arabic radio stations? What do they say?"

"Miss Zari, how are you? When can I make a visit and offer my condolences?"

"I'm not in the mood for that just now. Wait till some other time."

"God grant you patience. Why do you make it so hard for yourself?"

"How do I know? Everyone has a lot in life, Agha."

The neighbors began to return to their houses. The sounds of an ordinary winter evening began to fill the street.

"Good night, Professor Besharat," Nili said.

"Miss Nili, you are so young and you carry such a load on your shoulders. Will you allow me to help you take Mr. Bayat home?"

Nili drew her eyebrows together. "I don't understand, Professor Besharat. What do you mean?"

"You have so many responsibilities for someone so young."

"Oh, Professor Besharat, I like these responsibilities. I enjoy doing this."

Hadi Besharat shrugged and walked toward his house. If Farangu wasn't home by now, what would he do? Maybe he could call on Engineer Gharib. Maybe he could go to General Ghovanlu's and sit behind one of the cardplayers. Or he could finish his paper, "Angels from the Point of View of *The Book of Strange Creatures.*" He would discuss the angels who twist their thin brittle fingers in the air like morning-glory tendrils. Those with three- and five-point crowns, those with eyeless, eyebrowless white masks that make their faces look sorrowful.

As he put the key in the lock he thought of a famous sentence written by Sun Tzu, the Chinese military philosopher who wrote more than twenty-five centuries ago:

Oh, running sands of time, symbol of cleverness and secrecy, let us learn from you the art of concealment and silence so that we may hold in our hands the reins of the enemy's fate.

F I V E

As he went upstairs, a shaft of light passed through a crack in the door and folded like an accordion when it reached the edge of the stairway. Farangu must be back from her Mama Aliyeh's. He thought she might be ironing in the sewing room or maybe trying on clothes. He called, "Farangu?"

The sewing-room door opened slightly. Farangu peered through the crack with watery eyes. Hadi Besharat said, "Farangu, what are you doing?"

The door opened wider and Farangu stood in the middle of the light's rectangular frame. She looked like an opera singer. She wore her milky white silk negligee that she usually saved for holidays, and she stood on an imaginary stage as though awaiting the appearance of a storm's sea gulls or the return of a captainless boat, as though listening to the sailors' chorus, as though expecting the arrival of a fine sunny day or preparing to call someone from a distance. She tucked strands of her hair behind her ears and stood in silence. Hadi Besharat came closer and asked quietly, "Where have you been?"

Farangu put her arms around his neck, rested her head on his shoulder, and closed her eyes. She seemed tired and her breath smelled of alcohol. Hadi Besharat pulled back and looked at her face again. "Have you been drinking?"

She put her lips to Hadi Besharat's cheek. "Besharat, how cold your face is. What a cold wind's blowing outside."

"Don't you know it's dangerous to walk alone in the street when you've been drinking?"

"Cousin Sayid-jon drove me home."

She drew back from his arms, pulled a bobby pin from her hair, and clamped it between her teeth. Twisting her fingers, she rewound the coil of hair on top of her head and skewered it in place. Then she folded her arms and smiled carelessly. "Mama Aliyeh made a big dinner. We had a lot of fun. Tomorrow she's throwing a party."

"Mama Aliyeh's giving another party tomorrow?"

"They've just begun their traditional daily visits to welcome Sayid-jon home, and every day they're going to visit someone. Do you want to come?"

"I'm not so idle that I can waste time on such things."

"How humorless you are! If you don't want to come, then don't. But I'm going. I'm rotting away, sitting here listening to Agilax powder and the Angel Gabriel. One day you're going to open your eyes and find out the cradle is wet and the baby is gone."

But Farangu didn't change the relaxed expression on her face. She raised a hand to a tendril of hair hanging over her ear and smoothed it thoughtfully, as if she couldn't decide about a pattern she was cutting or some clothes she was stitching together. Then she placed her hands beseechingly to her heart and curled her fingers in a gesture of resignation and acceptance. Hadi Besharat wondered whom he was talking to. Why Farangu was behaving like someone who'd taken a drug.

He stepped into the sewing room and pulled over a chair. He sat down slowly; his joints didn't bend as easily as they used to. "I don't feel so good. My stomach is full of acid."

"You must have been eating junk food."

"What junk food? I avoid all dairy products, fruit, and raw vegetables. Only on occasion do I put a few pieces of boiled meat in my mouth without salt or seasoning. Even so, I have a heavy feeling. I should go on a diet."

"Well, do it, then."

"Why did you stay out so long? Is it because you're mad at me that you stayed at your Mama Aliyeh's all that time?"

Farangu said, "It's not because I'm mad. I just can't take it anymore. If I keep sitting here I'll go crazy."

"When you're gone nothing works right. The neighbors bother me constantly and don't let me write. They think writing books is not a real job. For a real job you have to go to an office and sit at a desk."

"You just need a servant, not a wife."

"How important is it for you to go to that party?"

"If I don't go Sayid-jon will be offended."

Hadi Besharat raised his eyebrows and said, "Well, go then. I'll keep myself busy somehow till your Sayid-jon takes his honor and returns to America. I fail to understand how you can talk to a ridiculous, pretentious person like Sayid."

"You just hate him because he likes to joke. But he doesn't do it out of malice. You don't want to forgive him for the Nobel Prize incident, but he only meant to tease you a little."

"I want none of it. I want to close our door, admit no one, and keep busy with my work. This evening I went to Mrs. Razi's to offer my condolences and comfort a grieving mother. Do you know what she said?"

"How come she let you in?"

"Because she's kicked Nili out of the house and there's no one to prevent it."

"Good for her. It warms my heart. That should teach Nili not to meddle in matters that are none of her business. If she comes here I'll treat her the same way. I'll slam the door in her face."

"All the time you were gone she hung around this house and searched every room. I suppose it's because she has no home. I mean no real home. Also there's no entertainment like in the old days. She doesn't know what to do with herself. She came here and asked me to give her lessons."

The Pilgrim's Rules of Etiquette

"Don't do it."

"Of course not. Do you think I'm crazy?"

"Besharat, never encourage her. She makes me angry."

Farangu turned and left the room. Hadi Besharat rose stiffly, slowed by the pain in his joints, and followed her down the stairs. He said, "Nili will be all right eventually. She's just young and inexperienced. But what about Mrs. Razi? Do you know she tried to sell me Mehrdad's clothes to send to Khosro in America. Can you believe it? The shroud on the poor boy's body is not yet dry and his mother is making a deal for his clothes. Strange. How confused the people of this land are! Have they lost their minds?"

Entering the kitchen, Farangu said, "I asked Sayid-jon to look up Khosro in America. Maybe he can find him money from somewhere. Mama Aliyeh said to me, 'Why doesn't Professor Besharat ask Mr. Bayat to pay back his debt to Khosro? Mr. Bayat is not a poor man.'"

"What business of Mama Aliyeh's is Mr. Bayat's debt? Since when has she been in charge of our lives? Basically, I don't want to take any steps for Khosro. I don't know all the ins and outs of his affairs. When are we having dinner?"

"Get something from the refrigerator."

Farangu spoke carelessly, placing no importance on her words. Hadi Besharat was annoyed. "Very well, if that's the way you feel —I don't have any appetite anyhow. I'll go upstairs and get busy with my work."

He climbed the stairs feeling hurt and angry. He thought of the streets in Whitehurst College, which every night seemed polished by the steely radiance of the neon lights. He remembered how the echo of his own steps had reached his ears like a sheet of glass breaking against the red brick walls. Each evening, with the arrival of darkness, the sole window at the police station would shine like a cat's yellow eyes as the police captain finished his cup of coffee. Oh, Whitehurst College! In 1969 Hadi Besharat had walked with Professor Humphrey along St. Peter Street and now everything that had happened there appeared before him, unbelievably interesting, almost miraculous. They had passed the First National Bank as a girl with braided hair ran among the trees toward City Park. An old man sat on a bench taking bread crumbs from a brown bag and scattering them on the dirt path for the pigeons. At the time Hadi Besharat had been preparing a history lecture for his students. He had wanted to analyze the details of an event so his students would gasp in amazement and ask where the truth is. What is reality. But how mistaken he'd been. In America he'd become conscious for the first time of that Eastern feeling, the sense of the instability of the universe and the transience of every moment and the eternal power of fate. Reality had pierced his heart like a spike.

He placed the magic lantern on his desk and began to clean the four brass angels with a cloth moistened in kerosene. On the surface there were no differences among the angels Israfel, Gabriel, Michael, and Izrail. Each held a horn to his lips, each raised his right leg toward the angel in front of him and bent his left leg behind him as they ran after each other in perpetual immobility. Whenever the candles were lit, the angels and the lantern would begin to rotate, their shadows passing over the wall—the shadow of the Garden of Eden and the Toba Tree of Life in Heaven. The Pit of Wailing and the bitter Zagghume tree in Hell. The shadow of the olive tree and the lamp burning among its branches, and the group of naked people listening to a song coming from the tree. The shadow of a celestial body with a crescent moon inside the sun's belly like a fetus. The naked angel spangling stars on a tray. The Angel of Death, Izrail, holding in one hand a soul flapping like a headless bird and pointing with the other hand to the bones in an open casket. The image of David singing his psalms. The scene of a heavenly visitation and the shadows of Mary and the newborn infant.

Cleaning that lantern not only took him back to 1969; it also filled him with the desire to travel and go sightseeing around the world. Circumstances being what they were, there was no possibility of his taking a trip. Instead he could only review the memories of past trips in his mind. Those had been possible because of the scholarship he'd received from Whitehurst College. He had traveled around the globe. First he'd gone nonstop to America. Upon his return he had visited Spain. He went to Morocco and, like a wandering Ulysses, sailed the shores of the Mediterranean. He visited the sites of the Byzantine courts. Reaching the Holy Land, he measured step by step the old quarters in Jerusalem like the thirteenth-century traveler Naser Khosro. He slept on the running sands at the edge of the Sinai Desert and grew lost in contemplation of St. Catherine Church. At the Dome of the Rock he went to sleep on the mosque's stone steps. An Israeli policeman woke him in the middle of the night and searched his pockets. As soon as he found out Hadi Besharat was Iranian he had smiled and escorted him to his hotel. In Paris he went to Père Lachaise Cemetery and stood for a moment in silence at the graves of Balzac, Alfred de Musset, and Sadegh Hedayat, the father of modern Iranian prose. Where was Hadi Besharat? Where was the Père Lachaise Cemetery?

After August of 1942 he had worked to earn his own pocket money as his father-jon had instructed. He watered graves in Mesgarabad Cemetery, charging the relatives of the dead twenty cents apiece. He went into the ice cream business as well. Each afternoon he rented a barrel of ice cream from Ramezan the ice seller. Painted on the barrel were a crown, two angels beneath it, and the Iranian flag. Hadi Besharat hawked his wares, spinning the wheel of his life with the profits. In the evenings he prepared his lessons. In the mornings he got straight A's from Fakhr Zanjani. Then a mere fifteen years later he was in the heart of Paris, standing at the site of Sadegh Hedayat's grave. What for?

He had wished he could stay in Paris, but eventually he ended up in Hamburg. He became lost in Hamburg's fish market and in halting German asked a few small children where he could find a toilet—*Toilette.* The children answered in a few broken phrases that he couldn't understand. As they walked away he heard one child say in Farsi, "What an asshole." He was forced to laugh at himself. The next day he packed, and, with no plan or goal in mind, went to London. Surprisingly, he felt calm in London. He went to a clothing shop in Covent Garden. He bought a black broadcloth suit, a white silk scarf, a blue nylon shirt, an orange tie, a bowler hat, and a rolled silk umbrella with a curved ivory handle. Wearing all his new clothes, he held the umbrella like a cane and began to walk with a raised head and a dignified gait. He passed Oxford Circus and Piccadilly Circus and arrived at Trafalgar Square. There he took the underground to Westminster Abbey. For three hours he visited the graves of famous personalities and historical heroes and the statues of Englishmen of letters. He stopped to read the plaque over the grave of Ben Jonson and couldn't take another step:

O rare Ben Jonson!

He could feel the depth of that rareness. Not only because Ben Jonson had been a rare specimen but because of his lack of presence. And he had felt a sense of pity as he viewed the golden painting of a bereaved mother with a newborn baby lying dead in her arms. His pity wasn't condescending. As each minute died, he too died.

He walked that night along the banks of the Thames. The next morning he canceled his lecture at the Oxford School of Oriental Languages. This was his soul's basic paradox. In the black broadcloth suit with the bowler hat on his head and the rolled silk umbrella in his hand, he could throw away all worldly possessions. Walking the streets with a sense of anger that was turning into rebellious arrogance, he could give up Oxford's honorarium and his high status. He felt that not only was he in need of nothing and indebted to no one, but also he was a rare specimen of the human race—as rare as the uninhabited islands in the Atlantic Ocean which he had seen for the first time while flying here. The islands were shaped like the palm of a hand, like an orange-tree leaf wrapped around the silky clouds. The ocean washed them silently and he had felt distilled just looking at them. O those rare and ownerless isles!

He lit the candles and the magic lantern began to spin. He brought the gallon jar from the closet to pour himself a little vodka. Then he changed his mind. He didn't want to get confused. The cares of the day had squeezed him like a dishrag and now God only knew how late it was. He should rest awhile. But he wasn't in the mood to change clothes and lie down on a proper bed. He stretched out on the couch instead, and his mind became filled with dreams. In the absolute silence of their house, he could hear Farangu singing in English.

> "Next time I fall in love,
> I'll fall in love with you. . . ."

Tomorrow, Farangu would don her fancy outfit again and go to her Mama Aliyeh's, leaving him alone. He would be awakened again by Ahmad Bayat screaming at Nili, "Next time I find you alone in the street I'll turn you over in handcuffs to the Revolutionary Guards and religious patrols so they can take you to prison."

Engineer Gharib would open his laboratory window and stick his head out. Even in such cold weather he would leave the window open awhile. Otherwise the air would go bad in the laboratory. In the warm, closed space, perfume essences smelled like rotten meat, like the smell in the street when the garbage wasn't collected. He had to keep the essences cold and dilute them with alcohol. Engineer Gharib always made sure his laboratory was as clean as a dining hall or a private bathing facility. Its black and white checkered tiles were even cleaner than those in a dissecting room.

Hadi Besharat felt he was calming down. His sailboat was nearing the shore of an uninhabited island. There the tongue of the ocean licked at the feet of the coastal ghosts, changing them into stone with the mariner's lullaby. The stone ghosts would turn to dust, crumbling at the touch of a hand. As in the legend,

Solomon leaned on his cane for a thousand years and no one knew he was dead until the termites ate the cane from inside and his body fell to the ground.

He woke up around noon and heard an uproar—the sounds of elegies and breast-beating, and from the Komité Building the mumbling of the judges trying drug smugglers, and from behind the Martyr Taher Nabavi High School the volleys of the Revolutionary Guards practicing to be a firing squad. He heard voices downstairs in the drawing room speaking gibberish. Farangu was begging everyone to eat. "Just a little—this little bit is not worth arguing about."

She must have decided not to go to her Mama Aliyeh's. Maybe she had postponed her trip because guests had arrived. It made no difference to Hadi Besharat. He wasn't in the mood for visitors or small talk. He just wanted to be left alone. He got up and went to his bookshelf to search for something. By chance he found an old book, *The Varasteh Method*. He had learned his English from that book. A thin book with an orange cover. Despite its thinness it felt heavy. Gilded English and Farsi letters, tightly printed, were pressed into the cover. He opened the book with care and read a few sentences. The memories of his high school years came back to him.

They served the meat on a broken plate.

The servant had brought small potatoes, but I liked the bigger ones.

Your ruler is longer than his, but shorter than mine.

My father hit him.

One of my cousins has seven servants.

How easy it had been to learn English from that book! He placed it quietly on the desk. Tiptoeing out of the study, he crossed the hall to the bathroom. He could hear Mrs. Gharib downstairs. "Nili is making up stories. She says all the television archives from the Monster Shah's regime are still hidden somewhere."

General Ghovanlu's wife said, "Miss, why do you encourage the girl? She doesn't know what she's talking about. Who can say where the television archives are hidden? There might be a chance of finding them if a bomb blew up the TV building."

Mrs. Gharib said, "*I* don't encourage Nili. She *forces* herself on a person. I don't pay any attention to her at all."

Farangu sighed. "By God."

General Ghovanlu's wife began to recite the story of their illegal trip to Pakistan. "It was Ashura, the tenth day of mourning for St. Hosein's martyrdom. We planned to fly to Zahedan first. My daughter Shehrzad said, 'Mama, you have to wake me early in the morning so I can tell you good-bye.' I said, 'Baba, I don't want to. You go ahead and sleep. Why bother saying good-bye?' I didn't know she was planning to give me a list of things that she wanted me to buy her in Zahedan."

The guests burst into laughter. Mrs. Gharib said, "Really. Didn't you tell her you had to look after Mr. Bayat and Agha Mojtaba? Things being as they were, how could Shehrzad expect you to buy her this and that type of shoes, slippers, and bangles?"

General Ghovanlu's wife said, "I told her, 'Shehrzad-jon, I won't promise, but I'll try if I get a chance.'"

Hadi Besharat closed the bathroom door, turned on the shower, and waited for the water to warm. Once he was in the shower he began recalling the interesting exercises that he had thought up when he was trying to learn English from *The Varasteh Method.* He had warned himself that learning a language is not a simple affair. But learning is a reward in itself, because it slows time. Haste moves horizontally and learning is a vertical journey to the deep.

He wrapped himself in a towel and tiptoed back to his study, drawing no one's attention. The guests were in the entrance hall now and evidently they were finding it difficult to part. General

Ghovanlu's wife was telling how they'd traveled on from Pakistan to America. "When we arrived in Los Angeles, I said goodbye to Mr. Bayat and Mojtaba. After a few days I thought to call Agha Mojtaba's home and ask how Mr. Bayat was doing. Agha Mojtaba's American wife answered. You don't know how beautifully Marguerite spoke Farsi. But, well, I could sense that her end-stresses were American and things like that. I said, 'I am a fellow traveler with your husband and Mr. Bayat.' Marguerite talked exactly like Iranians, saying hellos and pleasantries and admiring words and such, very warm and kind. She said, 'Agha Mojtaba is not at home. Mr. Bayat developed some discomfort and we had to take him to the hospital. Please give me your phone number and he will call you back.' I said, 'Is Mr. Bayat planning to return with us?' She said, 'No, miss. His life is in danger. We won't let him.' "

Mrs. Gharib said, "We weren't there, but we heard that Mr. Bayat had separated from his wife and was living all by himself."

General Ghovanlu's wife said, "Apparently he planned to find a woman, some nurse or companion who could take care of him."

Mrs. Gharib added, "Who could give him massages."

The guests burst into laughter.

Two years ago, when Mr. Bayat had decided to go to America, everyone had warned him and tried to change his mind. They had believed that traveling such a distance at such an age would kill him. But he insisted. He was going crazy because of the arguments among Ahmad and Heli and Nili as to who should look after him. He felt he had no choice. He had to go start a new life. And he did just that. But six months later, on the day of the Prophet's passing, which coincides with the martyrdom of St. Hassan, he returned with his arms longer than his legs. How thin he looked. He had lost at least ten kilograms, his hands trembling and his speech slurred and saliva dripping from his mouth. An old-timer cannot forget his country so easily. In a foreign country, even sweet water could not pass down his throat. He had to return.

The Pilgrim's Rules of Etiquette

Hadi Besharat heard Farangu and the guests leave the house. He was glad of the privacy. He dressed and put a pot of water on the heater. He straightened his desk top and brought a cup of tea from the kitchen. Sitting at his desk, looking out the window, he waited for Mehrdad to come. But that was foolish. The poor boy was gone.

Only once in a thousand times would you find a student like Mehrdad—just by chance, bingo. A student capable of comprehending something about the history of this nation. Why, even Hadi Besharat's own son, Khosro, had not been capable of that. Why, the only thing Hadi Besharat could do for Khosro had no connection with human thoughts and understanding. Only money could bring them together. Nevertheless he was ready to keep Khosro close to him in any manner he could.

He wished at least Khosro knew what a struggle it was, how hard it would be to go to Mr. Bayat and attempt to collect Khosro's debt. It was all for Khosro's sake. Sacrificing and forgiveness had been this nation's heritage for many thousand years. He had to pay a visit to Mr. Bayat and try to get Khosro's money back.

Still, he delayed. He picked up *The Varasteh Method* and put it down, gathered some papers from his desk and placed them on a shelf, took another swallow of tea. He even considered going on with his translation of *The Death of a Great Savior*. Then he realized that these were all excuses. Abruptly he clapped his beret on his head and took up his umbrella and set off for Mr. Bayat's.

Nili opened the door for him. He hadn't expected that, but he kept his frown in place. Nili threw him a slanted and meaningful glance, as if she had been counting the minutes behind the door. Her smile brimmed with triumph. Hadi Besharat took off his beret and unbuttoned his suit coat. He spoke with a decisive, emphatic tone. "Is Mr. Bayat in?"

Nili tugged the hair at her temples and turned away from him, saying in English, "Hello." Then in Farsi, "Professor Besharat, do you want to visit him?"

"If it's no trouble."

"What trouble? Come in, please." Then, continuing, in English, "Enter, please."

As he stepped into the courtyard Nili examined him up and down, down and up, curiously. As if overly curious about his black broadcloth suit, maroon shirt, and yellow tie. Hadi Besharat felt uneasy. He didn't know why she was behaving this way. Nili changed her expression and asked, "Would you like me to bring you some tea?"

"I just had my tea, miss. Thank you anyway."

Nili started laughing. "Professor Besharat, I like your yellow tie very much." In English: "Beautiful."

He was taken aback by her cheekiness and couldn't answer in a normal voice. He mumbled a little and said, "Thank you for your kindness."

Nili brushed lint off his shoulder, now laughing face to face. "You get offended easily. Perhaps Miss Farangu has left again and you don't have anyone to look after you."

Hadi Besharat looked at Nili's short hair, her sly, teasing eyes and free expression. She led him across the courtyard and into the house. She opened a door and when he had entered Mr. Bayat's room she smiled at him again and closed the door behind him and disappeared.

The room was connected to dark corridors, to curtained and heavily furnished rooms beyond. Time had turned the white walls yellowish, like old newspaper pages freckled with dried tea spots. There were all kinds of photos hanging on the walls in no particular pattern—photos of the Bayat family patriarchs of two or three generations past, wearing the special uniforms reserved for audiences with kings. Generations gazed down at Hadi Besharat imposingly: a photo of a swaddled baby with puffy cheeks staring at the camera; a photo of an old man and a bespectacled boy standing politely on snow-covered ground, tightly holding hands. The images of forgotten and dramatic family events; the souvenirs of secret marriages, sudden and scandalous deaths; suicides over love affairs; murders of illegitimate babies by sticking pins in their fontanels.

Mr. Bayat was stretched out on the bed, light as a feather. His head had fallen backward and his eyes were widened by the sheer force of staring. He raised his head courteously in recognition. But then he fell back. Hadi Besharat came close with measured steps, sat down on a chair next to the bed, and hung his umbrella on the headboard. He leaned forward and asked quietly, "How are you doing?"

Mr. Bayat gave him a suspicious stare. An uncertain smile glimmered on his face. Hadi Besharat said, "It is I, Professor Besharat. It's been a long time since we've had a real talk."

His mouth half open, his eyes fixed and empty, Mr. Bayat nodded a few times. Hadi Besharat said, "What news from your son, Agha Mojtaba, and your wife, Miss Monir, in America?"

Hearing the familiar names changed Mr. Bayat's expression. He grew excited and spoke as if he'd had a speech prepared. "Nothing at all is happening in America. You just run into a bunch of useless Iranians who are going here and there with no purpose in mind. Alas, those dumbheads won't give a helping hand to anyone. They only show off their money. It makes you sad. I swear by your life, this man was selling lime on Ray Street in Tehran. Now you go to Georgetown and see what pomp and pride he's gathered around himself. He's covered himself in gold and bought a house by the canal. Yes, Professor Besharat, these are the people who've gone to America. When they speak to you, tears well up in their eyes for the homeland. But you and I are different. Take yourself, for example. You're involved in your work. Whatever comes your way on the history of Iran, on Iranian literature and culture past and present, you collect and study. Well, this is a positive step. But these people are making a lot more money than you and they haven't taken a positive step for anyone. They say, 'Well, we're feeding ourselves. To hell with the rest.' "

Mr. Bayat paused for a moment. Talking seemed to have improved his spirits. But Hadi Besharat was running out of patience. He wanted to bring up Khosro's debt as soon as possible. Mr. Bayat reached for a glass of whiskey on the nightstand. He motioned for Hadi Besharat to pour himself a drink, saying, "Excuse me. I don't have the strength to do it for you."

Unwillingly, Hadi Besharat obeyed. Mr. Bayat raised his glass and said, "Well, let's drink to the health of the professor-jon. Let's drink to the health of Heli-jon, Nili-jon, and Ahmad-jon. Forgive me, I forgot, let's drink to the health of Khosro-jon, Mehrdad-jon . . . I don't remember the rest. Professor, what have you learned in this life, in this crazy world with no beginning and no end?"

Hadi Besharat took a sip of vodka and said, "Mr. Bayat, life is the distance between two borders. The border of coming into this world against your wishes and the border of leaving here against your wishes. They force you to come and they force you to leave. Happy are those who travel lightly the distance between those two borders. Alas, people are mostly in a hurry. Instead of giving depth to their lives, they shorten them."

"For me, Professor-jon, life is stretching out on this bed right here; life is being in my own country. Two days ago Ahmad and I were coming out of the National Garden. It was one o'clock in the afternoon. Ahmad had parked his Jeep in the Sepah Circle. Don't know what they call it now. The smell of soup meat hit my nose. You can't imagine. I told Ahmad, 'My, my, I'm about to pass out. Let's go have some soup.' Ahmad said, 'You're not the type to eat street soup.' I said, 'What's wrong with it? Let's go have some soup with the porters.' He said, 'Wouldn't you be embarrassed?' I said, 'It's my own country. Why should I feel embarrassed?' "

The door opened and Heli entered, a coffee tray in her hands and her head uncovered. Although she saw nothing, she walked around the table and chairs with delicate, almost sensuous movements. Without a word she presented the coffee tray to them. Mr. Bayat said, "Pretty girl, you don't drink coffee with whiskey."

Giving a Buddhalike smile, she bent her head. Instead of answering her father she turned to Hadi Besharat and said, "Professor Besharat, would you like me to put some cream in your coffee?"

Her voice was soft. It lulled him and prevented him from refusing. He stood up and said, "Allow me to help you."

"You can see I don't need any help. I can do it by myself. Professor Besharat, is that picture still on the wall of your house?"

He took the umbrella from the headboard and held it tightly between his feet. With his head lowered, he answered, "Miss, it depends on what you want to see and how you look at it. The picture Miss Nili has seen on the wall is only a mental picture. If you yourself were to look at it you would see a different picture."

"When I think of that poor boy I see him in that woolen sweater. I knitted a gray sweater for him while I still had my sight. Any time he wore it, it reflected shadows on his face the way gray often does with Iranians. Do you remember that black hair? That olive-colored, pale face? Those eyes sparkling like black diamonds?"

Mr. Bayat drank the last drop in his glass and said, "Just words, a bunch of rubbish, Professor-jon. How is the little fellow, what news from Khosro-jon?"

An opening had arrived. Now Hadi Besharat could talk about the real reason for his visit. He turned to Mr. Bayat and said, "As it happens, I had a phone conversation with Khosro just two days ago. He said his financial situation isn't that good. He's lost a great deal of money, and if he doesn't get more soon he'll go bankrupt. . . . Please don't think that he's pressing for the payment of your debt. It's just that he's in desperate need. He sent his greetings and asked you to mail what you owe for those girders."

He got it over with quickly. Silent and determined, he stared at Mr. Bayat. Mr. Bayat rubbed his unshaven chin and said, "Professor Besharat, why is it that our youth pack up and go to a foreign country? Are they distributing free halvah there? Tell him to come back to his own country. At least here people look after each other's interests and don't let a man paint himself into a corner."

"Is it possible for you to send him some money?"

"Tell him that at present I don't have much cash on hand. But I'll think about it. As soon as I get hold of some I don't mind sending as much as I can afford."

Mr. Bayat finished speaking with a sigh and a moan. He lowered his head to the pillow and closed his eyes. Heli stood vigilant above her tray, facing a painting with her eyes appearing open and shut at the same time. In the painting a rider in chain mail came down a slope of the Elborz Mountain. The touch of his spear caused lightning to flash and cracked the sky. Mr. Bayat had begun to snore and Hadi Besharat didn't want to disturb his sleep. He stirred a bit, indicating that he wanted to leave. Heli turned to him and bade him good-bye with a bow.

Arriving home, he looked for any sign of Farangu. Maybe the light in the kitchen was on and her shadow was moving across the floor. Maybe the shaft of light was passing through the sewing-room door and breaking at the edge of the stairs. Maybe he could hear her footsteps upstairs and the crackling noise of her changing.

But the only sound was the chirping of an insect that stopped as soon as he entered the house. He was in his study when he heard someone climbing the stairs. He thought it was Farangu returning from her Mama Aliyeh's house. Now, instead of being relieved, he felt angry. He didn't show it, though. He took off his beret and threw it on the daybed. It spun like a flying saucer before it landed. Then he heard his door open. He pretended nothing was happening and unbuttoned his cuff links. Nili walked in with an armful of laundered shirts and socks.

Hadi Besharat was flabbergasted but he didn't let it show. He immediately assumed a cold, scowling expression, meanwhile continuing to unbutton his shirt. Nili folded the laundry carefully and stacked it on the daybed. She didn't even glance in his direction. Satisfied with the arrangement of the clothes, she turned to leave the study. Hadi Besharat called, "Miss Nili."

Nili didn't say a word. Hadi Besharat planted his fingertips on his desk. He leaned forward and examined her face closely. She returned his stare. Hadi Besharat spoke slowly. "Haven't I pointed out that you should never step into this room without my permission? Haven't I?"

Easily and without any struggle, Nili said, "Yes. You did."

Hadi Besharat raised a finger to emphasize the second article of his accusations. But Nili's calmness and cool passivity had disarmed him. His finger was left in the air. He felt not so much angry as confused. He composed himself and asked, "Why did you come, then?"

Nili sat down in a chair across from his desk. She placed her hands together. Her fingers were chubby and rounded at the joints, with a dimple on each joint like babies' fingers. Hadi Besharat didn't move from where he stood. He was expecting some argument from her. But Nili remained relaxed and un-resisting. Hadi Besharat said, "Is that your answer? You don't have anything else to say?"

"I've made a chicken sandwich for you. Do you want me to bring it?"

"It's not dinnertime. What are you doing here at this hour of the day?"

"Miss Farangu hasn't come back yet. I thought someone ought to make your dinner. I love to cook. I'm responsible for most of the meals at our house."

He wanted to go on scolding her, but he couldn't bring him-self to do so. He asked more gently, "What do you want from me?"

"I want you to teach me English."

She clasped her hands together and leaned back in her chair, smiling. In her smile the air of victory was changing to one of need, forcing secrets out of him. But there was nothing invasive about her eyes. He could see his own reflection in them.

"You speak English all the time. Why do you want me to teach you?"

"My English isn't that good. I want to talk like Americans."

Crossly, he picked up *The Varasteh Method* from his desk. He leafed through the book with a frown and said, "You would find it too hard to be my student. I'm not easily satisfied. It's no reflection on you. In my student days I myself refused to do my lessons on many occasions. Our history teacher, the late Fakhr Zanjani, screamed at me and tore my examination papers to pieces many, many times. But at my age I don't have the time to waste. There are plenty of other teachers. You can go enroll in the Shokufeh Institute and learn as much English as you want."

"Professor Besharat, I want only to be your student."

Hadi Besharat didn't lift his frowning gaze from *The Varasteh Method*. "My expectations of my students are too high."

"What do you expect of them?"

"I expect them to be serious in their studies. They have to show their love of reading and their interest in this country's history and culture. Do you understand what I'm saying? Those who are my students must care about learning and knowledge."

"I know that. Poor Mehrdad told me everything. Professor Besharat, I want to say something."

For the first time Hadi Besharat, still frowning, raised his head from the book. "Please go ahead."

"I'm afraid."

Hadi Besharat looked at her. "What are you afraid of?"

"Promise me you won't be angry. I don't mean any harm."

"Miss, say what you want. Of course I won't be angry."

"I'm afraid of you. When you talk, it makes me nervous."

Hadi Besharat raised his eyebrows. "Miss, you're not afraid of me. You're afraid of your own ignorance and your lack of education. You think you're all-knowing and for every question you have a ready-made answer in your mind."

"You're right. I'm too uneducated, Professor Besharat." Nili set her elbows on the desk, cupping her face between her hands and looking at him with wide eyes.

Hadi Besharat drew back and wrinkled his nose. "Miss, of course study is the cure for that. Except that study is difficult. It tires you. A young lady your age prefers something that entertains her. It's not easy to spend all your time studying."

He opened *The Varasteh Method* and slid it over to her. Nili asked, "What is this, Professor Besharat?"

"Look at it carefully. See what you make of it. To learn English you have to like your textbook."

Nili sat straighter in her chair and picked up the book. She leafed through the pages. "I don't see anything wrong with it. I like the text."

"How about its print style? Do you notice that some of the phrases are underlined? That helps you distinguish between what's important and what's not."

Nili's eyes sparkled with joy and surprise. "Oh, Professor Besharat! You're going to teach me after all! I thought that maybe, after Mehrdad, you wouldn't like to teach anymore."

Hadi Besharat blinked and looked at her from the corner of his eye. There must have been some hesitancy, some distress in his expression, because Nili lost her joyfulness. He was sorry to have caused that, and so he said, "Well, why don't you come for a couple of sessions. Let's see how you progress."

Nili jumped up from her seat and kissed his cheek. "I feel very grateful." In English: "Thank you." In Farsi: "When are we going to start?"

Hadi Besharat wiped off her kiss and didn't lift his eyes from his fingers as he spoke. "Come in the afternoons. Mornings I'm busy with my own work and can't talk to anyone. Evenings I get tired and my mind doesn't work right. Every Tuesday, Thursday, and Saturday from two to four in the afternoon."

"Then I'll come tomorrow." Nili closed *The Varasteh Method*. She passed a hand across its cover as if making sure the book was real. She turned it over and read the English version of the title. " '*Varasteh's English Method for Iranian Students,* by Professor Manoochehr Varasteh, Ph.D., LL.D., Doctor of Philosophy in the field of Education (London University) and Doctor of Laws (La

Sorbonne).' Professor Besharat, anyone with so much knowledge is bound to be scary."

"Why?"

Nili hugged the book to her chest and looked at him with excited eyes. "That much knowledge has a magnetic pull, it absorbs you. I think anything so powerful is scary."

"Everyone is frightened of knowledge. I would like to ask you a question."

"Please don't ask any questions. Your questions always make me nervous."

"Just a tiny question. What was the quarrel with Mrs. Razi about?"

"About nothing. I was trying to comfort her. As soon as I brought up Mehrdad's name she jumped on me for no reason. In this district I don't dare say a word. People blame me for everything. Whatever garbage comes to their minds they say behind my back."

"Miss Nili, why be so bitter? Laugh a little. I keep telling myself what a pity. What a pity your youth and your freshness. In this land's garden, how easily the flowers shed their petals in the wind. What hardships has this country not endured in its long past!"

"Why do you always think of ancient periods in history?"

"Because, Miss Nili, it's the same all over the country. People are sitting in their corners recalling distant years. All of us have become travelers in time, cruising the centuries in our minds."

Nili laughed, and Hadi Besharat laughed too. Now he wanted to go on talking. He said, "Miss Nili, hearing you laugh is a blessing for me. Don't feel so sad. Things will all work out."

Nili rose from her chair and said, "Let me go get your chicken sandwich. Surely you must be hungry now."

"It's not necessary. I don't have any appetite."

"But it's almost dark!"

She was right. He reached for the light switch and pressed it. The electricity was off again. He took a pack of matches from his desk drawer and lit the candles on the magic lantern. He waited for the angels to start spinning. In the dusk the room was pale and Nili's milky face was shadowed. When she moved her head her short black hair grew distinct from the gray wall behind her. The candlelight licked her face, causing flowers and leaves to grow around her ears with the movement of the flames.

Hadi Besharat felt an unbounded happiness. A sort of happiness that required description, and yet he couldn't think of the right phrase. He thought only of the angels he had seen on the windows of the cathedral at Whitehurst College. They wore long dresses and held musical instruments under their arms. The light passed through them from behind, stretching a multicolored pattern across the chapel's damp, paved floor.

One winter's day, a Sunday to be exact, he had paused in front of the icon of the Virgin Mary. In the chapel's curved solitude and crusty darkness he was struck by a sort of mental paralysis he'd never experienced before. After many months of traveling from one country to another, he stood still and looked at the icon. Only in that stillness, in that silence, could he collect himself and yet at the same time forget about himself. That pause pulled him down to the depths of some kind of primitiveness. The spread of light, the patches of stained glass satisfied the hunger in his soul just as red meat satisfied his body. In the composition of the space there was a perfection that connected each line and curve and corner. How strange that such perfection had a flaw. A flaw like a mole or a clouded eye or a crippled foot. A flaw that symbolized the lower world and the physical body. It sapped the blood with the dread of death, soldering together the living and the nonliving, leveling all differences. Izrail's pulse beat close to his carotid artery, bringing to Hadi Besharat's nose the smell of dead bodies, lotus, and camphor. Winter was in the air, the cold wind bringing news of brittle, isolated white surfaces. Hadi Besharat understood how to be but not how to pass over.

"Miss, don't forget to mention this arrangement to your brother. You have to ask his permission."

Nili set the book back down on the desk. As she turned to go she said, "Did Mehrdad ask Mrs. Razi's permission?"

"That's different. He was older than you and, besides, in our society boys have more freedom than girls."

"I think of Mehrdad all the time. I hire hourly cabs and go see Bibi Shahr Banu Shrine all by myself. I go to Yahya Shrine where they have a rope tied to the trees in front of it. People tie wish-cloths to the rope. The wind hits the wish-cloths and swings them in the air. I tell myself that a wish-cloth is just some sort of wish. It's just a wish they tie to the rope. Professor Besharat, how easily the wind plays with people's wishes! You worked hard to educate Mehrdad and you taught him a lot. But what's the use? Now Mehrdad is dangling on a rope like a wish-cloth. The wind passes him by and he swings in the air."

"Really? What a strange idea!"

"We took his body to Yahya Shrine for the burial. Mrs. Razi wanted him buried in an ordinary shrine. She wanted him buried in a shrine that nobody bothers to visit. Yahya's a pleasant place. You can sit there and think of Mehrdad. Maybe I could hire a cab someday and take you there."

She tied a bandanna under her chin and started toward the door. Hadi Besharat followed her and said, "Miss, you do things that need a fearless head."

"What, going to Yahya Shrine? It doesn't take much courage."

At the door she turned back once more and said, "Thank you for visiting my papa-jon."

"It was nothing. He was feeling a little better, I thought."

"There's still some dragging in his voice."

"I know. I heard. He talks like a tape recorder with a weak battery." Then, fearing that he might have offended her, he added hastily, "But it's not unpleasant. It reminded me of the voices in dubbed Indian movies."

He shouldn't have said that last part. The more he spoke, the worse it got. He shut his mouth. Nili only smiled and started down the stairs.

After he heard the door close Hadi Besharat went over to his study window and looked down into the street. Nili was running toward her house. A small crowd of people milled around that poor boy's bridal chamber, tying their wish-cloths to it, singing elegies, and beating their breasts. The wailing made his hair stand on end, as if torturers from some ancient court were planting burning candles on his body, stretching him on the rack, hanging him from four nails on the wall. There wasn't a sign of Farangu.

All of a sudden the electricity came back on. Hadi Besharat blew out the candles in the magic lantern. He took the kerosene-soaked cloth and dusted off his desk. He collected the half-empty cups and glasses, two by two and three by three, and put them on a tray. In his mind he was making plans, carrying on some sort of internal conversation.

There was a knock on the door and Farangu stepped in. Hadi Besharat was ready to attack. She wore black nylon stockings and carried a black veil draped over her arm. There was something different about her hair. She smelled of perfume and her gold choker shone on her neck. Hadi Besharat picked up the tray and prepared to leave the room. Farangu raised her eyebrows, tilted her head, and looked around the study curiously. She said, "Besharat, what's wrong with you?"

He didn't answer. He walked out into the hall and started down the stairs. In the kitchen he switched on the light and stacked the glasses in the sink. Farangu appeared in the kitchen doorway. She leaned at a slant against the frame, her purse dangling from her arm by its strap. Then her arm dropped, her muscles relaxed, and her head fell to one side. "Besharat, do you know my migraine is completely gone?"

"Thank you, Lord."

"When I turn my head I don't have any pain at all. I'm feeling so much better that I even let Mrs. Gharib fix my hair for me. I was walking near the flower shop when she passed me in her car. She stopped and said, 'You need a hairdresser.' I said, 'Miss Farideh, in these days of mourning nobody goes to the hairdresser.' She said, 'Don't worry about that. Let's go to my house. I'll fix your hair in a minute.' We went to her house. She washed my hair in no time in her sink, did the combing and the curling better than any European hairdresser. The foreign hairdressers don't have our Iranian taste. Our own worst hairdressers are better than any foreign hairdressers."

Hadi Besharat screamed, "Why do you have your hair fixed by people who don't know anything? I like your hair the natural way—the way it used to fall on your shoulders."

Farangu patted her hair and straightened her head. She was about to leave the kitchen when Hadi Besharat said, "Are you going to your Mama Aliyeh's again tomorrow?"

Farangu didn't answer but went off down the corridor, her posture loose and undecided.

Hadi Besharat followed her. In the drawing room he changed his tone and said, "I talked to Mr. Bayat about Khosro's money. In the middle of my visit he went to sleep."

"We ought to call Khosro. We've left that boy in a foreign country, all by himself."

"Did you hear the plumbers came? They soldered the pipes in the bathroom. Day after tomorrow they'll bring a pump and clear the kitchen drain."

Farangu stretched out on the couch. She put the toe of one foot to the heel of the other, slid off her shoes one by one, and kicked them into a corner. Then she rested the back of her hand against her forehead. "These visitings and revisitings are tiring. God will reward Sayid-jon. He kept us entertained. He twisted a veil into a whip and we played the whipping game. He was the dealer and anyone who lost got a whipping from him. I got ten whippings. But Mama Aliyeh was condemned to death. Instead of stoning her to death, we threw pistachios at her, ha, ha, ha. . . ."

Her laugh sounded like hiccups. Hadi Besharat looked at her and said in desperation, "Dear God . . . God . . . God . . ."

He went back upstairs to his study. His desk top was clean but books, notes, a sugar bowl, and other odds and ends cluttered the bookshelf next to it. He closed the books and placed them upright side by side. He stacked his notes together and put them in a drawer, then set the sugar bowl on the table next to the daybed. Satisfied, he sat in front of the radio and turned it on. The needle of the dial passed through the shortwave and international bands. He heard the usual rumblings, the constant, fragmented static, the noises from far and near. BBC, Voice of America, Radio Moscow. People talking rapidly in Arabic, in Chinese, in German. He found a station that was broadcasting a beautiful symphony. The splendor of the music ascended through the static, landing around him like a languorous dust. Like that wintry day, back in 1969 . . .

Early on Christmas morning he had gone to the harbor near Whitehurst College and he had stood watching the sea all by himself. He saw the sea gulls circling the sky, crisscrossing each other like pairs of scissors. The children's chorus was singing in the cathedral but the scattered tumult of the sky and the sea made their words unintelligible. The waves tumbled in a swinging motion, pounding against the jetty, cascading downward in a blizzard of sparkling drops. The sun was rising behind a line of purple clouds, emblazoning the clouds' edges. A glowing red welcomed Hadi-jon and pulled him out of himself. The murmur of the rushing waves widened the space between earth and sky and moved him deeply. He expected to hear a voice, to hear somebody call him by name. He tilted his head, looking at the sea, waiting. He said, "Did you call me? Did you call my name?"

Across the street, on the balcony of a house, a young mother sat on a chair. Three children with naked arms and calves moved around her. They still had their pajamas on but they didn't seem to mind the cold, even with those pale arms and legs. They were looking at the sea, waiting for the sun to finish rising so they could go open their presents under the Christmas tree. They followed him curiously with their eyes, the way a dog's eyes follow someone. He noticed the traffic light that was always red. Again he thought he heard someone calling him. He echoed, "Did you call me? Did you call my name?"

His eyes fell on *The Varasteh Method,* which he'd placed on the shelf only minutes ago. He got up and took hold of it. Opened the cover. In his introductory note Professor Varasteh was telling the reader:

> It is clear to the knowledgeable that each language possesses secrets, mysteries and special complexities not apparent even to those who speak it. . . .

Now Hadi Besharat had found a student and he could start teaching once again. A gate was being opened for him and his head was dizzy with anticipation. A scene appeared to him, covered by mirror chips like a cloister in a holy court. The mirrors weren't reflecting anything. Instead they let the patterns flow on the walls like melted light. That pure light that represented the world of counterparts, the light of the earth and the sky, the glowing light of a glass lantern. The shining star that was lit by the blessing of the olive tree. A light that was neither Eastern nor Western. The light of a lamp that was burning, soft and eternal, without oil or flint.

> *Light*
> *Light*
> *Light*
> *Light over light*

He picked up a lump of sugar and put it quickly in his mouth. Then he straightened, looking all around to see if anyone had noticed.

S I X

That night he had a dream that he couldn't remember exactly. Although he heard no sound, the sky was crowded. He saw a handful of winged creatures riding tandem bicycles, flying like mosquitoes and zooming in all directions. Any time they met with an obstacle they changed shape and passed over it. He asked one of them, "What's going on?" Somehow it was conveyed to him that these creatures were planning to participate in an intergalactic conference on nuclear arms control. Hadi Besharat felt he had grown weightless. Happy and excited, he took a seat on a bicycle of his own and started flying too, a sort of flight that was most pleasant. He flew up and down, passed over buildings, and constantly increased his speed. Then he flew down a very long avenue without touching the ground. He traveled the avenue with the speed of lightning, paying no attention to anything at all. Suddenly a traffic light turned red in front of him. He was petrified. What if a traffic control agent arrested him for having such a good time? He put on his brakes. One of the winged creatures approached him and said he must take a special powder with a little water. Hadi Besharat asked, "Why?"

The winged creature said, "Because we want to blind you."

Hadi Besharat paled and said, "Why?"

The creature answered, "I'm sorry, I didn't say it right. We want to make you invisible."

Hadi Besharat put the powder in his mouth with a little water, sat on the back seat of the creature's bicycle, and flew along the avenue. Now he knew he could see everyone and no one could see him. The creature pointed to the other side of the avenue and he saw the late Fakhr Zanjani, his father-jon, his mother-jon, that poor boy, and even Khosro or someone resembling Khosro, all walking in a garden. Then he felt he was standing in front of his students in a classroom, intending to deliver a lecture. The students were singing a hymn about Mani's last journey, referring to the prohibitions against drinking wine, eating meat, and associating with women:

> *"Oh, Mani,*
> *You are the one we call by name.*
> *You are noble and possessed of a good name,*
> *You, the bringer of light.*
> *The Magi put chains on your body,*
> *Tied your hands and feet with iron,*
> *And kept you in prison for twenty-six days."*

The hymn changed into a song that he'd heard before, but he couldn't remember its name. A song that promised someone's return: "The lost Joseph will return to Canaan, don't be forlorn . . ." To his horror, he realized he had no clothes on. He was standing naked in front of his students and he couldn't recall the details of the Battle of Salamis. Searching his notes, he asked someone, "How did the Battle of Salamis end? Tell me how it ended."

Amidst the dust of the road Fakhr Zanjani appeared, walking away from him, holding an attaché case in one hand and his old umbrella in the other, stepping up into the bus like a cartoon figure.

The Pilgrim's Rules of Etiquette

He worked till afternoon on his lesson plans for Nili, breaking only once for a light lunch which he took back with him to his study. Downstairs he heard Farangu's voice, giving each guest a different excuse. She told General Ghovanlu and his wife, "My, why didn't you warn us? Besharat is finishing his hymn, 'Porturne for a Hanged Man.' He asked to be left alone. He apologized in advance and said he misses going to the park and visiting with the neighbors."

"Where is he?" General Ghovanlu asked.

"In his study. If I call him he'll be distracted. Then we'll have to listen for three days to his moaning and groaning."

When Engineer Gharib and his wife arrived Farangu found another excuse. "I don't know how to repay your favors. The booster pills you sent for Besharat work real miracles. He feels so good that he can't put his pen down even for a minute. He unplugged the phone so no one could disturb him. I'll go and call him if you wish."

Mrs. Gharib begged, "Please don't bother. He shouldn't be interrupted. What do you say, Engineer?"

Engineer Gharib said wryly, "Let him do what he wants. It makes no difference to me."

When Mrs. Razi arrived Farangu didn't need to make excuses. Mrs. Razi had come to show Farangu that poor boy's bundle of clothes and she had no reason to see Hadi Besharat. At the front door, where she must have caught a glimpse of the assembled guests, she pulled Farangu aside and said, "This is confidential. Can we go to a private place and talk alone for a few minutes?"

Farangu lowered her voice. "How about the sewing room?"

"Fine. Let's go."

Step by step, they started up the stairs. They paused halfway so Mrs. Razi could catch her breath. In the drawing room General Ghovanlu's wife was making herself the life of the party, once again reliving her illegal trip to Pakistan and America. Mrs.

Razi grumbled, "Mrs. General has given us all a headache with so much talk about that sickening trip."

The sound of their footsteps came gradually closer. Hadi Besharat was afraid they would enter his study without knocking. But Mrs. Razi raised her voice: "Miss Farangu, say something to your professor. I've heard he has agreed to give English lessons to Nili. If you ask my opinion, all those lessons he gave my hapless Mehrdad were enough for many future generations. He corrupted the mind of that innocent boy. If this is what kind of professor he is, it won't help a thing. You have to put these professors in a pitcher and drink the water. What's the difference between him and those who run like a dog after a few pennies, get married and have a baby every year like so many animal droppings?"

Farangu pretended not to hear. She said, "Be careful. Watch your step or you might fall."

"I'm extremely careful. My feet take very good care of me even though they're swollen. Do you know of any other mother who loses the apple of her eye and still keeps going like this? Don't judge me by appearances. I think of him all the time. You have to believe me. I think of that last furlough before he went to the front. He hugged me inside the bus and his head hit the ceiling. I said, 'Your mother dies for you. I hope that didn't hurt.' He said, 'No. Nothing happened.' Then he kissed my face and went away. . . . What a going away, miss. . . ."

He heard their steps growing distant, and then the sewing-room door closed. He got busy changing his clothes as quickly as possible. On his desk he arranged the exercises he'd prepared for Nili side by side. He had kept the level of the lessons high so that Nili would appreciate his seriousness. He put on his fur cloak, and the wall mirror showed the white fur sticking up around his neck, giving him a formidable appearance. He was pleased with his imposing figure. Let Mrs. Razi say whatever she wished. It made no difference to him. He had taught all his life and he couldn't change now.

He patted his walrus mustache and glanced at a marble statue of a dying hero that stood on a pedestal in the corner. The chilly folds of the stone gave the statue an air of limpness. Over the hero's naked body the timelessness of death's last moment kept flowing. The hero looked calm beneath the soft pleats of the sheet that covered him. The pleats slid downward, leaving the viewer with an impression of ecstasy and eternal sleep. In the presence of death the hero's contracted muscles relaxed, preparing the tired body for unconsciousness. The Angel of Fate sat on a stone bench, unwinding the string of life from a spindle. Hadi Besharat imagined somebody was calling him. As if Farangu were saying dinner was ready or telling him to get dressed for a party. Simple phrases, out of context and forgettable. Irrational thoughts that refused to die, descending on his mind like snowflakes.

He took *The Varasteh Method* off the shelf and placed it on the desk. Nili ought to be here soon. The idea of teaching obsessed him. He had specific exercises in mind and he had prepared notes and found booklets that might be of help to her. He thought of Nili's face waiting for an opportunity, drilling him with questions.

Once again he heard the guests' voices and their endless conversation. The general's wife was reciting the story of the flask they took with them to Pakistan. "All that was left for us was one flask which we filled with water so we wouldn't die of thirst in the Pakistani desert. The dirty Pakistanis kept coming to drink from it. I shuddered and I couldn't bring myself to touch the flask. Agha Mojtaba kept saying, 'Miss, give me some water.' I answered, 'If you want water, pour it yourself. I won't touch that flask anymore.' We were about to die of thirst."

Mrs. Gharib said, "Why did you allow the Pakistanis to drink from your flask?"

"Miss-jon, what could we do? This little Pakistani man comes and asks for water. Well, did you want us to fight him?"

"Pakistanis are very cheeky."

"Without our permission, this little Pakistani man came to

our train compartment. He carried his big belly over our heads and went to sleep on the baggage rack."

The guests burst into laughter. The general's wife continued. "Nonstop, Agha Mojtaba kept cursing our government. He said, 'These son-of-a-guns have done this and done that.' The Pakistanis kept nodding their heads like dead goats. Every minute they drank from our flask until we reached Karachi and went to a hotel. If you could call it a hotel. It was so dirty, worse than a latrine. So many flies were buzzing around that you didn't dare squat in a corner and smoke a cigarette with any peace of mind. Mr. Bayat gave the flask to the hotel owner and told him, 'Hold this for us. When we return we can take it back to Iran.' See how he kept account of everything."

"If he weren't so tightfisted he wouldn't have been able to buy that biscuit factory and save so much money in American banks."

"He pulled out all the money he had brought with him and said, 'Miss, you keep this money in your purse.' He held onto a little money for expenses on the road and gave the rest to me to hide in my purse. I didn't feel obliged, either. Whenever we encountered some expense I took a bit of Mr. Bayat's money and told him, 'Mr. Bayat, another twenty-dollar bill is gone.' He wasn't feeling good and couldn't talk much. All he said was, 'Very well, miss. Let that be the ransom for your health. We'll settle up later.' I thought he was about to pass away."

Hadi Besharat heard a banging at the door. Somebody came in without waiting for permission. The general's wife stopped talking and the rest of the guests stayed silent. He heard Farangu's footsteps again, running down the stairs to the entrance hall. She said, "Do you want something?"

Nili answered, "Where's Professor Besharat? I need to see him."

He didn't hear an answer for some time. Then Farangu said, "He's busy now. He can't see anyone."

He heard a commotion, and then once again the sound of the door slamming. From the guests' murmurs and the shuffling of

Farangu's footsteps on the stairs, he knew she had got rid of Nili. He felt disappointed. He was about to go downstairs and inquire when Nili entered the study with a sack in her arms. Hadi Besharat stared at her. "How did you get here, miss?"

Nili put her sack on the desk and took off her brown bandanna. "Professor Besharat, at any dead end there's at least one opening."

Hadi Besharat looked at his wristwatch and asked, "Why are you so late?"

"I had to look after my father. I couldn't come any sooner." She went over to the window and glanced out. "What a snow. How long is it going to snow?"

In surprise, he crossed the room to look over her shoulder. It was true, a heavy snow was falling. A crowd of stooped, dull-faced people was carrying a body through the street. The snow fell on their heads and shoes, which left imprints on the pavement. Hadi Besharat sat down at his desk. He picked up a pencil and started playing with it. Nili asked, "Did something happen?"

"Miss Nili, as I've already mentioned, I am willing to teach you. But only under certain conditions."

"Have I done something wrong?"

"I mean, if you want me to teach you, you have to be mindful of others. I don't like your offending Farangu."

"I apologize. I'll do whatever you want."

"You have to pay attention to your lessons and be on time. An education requires hard work and sacrifice."

Nili sat down on a chair and struggled out of her navy-blue coat. Now and then she peeped at him to see his reaction. She was wearing the poor boy's military fatigues. He recognized them by their large size and by the ink spot. After that fight with Mrs. Razi, he didn't know how she had dared go back to the boy's room and steal his clothes. He narrowed his eyes and said, "What you're wearing belongs to that poor boy. I've seen those on him many, many times."

She met Hadi Besharat with her proud, mocking eyes. "Yes, these are Mehrdad's."

"Why, Miss Nili?"

"When I wear these clothes it feels somehow as if we're together, as if he's here."

"But they're too big for you."

"That's why I like them. The way they hang loose on me, they make me feel so small. I like that." She took an object from her sack and unwrapped the newspaper around it. It was a bottle of whiskey. She held it up.

Hadi Besharat said, "What's this?"

Nili gave him the bottle and said, "Your wage for these lessons."

Hadi Besharat took the bottle and examined it closely. "Where did you get it?"

"From the crate my father smuggled in."

"What do I want with a bottle of whiskey? Do you have your father's permission to do this? Do you know how expensive this brand is?"

"He doesn't have much sense left to him. How can I get his permission?"

Hadi Besharat held the bottle up to the light and said slowly, "Miss Nili, let me ask you a question."

Nili placed her elbows on the table, ready for the challenge. "Please, go ahead and ask any question you want."

"Is there anything in the world that doesn't belong to you?"

"What do you mean?"

"Where do you draw your limits? This bottle of whiskey, those military fatigues, that sack—they don't belong to you, but you take possession of them with no trouble. It seems to me there are no limits or boundaries in your life. You think everything is yours."

"What's wrong with that?"

Hadi Besharat set the bottle in front of her and said, "Thank you very much for your kindness. But I can't accept this. This is not my property."

It was obvious from Nili's look that she didn't understand.

Maybe she couldn't believe him. She collected herself and said, "I beg you to accept it. You have to accept it."

Hadi Besharat began his lecture as if she hadn't spoken. "The mysteries and complexities of the English language appear different to different nations. For example, you are Iranian and you understand the English language one way, but a French-speaking person understands it quite another way. That's why I insist that Iranian students spend time figuring out the differences and take nothing for granted."

Whatever he said, Nili repeated in a soft voice. ". . . spend time figuring out the differences and take nothing for granted . . ."

Hadi Besharat slammed the book shut, leaned forward, and said, "Miss Nili, what is your trouble?"

With exaggerated politeness she answered, "Yesterday I started a diet and in just one day I've lost a pound."

"Why do you want to lose weight?"

"In order to be your student. Mehrdad told me that you don't accept just anyone as your student. Toward the end Mehrdad lost a lot of weight. I knew he was on a diet."

Hadi Besharat said, "Miss, you're mistaken. That poor boy fasted only a few days so that he could gain some experience of the Mandaean fasts. He wanted to experience the Mandaeans' baptismal ceremonies in action, the so-called Masbuta ceremonies. You're getting things mixed up that you can't possibly understand."

"That's exactly what I say. I can't possibly understand your lessons, but I want to be your student. I want to know all those strange things, the Masbuta ceremony and those other things you know. Like Mehrdad, I'll do whatever you tell me."

"How thickheaded you are!"

Hadi Besharat laid a hand on his forehead and frowned. Perhaps he was weary of so many confrontations. Like that afternoon when the poor boy suddenly appeared from around a corner after his father's execution and sat next to him on a bench in the district park. Hadi Besharat had drawn back and continued to read the evening paper. The boy wanted only to show how quickly he was learning his Coptic, his Soghdian, and even his Hebrew. It was Hadi Besharat who had given him the textbooks for those languages. Hadi Besharat had bought those books at the suggestion of Professor Humphrey. Yet, when the poor boy recited his hymn in Coptic, Hadi Besharat had tried not to hear, pretending he was confused.

Nili's face glowed under the light like raw copper. A glow that penetrated the dusk and cast a halo around her head. The crumpled military fatigues hung loosely on her shoulders, reminding him of the tobacco-colored uniforms the soldiers wore in the Battle of the Somme. She looked at him with the silence of a praying nun, waiting without insistence.

Hadi Besharat said, "Miss Nili, open your book. Look at the second page. Here we have to talk about different pronunciations in the English language. All these pronunciations exist in Farsi as well, except for two: a soft 'th' as in 'thought,' and a hard 'th' as in 'that.' You'll have to practice those. Now, I'll say in English, 'The pencil is on my book,' and you answer, 'Yes, the pencil is on your book.' Use your brain and let me hear it."

Nili moved a little on her chair and said, "Very well, I'll do it. But you don't seem very pleased that I'm on a diet."

"What does your diet have to do with me? Read your English!"

"I'll try my best and answer as much as I can manage. But you have to encourage me a little."

"Encourage what? Encourage your theatrics? If you're interested in fasting and singing Mandaean hymns, I don't have the time for that now. Please don't waste my time or yours."

He was almost shouting. Nili waited until he had finished. Then she said, "Do you think Mehrdad's face on your wall is only imagination? It's not real?"

"Miss, you just keep after your goals, learn your English, and go to America."

Nili lifted her sack and said, "Want me to tell you something?"

"Please."

"Engineer Gharib wanted to go claim the body from the city morgue. Heli and I begged him to take us along."

"Well, what's that got to do with me?"

"We wanted to see if we could recognize him after death. We wanted to know if his face had changed completely. In the morgue they had him stretched on a metal table. We looked around us. Everything was made of metal, very cold and empty. We heard nothing but our own footsteps on the tiles."

Hadi Besharat was curious. "How come they allowed you inside the morgue?"

"Because we introduced ourselves as the martyr's relatives. After that they didn't create any problem. They showed us a lot of respect. I felt very cold. The door was left open behind us and a draft was coming in. I went and closed the door again, and then I took Heli's hand and went to his table. Heli kept asking me to tell her what I saw. I looked but I couldn't say anything. He was all swollen, looking strange. He still wore his military uniform. His hat was on his chest. His hair was disheveled and frozen. I asked Heli to help. We combed his hair and washed the dried mud off his face. We talked to him. Engineer Gharib thought we were out of our minds and he went to sign the forms for shrouding and for the burial. Heli and I stood in front of Mehrdad and told him we loved him. We sang hymns to him. We plan to visit his grave before sunrise. The prisoners of the graves can hear your voice before sunrise and they'll answer you. After sunrise they hear your voice but they don't answer. We're going to visit his grave every Friday evening, too. Every Friday evening for a year the souls of the dead will return and walk around their own graves."

Hadi Besharat leaned back in his chair and looked at Nili suspiciously. Nili started putting her coat on. She buckled her belt, picked up her sack, and said, "You have too many guests. How loud they are! I don't want to bother you anymore just now. Next time I'll be on time and I promise you I'll work on my soft and hard 'th.' "

Hadi Besharat rose and went to the door to see her off. He said, "Miss, let me give you some advice."

"Please."

"To learn English, you're better off enrolling at the Shokufeh Institute. I'm very busy now. I've got a thousand projects to look after. I don't have any extra time."

"Do you mean I can't come back here anymore?"

"Miss Nili, it's beyond me."

"Professor Besharat, please let me come back."

With a determined expression, Hadi Besharat guided Nili out of his study. When she reached the top of the stairs she turned and said, "I'll be back again."

She rushed downstairs and disappeared in the dark of the corridor so quickly that Hadi Besharat had no chance to answer her.

At the top of the stairs Farangu was leaning on the newel post with her scornful glare fixed upon him. Hadi Besharat brought his hands forward to explain. But Farangu turned her back and went to the sewing room. The guests burst into laughter in the drawing room. The general's wife was still talking. "I was going to sleep from the tap-tap of the train. Mr. Bayat said, 'Miss, your purse! Watch your purse. Don't take your eyes off that purse.' I said, 'Poor me. I'm sleepy and I can't keep my eyes on this purse all the time. You take it for a minute.' Now we have been traveling for nineteen hours in that rickety local train and we're about to pass out from being so tired. Then the Pakistani official wants to take us to another compartment. We went to the new compartment. I don't wish you a bad day, but you can't imagine how dirty and dusty it was. We told the official, 'Baba, we have first-class tickets and you have to give us a better compartment.' The official said in English, 'I don't know. I am a proper person.' Then the train stopped and we came out of the compartment, asking ourselves what we should do. What shouldn't we do? What sort of a curse could we put on our heads? Then Agha Mojtaba came in and said, 'I'll sit here and watch our belongings. You go out and get some fresh air.' I thought that wasn't a bad idea. The heat was merciless. I desperately needed to sleep. I told Agha Mojtaba, 'Look, the Pakistanis are sleeping on the ground next to the train.' He said, 'Miss-jon, these are cows and sheep. You can't compare them with me and you.' I answered, 'Whatever they are, I have to get some sleep.' Agha Mojtaba had this rubber tire. He blew into it and it became a pillow. He brought a rug and spread it out for us on the ground. I couldn't feel anything at all. I put my head on the rubber tire, clutched my purse and Mr. Bayat's money to my bosom, and passed out."

Engineer Gharib's wife said, "At least you could have put the purse under the rubber tire for safety's sake."

"I was sleepy and I didn't think of that."

Hadi Besharat returned to his study and quietly closed the door. His confrontation with Farangu had left him feeling dejected. He thought again of Nili and that poor boy. He was confused. Perhaps because there was still something hard to understand about the boy. He didn't know how to sort out the major and minor parts of the argument for himself. For example, he thought of that afternoon when Mehrdad had arrived at the district park and sat on the bench next to him. Mehrdad had talked very fast. He had moved his hands rapidly, as if he were in some kind of hurry, leaving most of his sentences incomplete. He said he didn't wish to go claim his father. This was at the time when poor Colonel Razi had already been executed in somebody else's place by mistake. Mrs. Razi had had to draw a check from the bank to pay for the firing squad's bullets. Now she was waiting for the boy so they could go together and claim the body. But the boy wouldn't go along, believing it wouldn't be proper. He wanted only to talk about Mandaean ceremonies and Mani's visit with Bahram I. He believed that speaking in dead languages would connect him to the world of the dead. Then he pretended that he was the eunuch king Agha Mohammad Khan, of the Ghajar Dynasty. Sitting on the bench, he kept his feet apart, rested his fists on his knees, and addressed the war prisoners. "Sons of hell, you bring me women? You think you are painting an ass? Where are your jewels? Sons of bitches, tell me where they are if you don't want me to blind your eyes."

He heard Farangu ushering Mrs. Razi from the sewing room. Their voices were soft and friendly. He sensed that Mrs. Razi had persuaded Farangu to buy that poor boy's clothes. Whenever Farangu paid some penalty in order to get out of a difficult situation, her affection would blossom. She spoke compassion-ately: "By God, Mrs. Razi, be careful. God forbid, I'm afraid your heel will catch on the edge of a step and you'll fall."

"I am careful. Thank you very much for your kindness. Cer-tainly Khosro-jon will enjoy those clothes. Death keep away from his life, he and that poor boy had the same taste. God willing, maybe it's our lot that we'll go to America all together. I'm in fine shape for traveling. This Japanese doctor tells me, 'Miss, your heart works like the heart of a twenty-five-year-old.' "

"Me too. My migraines are getting better. I feel fine. But what am I going to do with Besharat? He's driving me crazy. There's always something wrong with him."

"Why don't you take him to my Japanese doctor? He's just opened an office on Revolutionary Guards Street. You can't imag-ine what kind of machines he's brought with him. He doesn't charge much, either. I went to him for my sinuses. He put a machine on my head exactly like a space rocket. It made a strange whistling sound. I said, 'God forbid! What is this ma-chine, snoring like a monster? Why do its lights flicker in the dark like an angry mouse's eyes? Doctor, who gave you permis-sion to import this machine?' He laughed. His glasses were so thick that I couldn't see his eyes."

"Have you ever known a Japanese without glasses?"

"It's because their eyes are so narrow that they can't see out of them. The Japanese are good at training dogs, too. This Japanese doctor has a dog that sits in front of his house every evening until they bring the newspaper. The dog pays for the newspaper, takes it in his mouth, and brings it to the doctor."

Their voices grew fainter as they reached the hall downstairs. No doubt it was still snowing out. Hadi Besharat slipped his fur cloak off and hung it in the closet. He sat down at his desk and prepared to write another letter to Professor Humphrey. His eyes fell on the bottle of whiskey. Nili had forgotten to take it with her. He wondered if her oversight had been deliberate. Turning the bottle by its neck, he heard the sound of water running in the bathroom. Farangu must be taking a bath after her guests' departure. Maybe she was getting ready to visit her Mama Aliyeh and Sayid-jon. He stood up to look out the study door. The two large brick-colored vases stood in their usual places at either end of the passageway, and the bathroom door was half ajar. Farangu wasn't bathing after all. He could see her in front of the mirror putting on makeup, twisting her hair around like a rope and fastening it with bobby pins. Then she came out to the full-length mirror in the passageway. She buttoned the front of her navy-blue dress. Hadi Besharat whispered, "Farangu, what are you doing?"

Farangu lifted her head and answered coldly, "Obviously, I'm dressing."

She turned toward him but kept her distance. The skin above her low neckline was so clean that it seemed opaque. Hadi Besharat came closer. He took her hand and said, "Feel my hand, how warm it is. I think I'm coming down with a cold."

"Well, if you are, you are."

She pulled her hand away. Hadi Besharat changed the subject. "Mrs. Razi finally sold you the goods, the boy's clothing."

"I couldn't refuse her. Why are you here all the time and never helping out? You always leave me alone with the guests. I've given them so many excuses, my tongue is growing hair. I can't look anyone in the eyes anymore. Then you bring in this girl, Nili, and give her English lessons. Why bother with someone so empty-headed?"

"At least giving English lessons is better than sitting with a bunch of guests and gossiping."

He put an arm around Farangu and kissed her cheek. Her face was soft and cool like a new bar of soap. Hadi Besharat became excited. Farangu pulled back and said, "Leave me alone. I have to go downstairs. I have things to do."

"Are you planning to visit your Mama Aliyeh?"

"Why shouldn't I?"

"Why shouldn't you? Because taxis are expensive and we don't have much money left in the bank. They've cut two thousand tumans from my monthly pension."

"You could buy a car like the late Mr. Lajevardi and become a cab driver. All those who used to have important positions are either driving cabs or they're selling goods in the streets. Work is nothing to be ashamed of."

She turned and went into the bedroom. Hadi Besharat hugged himself and stayed silent. He didn't know what to say. His mouth grew cold and the words froze behind his teeth. He heard Farangu walking about. He heard the sounds of furniture and objects being moved. The sounds of wooden and cardboard boxes that hadn't been moved for eighteen years. Contrary to her usual habit, Farangu walked quickly, making him suspicious about what was going on. He went to stand in the doorway. She was piling her jewelry into a fretwork box. She put the box in a suitcase that lay open on the bed. She took her dresses from their hangers and folded them into the suitcase. She did everything according to a plan and with determination. She paid him no attention. Evidently this visit to her Mama Aliyeh's was getting out of hand.

She closed the suitcase and staggered down the stairs with it. Hadi Besharat followed, saying, "Farangu, what's going on?" She didn't answer. In the entrance hall she put on her fur coat and her milky scarf. Then she was ready to go. She had her thumb hooked through her key ring, and she was squeezing the keys in her fist. Hadi Besharat said, "Farangu?"

Farangu half glanced at him and said, "Wait a minute. I want to call Khosro."

Sitting on the chair in an awkward position, she picked up the phone and hurriedly dialed. She crossed her legs and pressed the receiver hard to her ear. The house was so silent that Hadi

Besharat could easily hear the ringing at the other end and then Khosro's unintelligible voice. Their conversation didn't last long. Farangu just issued a few instructions about where to reach her, reminding Khosro of her Mama Aliyeh's telephone number. How strange that she didn't offer the receiver to Hadi Besharat. Gradually it was becoming clear to him that he was facing a crisis.

After she had hung up Farangu looked over at him. Worried and hesitant, Hadi Besharat asked, "When will you be back?"

"There's enough food in the refrigerator to last a week. The food coupons are on the kitchen counter. If you want something and can't find it, call me at Mama Aliyeh's. I'm going to be there for some time."

Then she picked up her purse and went to the front hall. Hadi Besharat ran after her and positioned himself between her and the door. He tried to seize her hand but she didn't let him. He felt bewildered. Finally he dared to ask, "Are you separating from me?"

"I want to be by myself for a while and think. Watch the house. Khosro has written a letter to Mr. Bayat describing his situation. Maybe Mr. Bayat will pay his debt now. Go over there again and see if he's still making excuses."

He heard the tap-tap of a taxi motor in front of their house. Farangu pushed him aside and went out the door, lugging her suitcase. Snowflakes hit Hadi Besharat in the face. The snow hung before the headlights of the taxi like a lace curtain. The taxi disappeared amid the whistling of the storm.

Hadi Besharat stood at the door dumfounded. His hand was frozen on the doorknob and any movement seemed beyond him. The snow kept falling on his face, on his walrus mustache and the shoulders of his sweater.

Finally he closed the door. He climbed the stairs to his study. He didn't have the heart to look into any of the other rooms. He knew he would see scenes that signified change. Cluttered scenes that made distant memories out of empty space. He was afraid to glance at the souvenirs of eighteen years of living in that house. Khosro's old toys. Farangu's old cosmetic bottles. At any moment it was possible that the toy soldiers would start marching, beating on their drums with those tiny sticks.

Instead he thought of Mrs. Helen Chadwick, whom he had met in Westminster Abbey by accident. He'd been standing in front of Ben Jonson's memorial plaque when Mrs. Chadwick bumped into him. He stepped aside and mumbled an apology. Mrs. Chadwick smiled and said, "It was my fault, sir."

Hadi Besharat answered, "I should have been more careful."

"Why do you accept the blame so easily? Where do you come from?"

"I'm Iranian."

He went back to looking at the memorial plaque. But Mrs. Chadwick wasn't about to give up. She stood next to him and said, "You are Omar Khayyám's compatriot. Have you seen Nishapur, his birthplace?"

When they left Westminster Abbey it was raining hard. They walked shoulder to shoulder. Hadi Besharat opened his silk umbrella and held it over both their heads. Mrs. Chadwick's blond hair was caught under the lapel of her raincoat. She put her fingers beneath her hair to free it, scattering it in the air. She was thirty, thirty-five years old. One of those British women who have a twist to their eyes and wide spaces between their teeth. She was working in the library at King's College and living by herself. She waved her arms like palm leaves and walked with some sort of absentminded, upper-crust manner. Her speech was episodic and instantaneous. In the middle of a sentence she invited Hadi Besharat to her apartment for a cup of tea. He was amazed when he stepped into the apartment. A whiteness the color of cream was spread everywhere—across the doors, the window frames, the walls, and even the furniture. He felt he had entered the domain of cleanliness, care, and attention. Everything was covered by white drop cloths in preparation for painting. The wooden floor shone with honey-colored shellac, and small patches of sunlight were scattered across it like a row of eggshells—patches as white as magnolia petals. Patches as light as a sleeping baby's hands, limp on the mattress. The Dutch tulips gave a wet, cool taste to the air. Simple earthenware vases guarded every corner and the freshness of the green leaves inside them thinned the space.

Hadi Besharat and Mrs. Chadwick talked quietly, and their conversation echoed off the walls. Mrs. Chadwick put a teakettle on the burner. Then she lifted the white cloths from the couch and two chairs in the living room. She threw herself on the couch, placing a tired hand on the couch's puffy arm and sinking into the hollow of its cushion. "Oh, Professor Bee-sharat. Am I pronouncing your name right?"

"You are pronouncing it right."

"Thank you. Thank you. Would you please brew the tea for us?"

"You want me to brew the tea? All right! No problem."

He searched for the tea canister but he couldn't find it. Mrs. Chadwick pretended embarrassment and hid her face in her hands. Her fingers were as white as white jade. "Oh, Mr. Bee-sharat, I forgot to buy tea. Would you like me to pour you some sherry?"

"Please."

Mrs. Chadwick got up and brought a sherry decanter and two glasses from the corner cupboard. She filled the glasses halfway and asked, "What sort of music would you like me to put on?"

"Whatever you like."

"No. You have to say what kind of music you prefer."

"Play 'Amapola.' "

"Oh, 'Amapola.' In England no one listens to 'Amapola' anymore. I have some tango records. Would you like me to put on 'La Comparsita'?"

"Please do whatever you like. It really doesn't make any difference to me."

She put the record on and as soon as it started, *bum-bum, baa, bum-bum* . . . she threw herself on the couch again, resting her long feet on the coffee table and tucking her skirt beneath her legs with girlish modesty. She held her glass between her thumb and two fingers and curved her little finger like a hook. Then she fixed her eyes on him and said, "You told me you're doing research in ancient history. Of course Persia is a very interesting country from a historical perspective. But it's also the country of roses and nightingales. Have you ever traveled to Nishapur? Have you seen Nishapur's roses?"

"There are plenty of references in the Iranian world of letters to the connection between beauty and truth. If you wish I'll tell you about it when the proper occasion arises. For now, the only thing I have to say is this. The rose is merely a superficial expression of Eastern beauty."

Mrs. Chadwick threw her head back on the couch and burst into laughter. "Oh, my poor Mr. Bee-sharat! Oh, my poor Mr. Bee-sharat! Do you believe in the return of things past?"

Hadi Besharat shrugged and said, "Anything is possible. I have an open mind and I don't want to be rigid about it."

Mrs. Chadwick brought herself so close to Hadi Besharat that the hem of her skirt touched the crease of his broadcloth trousers. She took his hand and said, "What you said is enough for me. We, I mean my friends and I, love ancient cultures very much. Every Wednesday night we study the cultures of Egypt, Akkad, and Assyria."

"What a coincidence!"

With a fingertip Mrs. Chadwick drew a circle on the palm of his hand. She didn't take her eyes from him. Hadi Besharat's soul was about to depart. Mrs. Chadwick went on talking. "Every coincidence is based on a certain predetermined plan. My dear friend, do you know how our relationship began?"

"How?"

"It was during the time of ancient Egypt. Three thousand years ago, we were worshipers in the temple of Apis, the cow. You were the special priest for the cow and I was a temple prostitute. Do you still insist that we ran into each other only by coincidence?"

Hadi Besharat sipped a little sherry from his glass, temporizing while he searched for an answer. He said, "I too believe that nothing happens coincidentally. Except that any happening has historical roots. How long has it taken for human beings to learn the baking of ordinary bread? Early man ate wild wheat. After a few centuries he discovered that grinding the wheat first made it easier to eat. He modeled the water mill after the chewing action of the jaws."

Mrs. Chadwick threw her arms around Hadi Besharat's neck and laughed loudly. "Oh, Mr. Bee-sharat, what a crazy human being you are!"

They danced to the tune of "La Comparsita." Inside her silk dress Mrs. Chadwick's breasts, arms, and shoulders felt soft and slippery and Hadi Besharat grew distracted. He tried only to listen to her conversation. Mrs. Chadwick said, "I want to give you an insight. You should not be afraid of evil forces. The forces of goodness are all around you. The farther you go, the closer you get to the source of goodness. Go to the West of America, go to Nebraska."

He woke up early the next morning. He realized he still had his black broadcloth suit on, and he was lying on Mrs. Chadwick's bed. His body smelled of a perfume that dusted his nose and mouth like powder. His eyes fell on a note that lay on the nightstand. Mrs. Chadwick had gone south for the weekend. She asked him to fix himself a continental breakfast and coffee, and not to forget to water the plants before leaving the apartment. Also to pour some milk for the cat, lock the door, and take "La Comparsita" with him as a reminder of last night.

He rubbed his eyes and looked around. The branches of light and the Dutch tulips were arching, reaching for each other, patting each other. His entire being was an ear, listening to the pause in Time. Whatever he wished, he had with him. He walked around the room with a watering can and watered the plants one by one. He poured milk in a ceramic bowl for the cat. He set the bowl on the floor and squatted down next to it. He put his hands under his arms and watched the cat drinking milk. Clean and pious, the cat made a fuzz ball of her paws, wearily put her pink tongue in the bowl, and began to drink. Hadi

Besharat felt a sense of refuge and privacy. He could be alone in the world like a grapevine, standing on its roots. He could easily put his head on a pillow, calm down with a half-open mouth, and forget to breathe.

Outside, Big Ben was facing the sunlight like a shield and people were walking on the sidewalks. The pigeons were landing on the steps in the middle of Trafalgar Square and the crowd was being swallowed by Charing Cross Station's entrance gates, wide open like a thirsty mouth. The railroads behind the station were stretching toward Dover, Boulogne, Paris, Strasburg, Alsace, and Lorraine. From the shores of the Mediterranean, Europe's news was being broadcast everywhere on the shortwaves. With a cane in his hand, a cigar in the corner of his mouth, Churchill raised two fingers in victory, shouting, "We shall fight them in the air, we shall fight them on the sea and we shall fight them on the ground. . . ."

The train station would be crowded, the soldiers' boots shuffling in front of the ticket booths, restless locomotives panting under the high rectangular ceiling, the rotating axles hiccuping, the engines hissing—the uproar of civilized barbarism, the fuss of chic primitiveness. Everybody would be bouncing on those sooty, oily, iron bars. With the paling of the air, the light was gone from Europe.

Hadi Besharat felt thirsty. The roof of his mouth was rough and he couldn't move his tongue on account of its weight. He picked up his silk umbrella and the recording of "La Comparsita," locked Mrs. Chadwick's apartment, dropped the key in her mailbox, and stepped into the street. Seeing the sunlight, he felt a window opening in his mind. In his disbelief there was true belief. As if he were amazed at the sight of a blossom blooming, as if he were filled with astonishment. He wanted to write Farangu and let her know of his decision to return. He had understood nothing and had imagined he knew everything. He couldn't believe that Mrs. Chadwick had made such a fool of him, that he had allowed her to use him like consumer goods. His ignorance was a window to the profound. Farangu's face smiled at him, a smile of compassion and endurance that belonged to him.

Now he shouted in his heart, "Farangu, Farangu, come back!"

He poured himself a little of Mr. Bayat's whiskey and drank it quickly. It tasted good. He poured some more and gulped it down. He imagined Farangu stretched out on the couch with her eyes closed, like a dead princess. As though she were longing for the arrival of a prince and the shortening of the camphor candles was calming her passion.

Among his old records he found "La Comparsita" and he put it on. He poured himself some more whiskey and listened to the record. Now he was quite high, throwing his arms around an imaginary dance partner, humming along with the music in a whisper, circling the study and dancing the tango.

> Bum-bum, baa, bum-bum,
> Bum-bum, bum-bum, bum-bum, baa, bum-bum . . .

He was floating through sheets of filmy veils, his glance passing over the antique objects. With his every turn and whirl Farangu's face appeared in front of his eyes. That summer day when they went together to Khezrabad to visit his mother-jon. That evening when they stood on a peasant's porch and watched the bent oak tree on the riverbank. At the touch of the old tree's branches, slanted parallel lines were drawn on the water. The house's reflection shivered.

> Bum-bum, baa, bum-bum,
> Bum-bum, bum-bum, bum-bum, baa, bum-bum . . .

He heard the weeping sound of a bird flying in the depths of the blue sky, its wings wheezing like an asthmatic patient. Spears of light pierced the heart of the sky and water cascaded from the stone fountain like a child dancing. A silver coin fell on the tiles, spinning and coming to rest in a corner. He heard Whitehurst College's cathedral chorus, rising from the winding corridors and reaching to the edges of the angels' wings. The unfinished smiles of the angels were testament to an ecstasy that anointed their faces, bedazzling their eyes with an indescribable view. In such a scene his entire life could be summarized and predicted. A scene that could make peace between death and birth, could make pattern out of color and color out of pattern. He had to seize the moment, to go on trying, to keep himself warm. He brushed his teeth and washed his face. He sat at his desk and wrote to Professor Humphrey in the voice of that poor boy:

Your Excellency, Professor Humphrey:

I hope you won't be offended by my boldness, repeatedly writing you letters. Please allow me to express my heartfelt thanks for helping with my college admission. If you wish to know about the condition of my health, I don't have many problems, except for the pains in my foot, my stomach, and my left ear, all of which are diagnosed untreatable by the doctors. Recently I was injured in an accident. They operated on my foot without much result. I even got worse. Now I walk with much difficulty and I don't believe it is possible for me to travel and come to see you. The doctors have forbidden me to walk and of course after a leg amputation this kind of pain is quite normal. They have diagnosed it and they say it is caused by bad nerves. They say it is psychosomatic. I want to make them understand somehow, but I can't express myself. They don't understand my language, they don't pay attention to my groaning.

Finally, I wish that God Almighty grant health to you and your honorable family. If it is possible for you, please respond to my small request and make me happy with an answer. I'll be very thankful.

Hoping to see you,

Respectfully,
Mehrdad Razi

The Pilgrim's Rules of Etiquette

Hadi Besharat reread the letter. He had distorted events. Rather than writing like that poor boy, he'd been speaking on his own behalf. How could a twenty-five-year-old young man moan so about weakness and disability? With one superficial glance at the photo on the boy's application form, Professor Humphrey would see it was impossible for Mehrdad to have written such a letter. He had always worn a childish, watchful expression that had made him look undetermined. He had stepped into any scene like an actor who hadn't yet decided what role to play, keeping his face rigid to gain control of his feelings.

S E V E N

He sat on the edge of his bed and picked up the crumpled
handkerchief next to him but he couldn't bring himself to blow
his nose. He didn't feel well and it was difficult to get up. Odd,
unrelated thoughts came to his mind. He felt as if a ghost were
climbing the stairs and searching the cupboards. The ghost of a
woman maybe his mother with fuzzy hair and a fixed stare,
stricken by a dream, prowling around the courtyard. She wandered barefoot from room to room, looking for something in the
drawers, in the tea box, and among Farangu's sewing materials.

He groped with his toes for his slippers. After he had put
them on he went to the bathroom. He shaved and brushed his
teeth, then returned to the study and looked for some socks.
Barely going through the motions, he got dressed. He hung his
fur cloak over his shoulders and went downstairs.

They didn't have an extra kerosene heater in the house. The
lower floor was as cold as the bridge between death and Resur-
rection Day. He blew on his hands to keep them warm. It was
like the first bell on Tuesdays. They used to sit around the coal
stove, waiting for the school janitor. The janitor was always late
and he wouldn't light the stove before Fakhr Zanjani arrived.
Fakhr Zanjani would enter the classroom with his face blue from
the wind. Acting as class monitor, Hadi Besharat would stand up
and shout, "All rise!"

The Pilgrim's Rules of Etiquette

Fakhr Zanjani was either indifferent to the cold or else so absorbed in his own thoughts that he paid it no attention. He would pull the scrolls from his leather briefcase and draw a map of a battle on the blackboard. Then he would fling out his arms in an exaggerated manner, like that clown in the Barnum and Bailey Circus who walked a tightrope at Whitehurst College so long ago.

Lord, what year was that? Was it the spring of 1968? Was it Christmas of '69? He remembered only that no one in the audience dared to breathe. The space inside the circus tent was swollen like a First World War dirigible. With their breaths caught in their chests, the spectators kept their eyes fixed on the clown. Sometimes he staggered on purpose, scaring them. Hadi Besharat could still hear the hypnotic waltz in his ears while he followed that mesmerizing walk. Finally the clown arrived at the other end of the rope, landing on the platform with a quick jump and bowing to the crowd. The trapped silence suddenly burst open and the spectators shouted bravos and their applause created an uproar.

In the classroom, using the same cartoon-like gestures, Fakhr Zanjani had made faces at the world, causing tension among his students. He raised his fist and pounded the desk. He talked in a deep and dreamy voice, clawing the air with his hands and puffing up his cheeks. Then he described for them how the sea was flogged at Xerxes's orders, how the Iranian naval vessels passed through the Hellespont. The warm glow of the fire lit a red spot on the stove, the air smelled of coal, and Hadi Besharat's fingers began to come alive in the heat.

He thought of turning on the gas burner and boiling some water for tea. But he couldn't get moving. The door to the drawing room had been left open and the curtains were twisting in the clear air. A half-filled tumbler waited on the kitchen counter for Farangu to put in the sink. He imagined Farangu standing in front of the mirror rubbing cream into the lines on her face, laying cucumber peels on her forehead and cheeks to obliterate the brown spots. Then she would lie down on the couch, close her eyes, and pass out. In the gray light from the window her tired face would grow cold and her half-open mouth would leave an unfinished sigh in the air.

But talking to Farangu's ghost was impossible. The silence was insanity's tied tongue, trailing continuously behind the noon siren which just now started blaring outside in the streets. A silence that he was incapable of explaining to Farangu. No doubt she had left because of his tactless behavior, because of his giving lessons to Nili and therefore allowing that nosy girl to enter their house. Maybe also because of Sayid-jon's slick tongue and the way his flattery could charm her out of her mind. Maybe because of other reasons that Hadi Besharat couldn't understand.

He wanted to turn his thoughts to the past but he wasn't able to come up with anything important. This indulgence in thoughts of the past was a kind of mental illness—a compulsion, like reading tombstones, or refusing to clip one's fingernails, or avoiding the sight of a hanged man. It would ruin his memory and cause him total amnesia. He had to shake himself out of this languid mood and bring Farangu back home. But just as he was deciding this the telephone rang. Hadi Besharat picked up the receiver and recognized Farangu's voice instantly.

Fortified, he shouted, "Miss, where are you? Why aren't you home with your family?"

Farangu paused in a way that worried him. He felt helpless. Farangu said, "I just wanted to tell you not to wait for me anymore."

"Why? What's happened?"

"Nothing's happened. I want to go to America to be with Khosro. Sayid-jon has managed to get me my passport. I'll go first to Pakistan via Zahedan. From there I'll apply for my visa and go to America."

He grew angry. "Then what about me?"

"I don't know about you."

Farangu seemed very far away. Her voice revealed such help-lessness—and yet there wasn't even a hair's-breadth of a crack in it. Hadi Besharat softened his tone and said, "At least let's talk it over. I'll come visit this evening. We'll go somewhere and talk."

Farangu said, "We don't have anything more to discuss. There's no way I can return. I feel terrible. I have to look after my own life."

A thought occurred to Hadi Besharat and he said, "Without your husband's permission, you're not allowed to leave the country. I won't give my permission."

"You are shameless. I didn't know you could be so low. Fine, then. Don't give your permission. It doesn't matter. I'll stay right here. But you won't see me again."

Anger gave Farangu a more precise and determined voice. Hadi Besharat grew nervous and said quickly, "Why do you go to pieces over a simple conversation? If it's just because of a fancy trip, to hell with it, I'll agree." He paused for a moment, searching his mind for the proper phrase. Then, more offhandedly, he asked, "Farangu, do you know where I am? I'm sitting downstairs, listening to the ticktock of the clock. The house is empty. I'm thinking of you. I imagine that someone is knocking on the door. I don't mean the door of our present house. I mean the Salsabil house where we got married. Do you remember the day after our wedding night? In the morning, when we first woke up? Why did we sell the Salsabil house and move to this house? Wouldn't it have been better if we'd stayed on there? Do you want me to beg? Come back to your home and family. Don't leave me here alone with a handful of memories."

When he finished that last sentence he disliked himself. But it was out of his hands. He had to tell the truth. Farangu said grudgingly, "If your nerves are bad, go to a nerve doctor. Go to the Japanese doctor."

"What would I do with a nerve doctor? All these memories take their toll. If you don't come back everything will fall apart. Let's discuss this one more time."

"No, I have to go now."

Hadi Besharat drew away and looked at the holes in the

receiver. He had used up all the tricks in his bag. He said deject-edly, "At least tell me why."

Farangu gave a cold sigh and said, "I don't know. Don't ask. It's hopeless."

"At least let's have a phone conversation."

"Forget it, Besharat. It's hopeless."

He couldn't restrain himself. "What a short temper you have! Just think about it a little."

Farangu hung up and Hadi Besharat sat paralyzed next to the telephone table. He felt a strong urge to get out of the house. He didn't know what to do. The house was eating him up. He had to hit the street and go somewhere. He had to look for some experience that would disturb his balance, that would drag him away from himself into the dust of a battleground scene where a group of soldiers marched down a dirt road far away. The pale columns of sunlight sliced the road into vertical bands.

The doorbell rang. No doubt Nili and Heli had come back again to surround him, to wash and dry him like a swaddled baby. He didn't need anyone's help. He went to open the door and saw General Ghovanlu and Engineer Gharib, their fists jammed into their coat pockets, their faces frowning. Engineer Gharib asked, "May we come in?"

Hadi Besharat felt obliged. He had no choice. "Please, do. I beg you."

He closed the door behind them and tried to take their hats and coats. But they shook the snow off their hats and hung their own coats on hangers. Hadi Besharat went out to the kitchen, sat down at the table, and placed his hands on his knees like a pair of yellow leather gloves. Engineer Gharib lifted his camera strap from his shoulder, tilted his head and examined the stairs. Then he glanced around the kitchen and asked, "How many rooms do you have in your house?"

Hadi Besharat was surprised by the question. "Seven. Why do you ask?"

Engineer Gharib sat on a chair and winked at Hadi Besharat.

"What is this face you've put on? Are you thinking of your small debts?"

"Two things ruin your business—small debts and small knowledge. It's not the small debts that make me look this way. It's the small knowledge."

General Ghovanlu rubbed his stomach, looked around, and said, "Don't you have a heater? You'll get sick in this cold weather."

Hadi Besharat forced a smile. "Do you feel like eating something, can I bring you anything? Have some oranges."

Engineer Gharib took an orange from the fruit bowl and said, "Are you worried about Farangu? You know women have a lot of tricks to make life difficult. She'll stay with her Mama Aliyeh for a little while. Then she'll get tired and come home."

Hadi Besharat waved a hand. "It's not important at all."

"Then why are you sitting here looking so miserable?"

"Forget it, it's not important. Let's talk about something else. Have some fruit. How are you doing? Enjoying yourselves? Engineer, why have you brought this camera?"

Engineer Gharib picked up the camera and held it in front of his face. "I want to take your picture."

Hadi Besharat looked suspiciously at the unmoving expressions of Engineer Gharib and General Ghovanlu. "Why do you want to take my picture?"

"You need six photos."

"What for?"

"For your passport." Engineer Gharib pulled a few printed forms from his breast pocket and placed them on the table. "Fill these out so we can apply for your passport."

Hadi Besharat rose slowly to his feet. "I haven't asked anyone to get me a passport."

General Ghovanlu said, "Professor, you have traveled the world over and you're experienced. This trip will be like those other trips of yours. It will take you out of this suffocating atmosphere. All your difficulties are due to a tired mind and the social pressures of living here."

Listening to General Ghovanlu made him nervous. He started collecting the plates, knives, and forks from the table. An unnecessary, aimless activity that calmed him, that eased his worries. Engineer Gharib was peeling his orange. "General, we have to think about how to sell the house, too. Real estate prices have been falling lately. It may be difficult to find a buyer. How much do you think this house will bring?"

The general glanced around and said, "It won't be easy. I know of a real estate agency. I'll find out from them and let you know."

Hadi Besharat said, "Who asked you to sell my house?"

Engineer Gharib said, "After you're in America you won't need this house. They'll come from the Martyrs' Foundation and confiscate it."

"I'm not planning to go to America."

Engineer Gharib closed his eyes with strained patience. "You have to take care of yourself. Look in the mirror and see those gray shadows under your eyes. You don't think of eating and sleeping. You stay in your study all the time, hiding behind a pile of books belonging to God knows what century." He spat orange seeds into an ashtray. "What's your own opinion, then? What do you want to do?"

That question gave Hadi Besharat strength and he said, "I want to write a paper on the historical roots of the war with Iraq. It's been a few days since I've listened to the radio or read a newspaper. What's the news from the front?"

The general looked at the ceiling with a desperate expression. "You're wasting your time. All wars are a sham. They've struck a deal. All the strategies are decided on the other side of the world. They want to cheat this poor nation. With so much education, how can you be so gullible?"

Hadi Besharat shook his head in defiance. "I have to see the front from up close. People don't go to the front for nothing. It's a human instinct, like the salmon's instinct that forces him to swim against the current to the mouth of the river. It's like the polar cranes' instinct that forces them to fly thousands of miles to the tropics. Mesopotamia has the same pull."

General Ghovanlu narrowed his eyes sleepily. "Don't say these things in front of other people. They won't understand and it could cause you trouble. Isn't that right, Engineer?"

Now Engineer Gharib was aiming his camera at Hadi Besharat. The flashbulb flashed as he spoke. "Another problem is his giving lessons to Nili."

General Ghovanlu's protruding lips made him resemble a sulky child. He told Engineer Gharib, "It's unwise for him to give Nili lessons. It creates difficulties for him. The religious patrols in the street will catch wind of it and in a week's time the stink will be everywhere."

The general was talking as if Hadi Besharat weren't there and it was making him angry. "General, what is this nonsense? I've taught all kinds of students in my lifetime. Maybe the Komité has sent you here. Obviously you're here at their orders. All this is the Komité's doing. If they have something to tell me, why don't they come see me?"

"You're wrong, Professor. What has the Komité got to do with this? It's our own good will. We thought to come over, to see if you need anything, and to offer our help. The neighbors say there's an excellent nerve doctor. He's written a prescription for Mr. Bayat, he's doing miracles for him. Mr. Bayat, who wasn't able to sleep a wink, now sleeps like a log every night."

"I don't need a nerve doctor."

The general said, "Look, you've been staying to yourself for some time, never talking to anyone, keeping silent wherever you go."

"Of course I keep silent. Talk belongs to the present and is forgotten with the passage of time. But silence always survives. Silence is the language of history."

"Very well, then. Sign these papers."

Hadi Besharat pushed the papers aside and said, "Do you think I'm out of my mind, that I'd sign these papers? Would you please leave this house and come back some other time?"

Engineer Gharib and General Ghovanlu looked at each other, thinning their eyelids, twisting their lips. Hadi Besharat shouted, "Please go, I beg you! If I feel the need for help I'll call on you."

The engineer and the general got up with some reluctance and went out to the hall to put on their coats. Hadi Besharat stood nearby, clasping his hands behind his back, bouncing on his feet like a spring and waiting for them to leave. When they were ready, he followed them to the door. As soon as he had closed the door behind them he felt he'd been freed from prison. He was happy now. Although he knew he shouldn't call this disgusted feeling "happiness." It was as if he'd entangled himself with a bunch of stupid students who repeated his words like parrots.

He rubbed his hands together to warm them and to forget about his anger. He went upstairs to the sewing room, looking for his old maroon shirt. He found it in a drawer of newly laundered clothes. He took a needle and thread from Farangu's sewing box, sat at the window, and started sewing a button on his shirt. The image of Farangu was everywhere—in the familiar atmosphere of the house, the smell of unwashed underwear, the dirty fingerprints and Scotch tape on the unpainted wall, the bottle of water on the ironing board that she used for sprinkling clothes, the calendar with the torn, curled corners, the old newspapers and magazines with their advertisements for Sony radios and Toshiba television sets.

This was exactly like 1942, after he left Khezrabad and started doing everything by himself, washing and patching his clothes and ironing with the charcoal iron. He had also learned to cook. Initially, his income wasn't that high. He wasn't the only one who chased customers through the Mesgarabad Cemetery with offers to sprinkle their relatives' graves. As far as the eye could see, children were busy sprinkling graves with water pitchers. In desperation he found a corner in the cemetery, put a tray on a table, and started selling things like cardamom-rosewater gelatin, Mama Jim-Jim halvah, Plato's Magic Electuary, and roasted wheat and marijuana seeds. If he was lucky he made fifteen or sometimes twenty-five cents a day. During the religious mourning periods of Tasua and Ashura his earnings went up to five tumans. Nevertheless he kept his stomach full mostly with grapes, goat cheese, and Barbary bread. After he started selling ice cream his income rose. A few times he went to a restaurant and ate a full course of rice and meat. Once he baked a pie decorated with sesame seeds, using a recipe he'd copied from an ancient handwritten cookbook in Fakhr Zanjani's library. The book was five hundred years old and it came from the kitchen of King Esmail of the Safavid Dynasty. How happy and satisfied he had been! He was complete in himself and he didn't need a soul.

That internal voice kept nagging him to make a decision. Encouraging him not to be intimidated by the avalanche and the closed roads, luring him to return on foot to Khezrabad. He wished he and his father-jon could take an afternoon walk in the silence of the highlands to read the message someone had carved in the mountain stone:

> If you have come from afar, if you are a stranger or broken-hearted, rent a peasant house and stay there. Take this narrow road and make a pilgrimage to Ghasem's Shrine. How pleasant are the narrow roads in Khezrabad! On your way you'll meet children, smiling and showing you the way to the shrine.

His father-jon would sit cross-legged on the bank of the river, tucking his feet beneath him, asking Hadi Besharat to light his cigarette with a magnifying glass. He would take a puff and whisper to himself, "In Khezrabad a mood comes over you that calms your nerves. The heaven people talk about has got to be right here."

Hadi Besharat decided to get out of the house and see what was going on. He had the impression that that visit from Engineer Gharib and General Ghovanlu was no coincidence. Only at Farangu's suggestion would they dare apply for his passport and try to sell his house. Perhaps Farangu was visiting the neighbors without his knowledge. Perhaps she was complaining over the phone to Engineer Gharib at this very moment.

He finished sewing on the button, took the fur cloak off his shoulders and hung it carefully in the closet. He put on his outdoor clothing and picked up his umbrella and stepped out of the house.

At the head of the street, he met Mrs. Kobra. She came close and tried to say something, but the edge of her veil snapped out of her clenched teeth, revealing her face dotted with brown moles like a burned flatbread. She fixed her filmed eyes on him and wailed, "Martyr Mehrdad Razi used to cry so much for St. Hosein the Oppressed. Brother, please give me a piece of the handkerchief he cried into. I'm going on a pilgrimage. I'm going to visit the shrine of my master at the deer sanctuary. When my eyes see his beauty I won't forget you. I'll tell him you gave me the handkerchief belonging to the martyr of his path . . ."

Hadi Besharat searched his pocket but he couldn't find the white handkerchief Farangu always put there. Helpless and frightened, he said, "Sister, please forgive me. I don't have the handkerchief with me."

Mrs. Kobra narrowed her eyes in disgust and said, "How come all you have is for your own enjoyment? You people are so used to being comfortable. You little old man! I watch the Bayat girls coming to your house all the time."

Hadi Besharat hurried to Mr. Bayat's house. As he opened the door he saw the sacrificial lamb hanging from a post in the courtyard. A young butcher was pulling out the entrails and steam was rising from the carcass. The butcher pointed the tip of his knife at Hadi Besharat. "Isn't it big? Isn't it?"

Hadi Besharat didn't answer. The butcher said, "Son of a gun, it's so big. What sort of grass was it eating that made it so big?"

He smiled admiringly at the carcass. Hadi Besharat went on into the house. Heli was standing on the stairs. As soon as he entered, she brought her hands forward and said, "I think it's Professor Besharat. Professor Besharat, is that you? Why don't you come in?"

"Greetings. How did you know who it was?"

"When you got close I knew right away. The air in the passageway changed. Your breath is striking my face right now. Are you tired? Have you walked a long way?"

"Not at all. Why do you ask?"

"I don't know. Maybe I'm the one who's tired. It feels as though they're carrying a body through the streets again. People lose their interest, they grow tired of being young."

"Go to the head of the street and count how many bridal chambers are planted there. Parents are walking by holding their children's hands. If you could see them you'd be surprised. The parents are so young themselves."

As he looked out at the wandering snowflakes, he began to cough. Heli said, "That's life. You have to accept it."

"Have you seen Farangu?"

"She was here this morning. She's getting ready to go to America. But don't worry. We won't leave you alone. Nili will bring you a portion of the sacrificial meat. We're going to look after you."

"Thank you very much. There's no need to trouble yourselves."

"It's no trouble. It makes us happy. Please come in and rest awhile."

"Much obliged for your kindness, miss. But I have to go now and find out where Farangu is. If you happen to see her again, could you tell her I'm expecting her?"

"Of course."

Hadi Besharat said good-bye and went to the head of the street. One after the other the signs from the road to the other world were drawing closer—the black flags, the green pennants, and a few Hezbolah motorcycle riders cruising the traffic circle in white masks and white aprons. The city ambulances arrived and their engines fell silent. A young religious student, holding a microphone in one hand and a machine gun in the other, stood shouting in the middle of the circle. But the soft snowfall had hushed the avenue. The parade of posters, rebellious faces, and hollow eyes proceeded soundlessly. Even the fountain of blood in the traffic circle couldn't express the agony of death. The agony of death needed a memorial monument made of white marble— a wounded rider who closes his eyes, sliding into the Angel Michael's arms from the back of his horse. A white horse standing on its hind hoofs in front of the monster War with bulging eyes and swollen neck arteries. An angel gazing at the sky, holding the wreath of victory over the rider's head.

In the avenue they were carrying bodies, and the cold had turned Mr. Bayat's face as sightlessly blank as the face of a clock. He was nodding rapidly while talking to his servant. "First you have to consider that the true Iranians live only around the city's main circle and below it. Above the city's main circle they're all gigolos concerned with nothing but getting their green cards. You put a marble on the city's northern boundary and let it roll down. Wherever it stops, that's where the true Iranians live. The true Iranian is an intelligent street Arab who fights alone, is spendthrift and a little bit cowardly." He saw Hadi Besharat, smiled hesitantly, and mumbled, "I apologize, but I don't recognize Your Excellency."

Hadi Besharat removed his beret, bowed, and said, "How come you don't recognize me? It was only two days ago I visited you at your house."

Mr. Bayat nervously pulled a handkerchief from his pocket and wiped his mouth. "This brain illness of mine is the cause of it all. You must forgive me. My wife has gone to America and left me here by myself. She didn't even wait two weeks for my condition to improve before she went."

A cold wind was blowing and Hadi Besharat had to put his beret back on his head. "Mr. Bayat, have you seen Farangu around here?"

"Of course I've seen her. What a lady! What an angel! She came to our house this morning with Engineer Gharib and General Ghovanlu. I gave her my word, Professor Besharat. At least I'll provide her with enough to cover her travel expenses. But she shouldn't be in such a hurry. It's not easy to find money, with the economy as bad as it is." He started coughing. "How do you dare to come out of your house in this blizzard?"

Hadi Besharat tried not to lose control. "You must give that money only to me."

Mr. Bayat said, "If anyone my age wants to stay alive he has to keep walking. Sitting still is bad for the heart and the joints. Did you move to this district recently?"

"I have already mentioned that I am Hadi Besharat."

"Very pleased to meet you." He brought his tilted head close and asked, "Pardon me, who has died?"

Hadi Besharat pulled his scarf over his face to protect himself from the snow. "What do I know? It seems they're bringing back the war martyrs."

"Where is Ramezan's casket, then? Didn't I hear he was executed early this morning for selling narcotics and having sexual relations with a married woman?"

"Do you mean Ramezan the ice seller?"

Mr. Bayat looked at Hadi Besharat and said, "How strange! You can't believe it. It was just two weeks ago that I ran into him in the little bazaar. By the way, your good name came up also. He said his friendship with you goes back to 1942. He said no one can compare you with the others. God have mercy on him, he was right. You are as pure as the Angel of Light. You are the gospel of mercy and goodness."

Now they were carrying three caskets. Mr. Bayat came closer and said, "I think the middle casket belongs to Ramezan the ice seller. The one in the front and the one in the back belong to the martyrs."

The servant said, "Agha, all those caskets belong to martyrs. They wouldn't mix up the casket of a smuggler with those belonging to martyrs."

Mr. Bayat raised his shoulders. "Even if they mix up the caskets it won't cause any trouble. You can always identify martyrs' caskets by the green leaves and the gladioli they put on them." He turned to Hadi Besharat. "Don't worry. God is great and eventually the money for the trip will come from some-where. You must only be patient and wait."

He lifted his hat to say good-bye and went away with his servant. Under the constant snowfall Hadi Besharat stood motionless. He couldn't keep from thinking about Ramezan the ice seller. He thought of his house behind the ice reservoir and Ramezan's small room in which he always felt the presence of someone. Someone always kept him company, like the lamplight that forced him at times to study till dawn. Then the window-panes emerged from the darkness like the white of an egg, and a concave picture of Ramezan the ice seller appeared beyond them searching his pockets for the house key as he left to collect his payments in the market. Every evening he drank arak until he was drunk and brushed against the street walls as he staggered along singing couplets in praise of St. Ali. At the end of the evening he bought a handkerchief full of fruits and vegetables and two flat, sesame-covered loaves of bread, and he returned to the house.

Hadi Besharat kept walking. The telephone lines sagged be-neath the snow, curving downward like the ropes of a sailing ship. The light froze in the air, coloring it the solid white of a night in Purgatory. The inside of his nose burned. He was afraid of catching cold and becoming bedridden. But he wouldn't allow himself to get sick. He would take some vitamin C and breathe some eucalyptus vapor.

As though chain mail and an iron helmet protected him against the blizzard, he was undaunted by the depth of the footprints appearing in the snow. On the contrary, he increased his pace. He had to pack up and go to the front. He had to visit Babylon's landscape, the pit of the angels Harut and Marut, the ruins of Lagash and Sipar. He imagined that the Angel of Death was passing through the winter air, leaving behind that silence that dwells in cold and covered spaces. A silence that could be revealed by X ray. The silence of a cathedral bell ringing on the hour, exhibiting the zodiac chariot in a window. The chariot of Gemini, of Leo, of Pisces. With the spinning of the magic lantern, the nursing infant grows to be a young man. The young man kisses a young girl's lips and three stars twinkle between their mouths. Then the young man takes a cane in his hand, grows a hump, and descends life's downward curve. The bony face of a clown laughs beneath a hood, reaping the stars with a crooked scythe. Darkness looms in the air like dust from a broom. The bearded moon rises and is hung on a hook in the sky. How could he deny it? By dead languages he couldn't understand or pronounce? By seas unable to reach each other, by vessels unable to sail the seas? By shore-dwellers searching the surface of the water for a lifeboat?

The day after his wedding he woke and saw Farangu asleep beside him. There were rose petals scattered around them, and sunlight stretching from the window onto the bed. He felt like sneezing. His nose was itching. He held still, screwing up his eyes and waiting. But instead Farangu sneezed loudly and sprang awake. Hadi Besharat burst into laughter, holding his stomach. As often as Farangu asked, "Why are you laughing?" he couldn't give her a convincing answer.

He sped on. With every step he lifted the tip of his umbrella and stabbed the frozen pavement. He passed the Martyr Taher Nabavi High School. They had already rung the bell for recess. But the students were still gathered at the windows, watching the avenue. In front of the Komité Building's guardhouse two Revolutionary Guards stood warming their hands over the flames from a tar barrel. Hadi Besharat approached them. He pointed the tip of his umbrella toward the slogan written on the wall and said, "Brothers, 'victory' is spelled with a *c* and not with a *k*."

One of the Revolutionary Guards glanced at the slogan and asked, "What is spelled with a *c?*"

" 'Victory.' "

The Revolutionary Guard took up a poker with a charcoal-covered tip and drew a curly *c* over the *k*. Then he went back to warming his hands. Hadi Besharat continued toward the Komité Building. He passed among the Benz and Paykan automobiles and climbed the stairs to the waiting area.

The waiting area was semidarkened, like the lobby of a seedy hotel in the southern part of the city. Men and women sat separately on benches that faced each other. Their voices and the cigarette smoke twisted in the air. Hadi Besharat grew dizzy from the sense of crowding and disorganization. The doors of the interrogation rooms were closed. Next to them was another door, partly open, leading to an office. In the middle of the hall some of the humbled masses were lighting their samovars and putting their food on their Primus stoves. The smells of boiled meat, fat spiced with turmeric, and burning kerosene lingered all around. Hadi Besharat felt he would suffocate. He didn't go to the reception desk and he didn't wait his turn. Instead he put the tip of his umbrella to the office door and peered through the crack he had widened.

Ahmad Bayat sat behind his desk, munching on a sandwich. With every swallow his Adam's apple bobbed up and down. Two Revolutionary Guards stood behind him. Ahmad Bayat was wearing an easygoing smile. The smile tightened the smooth skin over his cheeks.

Gradually Hadi Besharat was reminded that the Komité Building was in fact part of the old Mirza Isa the Minister High School. Instead of filing cabinets, rows of desks and benches filled the office. A grammar exercise had not been erased from the blackboard. A thousand unrelated details gave the room the air of a place untouched and idle—the fallen ceiling plaster, the worn-out picture frames, the maps of Iran and the world, the slogan THE BLOOD IN OUR VEINS IS AN OFFERING TO THE MARTYRS, the strange and obscure licenses on the walls all catching dust and turning yellow, all bearing their dates of issue and their general and particular numbers. The pictures of the martyrs were actually photographs enlarged from tradesmen's licenses or from passport applications or from students' report cards.

One of the Revolutionary Guards saw Hadi Besharat and told Ahmad Bayat, "Somebody's here and I think he wants something."

Ahmad Bayat said, "Tell him to wait till his name is called."

Then he continued talking with the Revolutionary Guards. Against his will Hadi Besharat sat down on a bench in the waiting area. Through the half-open door he saw Ahmad Bayat finishing his sandwich and lolling back in his swivel chair. His boots were propped on his desk and he was bouncing rhythmically, as if he sat on a train whose motion was putting him to sleep. His bony cheeks protruded like two stone islands, giving him the expression of one who has been totally consumed. Only his curling lips had any flesh; they made him look greedy.

Behind him the two Revolutionary Guards stood wrapped in blankets, speaking intently with outstretched necks. Hadi Besharat rose and put his umbrella tip to the door again, shoving it all the way open. He went straight to the desk and said, "Ahmad Agha, may I have a couple of words with you? I've waited so long that the grass is growing under my feet."

Surely Ahmad Bayat recognized him. But he didn't want to admit it. His smile faded. He motioned Hadi Besharat closer. "Please come here."

Perhaps he wanted to show off his position, Hadi Besharat considered, as he removed his beret and held it crumpled in his fist. He went forward and made a small bow to all present. Then he bent over the desk so he could speak at closer range. Ahmad Bayat pointed to the chair in front of him. "Won't you sit down?"

Instead of sitting, Hadi Besharat looked at the others. He wondered what they were waiting for. Why didn't they leave the room? Ahmad Bayat asked, "What sort of business brings you here, Mr. Besharat?"

Now he had recognized Hadi Besharat, but he still wouldn't address him as "Professor." Hadi Besharat lowered his eyes and said, "It's confidential."

At a glance from Ahmad Bayat the Revolutionary Guards moved over to the door. Hadi Besharat breathed easier. Now he could speak without inhibition. "Is this the Komité?"

Ahmad Bayat nodded and said, "Goodness, don't you know that yet?"

Hadi Besharat mumbled, "Have you heard from my wife?"

Ahmad Bayat raised one eyebrow. "Do you mean Miss Farangu? Are you referring to the payment of my father's debt to Khosro?"

"No, no, I just wanted to know if she's come to you for her passport."

"For her passport? Why here? She has to go to the Department of Passports."

"I know, but I thought she might have come to you for a recommendation."

"No, I haven't seen Miss Farangu today. Anything else? I have a lot of work to do."

"I've been waiting for half an hour. Nobody came to ask, 'Agha-jon, what do you want, what is your trouble?' I've come to register a complaint."

"What sort of complaint?"

"I want to go to the front."

Ahmad Bayat raised his eyebrow again. "I don't understand. No one has registered such a complaint before."

"I am complaining now. Write it down somewhere." He tapped his umbrella a couple of times on the desk.

Looking at him in amazement, Ahmad Bayat asked, "Well, so, do you want your money back?"

"I have a lot of problems, Ahmad Agha."

Ahmad Bayat said, "I don't understand what you're saying."

Hadi Besharat was silent. The students were singing together in one of the high school classes with voices as transparent as the olive oil in a crystal decanter, as pure as squares of light spreading beneath the arched ceiling and never reaching their limits. He scratched the bald spot at the back of his head. Then he raised his chin and said almost bashfully, "I apologize. It's not important. Let's talk about something else."

"You're so busy writing about history. Because of my religious obligations, I want to tell you something. If you like, take note. Otherwise, forget it. Studying angels and spinning threads around the world of counterparts deviates you. You become a stranger to yourself. You need to exercise instead." He stood up and started jogging in place. "Every morning you should run around your house for half an hour or so."

Hadi Besharat was caught off guard. He smiled artificially and started jogging also. "I should run? It's good for my heart and my nerves?"

Ahmad Bayat sat down again, nodding in satisfaction and approval. "It takes you out of yourself." Resting his index finger alongside his nose and his thumb beneath his chin, he leaned back in his chair and gazed at Hadi Besharat from a distance of a thousand miles. "Khosro has to return from America if he wants to get his money."

"Ahmad Agha, if Farangu pays you a visit, tell her I'm waiting for her at home."

"Professor, come out of your house more often. Instead of all this writing, pay more attention to the life of these people. Writing history is easy."

Hadi Besharat grew angry and brought his head forward with threatening force. "Ahmad Agha, writing history is not easy."

"Every day these people walk in front of bullets and write history."

Hadi Besharat thrust his chest out and said, "I want to go to the front. What would you say I should do?"

Ahmad Bayat smiled sarcastically, but he said nothing for some time. Hadi Besharat asked, "Why don't you answer?"

Ahmad Bayat pointed to a big poster on the wall. "Can you give up everything the way this ten-year-old child has?"

Hadi Besharat looked at the poster. The black smoke of an explosion was rolling across the sky. On the horizon a few soldiers were caught off guard, their knees bent and their arms upraised. In the foreground was the body of a child with his throat slit. Ahmad Bayat said, "This child wasn't martyred by a bullet. They slit his throat. Every morning I stand in front of this poster and kiss his throat."

"You kiss his throat? Why?"

"When I kiss his throat I think I am kissing the edge of the enemy's dagger." For a moment a softness appeared in his face. Then he frowned. Hadi Besharat put on his beret and picked up his umbrella.

Ahmad Bayat said, "You need help. You should take better care of yourself." He motioned to the Revolutionary Guards in the doorway. "See the professor out."

The Revolutionary Guards entered the office. But Hadi Besharat resisted and refused to move. Instead he spoke rapidly. "What do you mean? How should I take care of myself?"

Ahmad Bayat didn't answer. He gestured for the Revolutionary Guards to proceed. They came forward and led Hadi Besharat from the office. As they reached the waiting area, he struggled, trying to free his arms from their grip. "Leave me alone. What sort of country is this?"

Then he saw Engineer Gharib and General Ghovanlu in the crowd. They stepped forward to help the Revolutionary Guards drag him down the stairs and out of the building. When they arrived on the sidewalk he freed himself and shook his finger at the Komité Building. "Who are you? Are you God?"

General Ghovanlu put a hand beneath Hadi Besharat's elbow and tried to soothe him. "Professor! Professor-jon! Be a little calmer, be a little more considerate. . . ."

Hadi Besharat turned his eyes toward the crowd, but he didn't know what he was looking for. Maybe just for someone who was on his side. Someone who understood him and would back him up. Engineer Gharib and General Ghovanlu cared only about preventing a disaster. Hadi Besharat yanked his scarf from his neck, tore off his beret, and threw them both on the snow. He was about to take off his coat when Engineer Gharib seized his hands from behind. Hadi Besharat grew even angrier and shouted, "Engineer, are you losing your mind? Are you handcuffing me? Do you think I am a thief?"

Mr. Abolhassan Hashiyeh emerged from the high school and started running. Midway, he slipped on the snow and slid to Hadi Besharat's feet. He grabbed a cuff of his trousers and begged, "Master, I'm your devoted servant. You are our guide.

Let us please go to the school, have a cup of tea, and feel better. . . ."

Hadi Besharat shouted, "Take me to the mosque! I want to talk to the religious judge."

Ahmad Bayat stepped out of the Komité Building, pushed the people aside, and came over to Hadi Besharat. He looked at the crowd from beneath his eyebrows. Then he assumed a patient expression. Confidentially, he gestured to Engineer Gharib to let go of Hadi Besharat's hands. He bent to pick up Hadi Besharat's beret and scarf from the snow and gave them to him. He told him, "A person who wants to go to the front should not be so scared."

"Scared of what? Of you?"

"How could I scare you?"

Behind Ahmad Bayat the cloudy sky spread out, light snow-flakes twisting in the air and landing quietly on the soft ground. Ahmad Bayat said, "Now, go home and get warm."

He motioned for the crowd to clear the way and they stepped back. Hadi Besharat brushed the snow off his beret. Ahmad Bayat asked, "Would you rather come to the office for a few minutes' rest?"

Hadi Besharat brushed more snow from his beret and said, "It is exactly as you say."

"What do you mean? Do you want to come to the office or go home?"

"You are right."

He put the beret firmly on his head and started walking. The avenue was as crowded as in the days of mourning. The frozen surface of the pavement glared and the procession groups were getting ready. Some people were coming out and some were returning to their houses. Some were standing in line in front of the cooperative store and some were gathering in clusters, look-ing at the standards and banners passing by. A truck was driving away down the middle of the avenue, leaving tracks in the snow. A bus was stuck, spinning its wheels. Its passengers sat dazed behind the steam-covered windows. Although Hadi Besharat didn't know much about cars and engines, he began to think about some solutions for the problem of winter driving. Maybe they could wrap a few wires around each tire and connect the wires to the battery. When the car was stuck in the snow they could turn on the switch. That would certainly warm the wires, melt the snow, and free the car.

He noticed Mr. Hashiyeh walking beside him. The wind was blowing snow across Mr. Hashiyeh's wide flat forehead, across his dark face in which every line was delicately drawn. A face that could be seen only from train stations. A face in the window of a train approaching the station and then passing through without stopping. Mr. Hashiyeh had his hands in his coat pockets, and his breath came out between his beard and his mustache and rose in the air. Hadi Besharat said, "Did you say something?"

Mr. Hashiyeh asked, "Would you allow me to come with you?"

Hadi Besharat only nodded and kept going. After a few steps he said casually, "I like to walk a little in the street."

Mr. Hashiyeh looked at the snowy sky and pulled up his coat collar. "How about coming to my house? It's just around the corner." He pointed to the end of the avenue. "Behind the Mobilization Headquarters, two streets down."

Hadi Besharat didn't say anything. The two of them walked, pressing snow beneath their feet with a sound that rhymed with the pauses. Reaching Mr. Hashiyeh's house, they crossed a courtyard and a front hall, turned left, and entered a drawing room. There was a couch along one wall and above it hung a miniature poster of the national hero Rostam and his son Sohrab. Hadi Besharat saw two dolls on the mantel—a Spanish dancing couple, a man and woman, curling their hands over their heads like question marks. The room seemed smaller because of the clutter on the bookshelves. Old, moist smells made the air heavy. Mr. Hashiyeh had to open a window, letting the fresh air in. But the air was cold and they might get sick. Mr. Hashiyeh shut the window again. He pointed to the couch and Hadi Besharat sat down. He placed his elbows on his knees, leaned forward, and asked, "Do you have an alcoholic beverage or something that we could drink to make us feel better?"

Mr. Hashiyeh rubbed his hands together rapidly and said, "Of course, master. We have whatever you want."

He went to the next room and came back with a gallon jar of Engineer Gharib's vodka, a bottle of Coca-Cola, and pickles and other chasers on a tray. He poured a tumbler of vodka for Hadi Besharat and said, "First of all, it's not my place to show off in front of Professor Besharat, who is one of our scholars. But now that you have favored me and kindly come to our house I may be able to say a word or two. In my lowly opinion, martyrdom certainly takes a human being to heaven and bestows eternal life with peace. But death also lasts for all time. Constantly it wreaks havoc."

Hadi Besharat swallowed his vodka down. "No matter what life may be, it finally comes to an end. One day you put your head down and it's all over. But, with death, everything stays the same. Death is eternal."

Mr. Hashiyeh drank his vodka. "Professor Besharat, when will your next book be published?"

Hadi Besharat shrugged. "Nobody knows. The publisher says he's out of paper and can't print it now." He took another swallow of vodka. "It doesn't matter. Writing a book is never without its headaches. Whether you like it or not, you face a stone wall any time you write a book. Because it will never turn out the way you want it. It becomes something completely unrelated to you."

Mr. Hashiyeh sat on a chair opposite. "Like what, for instance?"

"Imagine you're sitting alone. Then a thought occurs to you in a flash. You decide to describe that thought to someone in ordinary language. You can't do it. It's impossible. Writing a book means to die. With the writing of each word, a piece of you dies. Take me, for example. I have written many books. But I still haven't been able to describe what I want to."

"You are so modest. I've read some of your writings two or

three times. Especially the article, 'The Hidden Faces of Death,' which in my opinion is quite vivid."

Hadi Besharat poured some more vodka for himself. "Mr. Hashiyeh, for the past forty, forty-five years I've been trying to describe a memory. Each time I've tried to write something about it I faced a stone wall. Maybe because originally I was a peasant. I come from Khezrabad and I don't have a talent for description. I remember well that it was September of 1941 . . . Lord, it wasn't then. It was September of 1940. That doesn't matter. Every evening I used to go and watch the young Tehranians dancing the tango on the veranda of the landlord's mansion." He threw his hands around an imaginary partner, closing his eyes, rounding his mouth like a blossom, and swaying as if he were dancing. "Those gigolos, those dandies, those don't-fart-at-me types who change their cars to match the color of their ties. Don't ask me about their antics." He stood up, gulped a little vodka, and continued. "Well, I was young. I had aspirations and I felt envious. Then just before autumn Naser Lotfi's band came to Khezrabad. They set up their tent in front of the bus station, next to the river. Early in the evening Naser Lotfi pulled out his croaking fiddle and started strumming with his bow. Then their dancing girl, who said her name was Huri, would begin to dance all by herself in an alfalfa field."

Hadi Besharat paused, not knowing how to describe his memory. He searched his mind for the proper words. Mr. Hashiyeh came to his rescue. "You were saying she danced in the field."

"Oh, yes. All by herself and in her bare feet. She wore a pistachio-green dress with white dots. As she danced her skirt puffed up around her calves and then wrapped around her legs. For more than forty years I have wanted to describe that dance somehow. But it won't work. Agha-jon, do you know why? Because if I did that I'd be finished myself. I would die. It's like looking at a very beautiful landscape, a heavenly view, and becoming possessed by it. That's no joke. You lose something, something will be reduced in you. This is the meaning of the experience of beauty. It means the final meeting between life and death. Something that will always be out of your reach. Sometimes I wish . . . Please keep this to yourself . . ."

With a twitch of his eyebrows and an intense look, Mr. Hashiyeh implored him to continue. "I beg you, don't be concerned about me. Please go on."

Hadi Besharat raised his hands above his head, put the tip of one boot forward, and glanced at Mr. Hashiyeh. "I apologize. Is it all right if I walk around with these boots on?"

"I beg you, Professor."

"Let me show you how Huri danced. At my age, I can't dance like her. These activities aren't suitable for me. Let me just give you a taste of her movements." He picked up the tumbler from the coffee table and emptied it down his throat. Then he paused a moment and searched for a picture in his mind. "Imagine we are standing in the Khezrabad bus station and the sky is barely growing dark. Naser Lotfi pulls his fiddle out of a dirty bag and rubs it on his sleeve to make it shine. He coughs two or three times, places the fiddle beneath his chin, and pulls the bow across it. Huri gets up like a windup doll, raises her hands from side to side, and dances barefoot in the alfalfa. Now, when I think of Huri, I can't recall her face. I can only see her spinning, moving her head to the right and to the left and smiling at her own arms' movements. You hear the moaning of Naser Lotfi's fiddle from afar and Huri keeps turning around just the same. Behind her is the darkness and she seems blurry, like the photo of an object in motion. With a jerk of her feet she stops and then she moves again: *Bum-bum, baa, bum-bum* . . ."

Now Hadi Besharat was very careful about the delicate movements he made with his feet. He held his fingers in snapping position above his head and he moved his hips ever so slightly, ever so softly. A sort of gyration that goes with the unscrewing of a bolt, always accompanied by the biting of the lower lip and the precise tensing of each muscle. Now and then he glanced over, making sure that Mr. Hashiyeh's total attention was fixed on him, that he was taking notice of the subtle virtuosity of Hadi Besharat's dance. Mr. Hashiyeh sat frozen in his chair, looking at him with glassy eyes. Coming out of his amazement, he asked, "You haven't heard anything from Naser Lotfi and Huri since then?"

"Not a bit. No news of them."

"And you haven't seen them since September of 1940?"

"Oh, yes. But only once. And that was on Ramezan the ice seller's wedding night. In the evening I went to the head of the street to rent a bicycle from Hassan the wheel. He was sitting on a stool in front of his store, holding a fresh walnut in a rag on his palm, hitting it with a knife blade, breaking it open and throwing the kernel into a bowl of water. He had leaned a double-trunk bicycle against the front of his store. As soon as he saw me he smiled and said, 'I just got a beautiful double-trunk bicycle with pedal brakes. Wouldn't you like to try it?' I asked, 'How much an hour?' He said, 'It's not even worth mentioning. I'll charge you three cents.' It's strange, Mr. Hashiyeh. Some scenes stay in your mind so vividly and yet their description is beyond you. I looked toward the end of the street. As you expect with any wedding, I saw the gasoline lantern on a tall stand and the bentwood chair in front of Ramezan the ice seller's house. There was also the usual policeman guarding the door, standing with his fists on his hips. Hassan the wheel was supposed to start the fight at the end of the night. Not a real fight. Just enough so that Ramezan could see blood before going to the bridal chamber. Otherwise he wouldn't have set foot in there. As the men arrived at the wedding the policeman opened the door to the courtyard for them with the heel of his shoe. In front of the stairs Ramezan's flunkies bowed to the guests and whispered, 'If you care for some medicine, please go upstairs.'"

Those who cared to drink went up the damp stairway to the second floor. But the rest of the guests went straight to the courtyard. Surrounding the pool were row after row of tables bearing cake stands laden with pastries and fruit. Hadi Besharat stood in front of Naser Lotfi's band, watching Huri, who wore a new outfit and was putting on her makeup. When she had finished she started shaking her shoulders, biting her lips, and dancing without a thought in her head. The music grew faster and Huri placed the tip of her index finger under her chin, wobbling her head, smiling in regret as if giving a friendly warning. Her smile said, "The world is like this. The fickle heavens always turn. You have to come to terms with it, dear boy."

Then she spun much faster, and then she started doing handstands on the wooden cover of the pool. She bent her legs in the air to form a scorpion. She opened her mouth for the guests to reward her with five- and ten-tuman banknotes which they placed between her teeth. The music climbed three octaves higher, the women began yodeling, and the party came alive. The four-measure beat created an uproar in Hadi Besharat's mind. His heart went crazy.

He pulled an imaginary bow across his shoulder in ecstasy and closed his drugged eyes. Standing in front of the band and indifferent to all around him, he pretended he was singing in the highest possible pitch. Everyone else was busy doing something. The children had their eyes riveted to the cake stands, waiting for the bride's family to call them to dinner. Then they could run to the five-doored room that faced Mecca. They could stuff themselves to their hearts' content. But Hadi Besharat kept pulling the bow of his fiddle just the same, bending and straightening, twisting and turning to the tune of his private symphony. One of the flunkies tugged his sleeve and said, "Don't block people's view, boy."

Hadi Besharat gave him an inquiring look and said, "Why not?"

"What do you call that? Why are you standing here, pretending you're playing a fiddle?"

Shouts came from the crowd. "Why do you bother him? Let him play his fiddle."

"My foot. This is not the auntie's house where anyone can come and play his fiddle."

"I'm playing just for myself. I'm not bothering anyone."

"Boy, you're blocking people's view."

He pulled Hadi Besharat aside. The guests were all watching a comedy show that was taking place on the pool's wooden cover, and no one paid him any attention. He took advantage of this and put the imaginary fiddle back under his chin to play a symphony just for himself. The symphony gave him wings, made him feel weightless. He played melodies as pure as melted light, as white as the skeleton of a camel in the desert. The smell of coffee and cardamom floated in the air and his heart was lit by the shining of raw silver.

Hadi Besharat stopped talking and held the tumbler out to Mr. Hashiyeh for a refill. Mr. Hashiyeh obliged him. Hadi Besharat drank the vodka to the last drop and said, "Let me tell you something. . . . Sometimes, I think I ought to just go to the head of the street and pull my heart out of my chest." With one fist he pulled something from his chest and held it high. "Just like that. Just so. Have you ever thought of doing that? Keeping your heart over your head like a lantern as you walk?"

A woman's voice descended from the second floor. "Abolhassan, when are you coming to eat? Your dinner's getting cold."

Mr. Hashiyeh answered without looking around. "Just a few minutes. I'll be up shortly."

Hadi Besharat gazed wearily at the ceiling and said, "How dark it is! Is it night already?"

Now he was aware of the silence. The sounds of the street, the rush of the people gradually faded away. Only the elegy singers could be heard in the mosque:

"Tonight the king of the religion is a guest in his own court
Tomorrow his body will lie under the horses' hoofs.
Oh, dawn, don't appear,
Oh, dawn, don't appear. . . ."

Hadi Besharat stood up and searched for his umbrella, he buttoned his coat, and wrapped his scarf two or three times around his neck, covering his ears and chin. Mr. Hashiyeh said, "Why so soon, Professor?"

Again the woman's voice came from the second floor. "Abolhassan, the children are getting sleepy."

Hadi Besharat started toward the door. "I have to leave. It's late. I have to pack my suitcase for tomorrow. I'm going to the Mobilization Headquarters to become a volunteer." He paused at the door. "If you want to study death, don't look for its whys and hows. The study of death is like the perception of beauty. You should let death take the awareness from your senses. Let it take you to that sleep that doesn't know time. It's because it doesn't know time that death is eternal and continues forever."

He left Mr. Hashiyeh's house, braving the snowstorm and the cold wind. Staggering, he tried to find his way. A hollow feeling cautioned him against returning home. The thought of his house didn't appeal to him. He tried to distract himself by watching the passersby. No one paid him any heed. A few scattered people were hurrying home with bowed heads. In his condition he feared he might get caught and end up being flogged by the Revolutionary Guards.

A force was pulling him toward the mosque. An indescribable force that he didn't recognize and at the same time could not forget. The cold wind made the mosque's vestibule look frozen. From the courtyard the frozen blades of light reached the chalky walls, pointing to the lights' sources. He grew excited by the strange solitude and the revelation of space. Winter was giving him more concentrated images, much better defined. He entered the mosque's vestibule, found a stone bench close to the superintendent's office, and sat down. He pulled up his coat collar, stretched out on the bench, put his beret on his face, held his umbrella in his arms, and went to sleep.

E I G H T

Somebody shook him awake. He didn't know where he was. The room was very dark and a flashlight beam was hurting his eyes. Then the flashlight circled the vestibule of the mosque, leaving its trace in the dark as though it had weight. Hadi Besharat shielded his eyes with one hand. "Please turn that off. You're blinding me."

The tube of light sheathed itself. He saw the profile of a woman, the sharp edge of her veil sticking out like a bird's beak. A masked woman, her face as white as the lime-covered walls of the vestibule. The words emerging from her mouth had no resonance. "Get up, please. I thought you'd frozen to death."

Hadi Besharat stared at her. "Miss Nili, what are you doing here?"

She took hold of his arm and helped him up. "I've been looking for you everywhere."

Hadi Besharat collected his umbrella and beret and moved out into the street. He said angrily, "Miss, what do you want from me? It's late. If they see us, all kinds of thoughts will pass through their minds."

Nili tugged his arm. They walked cautiously till they arrived at his house. Entering the front door, Hadi Besharat turned on a light and searched the corridor and the drawing room for

Farangu. The untouched look of the furniture told him she hadn't returned.

Nili took off her veil and threw it on the table. All excited, she ran to the kitchen. "I'll bring you a cup of tea. See how fresh I can make it. One of those teas that burns the gums and warms the bones."

Hadi Besharat went upstairs and threw himself on the daybed without changing clothes. The heater was still burning and the vapor of eucalyptus leaves rose from the bowl, infusing the air, mixing with the smell of orange peels, and soothing the scratchy sensation in his throat. His nerves felt as if they were being kneaded and a cold sweat gathered in his armpits and groin. The daybed smelled of old people and rest homes. Tall and short medicine bottles were lined up on the table like the skyscrapers of a city by the sea.

He tossed three vitamin C tablets into his mouth. Then he got up. He burrowed through the closet for the suitcase he'd bought in Seville and he opened it on the daybed. Inside he arranged his socks, underwear, and shaving kit. He added his notes, some books, medicine bottles, sweets and rock candy. He saw Nili standing in the doorway. She seemed thin and delicate, watching him over the tea tray in her hands. She wore a black dress under her brown jacket, which made her look thinner. Or was it because of her diet? Was she still fasting? Was she trying to perform the Masbuta ceremonies as that poor boy used to do? He raised his head indignantly and said, "What are you doing here? Who gave you permission to come into our house like this?"

Nili paid no attention. She placed the tray on the desk. Then she closed the door and sat down on the edge of the daybed. She took a notebook and pen from her bag. Hadi Besharat said, "Miss Nili, what can I tell you? How can I make you understand that I need my rest?"

Nili put a hand to her forehead and thought for a while. She patted the pillows and pulled the edge of the spread over them. Then she opened her notebook and read aloud in English:

"Whose stick did thee break?
Who did break the father's chair?
I tasted your soup before your arrival.
Did your younger brother break somebody's pencil?"

Hadi Besharat shouted, "Miss, what is this you've written? What sort of mixed-up language is this that you call English? You have to print your letters clearly, double spaced, on the left-hand page and working from the left. In English, the second-person pronoun 'thee' is used only for God and His prophets."

After he'd finished speaking Nili asked, "When is Miss Farangu coming back?"

"I don't think she'll ever come back."

"That's impossible. She'll be back."

Hadi Besharat forced his head up. "Miss Nili, I'm very tired."

"She'll be back in a while. You have to bear with this separation."

"What should I do? I can't sit home and stare at the walls."

"Go hiking. I'll take you to St. Yahya's Shrine. Let's go visit Mehrdad's grave. I'll rent an hourly cab and we can drive there."

"In this snowstorm?"

"The snow is stopping. It's not much longer till the first day of spring, New Year's. Everybody's going somewhere. General Ghovanlu and his wife got their passports and they're planning to go to America via Pakistan. They don't discuss it with anyone, but Mrs. Razi knows about it. I think she's planning to go too. She's preparing to join Nurdad, even though she doesn't say so. Her mood has changed. She gets up in the middle of the night, goes down to the kitchen, and stuffs her mouth with handfuls of sugar lumps. She hides flatbread under her mattress. Mrs. Gharib asked her, 'Why?' and she said she can't help it."

Nili uncapped her pen and began to write in her notebook. Hadi Besharat rose to a half-standing position and peered over her shoulder. "What are you writing?"

"This is my homework."

He sat back down and listened to the scratching of her pen

across the page. "Miss Nili, do you really believe in what you're doing?"

Nili answered simply, "Why shouldn't I? Don't you?"

Hadi Besharat said, "If I believed the way you do, I would think I needed a doctor."

He got up and went to the closet, where he faced away from her and breathed deeply. Nili asked, "What are you doing there? Do you want any help?"

"Miss, please go home and leave me alone."

"No! If I go, who'll look after you?" Then she added in English, "You'll die."

Hadi Besharat turned from the closet and assumed his usual serious expression. Intending to start reading, he opened the epitome of Mani's confessions and sat cross-legged on the rug in front of it. But his mind wasn't working. He noticed that Nili was looking at him in silence. He felt remorseful, and he thought he ought to apologize. As a gesture of atonement, he asked, "Why don't you get married?"

Nili answered jokingly, "Professor Besharat, where would I find a husband? Do you know of a dashing rich man I could marry?"

"Pick out an ugly girl friend. Many men look for an ugly girl who will introduce them to a beautiful girl. They know that beautiful girls don't get along with each other. All their friends are ugly. Albinos and people with yellow lashes don't like each other either."

Nili lowered her eyes girlishly and bashfully. A nice smile tugged at the corners of her mouth, revealing that injured elegance in her face, that enduring weakness that pained Hadi Besharat's heart. That erosive helplessness of hers that lanced his veins and wouldn't leave him alone. He looked through the door and saw the corner of Khosro's bed. The cat was licking a paw in front of the mirror. Nili's voice came to him from a distance like the sound of a river running. He could almost say the words along with her: "It's necessary to help your students recognize their mistakes and correct them. In this way one prevents them from repeating those mistakes. . . ."

Hadi Besharat went into a comalike sleep on the rug. A stupor mixed everything in his head and reminded him strangely of events belonging to forty years past. He was thinking again of Ramezan the ice seller's wedding night. Late in the evening a flunky became the cupbearer, pouring arak for the street Arabs with finesse, leaving a line around the cup's rim like a circle of silk thread. Then the other flunkies and the knife wielders began to find fault with his manner of serving. Hassan the wheel said, "Abbas Agha, you changed hands in the middle of pouring. You don't measure up. The medicine is getting to us and we feel terrible. Last Friday night it was Ali the limp's turn. Until the crack of dawn he poured for us, each cup in exactly the same style. Each cup had the same silk thread around its rim. You should have been there and learned how it's done."

They started to fight, making seven or eight pistachio slits in each flunky's neck before the policeman took them downtown. But on the way they made up and returned all together. They gambled at knucklebone till the early hours of the morning and they ate rich, cardamom-syrup ice cream from the barrels that Ramezan the ice seller rented to children for their business. Then they heard the call for the strangers to leave. The guests left the house and the sounds gradually faded away. Hadi Besharat stood at the edge of the courtyard pool, mesmerized by the lights dying off one by one. In the dark he heard the sound of a running stream and the breeze passing over the rooftops, he saw the moonlight and the shadow of the water pitcher and the fish swimming in the pool, he felt the air's moist thin sheet touching his skin. If he could find a double-trunked pedal-brake bicycle he would ride it around the pool. He would pass through the flower beds and play with his moonlight shadow. How could people sleep in such beautiful weather? He went upstairs to the veranda and opened the bridal-chamber door. Ramezan the ice seller called, "Who is it?"

The Pilgrim's Rules of Etiquette

Hadi Besharat recited the famous verses by Saadi that he had just memorized:

> *"The clouds, the wind, the moon, the sun, and the sky*
> > *are working,*
> > *So you can win a loaf of bread, eat it,*
> > *And not be blind to the beauty of creation."*

Ramezan looked at him. "Hadi, are you out of your mind? Don't you feel sleepy? Why aren't you asleep?"

"Oh, how beautiful. Get up, come look at what the moonlight's doing. How can a person go to sleep in weather like this?"

Grumbling to himself, Ramezan pushed aside his quilt and came out to the veranda. The bride was in a deep sleep and didn't move. Ramezan tightened his pajama belt and said, "What a sick-head you are." He looked at the moon and the stars. "But what a wonder this sky is. Would you like to share a few drops of arak? This weather dies for medicine drinking."

"I don't know how to drink."

"What do you know, then? Do you know how to play knucklebone? Do you know how to play chemin de fer?"

"No."

"How about ace?"

"No."

"Don't you know anything?"

"Well, I can make music all on my own."

"You're a musician?"

Hadi Besharat pretended again that he was playing a fiddle. Ramezan said, "Just that? Balls, did you wake me up just for that?"

He turned back to the bridal chamber, taking with him the bottle of arak and a tumbler. He squatted in the doorway and poured himself some arak. Raising the tumbler toward Hadi Besharat, he said, "To your health."

"What are you going to do tomorrow? Are you going to the vegetable market?"

"I'll go to the old soap factory. It's Ali the limp's turn. We play knucklebone there." He held the imaginary knucklebones of a sheep in his hand, threw them into the air, and slapped his thigh. "I deal the knucklebones pretty well. I swear by your life, by St. Hosein. I'll tell you the truth, you're like me."

The two of them squatted and watched the moonlight for an hour. They heard the fluttering of a moth in the dark.

Now he woke up on the rug in his study, and he felt excited. He wanted to get out of the house no matter what. He couldn't even wait to change clothes. The snow had stopped. Everything, separate and distinct, touched the skin of his body. He listened to Nili's footsteps in the kitchen as she made breakfast. Without his permission, without any hesitancy or consideration, she walked about and sang in a nasal voice:

> *"Next time I fall in love,*
> *I'll fall in love with you."*

It no longer mattered to Hadi Besharat. He wasn't connected to anything. He even enjoyed the commotion that disturbed the house's silence. He went downstairs, feeling alive at the touch of the air's pleasant warmth. The smell of toast made him hungry. Nili pointed a spoon at him and said in English, "Hello, good morning." Then in Farsi, "Go ahead and drink your grape juice. After that I'll serve you bread and butter and tea."

A glass of grape juice was waiting for him on the table, the sunlight breaking along its side. He wrapped his fur cloak around himself and sat slowly on a chair. "Aah . . ."

"Professor Besharat, how nicely you're dressed." In English, "Very good, very good." In Farsi again, "It looks like you're going out. Where's your umbrella, then?"

"I want to go to Mobilization Headquarters."

"Oh? Mobilization Headquarters? Does this mean you're excusing yourself from traveling to St. Yahya's Shrine?"

"Miss Nili, I'm amazed at how you entertain yourself with these silly ideas. What news from Farangu?"

Nili giggled. "If Miss Farangu were back, what would I be doing here?"

Hadi Besharat cupped his chin in his hand and looked out at the courtyard, thinking of the spring days heading his way. Burning sunlight needled the snow, dizzying the air so he couldn't tell the difference between cold weather and hot. Spokes of light passed through the cracks in the walls, neutralizing the lingering smells of the house. It was like standing on the sharp edge of anticipation. A sense of spaciousness heartened him, priming him for good news or an important letter. He reached a hand into his pocket, but his hand didn't feel like his own. It was something new for him to touch his key ring, the coins and bits of lint in his pocket. He felt he was in someone else's body. Nili called, "You're dragging this out too long." In English, "Hurry up." In Farsi, "Eat your breakfast. Why haven't you started eating?"

Hadi Besharat dropped a sugar lump into his tumbler of tea. He stirred it and said, "Miss Nili, how vast this life is, how complex."

Nili sat down, resting her elbows on the table and smiling delightedly. "Don't you want to go out and amuse yourself?"

"Not to amuse myself, no."

Nili sighed. "Don't you want to go visit Mehrdad's grave?"

"How time flies. How soon we get used to anything. When was it that poor boy passed away? We seem to have lost track of the days."

Nili grew thoughtful. "Even the face on your wall is fading." She looked at Hadi Besharat. "I'd better get the dishes washed before we leave for St. Yahya's Shrine."

"No, no, I have something else to do. You go on home. Then, if you like, come back in the afternoon."

"I'll keep busy right here. Don't worry about me. I won't bother you."

She took the tray back to the kitchen. Hadi Besharat stood up and gazed around the room. He ought to plant hyacinth bulbs in the vases, in preparation for the New Year. Also, the house needed a good cleaning. Now his feeling of anticipation was changing to a ticking worry, like a star giving off the light's heartbeat, the pulse of life making a galaxy infinite with each beat, generating a fear of falling. He collected the food coupons from the kitchen counter and put them in his pocket. Then he picked up his shopping bag. Nili saw him and asked, "Where are you going?"

"I'm going to Mobilization Headquarters, and I'll shop for some food on the way. We're out of meat."

"Don't buy bread. We already have plenty. You just go to Mobilization Headquarters. I'll do the shopping myself. You're not experienced in these things."

"No need to worry about it. I'll learn."

Nili smiled with her eyes wide. "Professor Besharat, see how mean you are? You won't let a person do you any favors."

Hadi Besharat puffed up his cheeks, raised his shoulders, and put on a self-mocking expression. Nili patted him on the arm a couple of times. "Now you run along, but remember I'm here and I'm ready to do whatever you want."

"I am indebted, Miss Nili."

After he had put on his wraps he left the house and walked slowly toward the avenue. He asked a boy where the butcher shop was. The heavy and foreboding mood lifted from his heart. The passersby didn't seem as tough-looking as usual. They passed him softly like shadows and they stood in lines in front of the shops. He saw no difference between them and the ancient warriors. Both groups had crossed the boundaries of possibility, transforming their struggles into some sort of endurance, some sort of immunity against the hardships of time. It seemed that the city was disarmed by these people's natural simplicity.

He felt he was looking at the streets through the wrong end of a telescope. The streets followed each other, long and narrow. Vehicles panted at the stoplights. There was a sense of persistence in the way the black and green banners hung. There was a wasted look in the unfinished buildings and a languor in the rusting cranes. No doubt a mourner stood waiting for a bus on the corner. A military commander was dreaming of hills and fields under the ceiling of the night porch in the mosque. A shrouded volunteer was preparing himself to go to the front, searching for Mobilization Headquarters in the city's back alleys.

Hadi Besharat stood in line in front of the butcher shop. When his turn came he realized he'd mistaken the bakery for the butcher shop. Even so, he took out his billfold, counted the banknotes, bought two loaves of flatbread, and put them in his shopping bag. He asked a middle-aged man, "Which way to the butcher shop?"

The man puffed on his cigarette and smiled to cover his scorn. "Agha-jon, there are plenty of butcher shops everywhere. But you have to stay in line for seven or eight hours. Go to the traffic intersection. I know a man there who can sell you meat at black-market rates."

"Are you retired?"

"Me? Retired from what?"

"Retired from your position. Like everybody else. I didn't mean anything specific. I just wanted to make conversation."

"It doesn't matter. No harm done. Yes, I'm retired."

Hadi Besharat kept going till he reached the traffic intersection, where he bought one kilogram of boneless meat at black-market prices. Then he walked up the avenue to the Shahin Bookstore. The sun had warmed the air and his galoshes sank into the snow easily. How long before the first day of spring? How long before the New Year celebration? Soon they would bring hyacinths and daffodils to the market. Once again the wax ducks would spin on top of the water in ceramic bowls. The wheat and lentils would sprout in the traditional copper plates and the violets would bloom. The earth would turn warm and his heart would long for travel in a grassy land. Spring had to be near.

Rather than bearing news of the future, spring always reminded him of the world's unreliability and the fickleness of life.

It is springtime, rise
And let us go sightseeing.
You can't trust the days
To bring back the springtime once again.

At the back of his head, from somewhere in the back alleys, moment by moment he heard the sound of a pickax hitting gravel, repeating in his ears a sound like coins being counted:

Dang, dang,
Dang, dang.

With each step he took a stronger apprehension pierced his heart. He walked toward Mobilization Headquarters and imagined it was behind this building that they were digging. Schoolchildren followed each other and disappeared one by one into the emptiness of the alleys. Under his breath he began to recite a prayer. "I beseech the One Whose hand unties the knot in any trouble and the One Whose power makes any hardship easy to endure . . ."

Dang, dang.

He passed through the crowd to enter the Mobilization Headquarters Building, mumbling under his breath, "God forgive those who are gone from this world. Let the light of mercy shine on their graves."

Dang, dang.

An old man took a handful of dust from the ground and scattered it into the pit.

Dang, dang.

That sound awakened the memory-monster in his mind, taking him by the hand and leading him through the orchard paths of Khezrabad. His late father and Fakhr Zanjani were talking in front of Khezrabad's passion-play theater. A trained parrot sat on Fakhr Zanjani's finger, picking sunflower seeds from his mouth. The coal trucks were arriving from Shemshak. The summer people were packing their belongings, climbing into the dusty cars and buses, and heading back to the city. With the coming of fall the leaves were turning a saffron yellow.

They stood there looking at the Guchak Pass until the helmets, sabers, and shields emerged from the dust. The passion players were returning like a defeated army. In their green turbans and yellow robes, they would sing their lament for two weeks. The peasants would poke their heads out of the wheat and alfalfa fields. Then they would follow the passion players.

Fakhr Zanjani recommended that, if Hadi Besharat's father wanted to improve his harvest, he should bury bones and dead animals on his farm. It was a mistake to think that a cemetery was unsuitable for farming. He knew of a cemetery with plum trees planted all over it. "Agha, you haven't seen plums so big in your life." He made a cluster of his fingers. "This big, very sweet and juicy. Cemeteries get fertilized in a natural way."

His father pushed his hat back on his forehead, wrinkling his meaty, thick-skinned face. "The water in cemeteries has lime in it. It gives you amnesia."

"Nonsense. Don't listen to that."

They walked slowly toward a tent before which Fakhr Zanjani had put a suitcase, a pitcher, and a Primus stove. As the evening shadows stretched across the fields Hadi Besharat felt sad. The water was tumbling in the river, reminding him of the fairy tales hanging in the lost mists of time—the stone-throwing parapet, the emerald castle, and the prince who is sleeping in a silk bed waiting, the sister who is washing her brother's bones in rose water and burying them in a flower bed, the rose that is growing in the flower bed and blooming in the evening breeze, the wandering nightingale that is warbling on a trellis and won't go to sleep till the white of dawn.

Now, row after row, the shrouded volunteers stood in prayer.

He had seen it all before and should not have been surprised. The opening of "Porturne for a Hanged Man" came to his mind like a heavenly message:

> In the precious night when the night rests peacefully,
> The angels and the spirits are descending to earth.
> Your greetings unto him until the dawn.
> O Lord, grant him eternal peace,
> O Lord, shed the light of mercy on his grave,
> O Lord, never forsake, never be wrathful to him.

He crossed the entrance hall of Mobilization Headquarters and climbed the stairs to the second floor. The building was empty, its walls covered with official memoranda, graffiti, and framed photos. The door at the top of the stairs was ajar. Inside this room Haj Ghadam, the Koran reciter, sat cross-legged on a wide chair—just the person to speak with, in these times when religious people were the ones in charge. His beard encircled his face like a woolly rope and he wore a straw nightcap under his little turban. He was playing with a string of worry beads, reciting a prayer with closed eyes and an absorbed expression. Not only his lips but also his jaws moved as he prayed. The movement of his jaws created a looseness in his face as though the lower part were disconnected from the upper part, giving the impression that something had snapped out of place. Even though his eyes were closed, he seemed aware of Hadi Besharat's presence. Eventually he looked up, motioning for Hadi Besharat to be seated. "Greetings. Please sit down."

He spoke so softly that Hadi Besharat could barely hear him. "I don't want to interrupt you."

In the same hushed voice Haj Ghadam asked, "Why not?"

"I thought perhaps you were closed on account of the snow."

"Didn't you come in off the street?"

"Of course."

"Didn't you see the beggars sitting there begging?"

"Of course."

"They haven't closed shop. Why should we?"

"That's how I thought too."

"Welcome. Your visit is a blessing. I don't know what's going on today. No one has come in yet, and sitting here all by myself is wearing me out. There was a time when I had a good voice. Then during the reign of the Monster Shah they fed me collyrium. It ruined my voice and now I can't recite the Koran. Brother, be kind and recite us a verse from the good book and let our spirit rejoice."

Hadi Besharat searched his mind for a suitable passage. A few lines from the chapter "The Merciful" occurred to him:

> *"For the one who fears the station of his Lord,*
> *There will be two gardens.*
> *Oh, which one of your Lord's bounties will you deny?*
> *There will be*
> *Two fountains of running water.*
> *Oh, which one of your Lord's bounties will you deny?"*

"How beautifully you sing! Every word is a cup of rose water, a cup of meaning. You opened the door of a garden for us. You brought us joy."

"Thank you. You are kind. Let me tell you the reason for my visit. I would like to have the honor of going to the front. Is that possible?"

"You want to go to the front for what?"

"To see from close up what's happening."

"Brother, at your age the front would be too much for you. Aside from that, you can't see a thing there. You have to hide yourself in a hole all the time and come out only during attacks. Military attacks usually happen at night. You can't see anything. Would you permit me to risk offending you and share a thought?"

"The choice is yours. I beg you."

Haj Ghadam locked his hands in front of his stomach. Humping his back in a supplicating posture, he said, "I'll write some-

thing for you in the air. If you can read it, you're very clever."
He raised his hand and wrote something in the air with looping
movements of his fingers. He said, "What did I write?"

"You wrote, 'There Is No God But Allah.' "

Haj Ghadam wrote again in the air and asked, "Now what did
I write?"

Hadi Besharat had studied with Fakhr Zanjani the art of
drawing arabesques in the air and inscribing words inside each
other. He nodded and said, "You wrote, 'Glory be to the Lord's
Majesty.' "

Haj Ghadam smiled with satisfaction. Stroking the curve of
his mustache, he said, "Excellent. God bless you. Where did you
learn the art of arabesques?"

"Our history teacher in high school knew the ancient arts.
During the typhoid epidemic of 1942 he came to our village for
summer vacation. One day I saw him in the field teaching a
peasant how to draw arabesques. I asked, 'What are those designs?' He said, 'What are you waiting for? Sit right down and
learn how to do it.' It made an impression on me. I sat down and
learned the art of arabesques."

"God forgive his sins."

Haj Ghadam pulled out a form and placed it in front of Hadi
Besharat. Rubbing his hands together and tilting his head, he
said, "Well, please fill in this questionnaire carefully. Give your
name, address, the number of your identity card, the date and
place of its issuance. It won't hurt to write a short explanation of
why you want to go to the front. God willing, going to the front
is a blessing. Don't forget to remember us in your prayers."

Hadi Besharat went over to a corner and sat on a chair.
Resting one ankle on his knee, he placed the form on his foot
and began to write:

In His name, the Almighty,
  Whereas each individual is basically a human being before possessing a nationality or a religion, whereas the human soul is thirsty for the knowledge of truth and experi-

ences history in its mathematical form, this servant of God has decided to go to the front on account of his natural talent, trying to see what is the truth in the world. Verse:

> The thirsty always dream of water,
> The hungry always fancy the flatbread.

The ancient as well as contemporary scholars have always studied mathematics before studying philosophy and history. If my works are considered valuable at all, it is only because of the theories I have advanced regarding mathematical history. I am well aware that the mathematical sciences do not belong to Iranians alone. On the contrary, the zero was invented in India and no one can deny the importance of the Arabs' contributions to mathematics (especially in Ibn Hathim's work). Nevertheless, only Iranian thinkers like Avecina and Abu Rayhan Beiruni have raised the basic philosophical questions and I would like to give a couple of examples.

One question asks why underground waters are warm in winter and cold in summer. Another question asks whether sunlight is warm in itself or warms up when touching objects. In my opinion it is warm in itself, as Avecina proclaimed. But also I would like to join Abu Rayhan Beiruni and state, "Our time is pregnant with wonders." I am thirsty to know these wonders. Each limb in my worn-out body is burning with the fire of this thirst. (A strange and torturing fever which a delicate individual like me does not have the strength to fight—alas!) I request permission to go to the battlefield. I want to go!

At the foot of the form he jotted down his name, address, family history, and educational background. Then he handed the form back to Haj Ghadam. Haj Ghadam read it carefully. Then he placed it on the desk and looked straight into Hadi Besharat's eyes. "How strange, Professor Besharat! You are a rare human being, like that mythical bird Angha. But I think you are mistaken and you're going the wrong way. It's better for you to follow your studies right here and educate our people's children."

"Would you allow me to share a basic idea with you?"

Haj Ghadam knotted his brows and narrowed his eyes. "Please go ahead, Professor."

"Your Excellency doesn't know why it's important that I go to the front. It isn't just for me. My presence at the front can be very helpful to our young military commanders. I am a professor of history and dead languages. I've studied strategy and military tactics. It's true I haven't traveled to Mesopotamia before. But I know every inch of that land like the palm of my hand. I can help."

"How can you help?"

"I'll describe a situation as an example. The present-day commanders depend only on material instruments. They figure out how many bombers, rockets, guns, tanks, and spare parts they need. But ancient military commanders paid attention to another matter as well. They had a respect for land and water. Land and water speak the language of allusion. Among all the ancient commanders, Xerxes was the only one who flogged the ocean. But his naval force was set on fire by the Greeks."

"Forgive me, brother, what are you talking about?"

"I didn't mean to insult you with too many complicated phrases. When I was a child I never slept on our rooftop with my back to the sky. Because that would be an insult and insults make human beings lonesome. You'll get lost in yourself. You look at the wall and see a monster."

"Are you living alone in the house now or are you with somebody?"

"My wife has been gone for two days and she's left me all to myself. Being retired is also a problem. Even if I were not retired, it's difficult to find a good student in this day and age. I had one student who read his lessons well and understood them. He had a passion for ancient history. But he went to the front to see ancient history from close up. Now they say he is martyred. How I cautioned him! I told him a hundred times, 'Agha-jon, always hide in well-covered places and always hold your gun ready.' I'm afraid he might have missed the point."

"You should trust God. Your student is in Paradise now and keeps company with the innocent saints as his reward."

"I told him, 'If you see frightened animals in a field, that means the enemy is making a sudden assault. Dust in the air is a sign of an approaching army. Birds fly over only that land that's already vacated by the enemy.' But unfortunately today's youths don't lend their ears to old people like us. As the poet says, 'In this world, there should be two lives for the wise and the artful. They should gain experience in one life and use that experience in the other.' "

"Professor, do you want me to take you home?"

"No need to trouble yourself. I can go there on my own. But the human being always has his problems. Just look." He extended his clawed hands and then burst into laughter. "I don't know how to move my own hands anymore."

"Why are you laughing?"

"Think about it. I have lived in this district for a long time. I know its every nook and cranny. I've known everybody here for eighteen years. But now I come to you to pour out my troubles. If you were in my place, wouldn't you laugh too?"

"Agha-jon, why should I laugh? We're all each other's brothers. No one is a stranger among us." Haj Ghadam pinched his lower lip and smiled. "I have a story I want to tell you. I think you're going to like it. Today I was praying at dawn and I heard a breaking sound coming from our tree in the courtyard. Our tree doesn't have any leaves. In the middle of this snow, it's standing dry and bare. But you could tell from that breaking sound that the sap is moving in its veins and spring is on its way. Brother, the ointment for life's wounds is the passage of time."

Haj Ghadam stood up and gave Hadi Besharat a bear hug. Hadi Besharat looked for his umbrella and shopping bag. But before he left he laid a hand on Haj Ghadam's sleeve and said, "How long till I'll have an answer?"

"Stop by in a day or two. Meanwhile, don't forget. If you need something give me a call. Maybe I can find a way out, God willing."

"Could I ask you a favor?"

"Please."

"My home is nearby. If you wish, honor me and come for a visit."

"By God, I don't have much free time. I'm so busy. But if I find a minute, of course I'll visit you."

"Should I give you my phone number?"

"Not a bad idea. Here, use this."

Haj Ghadam handed him another form, and Hadi Besharat wrote his number on the back of it. Haj Ghadam looked at it closely. He said, "This is a wrong number. One digit is missing."

"You see? I made another mistake."

He added the final digit. Haj Ghadam said, "No problem. At night, look toward this window. I'll draw arabesques in the air with a flashlight."

"Why would you want to do that?"

"To let you know I'm here."

Hadi Besharat bent his head. He said, "I thank you for your kindness. I hope you'll be even more kind."

"May the hand of St. Ali be your protection."

Hadi Besharat picked up his shopping bag and went downstairs and out into the street. But he didn't want to go home. Now he was thinking about finding an empty house with no known owner. He could take possession of it, the way the humbled masses did. He looked down the street toward the stain on his wall. The dampness had been absorbed in the warmth of the sunlight, leaving a circular pattern behind. It was like the patterns made by wind on a salty shore, like stripped, plowed land extending to the edge of the horizon. He imagined himself with a knapsack on his back and his robe on his shoulders, heading toward an uncertain fate. That sense of isolation helped him to wait for events without any forced planning. He thought of Mani's silhouette in the corner of his prison cell and the moonlight slanting down to the floor from the barred window. It was an echo of his own disturbed mind, recalling the hanging at dawn.

> *In the precious night when the night rests peacefully,*
> *The angels and the spirits are descending to earth.*
> *Your greetings unto him until the dawn.*
> *O Lord, grant him eternal peace,*
> *O Lord, shed the light of mercy on his grave,*
> *O Lord, never forsake, never be wrathful to him.*

He arrived at his house. He was taking off his coat and galoshes when he heard Nili and Heli talking. It was as if they were preparing the house for the New Year celebration. There were signs of clutter and disorganization everywhere. One of them was walking around upstairs. From where he stood he could see that his study door was open. Obviously they had searched every corner, perhaps disturbed his notes and writings as well. He climbed the stairs quickly and stuck his head into his study.

Nili was sitting on the floor reading a thick book. He couldn't see Heli. He only sensed that she was walking around barefoot in Khosro's old room, no doubt groping through his toys, his paintings and plaster busts.

Without a word he returned to the first floor. He listened to the sounds of the house with some sort of indifference, some sort of peacefulness. It seemed as if he had crossed an ocean and now he was stepping onto a safe shore. Just as he'd been expecting for so long, everything was matched by its counterpart, everything confirmed a truth. He was awakening to find himself in a world where events moved slowly, as if he'd been drugged. He was standing in a place that looked familiar despite its total strangeness. A feeling came over him. Surely this was how the poet Rumi had felt when he met his spiritual guide Shams of Tabriz, or how St. Augustine had felt in Cassiciacum. He had suddenly opened his eyes and the brilliance of the landscape dazzled him like a sheet of burning copper. He told himself, "How strange! This is how it is, then. Why didn't I know this before?"

His joints felt loose and a sweat appeared on his forehead. He sat down very slowly in a chair and gazed around him. He saw Heli descending the stairs. For some time now he had failed to notice the details in the blind girl's face. Her wavy hair was almost silver blue, graying prematurely. A purple patch spread around her membrane-covered eyes. It was defined by a clear border, like a country on a map, as it reached her pale lemon skin. It gave her mellowed face an expression of adjustment to her blindness and acceptance of the dark. The words of a prayer came to his tongue like soap bubbles: "No evolution and no power exists but by Allah's will."

Heli approached him, bent her head toward him, and said, "Professor Besharat, when did you come in? We didn't hear you."

Hadi Besharat held up the shopping bag and said absentmindedly, "I bought these."

"What did you buy?"

"You said you can see everything. See what I've bought."

"How can I see? I can only sense things. I don't think you're feeling well. Are you angry at Nili?"

"What for?"

"Maybe because she goes to your study without your permission. Maybe because she opens your books and reads them."

Hadi Besharat said, "Miss Heli, that's not important to me anymore."

Heli rounded her mouth in disbelief. "Oh."

Hadi Besharat stood up to carry the shopping bag to the kitchen. But then he stopped and asked Heli, "Do you need meat and flatbread?"

"Why?"

"Take these to your house."

"Professor Besharat, don't you want them? It's bad for you not to eat. You'll get weak. You have to think about your future."

"Miss Heli, what is the future? The future is now."

"If the future is now, I wouldn't have any reason to tell your fortune. Wait, I'll read your fortune in your coffee cup."

With her sightless face, Heli searched the entrance hall, and then she turned and went out to the kitchen. Hadi Besharat thought of a spring breeze that had awakened him many years ago. The breeze had come in a rush, paused, and then once again hit his face. When he lifted his head from the pillow raindrops were falling from the willow branches onto the courtyard pool, mixing up the patches of light. The echo of the raindrops' tapping resonated in the air. The cistern in the basement breathed in harmony with weightless moving images. It was like leaves stirring in their places in the quiet of the afternoon, like the reflection of the water rippling intermittently on a damp lime wall.

Nili came downstairs very slowly. She held an open book in her hands and the hem of her black skirt dragged behind her on the stairs. A lock of hair fell by one ear, as if it were taking a drink from her fair cheek. But Hadi Besharat wasn't concerned with the content of what he saw. He was concerned only with rotations, evolutions, and transformations. He felt the vibration of an angel's wing on his face. There was a name on the tip of his tongue that he couldn't pronounce. He was experiencing something that would never reach completion. To understand the experience was beyond him and therefore the experience kept repeating itself. He sat back down on his chair and looked around in amazement. Nili came over to him and said, "Professor Besharat, how bright the sun is today. We ought to go sightseeing."

Hadi Besharat held his head between his hands and began weeping quietly. He might have been sitting in a passion-recital party, listening to the tragedy of the Prophet's household. Nili said nothing. She just stood looking at him with childish sympathy. Finally she broke the silence. "I swear to God, please don't take it so hard."

Hadi Besharat stopped crying. He raised his damp face and said, smiling, "You misunderstand. These tears are making me happy. I don't know how to say it. I didn't expect this feeling. It's new to me. It's not something I have borrowed from the past. It's not history. My dear, the discovery of history depends upon our hearts."

Nili sat on a step, hugging her knees. She said, "Didn't you talk to Mehrdad the same way?" In English, "Very intelligent!"

"Oh, Miss Nili, you are kind. You embarrass this poor soul wandering in the desert of bewilderment. How forgiving! How generous!"

"What forgiving, what generous? All I said was the truth."

"No. You're not aware of your feelings. The meaning of being young is just that. You don't know what you're saying. Oh, ignorant and innocent youth! As soon as you become aware of your feelings the innocence will leave you."

Heli appeared with a tray of Turkish coffee in her hands. Nili looked relieved and said, "Heli has made Turkish coffee and wants to read the grounds for us."

With a trembling hand Hadi Besharat took a cup from the tray and drank half the coffee in a gulp. He tasted a few of the grounds in his mouth and said, "Miss Nili, please put on a record for us. Let's listen to a little music."

"Professor Besharat, we have to be quiet now and let Heli tell your fortune."

Hadi Besharat took another gulp and said, "General opinion has it that the word 'music' is taken from 'Musa,' the goddess of art, knowledge, and song. But I believe its true origin is Syriac. In Syriac, *mu* means 'air' and *zic* means 'to knot.' In other words, music is the art that delicately knots the empty air. Some others believe that 'music' is a synthesis of the Arabic phrase, *Musa, ghee,* which originally was addressed to Moses. It means, 'Moses, memorize these melodies.' "

He set his empty cup upside down on the saucer and passed it back to Heli. Heli stood holding it and waiting for the grounds to dry. She said, "Today we have to go to the airport and see General Ghovanlu and his wife off."

Nili said, "God kill me. I'd forgotten all about it. Mrs. Razi is going too."

Heli said, "They've been granted their passports and they'll travel to Zahedan this afternoon. From there they fly secretly to Pakistan. They don't want anyone to know about it. I told them, 'Bon voyage, where are you going?' They said, 'We're going to Mashad for the New Year holidays.' "

Hadi Besharat stood up, clasped his hands behind his back, and paced in front of the door. "I asked the late Fakhr Zanjani, 'What is the meaning of the expression, "shaking one's sleeves on the two worlds"?' He said, 'It means to part with all your worldly possessions and grow solitary. . . .' "

Heli asked Nili, "Nili-jon, what do you see in the cup?"

Nili took the cup from her and turned it right side up. She examined the patterns left by the coffee grounds. "In this corner something is curled around itself. There's a white spot, too. It has wings like a butterfly. Heli-jon, you tell me what it means."

Heli said, "Undoubtedly that is the picture of a bride wearing her lace dress and sitting in the bridal chamber. She should have a tiara on her head. Her tiara should look like the full moon."

"I don't know what this other spot is. Something like a wheel with seven spokes, like a spindle. Something, I don't know what."

Heli said, "The picture of a bride is a good omen. It means that someone is dreaming in front of the wedding tray. She's waiting and thinking of the future."

The two sisters were so absorbed in his cup, they didn't even notice when Hadi Besharat rose and left them. He climbed the stairs to his study, took his suitcase from the daybed, and carried it back down with him. He opened it out on the little table in the hall. Carefully he rearranged his socks and underwear. He rubbed his fingers in the air, looking hesitantly at the suitcase to see if something was missing. "Do you see this suitcase?" he asked the sisters. "I bought it in Seville. You have to see Seville. For eight centuries it hasn't changed at all. You walk in the Santa Cruz district and all of a sudden the smell of jasmine hits your nose. The jasmine trees there are very tall. The cathedrals in Seville have minarets. What a sun, miss! The Spanish sun drives you crazy, like the scent of jasmine."

Under his breath he counted his rolled socks one by one. He saw the package of rock candy and he raised his eyebrows. "Miss, the warm sun in the south works miracles for arthritis. When I get to Dizful, every day I'll stretch out in the sun for half an hour till the sweat rolls all over my body. Oh, Lord, where did I put my shaving kit? It was right in front of me a minute ago. When you get up in age, forgetfulness hands you a cane." He took his eyes from the suitcase and looked at Nili. "Miss, you . . . you being so young, how can you understand forgetfulness?"

Nili's face radiated a smile and she squeezed the coffee cup between her hands. Heli leaned against the banister and continued her fortunetelling. "Maybe it's also the picture of a person whose dear one is in a distant land. . . ."

Hadi Besharat asked, "Can you tell me what I can expect from my travels?"

"Professor Besharat, this fortunetelling is only for our amusement. I don't know what you'll run into during your travels."

Hadi Besharat thought for a moment. "Any time I go on a trip, I think I'll run into Fakhr Zanjani. It's unbelievable, miss. This idea just now occurred to me. Sometimes I'm sitting and thinking. All of a sudden I want to get up and leave the house. But in truth I expect to run into Fakhr Zanjani at the head of the street. Really. I want to know how he'll react after nearly forty years. Will he recognize me? Will he recognize Engineer Gharib?"

Nili said, "He couldn't possibly recognize you after nearly forty years."

Hadi Besharat sat down again. "I don't know. You can't imagine. You arrange certain scenes in your mind all the time. You picture the late Fakhr Zanjani in various situations and you try to guess what he would be saying to you, how he would behave."

Heli said, "It sounds to me as if you really didn't know the late Fakhr Zanjani. You put him in those situations as a way of trying to get acquainted with him."

Hadi Besharat was taken aback. She was right. He had traveled the world over. But it occurred to him that he hadn't moved even one step from the traffic intersection in his own district. How was it possible to wait at a traffic intersection for the length of a lifetime? Such immobility would stiffen a human being's knees. Termites would eat the inside of his cane and turn it into dust. Instead of grass, a jungle would grow beneath his feet. He wished Professor Humphrey were there so they could discuss this. He could explain to Professor Humphrey that all his travels were actually a prolonged state of expectation. He hadn't taken even one step beyond the traffic intersection. Maybe Professor Humphrey knew that already. At the New York airport he had told Hadi Besharat, "You're not returning to Iran just to see your homeland. You're going back for a person who doesn't exist anymore."

Hadi Besharat had been so anxious to get home that he'd paid no attention to Professor Humphrey's words. A gigantic poster of the Statue of Liberty covered the entire surface of one wall in the terminal. He pulled out his camera, climbed a few steps, and held his camera in such a way that every bit of the Statue of Liberty, from her pedestal to the tip of her torch, was included in the viewfinder. Professor Humphrey had laughed. "Are you taking a picture of a picture? Why don't you buy a postcard instead?"

Hadi Besharat closed one eye and bent his knees as he spoke. "A postcard's no good." He advanced the film in his camera. "I want to take a picture from way up high, so people in Tehran will think I've photographed the statue from a helicopter."

The windows of the Mobilization Headquarters Building could be seen far beyond the courtyard. Sunlight smoothed the white of its walls. Hadi Besharat said, "Miss Heli, I'm indebted for the comment you made. I don't know how to thank you."

Heli said, "Don't think about it. It was nothing."

"Oh, no, miss. You spoke beautifully. What can I say with my ordinary words? One can speak like you only with the language of allusion."

Nili broke in and said, "You've done it again. I'll kill you, Professor. You're too complimentary."

Hadi Besharat pointed to the sky. "What do you do when you arrive in a strange country and you want to ask for water? Either you have to point to water or you have to mimic the act of drinking. You can speak only in pantomime. Pantomime is the language of allusion. Miss Heli, we can use other mediums for the blind. For example, if I want to tell you how indebted I feel for your kindness, I could kiss your hand this way."

He took hold of Heli's fingertips, lowered his head, and soundlessly kissed the back of her hand. Heli smiled. "Why, Professor Besharat? You don't need any other language. You talk very nicely."

Hadi Besharat kissed the back of her hand one more time, and his shoulders trembled with silent weeping. "Oh, Miss Heli, you are so kind to me. Listening to your voice is like listening to the angels singing. . . ."

The telephone rang. Hadi Besharat jumped up from his seat. He wiped his eyes with his palms and looked around him. He was afraid to pick up the receiver and hear Farangu's voice. Nili said, "Professor Besharat, run! Maybe it's Miss Farangu." She clapped her hands together and pretended to be running as she stood there. "Hurry, now. Get to the phone quickly. Otherwise they'll hang up."

Slowly Hadi Besharat crossed the corridor and picked up the receiver. Voices came to him from the bottom of a long, distant funnel. The misconnections in the international lines mingled several conversations together. On the other side of the ocean a woman was saying good-bye. But she couldn't bring herself to hang up. Behind her whispers another person waited in silence. Hadi Besharat guessed that it must be Khosro. But he wasn't certain. It could be Professor Humphrey himself. He pressed the receiver very hard to his ear and said, "Hello? . . . Hello?"

He heard Khosro's distant, croaky voice. "Papa-jon, Papa-jon, is that you?"

"Yes. This is me. How are you feeling?"

"Did you hear that Mr. Bayat never sent my money and now I'm bankrupt? If I ever come back I'll put a bomb in front of his house. Whatever I had or didn't have, all went down the drain. He ruined me."

"Aah, why?"

"Why? Because we had too many expenses and not enough customers. For one whole week we've been standing in front of the car wash and not a single customer showed up."

"Where is your car wash?"

"In the middle of nowhere."

"Well, was it so hard to find a good place? Why did you open a car wash in the middle of nowhere? Anyone who doesn't live by logic ends up like this. Then you want to put a bomb in front of a person's house?"

Khosro raised his voice. "Please stop lecturing me on how to live. I learned my lessons in the arms of a sacrificing, pure, and matchless mother. That mother has to wander in the streets so you can lecture me on how to live."

"Khosro, who's lecturing you on how to live? You've dug a pit for yourself and now you want to blame it on me?"

"You don't know anything about my style of living, my style of thinking, my beliefs and disbeliefs. You told Mr. Bayat that the basic foundation of my life is wrong and you need to correct it. You are determined to save me, to save this lunatic from his own stupidity."

"What sort of Farsi is this language you're talking? What beliefs and disbeliefs? What basic foundation?"

"You are very much mistaken. I prefer my homeless mother's lectures to yours. I prefer to fill my stomach forever with a bullet rather than extend a begging hand to you."

Khosro fell silent. No doubt he was expecting some jaw-breaking answer. Hadi Besharat glanced at Nili and Heli, wishing to reassure them. He covered the receiver with his hand and told the sisters, "Nothing important. It's Khosro. He likes to nag a little." Then he removed his hand and said loudly, "Khosro, you were brought up by your father, who always made sure you wouldn't lose heart when confronted with life's hardships. Of course, you shouldn't extend a begging hand to anyone. You shouldn't ruin your brain cells by eating that odd country's moldy bread and worm-infested cheese. If you did that, of course I am the guilty one and I should compensate for my faults."

Khosro took a fresh breath and asked more quietly, "When are you going to send me the twenty thousand?"

"Son, there's not even a sigh in my pocket. If I send you anything, it'll be my fatherly affection. In my opinion that is much more valuable than any money."

"Papa-jon, Papa-jon, you have to do something! I'm stuck here. I can't pay my bank debts with fatherly affection. Also Mama has bought her plane ticket and she'll be landing here in three days. How can I take care of her? Don't let her come."

"Mama has gone to her Mama Aliyeh's for a while. She doesn't listen to anyone. I'll write you a letter explaining."

Khosro spoke with passion. "I can't make any sense of your letters! You always write in secret codes. Good-bye, Papa."

Khosro hung up. Hadi Besharat held the receiver away from him and looked at it for a few seconds. Heli asked, "How's he doing? Did he get his diploma?"

Hadi Besharat absentmindedly put down the receiver. "He'll get it. He has some problems. Time has no meaning for young people. Whatever they want has to appear in front of them immediately."

He put his hands in all his pockets, making sure that his billfold, notebook, and fountain pen were in their places. Generally he was resigned. It seemed to him that someone had lived in this house who was already gone. Someone who did not have flesh or skin or bone anymore but was a pure spirit. A blind person who saw no light but was light. A deaf person who heard no sound but was sound. For him this sound was changing into the whisper of an unceasing song. A song from the East wandering through the protracted centuries, searching hard for words. Children cheat their parents with their secret hurts and get even. They are unfamiliar with the voices of the past. They bear on their shoulders only the weight of the future.

The house seemed dark and choked. He didn't have the heart to stay there any longer. The light was still on in front of Khosro's room. Recently he'd been turning it off every morning, leaving it burning only at night. He went upstairs to see to it. Nili called after him, asking, "What do you want to do now?"

Surprised, he turned to look down at her. A thought occurred to him and he said, "Call a cab. Let's take a cab and go out. I'll pay for it."

"Where do you want us to go? To the airport? To see the travelers off?"

Hadi Besharat flicked the light switch. Then he stood in front of Khosro's room. He was about to close the door but something stopped him. Farangu's door was open too. He saw her negligee. She had forgotten to take it from its hook on the wall.

He entered Khosro's room and sat on a chair in the corner. Farangu had cleaned the room very thoroughly. The books and the clothes were neatly arranged in their places. The shadows were gathered around the pale shafts of light, making the room seem emptier. The ranks of toy soldiers extended one behind the other, and a perpetual peacefulness watched over the room. From downstairs Nili's voice reached him. "Professor Besharat, the cab will be here soon. Let's go."

He answered, "I'm coming, I'm coming."

His knees didn't help as he struggled to his feet. Since Farangu had left, a thin layer of dust had fallen on Khosro's desk. He went over to the desk and passed a hand across it. Then he glanced at his palm. It was gray with dust.

N I N E

Hadi Besharat waited outside his house while Nili took Heli home. Heli was supposed to look after Mr. Bayat until they returned from the airport. Everyone else was at the airport already, saying good-bye to General Ghovanlu and his wife and Mrs. Razi.

For a moment Hadi Besharat thought something seemed different. It was true that people were quietly going about their business, and up the avenue, the traffic flowed in a natural way. But underneath was an ambiguous silence. He asked himself, "What's going on here? What's happened?"

A few steps away the cab sat idling. The driver was counting his money behind the wheel while he listened to the radio. The radio was broadcasting the passion of St. Muslem's children. The passion reciter was so grief-stricken that he couldn't control his voice. He wailed:

> *"Oh, Hosein, if my heart*
> *Did not accept your burden of your loss,*
> *It carried the burden of your tragedy all alone.*
> *Hosein, Hosein-jon . . ."*

The mourners' sobs resounded like the clapping of hands in the highlands. From somewhere far away, the lamenters set up a cry:

The Pilgrim's Rules of Etiquette

"Hosein-jon,
Hosein-jon,
Hosein-jon . . ."

The passion reciter continued: "Let me give an introduction to prepare you and then I'll sing you the tragedy. They say that when you go from Karbala to Damascus you see two tiny domes near the place where the massacre occurred fourteen centuries ago. . . ." He was referring to the shrines at the burial site of St. Muslem's two children. The crowd wept and the passion reciter started to sing, "Hosein, Hosein-jon, tonight is the night to be kind to orphans. Orphans like whom? Like St. Muslem's children . . ."

Hadi Besharat could imagine the passion reciter standing at the pulpit, raising and lowering his hands for the mourners, putting his fingers together like a cone, pounding a fist to give weight to each word. First he described some unrelated events. Then, bit by bit, he discussed children in general and children's relationships with their parents. After that he made a few indirect references to the martyrdom of St. Muslem's two children. Suddenly the mourners started keening and slapping their faces. Hadi Besharat began to worry. He felt as though he were listening to the actual massacre.

Finally Nili emerged from her house and went over to the cab. She saw Hadi Besharat standing in the street. She frowned and held the cab door open for him. Hadi Besharat slid into the rear seat next to her without a word. He pulled his beret low on his forehead and leaned back. Perhaps with Nili there to watch for the unexpected he could take a short nap while he listened to the tragedy of St. Muslem's children.

A band of people rushed along the sidewalk. Buses in the streets and slogans on the walls kept passing him by. Nili tilted her head against the cab window. Beneath her veil she wore earphones, and she hummed along with her cassette recorder in a whisper. Was it just that she didn't want to listen to the tragedy of St. Muslem's children? Or was she cross about something? Hadi Besharat was in no mood to ask. It was enough that the cab was traveling farther and farther away from his own house.

The wailing on the radio was growing too loud. Little by little the passion reciter's story was nearing the day of the Ashura Massacre. Now he had reached the scene where the children embraced each other for the last time. "The closer Ashura came, the more the children worried. Sometimes they walked around Abbas, Hosein's brother, sometimes around Akbar, Hosein's son, sometimes around Hosein himself." He started singing a verse: "Love put the chain of madness on my heart and locked it . . ."

The mourners groaned loudly and shouted in grief. Hadi Besharat listened to the pleasant symphony he had composed in September 1941. When he was alone he used to go to a corner of the little room he'd rented from Ramezan the ice seller and perform his symphony. He would put his imaginary violin on his shoulder and draw his bow across it. Then he would step out into the street, stand in front of Hassan the wheel's shop, and enjoy the sunset. When darkness arrived it seemed to build a dome and court inside the mosque. The stretch of marble at the base of the walls gave the mosque's night porch an unadorned solitude, creating an atmosphere of purity and simplicity.

Hadi Besharat tapped Nili on the shoulder. When she turned to him he asked, "Are you listening to a cassette, miss?"

Nili nodded. "Yes."

Hadi Besharat said, "There's nothing wrong with that. Just make sure no one else notices."

Nili shrugged and pursed her lips, meaning that that was none of her concern. Hadi Besharat pretended he was playing a violin. "Do you know how to play a violin?"

Nili shook her head and smiled apologetically. Hadi Besharat pretended he was playing a sitar. "How about a sitar?"

Nili shook her head again. Hadi Besharat closed his eyes and drew the imaginary bow across his shoulder, putting on an expression of ecstasy. He pretended he was lost in the violin's melody. In his mind the complicated music sometimes ascended, sometimes descended, and sometimes crashed cymbals in an up-roar.

Hadi Besharat's private symphony was often performed by an imaginary orchestra under his own baton. It would take him to a mountain where he could watch foot soldiers and battleships proceeding in rows at his feet. The infantry and naval forces moved in parallel bands. Stone ghosts appeared on the shore as they passed. These statues held their faces upward to the sun, expecting a god to appear from the sea. A strange god who knew no victory or defeat, no mosque, no cathedral, and no temple. A god who drew a map of the world, creating continents, mountains, and oceans from scratch. Like an old nurse who kept constant watch over Hadi Besharat, never speaking a word. Every day this god came out to meet Hadi Besharat like the radiance from a pure light, passing over his desk, books, notes, and index cards. Gradually the light made everything emerge, like a picture being developed. Hadi Besharat imagined himself walking through wheat fields, passing mud houses. The weeping willows hung on both sides of the field. With each step he took, branches bowed down, assuming a rusty color.

Nili seemed happy and absorbed. She said, "I think we're getting close to the airport. Mesgarabad and Behesht Zahra Cemeteries must be south of us. Professor Besharat, weren't you living around there when you came from Khezrabad after the war?"

Hadi Besharat said, "That's right. Somewhere in that area."

Nili said, "I've been there. It has lots of twisting alleys. You can easily get lost."

Hadi Besharat's mind was focused on a voice that came from within, suggesting a prayer. He heard a song floating toward him from the orchards of Khezrabad:

> It is springtime, my beloved,
> And my heart is impatient.
> From the tree branches
> In the middle of the orchards and the gardens
> It rains blossoms, my beloved. . . .

Nili took off her earphones and said, "You love music so much. Why haven't you learned to play an instrument?"

"To play an instrument you need a receptive environment. You can't play just anywhere."

Now the passion reciter had reached the scene where the murderer Hareth finds St. Muslem's children. "The two children are standing in prayer. One of them says, 'Brother, I have seen my father in a dream. I have seen the Prophet in my dream.' The young children throw their arms around each other's necks. That murderer, that bastard lecher, hears their voices . . ."

"What did you say, Professor Besharat? I can't hear you."

"We've reached the airport. I'll tell you later."

"I didn't hear what you said. Will you tell me later?"

Hadi Besharat counted out the cab fare. Nili bent over and told the driver loudly, "Wait right here. We'll be back in half an hour."

Instead of answering, the driver slapped his forehead and his shoulders trembled with sobs. Nili glanced at Hadi Besharat, not daring to say anything else. Hadi Besharat asked the driver, "Will you wait for us?"

The driver nodded rapidly but he couldn't stop crying. He could only motion for them to get out of the cab.

Feeling awkward and embarrassed, Hadi Besharat hurried toward the airport terminal. Nili turned back midway and called to the driver, "Are you all right? Do you need any help?"

The driver wiped the tears from his face and said, "I'm fine. I'll be waiting here for you."

Hadi Besharat said, "Miss, don't bother him. He enjoys crying."

Inside the terminal the first thing he noticed was the size of the crowd. Disorganized lines of people waited in front of the ticket counters and the customs officials. Deep, unintelligible voices echoed beneath the ceiling. Now and then a voice came over the loudspeaker, requesting passengers and well-wishers to follow official procedures. Hadi Besharat looked around in bewilderment. He realized that Nili had remained at the entrance and seemed unwilling to venture further. He returned to her and asked, "Miss, what's your problem now?"

"Go ahead by yourself. I'll wait for you here."

"Why?"

"Nobody wants me here. They don't like me."

"Show a little courage. Go over to them. If they like it, fine. If not, that's fine too."

"I'll stay here."

Hadi Besharat craned his neck at the crowd. Children of all sizes were loitering at the passengers' feet. He asked Nili, "How much longer before the plane leaves?"

Nili looked at him in surprise and asked, "Are you getting tired already?"

"Of course not, miss. It's just that I don't want to keep you waiting here a long time."

"The plane to Zahedan takes off in half an hour."

"I'll be right back."

He recognized General Ghovanlu from a distance. The general had his leather jacket on and he was screwing up his face in an effort to stay awake. Then the general put two fingers inside his breast pocket. He took out his passport and some folded documents, which he tapped regularly against his wrist. His wife gave him an angry look, ordering him to hide his passport and not draw the Revolutionary Guards' attention. The general put his passport back in his pocket and compared the clock on the wall with his wristwatch. The Gharib and Ghovanlu children were gathered in a corner, talking in low voices, their eyes shining with laughter. Nearby, Mrs. Razi sat among piles of suitcases, sacks, and handbags. Seeing Hadi Besharat, she wrapped her woolen scarf around her neck and pushed her glasses higher on her nose. The general's wife took some nuts out of her purse and offered them to everyone. A voice came over the loudspeaker: "Honorable passengers, because of a local windstorm the flight to Zahedan will be late. Please cooperate with the officials until further notice."

Catching sight of Nili, the general's wife stood on tiptoe and called, "Agha Mojtaba wants your father to come to America. He wants to put him in a hospital for treatment."

Nili pointed to herself and asked, "Are you talking to me?"

"Yes, I'm talking to you. Why don't you come over near us?"

But Nili stayed where she was.

Mrs. Razi's voice rose from behind the suitcases. "Her father will never leave. He's lived two years in his present condition. Why should he spend all that money now to go to America? Mr. Bayat knows how to count his pennies."

Engineer Gharib said, "Money doesn't mean that much to an eighty-two-year-old man."

Engineer Gharib's wife said, "What? He's not eighty-two. He's only seventy-some."

Mrs. Razi said, "Even if he were a hundred years old, even if he were a hundred million, he would still think of the future. He would still worry all the time about what will happen to his wife and family, what his end will be."

General Ghovanlu looked at the ceiling and said, "It's a very good thing that he does that. We Iranians think only of the past. We don't care about the future and we don't want to bother with the present."

The general's wife said, "Mr. Bayat is a very sociable and intelligent man. Sitting and talking to him is a pleasure."

She glanced over at Nili. Obviously she thought Nili might be listening.

From among her piles of luggage Mrs. Razi said, "Mr. Bayat is an ugly man. He's so ugly, you don't want to look at his face."

The general's wife took on an anxious expression. What if Nili had heard this? She interrupted Mrs. Razi and said loudly, "Baba, what is so ugly about Mr. Bayat's face?"

Mrs. Razi said, "I swear to God. He's so ugly—"

The general's wife said, "What business is it of ours whether he's ugly or not? Besides, when you look at him closely he doesn't seem ugly at all."

Mrs. Razi said, "What are you talking about? With that big

nose of his? With that big mouth of his? Any ugliness you can imagine, you'll find in the face of that chimpanzee."

The general's wife said, "When you study his face closely it's not so bad. There are many people who look fine if you consider each one of their features separately. Even though their faces as a whole don't seem attractive."

Mrs. Razi said, "Let's say he's attractive, then. But that little man is basically stingy. Have you seen his storage room? He's bought big cans and jars and sacks of food, as many as he could find, and hidden them in his storage room for a rainy day."

Engineer Gharib's wife asked, "Why?"

"Because he's afraid of a food shortage. He doesn't want to die hungry. He's gone everywhere comparing prices and buying the cheapest food. To make a long story short, he's hoarded enough food for the next six months. Ahmad Agha gives him the Komité's Jeep to go shopping. When Mr. Bayat is at the wheel, you can't imagine what tantrums he throws. For example, if a lady passes in front of his Jeep or another car brakes suddenly, Mr. Bayat loses his temper. He attacks like a dog going for your legs. 'Son of a bitch! Shit on your father's grave!' He keeps cursing. Ahmad Agha tells him, 'Agha-jon, why are you cursing like that? No one's listening to you. You only aggravate yourself.' Instead of answering, Mr. Bayat says, 'Ahmad, a right is something you take. It's not given to you.' "

Everyone glanced sideways at Nili, concerned that she might be offended. Hadi Besharat stood absentmindedly among them without saying anything.

Suddenly he felt himself pushed forward. The pressure of the crowd propelled him toward the exit gate for passengers traveling abroad. But he put up no resistance. Instead he took off his beret and waved to the others. He didn't do this consciously. It was an old habit. Whenever he grew distant from people his hand rose of its own accord and plucked his beret from his head. He was always ready to travel without even being aware of it.

One of the veiled women who was searching the suitcases saw him and shouted, "Uncle, where are you going?"

Hadi Besharat lifted his shoulders, indicating that it wasn't his fault. "Sister, it's not up to me. You'll have to say something to these people behind me."

"How did you manage to get here? Where's your passport, where are your foreign currency papers?"

"I didn't come here on purpose. People are pushing me."

A Revolutionary Guard tried to reach him. But the crowd was packed together and it was impossible. He could only call, "Father, stay right there until I can get to you."

Hadi Besharat clung helplessly to his umbrella as he continued to be pushed forward. A warning came over the loudspeaker. "Passengers to Frankfurt, proceed to Gate Number 3. Please have your passports and foreign currency papers ready."

An official was standing next to him with his hands on his hips. Hadi Besharat asked, "Brother, is this Mehrabad Airport?"

The official looked down at him from above and said, "Yes, it is."

"Why haven't they changed its name? It was Mehrabad even during the reign of the Monster Shah."

"Get your passport and documents ready. Hurry up. Bon voyage."

Hadi Besharat raised his chin and looked at the crowd. "Are we going to Frankfurt?"

"Father, do you have someone to help you or are you traveling alone?"

Hadi Besharat was offended by the official's calling him "father." But he didn't show it, and he said, "I always travel alone."

Nili appeared at the gate, glaring at him commandingly. She held the palms of her hands together. The edge of her veil made curved folds around her face, and the folds slid down to her shoulders in straight and slanted lines. Hadi Besharat asked the official, "How long is the flight from Tehran to Frankfurt?"

The official answered, "A little more than five hours."

"It was almost that when I returned from Frankfurt to Tehran fifteen years ago. I think this ought to take longer."

"Why?"

"Because from our direction it's uphill."

"The air is not like a road that has an uphill. Are you sure you've traveled between Frankfurt and here alone?"

Hadi Besharat grew angry. He opened his notebook in front of the official and said, "When you travel from the direction of Iran the wind blows against you. It slows down the plane. Agha, I have traveled from Frankfurt twice. You look at this notebook yourself. I wrote these notes during one of my stays in Frankfurt."

On the page that he showed the official he had written himself a memo:

What Do I Need for My Future Trips?
Glue + Scissors + Small pocketknife + Life insurance + Sport clothes + Camera film (twice as much) + Plastic bags + Rubber bands (a few more than usual) + One or two small pillowcases + Bottle opener + Playing cards . . .

The official patted his beard and smiled. Hadi Besharat shook an index finger at him. "Mr. Official, I have traveled the world over. I have talked to every country without knowing its language and I haven't once got stuck."

"That's right, I know, Father."

"Mr. Official, everybody sees the world from his own point of view, and everybody's point of view is like a circle." He drew a circle in the air. "Tehran, Frankfurt, New York, London, as well as Hadi Besharat and the Revolutionary Guards, are all in this circle. The superpowers and the third-world countries are in the circle too."

The official interrupted and said, "Keep moving. People behind you are waiting."

Hadi Besharat looked back and continued speaking. "Whatever you experience is in that circle. If two circles overlap they form intersecting arcs and they resemble each other. That's why people in this world can understand each other."

Nili's voice came from a distance. "Stop that gentleman. That gentleman is not a passenger. He's in the passenger area by mistake."

The official looked from Nili to Hadi Besharat. He asked her, "You mean this gentleman?"

Nili stood on tiptoe and pointed to Hadi Besharat. "That gentleman. Bring him back to this side of the gate."

The official took Hadi Besharat's arm and pulled him over to the gate. Hadi Besharat resisted, shaking his umbrella in the air and shouting, "Agha, I'm going on my own. Why are you pushing me?"

The official shoved him forward and told Nili, "Sister, you have to watch over your relatives."

Nili shouted back, "In the middle of this bedlam, how can I watch anyone?"

She got Hadi Besharat through the gate, took his hand, and forced him toward the well-wishers. "You've kept everybody waiting. Say your good-byes and we'll go home."

Hadi Besharat resented being dragged about like this. He said, "I don't want to go home."

"Don't worry. Heli and I will look after you."

Hadi Besharat stopped walking and smiled at Nili. He was feeling Nili's soft fingers around his wrist. He wanted to thank her for her care and kindness. But instead he just looked at her.

Engineer Gharib shook the travelers' hands. His wife put a spray of gladioli in Mrs. Razi's arms and wiped her eyes with the corner of her handkerchief. Hadi Besharat couldn't understand why everyone was so upset. Separation wasn't a bad thing. It deepened people's souls. A good example of that was a trip he'd once taken with his parents to Ghum for the New Year's celebration. They had bought tickets to return by train. When they arrived at the station the train was just leaving. He ran forward and with one leap he landed on the steps of a car. But when he turned and looked back he saw that his mother-jon and father-jon were still on the platform, wearing expressions of consternation as the train pulled away. His father-jon waved to him and shouted, "Hadi, when you reach the station, don't go anywhere. We'll be there on the next train."

His mother-jon lifted her arms at her sides, her eyes surprised and her mouth wide open. Boxes of candies and cookies hung by strings from her hands. Hadi Besharat's mind registered the movement of the train, the faces that grew smaller by the second. For him, that view was forever fixed against the backdrop of the night. The distance had made a painting of his parents that could be admired on a museum wall. The event was lifted from the realm of ordinary life, and for that very reason it couldn't be forgotten. He didn't feel a trace of sadness or homesickness. He saw that every moment could become an eternity, transforming every face into shadows of mythical events and historical heroes.

Mrs. Razi approached him to say good-bye. Hadi Besharat felt they hadn't seen each other for a long, long time. He squeezed her hand and said, "Miss, don't be unkind. These days you walk with a heavy shadow. Think of us poor folks once in a while."

Mrs. Razi showed him the bundle of that poor boy's clothes. "I promised Miss Farangu I would take these clothes to your Khosro-jon. In return, you have to keep watch over my house. The key is with Miss Farangu. If you can find a tenant, go ahead and negotiate the rent. We don't have anyone here anymore to look after our business."

Hadi Besharat squeezed Mrs. Razi's hand even more tightly and said, "Don't worry. I'll do whatever needs to be done. When did you speak to Farangu?"

"Just a minute ago. Haven't you seen her?"

Hadi Besharat looked around the crowd but he couldn't find Farangu. "I don't see her. Is she flying with you?"

"Nothing like that. She's postponed her trip. Professor Besharat, could I ask another small favor?"

Hadi Besharat's eyes were still searching the crowd. He said, "Please go ahead."

"I've left a few pennies with Miss Farangu. For the sake of that poor boy's soul and his late father's"—she started crying and had trouble continuing—"once each year at the time of Ashura distribute some bread and halvah among the poor."

"There's no need for money. I'll water their graves each Friday night. I'll give alms for them." Pounding his chest, he said, "I'll do it, miss. I'll do it."

Mrs. Razi's dentures were loose again and she was talking with the tip of her tongue. She turned and asked the general's wife, "Have you brought a flask? You have to bring a flask when you go for a long trip."

The rest of their good-byes proceeded calmly. They went toward the plane in silence. In the end Nili took courage and waved to the travelers. But the travelers paid no attention; nor did the well-wishers, not even the Gharib and Ghovanlu children. Nili went over to Hadi Besharat and hid behind him. Hadi Besharat kept lifting his chin, searching everywhere for Farangu. When he looked toward the airport exit doors he suddenly saw her. She was wearing black from head to toe, squeezing a white handkerchief and scratching the edge of the railing with her long fingernails. Hadi Besharat was surprised to see her in that outfit. People don't wear black every day. Once in a blue moon when someone dies, the black dress comes out of the clothes chest. That's why black dresses always smell like a hot iron. Hadi Besharat shook his umbrella in the air and shouted, "Farangu! Farangu!"

He hesitated over whether to approach her or stay put. He felt uncertain. Farangu hid her profile behind the edge of her veil and pretended to look at a poster on the wall. Hadi Besharat waved his umbrella at her. Then he ran toward her. Like lightning, Farangu dashed to a corner of the terminal. Hadi Besharat called, "Farangu! Farangu! Stay right there!"

Nili hurried after Farangu. She blocked her way and spoke to her urgently. Hadi Besharat drew nearer. Nili and Farangu turned and looked at him. He slowed his pace, coming to a stop some twenty feet away. Farangu spoke into Nili's ear. Then Nili rushed over to him, saying, "Professor Besharat, are you feeling all right? Are you running a fever? Are you coming down with a cold?"

Hadi Besharat looked around in disbelief and said, "What do you mean? Is it Farangu who's asking all these questions?"

Nili turned toward Farangu with inquiring eyes. Then she told Hadi Besharat, "Miss Farangu is worried about the cold weather. You might catch cold."

"There's nothing wrong with me. I break the ice and swim in our pool in the dead of winter. Let me talk to her myself." He cupped a hand to his mouth and shouted, "Farangu, do you remember that I used to break the ice in our Salsabil pool and take a dip?"

Farangu pulled her veil closer and turned away. Hadi Besharat asked Nili, "Why is she doing that?"

Nili ran back to Farangu. Again they said a few words to each other. This time Nili took a woolen sweater from Farangu and returned to Hadi Besharat. "Miss Farangu doesn't want to talk to you face to face. She only wants you to wear this sweater."

"I don't need it. I have to talk to her."

"Miss Farangu wants to know if everything's all right with you."

He was so angry that he didn't know how to answer. He said, "I don't need this sweater. Take it back to her." He turned to Farangu and in a louder voice said, "Stop these childish games. This playacting isn't becoming. Let's go home."

Farangu didn't utter a word. Hadi Besharat asked Nili, "Why is she acting like that? Why isn't she talking?"

"I don't know. Maybe she's afraid you'll catch cold and get sick."

"If she's so worried about me, why doesn't she want to talk to me?"

"You have to go talk to her yourself. You have to let her get it off her chest."

"I refuse to take even one step toward her. Farangu has to come to me and explain the meaning of this behavior."

Farangu was rushing toward the airport exit now. When she

opened the door the wind blew her veil so it fluttered and lifted its tail in the air.

Hadi Besharat thought the avalanche should be cleared from the road to Khezrabad after the New Year and he would be able to travel. He ought to be moving on. He ought to go to the highlands, somewhere far away from the madness of the city. Nili said, "It's a crying shame. You should have followed her."

"Is Farangu going home?"

"No. She's going to her Mama Aliyeh's. You'd better get started too. We have to go back."

"I don't want to go back. If you want to, go on your own."

"And leave you here by yourself?"

"It's too early to go back."

"What should we do, then?"

"Let's visit St. Yahya's Shrine."

Nili looked at him in amazement. "You really want to go to St. Yahya's Shrine?"

"Why not? You know the way and the cab is waiting for us."

The driver was sitting in the cab, still listening to the tragedy of St. Muslem's children and still crying. But now he cried more quietly. He kept searching for something in the glove compartment, not looking at Hadi Besharat or Nili, pretending to be unaware of their presence. Nili's mind seemed fixed on the tragedy and the weeping driver. The cries of the crowd had changed into some sort of harmonious chorus. First the wailing soared and then it calmed down as breaths were caught rhythmically:

> "Heeeey, hey hey hey hey,
> Hey hey hey,
> Hey . . . hey . . ."

The emotional voice of the passion reciter trailed behind the chorus. "Hosein's sister, Zaynab, keeps talking in riddles."

The crowd answered:

The Pilgrim's Rules of Etiquette

"Hey hey hey hey hey,
Hey hey hey hey hey."

The passion reciter softened his voice. "Why do these children love Hosein so much? Why are they so wild about Hosein? Why is it that as soon as Hosein's name is brought up Zaynab cries and the children cry too?"

The lamenters' chorus began:

"Hosein-jon,
Hosein-jon,
Hosein-jon . . ."

Hadi Besharat gradually realized how much he was dreading the visit to Mehrdad's grave site. He began to worry. He asked Nili, "Do you do well in school?"

"Last year I had to repeat a few subjects. Of the fourteen students who had to repeat, only two passed their finals. The rest came out of school crying. So I didn't have much hope myself. I was afraid I'd be embarrassed in front of the school principal. I opened the door to the principal's office and went in very nervously. Our principal said, 'My dear, dear child, you have restored our pride.' It was obvious I'd passed my exams. I went home completely happy. My father was sitting on his prayer rug. He finished up his last glorias quickly and asked, 'Dear, what's the news?' I said, 'I passed.' He said, 'You passed?' I said, 'Yes.' He said, 'Why didn't you get it in writing on a piece of paper or something? If you go there tomorrow and they deny you passed, then what?' "

"Thank God, this year you'll finish high school. Then you have to think about getting married."

"Please don't talk about my getting married. I don't like it."

"Why not? You're the proper age."

Nili frowned. Hadi Besharat said, "It's a shame you keep thinking about that poor boy all the time. You've taken him enough halvah and saffron rice pudding."

"He came to ask my father for my hand."

"Really? I didn't know that."

"I swear to God. He suddenly got the idea in his head and no one could stop him. He snuck five thousand tumans out of his mother's purse and bought a heart-shaped diamond. He got drunk and came staggering to our house and presented it to me in front of my father. My father took the heart-shaped diamond, examined it, and said, 'How much did you pay for this?' Mehrdad told him a much higher figure. I mean, he gave its real price multiplied by three. He didn't know who he was talking to. My father can tell the price of anything down to the last penny from a hundred feet away. When Mehrdad left our house my father said, 'Basically, you have to look after your education. Get married? What for? First try to be a human being and never let some cuckold tie you down.' "

"A few times Mr. Bayat did inquire around the neighborhood about the boy's background."

"We used to rendezvous in front of the Iranian-French Association. Ahmad knew it. He used to follow us everywhere we went. That was why Mehrdad didn't dare get close to me. Only when we went clothes shopping he would pass me letters under the fitting-room door."

The passion reciter was speaking in a dragging voice. "There are a lot of people who were tortured and killed by the ex-Shah's hatchet men. But I want you to imagine the Prophet's household in the wastelands of Karbala. Think of the apples of Zaynab's eye. Think of the newborn son of St. Hosein, and Ali Ashgar's thirsty lips. Ah . . . Hosein-jon, dear heart, what have you done? Why do you color this wasteland red with the blood of your children? Why do you water the desert with the blood of your precious children, Agha-jon?

> "Our garden is so fruitful,
> Now the rose blossoms smell of Hosein.
> Hosein-jon, Hosein-jon . . ."

The crowd chorused back:

> *"Hosein-jon,*
> *Hosein-jon,*
> *Hosein-jon . . ."*

They were driving up the slope of a hill. The snow had begun to melt and newly sprouted grass was visible beneath. At the top of the hill the shrine's blue dome gradually came into view, rising in the sky. Then Hadi Besharat saw the rope and the wish-cloths people had tied to it, each cloth swinging drunkenly in the wind. The leafless branches of an old mulberry tree stretched above the shrine. Hadi Besharat was familiar with every detail of that scene. He had come a long way and now he was approaching a place that was like a chapel to him. A small shrine built by the hands of a loving people many years ago. The wind blew it and the shade of the mulberry tree protected it from season to season. As though this courtyard and this shrine had been waiting for him according to an appointment made in the distant past.

Hadi-jon, appreciate the present! Hadi-jon, shake the sleeves of contentment on the two worlds! Hadi-jon, get moving, fight to the bitter end!

He could hear "Amapola" from far away. The young Tehranians were spinning with their arms around each other's necks. His private symphony had reached the tumultuous part where the cymbals crashed together. A chorus ascended from the slope of the hill, making the sky seem as shoreless as an ocean. Hadi Besharat seized Nili's hand and said, "Thank you very much."

Nili stared at him. "What's wrong with you, Professor Besharat?"

"You have made me your devotee. Oh, miss, how pretty you are. Where have you come from? Where do you belong?"

Nili pulled her hand away and said, "All right, Professor Besharat. It's all right."

"You have to believe me. You have to pay attention to the truth in what I'm saying."

Nili lowered her voice. "All right, I said. All right, Professor Besharat."

It was hard for Hadi Besharat to leave the cab and enter the shrine's courtyard. Instead he wanted to go on talking. But Nili opened the cab door quickly and jumped out. She tipped her head back and looked up at the turquoise-colored dome. "Oh, baba, today the shrine is closed, but the door is open. Why isn't anyone here? Yoo-hoo!"

Hadi Besharat stepped out of the cab. He hooked his umbrella over his wrist and asked, "Which way?"

"Let's go this way."

He looked down at the gorge and said, "Spring really is coming. What air! What exhilarating air. How this place resembles my own Khezrabad. Smell it, miss. The fresh damp smell of grass is in the air."

The sunlight of late afternoon was climbing the wall, pulling its tail after it. Many hands had rubbed the huge bolt on the courtyard gate so that it looked glassy, like an old, well-polished shoe. Hadi Besharat swung his umbrella and stepped into the courtyard. "Oh, Miss Nili, what is life? Why do we have to worry about it so much?"

They went to the rear of the courtyard and walked among the rows of old graves. At the far end, beyond the slabs of stone, the ground was unpaved. The moist brown earth was mounded over that poor boy's grave. They both paused. Something prevented them from drawing closer. Hadi Besharat put his hands at his back, bent over, and inspected the surface of the mound. A few pieces of gravel had strayed onto the grave. With the toe of his shoe he nudged them back onto the gravel path. He told Nili, "This place needs a gardener."

Nili had turned her back to him and she was crying. Hadi Besharat said no more. He bent to pull two or three weeds. He patted the mound of earth, smoothing it. "Sleep, son."

Nili ran up onto the porch of the shrine and hid behind a pillar. Hadi Besharat kept rearranging the earth on the grave. "Sleep, son."

The Pilgrim's Rules of Etiquette

He thought of how far Mrs. Razi must have flown by now. No doubt their plane was already circling Zahedan. Had the local windstorm stopped yet? He laid his umbrella aside and went over to the water faucet. He filled the pitcher that sat next to it and then he watered the grave, mumbling to himself. He put the water pitcher down again. He dried his hands on his handkerchief and climbed the steps to the porch. Nili was still hiding behind a pillar. Hadi Besharat stood in front of the pillar and spoke very gently. "Miss Nili, you must forgive me."

Nili emerged, and with tears in her eyes she said, "I know enough English to get by in America. I want to go to my mama in America."

"I wish you success, God willing."

"Are you still planning to leave for the front?"

Hadi Besharat nodded a few times, scraping a floorboard with one shoe. Nili said, "I'm sure you would have gone to Khezrabad instead, if the roads weren't closed."

Hadi Besharat pointed to himself. "The real Khezrabad is here in my heart."

"Wouldn't you have gone there if the roads were open?"

Hadi Besharat didn't answer.

Nili persisted. "Can't you go to Khezrabad on foot?"

Hadi Besharat shook his head.

Nili asked, "How about by horse, or mule?"

"Mule! You can't make a pilgrimage by mule. Don't you know the etiquette?"

Nili said, "Sorry."

Hadi Besharat turned and looked down the gorge from the edge of the porch. He opened his arms wide as if he could embrace the gorge. "Oh, World!"

Nili said, "Watch out! Don't fall."

"If you could see the way I do, you would fall too. So much beauty would make you dizzy."

"What are you seeing down there?"

"Beauty and harmony. Symmetry and proportion. Everything is in its right place and you can't pass so much as a hair through the cracks. Everything is exactly where it's supposed to be. If it weren't for my tongue's shortcomings I could describe it much better than this."

The driver called from his cab, "What are your plans? Shall we go or stay here?"

Hadi Besharat called back, "Give us a few more minutes and then we'll go."

He counted out some banknotes from his billfold and handed them to Nili. "No doubt he's worried because we're taking so long. This ought to calm him down."

Nili accepted the banknotes and removed a sandwich from her bag. She ran down to the cab and passed the money and the sandwich through the window. "Agha, we'll be ready in half an hour."

Then she returned. She took another sandwich from her bag and offered it to Hadi Besharat. He lowered his eyes in a pretense of shyness, smiled mischievously, and said, "What a huge sandwich! Are you playing a trick on your English teacher? Anything is possible. You surpass everyone for sneakiness."

He ate his sandwich without worrying about indigestion. Nili began eating too, taking delicate bites from her own sandwich. Halfway through, she set her sandwich down, wiped her fingers, and took the cassette player from her bag. She said, "Would you like to listen to some music?"

"Put on one of your tapes."

She started the player, and dulcimer music began floating through the air.

Hadi Besharat said, "Pythagoras invented music after hearing the sound of a blacksmith's sledgehammer and listening to the wind passing through the holes of a dead man's skull. In Mani's religion music was considered very important because it is basically related to death. Abu Rayhan Beiruni believed that the art of music is one of the first to disappear at the time of cultural decadence and disintegration."

He felt happy and full of energy. He stood enjoying the landscape, stroking the curve of his mustache, playing with the strands of hair that stuck out from under his beret. He turned and said abruptly, "Miss, why don't you go to the front? You're so eager to visit ancient sites. Why don't you go to the south? Do you know of any other land as ancient as Mesopotamia? Go there and listen to it. Ancient lands speak with the tongue of the heart and not with the tongue of the mind. You listen to them with the ear of the heart and not with the ear of the intellect."

He began snapping his fingers to the rhythm of the dulcimer, moving his body from the hips ever so gently. Nili sat in a corner of the porch, letting her veil slip down from her head. Not only did she seem unsurprised by Hadi Besharat's behavior but she even started clapping in time with his dance. A smile came over Hadi Besharat's face. Out of the corner of his eye he looked up and down, up and down, nodding to the fourth beat of the scale. Then he went to the edge of the porch, raised his hands, and recited his "Porturne for a Hanged Man."

> *"In the precious night when the night rests peacefully,*
> *The angels and the spirits are descending to earth.*
> *Your greetings unto him until the dawn.*
> *O Lord, grant him eternal peace,*
> *O Lord, shed the light of mercy on his grave,*
> *O Lord, never forsake, never be wrathful to him."*

He stretched each phrase mysteriously, creating a foggy and faraway atmosphere by pulverizing the words in his mouth, keeping his eyes half closed, passing cold sighs through the distances between words. Nili screamed, "Watch your step! God kill me. You're going to fall."

Instead of looking down at his feet he turned, trying to understand the reason for Nili's anxiety. He frowned and said, "Miss, why do you scare me?"

The end of the sentence was still on his lips when he slipped and fell off the edge of the porch onto the paved courtyard below. Nili screamed, "God kill me! What happened, Professor Besharat?"

"Ouch, my ankle. Ouch, my ankle. I've broken my ankle. Ouch, Mother-jon."

Nili ran down the steps to the courtyard, took hold of his ankle, and examined it. "Professor Besharat, thank God you're all right. Nothing is broken. See, you've escaped disaster again. For God's sake, get up and say something."

Hadi Besharat retrieved his beret and hit it against his knee a couple of times to shake the snow off. Then he struggled to his feet. He examined his arms, legs, head, and face, one by one. He was reassured to find he was still in one piece. He said, "Thank God, there are no serious consequences. But believe me, my left ankle is aching badly. I have to be careful. An injured ankle can easily become very painful."

He limped back up the stairs to the porch, sat on a bench, and looked at the sky with worn-out eyes. Nili said, "Why are you sitting there? What are you waiting for?"

Hadi Besharat threw his hands up. "I was thinking of America. The Russian circus came to Whitehurst College once. You had to see the acrobats with your own eyes to believe it. There was this donkey that they'd taught to jump over a rope. I told Professor Humphrey, 'Agha, see that? Once you show a donkey how to jump over a rope, he never forgets. But show the same act a hundred times to human beings, and they still trip and fall to the ground.' "

Nili looked down the hill toward the road and said, "It's getting late. Let's start back."

Hadi Besharat said, "Imagine the arrogance of human beings. They consider themselves all-knowing and yet they can't understand as much as an ass."

"Let's start back. It's getting dark."

Nili shut off her cassette player and put it in her bag. Meanwhile Hadi Besharat sat on the bench, rubbing his left ankle. Then Nili handed him his umbrella, and they started slowly down the hill. When they reached the road the driver got out of the cab to help Hadi Besharat in. Hadi Besharat didn't put up any resistance.

The Pilgrim's Rules of Etiquette

The cab sped toward the city. The streetlights were lighting up one by one against the purple sky. The snow didn't seem to be freezing again even in the cold evening wind. Melted snow splashed everywhere as if this were midday.

Now Hadi Besharat's ankle was growing chilled and it felt much worse. He laid his left foot across his knee to examine it. Fortunately there was no swelling and everything looked all right. He was tempted to massage it but he worried that he might not be able to stand the pain. At the same time he had trouble leaving it alone.

No one was as familiar with the complexities of his frail body as Farangu. She knew so well how much pressure to apply and at what point, where to touch and where to avoid touching. She was aware of all his body's peculiarities.

He didn't dare tell Nili how much he missed Farangu. It would offend her and she would consider him ungrateful. Instead he kept up a constant moaning. Nili listened with no reaction. She was bowed beneath her veil like a pilgrim woman from medieval times, keeping watch over the night and the burning camphor candle. Despite that he felt they understood each other. How many months of crisis lay behind them? Who could say? He had long ago lost track. He knew only that a precious being like Nili should not be wasted, she shouldn't be scattered like the petals of a flower. He bent forward to look directly into her face. Nili caught his glance. "What is it, Professor Besharat?"

"I don't know what to say. You don't need to go to the front. Forget what I told you about Mesopotamia."

Nili put a thumb beneath her chin and rested her fingers against her temple. "It doesn't matter about that."

"Why? Are you tired of living?"

"I'm just sitting next to you. I'm just listening."

Nili's face had lost its girlish look, assuming a self-possessed, resigned expression. Hadi Besharat couldn't take his eyes off her. He said, "What can I tell you? Maybe it's better not to say anything."

The cab circled the station and parked at the corner. After he had paid the driver Hadi Besharat stuck his head out and held his umbrella high so he could open it. Instead of snowing, it was drizzling. They had removed that poor boy's bridal chamber and it seemed to have left an empty place.

Hadi Besharat limped down the street with Nili's help. The closer they came to his house the more apprehensive he grew. Maybe he should visit Mr. Hashiyeh instead. Maybe he should pay a call on Engineer Gharib. But the lights were off in Engineer Gharib's laboratory and it looked blind and deserted. There wasn't a trace of the engineer. Probably he'd gone home for supper.

It was like those evenings after they first moved to this district. Every night he would go up to Khosro's room to keep him company. Both of them were waiting for Farangu to come home from the theater. One night Khosro rearranged the table and chairs to make a fort. Hadi Besharat sat in a corner and watched him pulling chairs under the table with much effort. He spread a blanket over them to make a roof. Then he dragged a little plastic chair inside the fort. He said, "Papa, turn off the light."

Hadi Besharat obeyed. Khosro sat on the plastic chair, leafing through his fairy-tale book and rocking himself in the dark. For a long time Hadi Besharat didn't speak. He only watched Khosro. Then he broke the silence and said, "Khosro, how nicely you keep yourself occupied."

Khosro kept rocking on the chair. Without turning his head he said, "Ssh, Papa-jon. Ssh, Papa-jon."

"What are you doing in there?"

"I'm becoming a ghost. I'm not here anymore."

"Why do you want to become a ghost?"

"I want to take revenge."

Khosro emerged from his fort and made a scary face at Hadi Besharat. Hadi Besharat pretended to be frightened. Falling to his knees, he begged, "Mr. Ghost, take pity on me. You scare me with your behavior."

"I don't have any pity. I want to kill."

"Mr. Ghost, don't you feel pity at all?"

"I'm a statue. Statues don't feel pity."

Hadi Besharat smiled at him and then glanced toward the stairs. Farangu still wasn't back. Early in the evening, before she left for the theater, they had all three been playing "The Crow Flies" and "Twisted Rope." Hadi Besharat had thrown the twisted rope around Farangu's neck and pulled her toward him. "Little lamb, say 'Baa.' "

Farangu had burst out laughing and kissed him on the lips. Then she'd pulled a handkerchief from her pocket and wiped away the wet spot she'd left.

Now Mrs. Kobra and a Revolutionary Guard were standing in the middle of the street glaring at them. Hadi Besharat approached and asked, "What are you doing here?"

Mrs. Kobra said, "Where have you been all this time?"

"We went to St. Yahya's Shrine. Is it any of your business where we've been?"

Mrs. Kobra motioned to the Revolutionary Guard. "Brother, take this girl home. Her brother is looking all over the city for her."

Nili said, "Wait a minute. We just went to the airport to see the passengers off."

Mrs. Kobra came closer. She wrapped the edge of her veil around one finger, wet it with her tongue, and rubbed Nili's lips. "You talk more than you should. It's been two hours since your brother took his car and went looking for you two."

She held Nili's face under the streetlight to examine it for any traces of powder. Nili said, "You see? There's nothing on my face."

Once again Mrs. Kobra rubbed the edge of her veil across Nili's lips. She said, "Then why is it your lips are as red as a monkey's asshole?"

"They're naturally red. If I were wearing lipstick it would show on your veil."

"Do you think we're stupid? This is Mecca lipstick. It doesn't rub off."

Hadi Besharat was taken aback. He moved forward to lead Nili to her house. Nili stood frowning at him out of the corner of her eye. She had wrapped herself tightly in her veil as if to avoid anyone's touch. She spoke with her jaw set. "You just run along. Go home."

"Let me see you into your house first and then I'll go."

"Don't worry about me. Don't stand there wasting your time. You'll cause trouble for both of us."

"I'm not going home anyhow. I'm going to the Komité to see if Farangu has left a message for me."

"Miss Farangu will return on her own. You go home."

"I can't, Miss Nili. It's beyond me."

Nili turned angrily on her heel and hurried away. Hadi Besharat waited until she'd opened her door and disappeared behind it.

Now he could see another Revolutionary Guard standing in front of his house, squeezing a radio transmitter in his fist. Mrs. Kobra and the first Revolutionary Guard were deep in conversation.

Hadi Besharat squatted down and curled his fingers around his ankle. But when he tried to straighten up again he couldn't. Suddenly all his muscles contracted as if he were frozen on the threshold of an epileptic seizure, as if the light had vanished from the world. He put a hand to the pavement but still he failed to rise. He felt he'd been shot and was about to fall to the ground from the back of a horse, a horse rearing up without a sound. He was falling into a dark pit, connected to nothing between heaven and earth. Far below, a wide expanse of field extended and the sky had ceased to move. The grumbling of the First World War artillery rattled in his eardrums. It was rumored that the Seventeenth Plan had been carried out and that the French army was returning from Alsace and Lorraine. The victory had left no effect on them. They walked wearily and carelessly. Then he thought of the Nazis' blitzkrieg during the Second World War, piercing the Russian defenses. Whatever had been left of the

Russian army kept joining the line of defense just behind, creating a much stronger defense. The Germans wondered why the Russians didn't come out of their cities and establish a position along the border. Why they kept retreating. Even General von Schlieffen hadn't foreseen that.

For some time he remained in a squatting position in the street. Then gradually he elevated his shoulders. He pushed himself upright stiffly and started walking. It was completely dark now and the street seemed spacious. He passed Engineer Gharib's house and reached the avenue. The avenue glared with melted snow. Headlights shimmered on the polished pavement, making faces like the reflections in a fun-house mirror. He passed the next street. All of Mr. Hashiyeh's windows were dark except for one downstairs. Nevertheless he drew closer and stopped in front of the house. The shadow of a woman crossed the window. She lit the light in the entrance hall, ran up the stairway, and turned the light off again.

He returned to his own street. Two women and a man stood together in front of Mrs. Razi's house, and they cast a worried glance in his direction. He knew the man right away. It was Mr. Hashiyeh. Then he recognized Nili and Heli. He felt removed from them. Everything was very far away. Even his own behavior struck him as strange and complicated. Why was he acting like this? What for? What was the meaning of it?

He tried to leave again unobtrusively. He took the dark side of the street and limped toward the Komité Building. But Mr. Hashiyeh and the two sisters followed him at a distance. The sound of their footsteps established a hidden conversation among them—a conversation of walking in step, pausing, and walking again. He bowed his back and hurried on. He saw the three stick shadows stretching from behind him, hand in hand. The darkness spoke clearly for him and he had no need to open his mouth. He huddled beneath his umbrella, walked favoring his left ankle, and instead of shouting kept his silence.

T E N

The pain in Hadi Besharat's left ankle was slowing him down. At the entrance to the Komité Building he paused and turned. He bowed briefly to the three shadows following him and said, "I beg you, please go home."

Mr. Hashiyeh and the two sisters looked at him. Hadi Besharat took a deep breath. The smell of dahlias hit his nose, wet and salty like the rain that was just now coming to a stop. It was the smell of a florist shop, the smell of the ceremony for the seventh day after a burial.

Closing his umbrella, he entered the Komité Building and climbed the stairs to the waiting area. An officer stood reading a file in front of the reception desk. Behind the desk sat a Revolutionary Guard whom Hadi Besharat recognized. It was a former student of his. In the old days he used to be called Shahbaz, but after the recent turmoil he had changed his name to Yar Ommat. As far back as Hadi Besharat could remember, Shahbaz had been a careless student who dressed in thick, shabby clothes. Even in winter he'd worn ragged tennis shoes. He had walked informally, as if unwilling to stand on ceremony with anyone.

The officer surveyed Hadi Besharat with a cold, indifferent glance. Then he returned to his file. Limping, Hadi Besharat approached the desk. He told Yar Ommat, "A greeting to you. Is it possible to talk privately with Brother Ahmad Bayat for a couple of minutes?"

Yar Ommat lifted his head and looked at him blankly. "It's late. Come back tomorrow morning."

"This is important."

Yar Ommat shrugged. "Then take a seat and wait till he gets here."

"I suppose you still live in this district. Have you seen my wife? I mean Mrs. Farangu Besharat."

"Go sit down till your turn comes."

Hadi Besharat sat on an empty bench and propped his umbrella between his feet. It had slipped his mind that he didn't have his identification card with him. If they were to ask his ID number and the place and date of issue he wouldn't be able to give a decent answer. Probably his best defense was to claim he was one of the humbled masses. Or maybe Yar Ommat would come to his rescue because of their past relationship. Hadi Besharat had begged many times during the course of his life. Now he would have to beg again. He felt he was really in need and he wanted to make an official complaint. Someone ought to listen to what he had to say. It was a shame that so much devotion and sincerity was going to waste. He stood up and cried out, "Yar Ommat!"

Yar Ommat didn't seem to hear him. Hadi Besharat limped closer. He said, "Yar Ommat, there's an urgent matter. I have to talk to you."

Yar Ommat tapped a pencil on his desk. Hadi Besharat said, "Aren't you going to answer?"

With the end of his pencil Yar Ommat pointed and said, "Just sit on that bench till your turn comes."

Hadi Besharat shuffled back to the bench and sat down again. What was he waiting here for? It was high time Farangu stopped her childish games and talked to him. He needed to hear the sound of her voice. He worried about what had been left unsaid. The images on the magic lantern meant no more to Farangu than a handful of shadows. Yet she had kept watch over those shadows all these years. Perhaps she was thinking now that all her hard work had been for nothing and her whole life's labor was gone with the wind. How mistaken she was!

Yar Ommat was looking away from him, deliberately ignoring him. He was admitting a man who'd arrived after Hadi Besharat. Hadi Besharat coughed a few times to catch Yar Ommat's attention. Yar Ommat pretended not to hear. Hadi Besharat raised his voice. "Yar Ommat, my turn comes before this gentleman's. If our turns are based on order of appearance, it's my turn now."

"You can see I'm busy. When I find time I'll listen to you."

"But my turn comes before this gentleman's."

"This gentleman has had his appointment since yesterday."

Hadi Besharat got up and walked around the waiting area, stabbing the floor with his umbrella and muttering a prayer, "When a Distressed One Is Answered." He did it in such a way that Yar Ommat could hear. Yar Ommat rose and came over to him. He said, "What's wrong with you? Why are you bothering people?"

Hadi Besharat refused to be pleasant to him. He swallowed and spoke from the depths of his throat in an Arabic accent. "God's greetings, mercy and blessings unto you."

Yar Ommat said, "I know you. Who incites you to write your books? Who pays to have them printed?" He came closer and said, "Think about it. Refusing to answer is not in your best interest."

Hadi Besharat looked toward the interrogation rooms. He was filled with fury. His former student refused to recognize him and spoke to him as if he were a stranger. Hadi Besharat was about to unleash his tongue. Yar Ommat said, "Well? Have you thought it over?"

Hadi Besharat turned and said fearlessly, "What should I think over? You were this high"—holding his hand near the floor —"when I taught you everything you know. Then you come to me and order me to think? You should be ashamed of yourself. You people don't understand the truth. No, you have made a mistake. You are talking to a person who is innocent of lies and cheating."

In the middle of his tirade the officer who'd been reading the file called, "What's all the fuss?" He came over to them.

Yar Ommat told the officer, "Never mind, this man is only pretending to be angry. They think if they pretend they're angry they can escape punishment."

Hadi Besharat gave Yar Ommat a scalding glare. The officer drew up his shoulders and sucked in his belly. Leaning back, he asked Hadi Besharat, "Do you know the punishment for talking like that? It's death by firing squad."

Hadi Besharat stood taller and stuck his face into the officer's. "Why don't you shoot me, then?"

The officer tossed a candy into the air and caught it in his mouth. He said, "Why should we? Do we have extra bullets to waste on the likes of you?"

Hadi Besharat was surprised by his own behavior. In the battles of everyday life he had always used silence as his ultimate weapon. He couldn't recall any important military commander who had employed the weapon of silence so shrewdly. Unlike the great commanders, he had poured out his secrets in public. He had opened his arms to encourage attack. He had exposed his chest freely so the enemy could aim and fire. The only thing he had kept for himself was his silence, the core of his being.

Now he regretted leaving Whitehurst College. Whitehurst College had removed him from his usual surroundings. It had changed the texture of the light for him. The old scenes returned to him, piece by piece. Surely St. Peter Street still stretched like a dark band every night, reflecting the First National Bank upside down. He used to go to the harbor for a walk in the evenings. In the fall the tall ships had approached the harbor, their sails dripping wet. They had anchored by the shore in rainy weather. Sometimes an old man had appeared on the Black Tulip Bar's balcony and drawn circles on the garage wall opposite with a lighted flashlight. Hadi Besharat had imagined himself standing on a deck and preparing for a long journey like an old sea captain. He could hear a volume of water moving around him but he couldn't see the water itself. The swaying of the ship made him stagger, tilting the horizon up and down. A heavy fog spilled from a cloud's gray mouth, floating on the wet pier and moving out to sea. Intermittent drops hit the pavement, leaving behind a host of indefinable sounds like pages rustling in the evening breeze. He heard the rhyming words of a prayer that was repeated like empty chatter. He recited to himself, "In a night so dark and a whirlpool so overwhelming, how can the shore dwellers comprehend our situation at sea?"

The monotonous ticktock of the wall clock kept stretching the silence beyond its limits. It showed the time as six past eight. He figured it must be close to noon at Whitehurst College. No doubt the students were coming out of the lecture halls wearing their blue jeans and their yellow, green, and red shirts. They were passing the tennis courts, waving to each other and calling, "Hey, where've you been?"

The outside door slammed and Ahmad Bayat entered the waiting room. He was wearing a wet, wax-colored raincoat. The hood was pulled up over his head. He seemed exhausted and out of patience. With curious eyes he scanned the crowd as he undid his raincoat buttons one by one. When his gaze met Hadi Besharat's he came to a halt. A puff forced itself from his tight lips and he suddenly attacked. "Professor Besharat, why do you cause so much trouble? Why don't you listen to anyone? If I hadn't come when they sent for me you'd be headed for Evin Prison by now."

He seized the file the officer was holding and strode into his office without a backward glance. Maintaining a stubborn silence, Hadi Besharat followed him, with the officer close behind. Ahmad Bayat hung his raincoat on a hook and then flung himself into the swivel chair behind the desk. Motioning the officer closer, he mumbled something in the man's ear. That changed the officer's attitude. He turned to Hadi Besharat and assumed a much warmer tone of voice than he'd used earlier. "Don't think we're unaware of your twenty years of scientific struggle. Not at all. We are fully aware and we have no interest in prosecuting you."

He ushered Hadi Besharat to a chair in front of the desk and Hadi Besharat sat down stiffly, scowling at him. The officer pretended not to notice and continued speaking. "When a man reaches a certain age he becomes sort of childish." Turning to Ahmad Bayat, he asked, "Do you remember how children in the old regime used to watch television? Didn't they start dancing in front of the television when they could find a musical program? These people are like that. They find an occasion and they become children again." He asked Hadi Besharat, "How old are you?"

Hadi Besharat forgot his stubbornness and the words jumped out of his mouth. "How old do you think I am?"

"Sixty-four, sixty-five. Am I right?"

"Why do you distort the facts? Anybody can guess a person's age. Maybe with two or three years' margin of error. But not seven or eight."

The officer paused and a bemused smile appeared on his face. "We weren't supposed to be angry with each other, Professor. Were we?"

Hadi Besharat didn't like the officer's tone. The man was so close that Hadi Besharat could hear him breathing. The officer said, "Well, Your Excellency the Professor, we have received a report about your trip to St. Yahya's Shrine in the company of Ahmad Agha's sister. No problem with that at all." Turning to Ahmad Bayat, he asked, "Is there any problem with that, Ahmad Agha? Of course not. The professor is as old as your father. As the expression goes, the sunlight has reached the roof of his life."

Ahmad Bayat waved a hand toward the officer. "That's enough," he said. "You can leave now."

The officer seemed about to say more but he changed his mind. Without looking at Hadi Besharat he turned and walked out of the room.

Then Ahmad Bayat rose and came from behind his desk to

stand in front of Hadi Besharat. He said, "Get up and I'll take you home. Let's go."

Hadi Besharat gathered himself in his chair and hunched forward, resting both hands on his umbrella. He was determined not to move. Ahmad Bayat threw his arms out helplessly and told the ceiling, "He doesn't understand. He doesn't realize he's playing with fire." He bent over and shook a finger in Hadi Besharat's face. "Why do you refuse to listen to logic? Do you want them to arrest you? Grill you tomorrow in the interrogation room?"

Hadi Besharat tightened his grip on his umbrella and looked at him with frowning eyes. After a pause Ahmad Bayat threw out his arms again. "That face isn't really yours. That face is your reflection in a fun-house mirror. Go ahead. Do what you wish. You'll pay for it."

He left the room. Hadi Besharat gazed after him calmly. It seemed to him that the whole world was a reflection in a fun-house mirror.

The side door of the office had been left part way open. Hadi Besharat could look through it and see the long hall that had once been part of the old Mirza Isa the Minister High School. The humbled masses were carrying their Primus stoves and their samovars down the hall to the various classrooms that led off from it. Without planning to, Hadi Besharat stood up and stepped through the door into the hall. The weak light gave the walls the color of yellow soup. The classroom doors followed each other in two long rows, repeating themselves at equal distances and leading his eye to the end of the hall.

Just standing here made his mind start working. He remembered everything—the hall, the classrooms, the athletic field, and the stairway. There was a smell of chalk dust around him. The smell revived all the old scenes. He had often walked this hall between bells. Always the sound of scattered voices had trailed through the corridors. Students had kept coming toward him and when they got close they zigzagged around him and he had returned their greetings.

One of the classrooms was unlit. He opened the door wider with the tip of his umbrella and stepped inside. He could see the blackboard, the benches and desks. Everything was still there. He imagined that the room was crowded and students were walking up and down the aisles. Their voices couldn't be heard and they were unaware of his presence. He stood smiling at their soundless laughter, at their roughhousing, at their gray uniforms and their short hair that had been cut with a Number 4 clipper.

Yar Ommat and two other Revolutionary Guards appeared in the doorway. The reflection of the hall lights behind them danced on their machine guns. Hadi Besharat touched his beret with a fingertip. The beret was soft, like the muffled sounds from the hall. He turned away slowly and mumbled to himself, "Oh, there's the window."

He heard Yar Ommat asking, "Agha, what are you doing here? Who gave you permission to come in here? How would you like to go to Evin Prison?"

Hadi Besharat placed a palm on the windowsill and leaned forward. He tried to guess his distance from the ground. It seemed about ten meters. Melted snow glared in the street. The store windows were as shiny as camera film and there was no one in sight. Still the tired, heavy steam kept rising from the guardhouse. He laid aside his umbrella so he could open the window. Then he poked his head out and looked toward the Mobilization Headquarters Building. He drew a deep breath and felt dizzy with the smell of fresh air. When he turned back the wind swept in and took his beret.

Yar Ommat shouted, "What are you doing here? Why did you sneak into this room?"

Hadi Besharat backed up against the window. He wanted to put one of his legs over the sill and let it hang above the avenue. But Yar Ommat barred his way with one arm. "Are you trying to kill yourself?"

Hadi Besharat waited, watchful and prepared to jump. Yar Ommat altered his approach. Lowering his arm, he spoke more quietly. "Agha, what's all this about? If you want to stay here overnight, well, be my guest." Seeing that Hadi Besharat wasn't answering, he said, "Don't you have a home?"

Hadi Besharat's hand kept searching his head for his beret. He was looking at Yar Ommat and the two other Revolutionary Guards, but his mind was on his beret. How had it flown off so easily? Where had it gone? He blinked to keep himself awake. He rubbed his forehead and raised his eyebrows. He lifted his chin, meaning that they should leave him alone. Yar Ommat asked, "Aren't you going to answer me?"

Hadi Besharat placed his hand on his cheek, indicating that he was sleepy and wanted to rest. Yar Ommat thought for a second and then said, "Stay right there. I'll get Ahmad Bayat. Maybe he can make sense of this."

Hadi Besharat heard the sound of the door closing and the key turning. Again he looked around the room. He could see the details better now that his eyes had grown accustomed to the dark.

He had lectured in this very room many, many years ago. And the late Fakhr Zanjani had lectured here before him. It was a large room, so tall that the walls seemed to disappear in the dark before they reached the ceiling. It smelled of dust and old houses. Thin bands of light passed through the seams around the closed door and through the keyhole, breaking at the edges of the desks and benches. The stoplight in the street below turned on and off intermittently.

Red,
Black,
Red,
Black . . .

With the others gone, he wasn't sleepy anymore. In fact he felt wider awake than usual. Now he was stuck as to what to do next. What time was it? Ten P.M.? Midnight? A sneeze tickled his nose. He held his arms extended as if he'd been struck by lightning. For some time he stood there, immobile. Still he couldn't sneeze. He took his folded handkerchief from his pocket and shook it in the air until it fell open. Then he walked among the rows of benches and desks, giving them some order, arranging them row by row. Dust had covered everything. Starting with the first row, he began dusting benches and desks with his handkerchief. He kept hearing the sound of raindrops from outside. Headlights moved on the pavement like stretched elastic bands. The night's shine played over their metallic bodies. Absentmindedly he went on dusting, moving from one side of the room to the other.

He couldn't remember exactly. He knew only that they'd put the theater backdrop next to the blackboard. It showed Xerxes's army passing through the Hellespont. Fakhr Zanjani sat behind his desk, tilting his head and examining the backdrop carefully. But he was also watching Hushang Gharib out of the corner of his eye. Hushang sat at the rear of the classroom, showing a picture to the student next to him. Fakhr Zanjani got up very silently and tiptoed toward Hushang Gharib like a lurking cat. The other students stopped breathing. They looked in distress toward Hushang Gharib, who was completely unaware of what was going on around him. Fakhr Zanjani seized his opportunity, leapt forward, and slapped Hushang Gharib on the back of his neck. Hushang jumped up like a firecracker and rubbed his neck. He moaned, "Agha, why did you hit me? I was just trying to get my notebook out of my bag."

Fakhr Zanjani waved the picture of a nude woman in the air and screamed, "You call this trash a notebook? You incompetent ignoramus!"

In front of all the students he tore the picture to pieces and sent Hushang Gharib to the vice-principal. Then he tightened the knot on his tie, made a swallowing motion, and continued his lecture. "Pay careful attention. These are the Iranian vessels, sailing unfamiliar waters. They are passing through the Hellespont. Of course they are bound to fall out of formation. The pass is too narrow. Please look at the map of the battle. See how easy it is for the Greeks to attack these vessels." With a stick he pointed to the map on the blackboard. "To have a lot of ships or a superior army is not important. What is important is organizational and administrative ability. This removes the element of personal error. The Greeks are all huffy with arrogance. They say to each other, 'The Sea of Marmara will be red with the blood of the Iranians. . . .' "

To attract the students' attention, his voice assumed a sly and exaggerated tone. Standing on his toes, he rounded his lips and stretched upward so he looked as narrow as a paintbrush. His bony face resembled a piece of varnished wood. His wavy hair grew from a point in the center of his forehead and spread backward over his head in a fan shape. He blinked at his students beneath lowered lids. The students were so fascinated, they didn't even breathe. He put on a warning expression. To mock the Greeks, he lowered his voice confidentially and he smiled sarcastically. He closed his eyes to indicate caution, making sure the Greeks wouldn't hear him, and he said, "The Iranians don't give this nonsense the attention they would give a dog. They soak their national banner with the red of their blood, proudly holding it high for everyone to see."

Hadi Besharat thought that Nili and perhaps Farangu were standing outside in the street, keeping watch over him. He needed them to watch. If he wanted to lie on a bench and take a nap, at least they would be near to see what was going on. It was getting very, very late. The night was passing in slow motion. The pause in every moment affected his senses. One by one, images kept coming to his mind. They faded away and came back again. Perhaps Engineer Gharib was in his laboratory, putting a pipette into a tube and titrating the alcohol for his new batch of vodka. Perhaps the night was ending and the faithful were walking to the mosque. Perhaps Ahmad Bayat was about to come out of his house and start jogging around the block. Perhaps Nili was in her room preparing her English lessons. Perhaps Mr. Bayat was still in bed, dreaming about his illegal trip to Pakistan.

The Pilgrim's Rules of Etiquette

——

Behind the windowpanes the white of dawn was thickening and people were emerging from the darkness on the avenue. He rose from his bench to look out and he recognized Nili. She was standing across the street, gazing up at his window with an injured expression in her eyes. Hadi Besharat clapped his hands to get her attention. From inside her veil Nili brought forth his wool sweater and waved it in the air. She called, "I'll throw it up to you. Catch."

Hadi Besharat asked, "Where's Farangu? Hasn't she come back yet?"

Nili tossed up the sweater. But it didn't quite reach him. Instead it twisted and fell down again and Nili caught it herself. She raised her shoulders and curved her lips. What could she do? She couldn't throw it any higher. She waved at him, standing on tiptoe. "You go back home. Miss Farangu will return." In English, "I swear."

She covered her mouth with the sweater, laughing sound-lessly. She said, "Professor Besharat, are you taking good care of yourself?"

Hadi Besharat didn't want to attract the Guards' attention, so he merely spread his hands, meaning she shouldn't worry about him. Then he put his index finger somewhere in the middle of his bald spot and took it away again, meaning that last night the wind had blown his beret off. He looked pointedly downward, hoping this would lead her to search the pavement. Maybe the beret was still there. Nili walked around and looked everywhere. Then she raised her head and called, "I don't understand. What do you want? I don't see anything here."

He placed his palms together, meaning that she should wait till it got light. Confused, Nili narrowed her eyes. A thought occurred to her. She held up her fingers one by one and said, "Your books? How many books do you need? Do you need paper and pen?"

Although she hadn't understood him, Hadi Besharat nodded

happily. Nili said, "That's not a problem. I'll bring books, paper, and pen. I'll give them to Ahmad for you."

The wind took words away from her sentences and her voice reached him in separate pieces. But still he caught most of what she said. He put a hand to his chest and thanked her with a smile. He hooked his thumbs in the armholes of his vest, lifting his head as if preparing to whistle. Nili didn't understand. She stood on the sidewalk and stamped a heel helplessly on the ground. Hadi Besharat showed her a palm to calm her down. Someone out in the hall called, "Hadi Besharat! Where is Hadi Besharat?"

Somebody else answered, "Down the hall, in the middle classroom."

Hadi Besharat hurriedly closed the window and turned away from it. Then a key rattled and the door opened. A Revolutionary Guard stuck his head in. "Who is Hadi Besharat?"

Hadi Besharat looked around. He was the only person in the room. He didn't want to break his silence. The Revolutionary Guard asked, "Are you deaf? Can't you hear?"

Hadi Besharat still refused to answer. The Revolutionary Guard said, "Why don't you speak?"

Ahmad Bayat pushed the Revolutionary Guard aside and entered the room. This time he didn't have his raincoat on, but his boots were wet and muddy. He set both hands on his hips and told the Revolutionary Guard, "You can leave now. I'll be along in a minute."

The Revolutionary Guard disappeared. Hadi Besharat stood still and waited. Ahmad Bayat came close, sat on the edge of a desk, and said, "Professor Besharat, did you get any sleep?" He received no answer. He went on talking. "That incident last night was only a misunderstanding. These people mean no harm. They would love to hear your apology so they can release you."

Still Hadi Besharat didn't answer. Ahmad Bayat rose from the edge of the desk and came closer. "Don't you believe me? You have to believe me."

Hadi Besharat turned his head toward a corner of the classroom and spoke to an invisible person. "This gentleman insists that I believe him. He says the Revolutionary Guards have made a mistake and it's all a misunderstanding. What do you think? Should I believe him?"

Ahmad Bayat asked, "Who are you talking to?"

Hadi Besharat blinked and said, "I'm consulting a friend. I'm asking for his help."

"What friend?"

"Never mind what friend."

"Well, what is he saying?"

"He says it doesn't matter if I believe you. You have to believe yourself."

Ahmad Bayat spoke more gently. The softness made his voice seem unsure. "Let's go downstairs. We'll get something to eat."

Hadi Besharat put a hand in his pocket. He was searching for his Agilax powder but he couldn't find it. He took his umbrella from the windowsill and followed Ahmad Bayat out of the room. In the hall Ahmad Bayat turned to him and said, "The weather's getting warmer. You ought to start exercising. The more you run and the more you sweat, the easier the blood will reach your brain."

Hadi Besharat walked more quickly. With the arrival of spring, the road to Khezrabad would be open again. Perhaps he could find some means of transportation. Perhaps he could find a narrow road in the middle of nowhere and get himself to Khezrabad.

He felt he was traveling a grassless, waterless desert. He was consumed by the passion of the pilgrimage and, as the poet had put it, he didn't mind the desert thorns hurting his bare feet. For him, that precious night was brighter than a thousand moons. It caused the ground to swell and fall back again as if it were breathing. The angels kept descending until the break of dawn.

They went downstairs to the dining hall and took a seat at an empty table. The sun had not yet risen and Hadi Besharat couldn't see anything outside the windows. From somewhere he heard the metallic sound of silverware rattling together. No doubt breakfast was being prepared. He felt safe, reassured that the Revolutionary Guards weren't planning to do him in. They wanted only to stop him at the gate and show off their power like any other gatekeeper. Ahmad Bayat said casually, "Miss Farangu has brought you a package."

Hadi Besharat said, "Farangu? Is she here? Can I talk to her?"

"You can talk to her. But it has to be a very ordinary conversation. This is not the place to solve family disputes."

Hadi Besharat reached out a hand. "Where's the package, then?"

"I don't have it. She'll bring it to you herself."

Hadi Besharat rose halfway and looked around. Ahmad Bayat said, "These Revolutionary Guards have made a mistake, that's all. Don't you notice how much they respect you? Wherever you go, they stand up in your presence."

Hadi Besharat was about to walk off. But Ahmad Bayat grabbed his sleeve and said, "Other people who receive a package here have to claim it from a Guard. But I'm allowing Miss Farangu to give you your package personally."

Hadi Besharat placed his hand on his chest and thanked him with a smile. But he didn't sit back down. Ahmad Bayat said, "Don't you want to wait for your breakfast?"

"I want to see Farangu."

Ahmad Bayat sighed, but he stood up too. He said, "Very well. Let's go to the visitors' room."

They walked down the hall to a large room with all its windows boarded over. A long wooden table ran down the center and straight-backed chairs were lined up on either side. As soon as they opened the door Hadi Besharat saw Farangu preparing to enter through another door opposite. From where he stood it was hard to make out her face. She had wrapped herself in a black veil whose ironed folds covered her entire body. She was carrying a package tied with string.

Ahmad Bayat stayed by the door, but Hadi Besharat went over to sit on one of the chairs. He propped his umbrella at his feet. Watching Farangu approach, he felt weak and ill. She settled slowly on the chair across from him and laid the package on the table between them. She forced a smile and searched through her purse. Eventually she took out a handkerchief and dabbed the tip of her nose. She looked at Hadi Besharat as though she'd caught sight of him merely by chance.

The scene reminded Hadi Besharat of their first meeting. *Tosca* was playing at the Saadi Theater, and as soon as the curtain came down Hadi Besharat had gone backstage with a branch of ice flowers. Farangu had been sitting in front of the mirror in a green satin dress. The light glared on her makeup—on the black shadows around her eyes, the unnatural concentration of rouge on her cheeks, the red shining on her lips like some sort of shoe wax. Hadi Besharat had been completely overwhelmed by her presence. He had looked at her with nervous admiration and extended the ice-flower branch. She patted her tubular curls, wiped the extra powder off her face, and spoke to his reflection in the mirror. "Why are you standing there?"

Hadi Besharat extended the ice flowers closer and still said nothing. Then Farangu noticed the flowers and her face lit up with a smile. She turned quickly, cupped her hands beneath a blossom, and said, "Did you bring these for me?"

She accepted the flowers and stood up to kiss his cheek. Then she took a tissue from her dressing table and wiped the lipstick from his face. Hadi Besharat said, "I wanted to bring you something even better."

"What did you have in mind?"

"I've written a song. But it needs someone to compose the music for it."

"That's a shame. I wish I knew how myself."

Then the lights were dimmed for the curtain call. Farangu spun around, smoothed her satin dress, and tiptoed through the door.

But now that more than thirty years had passed, what did they have to say to each other? A strange feeling of annoyance filled his heart. After a few moments of indecision Farangu pulled her chair closer and said, "I have something for you. I came to give it to you."

She handed him a blue envelope. Hadi Besharat glanced first at the envelope and then at Farangu's face. He unsealed the flap of the envelope. Inside he found a reprint of an article by Professor Humphrey. Instantly he guessed that there must be a letter as well. He flung the reprint on the table without reading it and pulled out a sheet of white paper. As soon as he unfolded it he recognized Whitehurst College's official logo—a Sumerian cup that had probably been used in the sacrificial ceremonies in Lagash. The body of the cup showed two serpents twisted around two pillars, while lion-birds held staffs and guarded the serpents on both sides. He glanced at the handwriting. Professor Humphrey had written in haste, but the words were well spaced and evenly slanted.

January 29, 1983

Dear Hadi,

I have to apologize for being such a poor correspondent. I'm sending you a paper of mine on American tombstones that was published just recently in *Archeology Studies Review*. This is an offering, or shall we say a payment for my sins of omission during the past few years. I hope you'll accept it.

Today Nancy and I went to see the Vietnam War Memorial in Washington. The memory of your visits to Whitehurst College came back to me as we walked along that black granite wall. People were touching the names of the dead, leaving flowers and other mementos on the ground. The hubbub of the living made such a contrast to the silence of the dead. It seemed that we the living were speaking for the dead and the dead were reproaching us with their silence. But it's futile to try explaining it. All I can say is, I had just found the name of my poor Woolfy when I saw my own reflection on the wall. There I was, holding Nancy's hand in mine, looking at my poor Woolfy and fifty-eight thousand and God-knows-how-many others. Then I thought of your last visit to Whitehurst College— that evening we dined together and you quoted a poem of Rumi's. I can still hear your voice: "With the next fit, I'll die from being human. I'll grow angels' wings and feathers. Once again I'll soar above the angels and I'll become that which is beyond imagining."

Frankly, I have to confess that I didn't pay much attention to the meaning of that poem at the time. But there by the Vietnam War Memorial, I became aware that there's a certain relief in destruction, and that is what it's all about.

Although I'm not able to answer the questions you sometimes ask, your letters have been a necessary reminder and I want to thank you for that. I hope you'll find the time to write again. I'd be most grateful. Really!

Nancy and I send our greetings and our heartfelt warm wishes.

As always, your friend,
Rudolph P. Humphrey

Hadi Besharat felt stunned. Without intending to, he crumpled the letter in his hand. He leaned back in his chair and tilted his face upward, gazing at the ceiling. He was very happy to receive that letter. Happiness caused the blood to rush to his head. His heart was pounding with elation. He wanted to sit there a long time reviewing Professor Humphrey's words. He opened his fist and looked again at the crumpled sheet of paper.

Then he noticed the people around him. Ahmad Bayat was still standing next to the door and Farangu was watching him from the chair opposite. Hadi Besharat began to calm down. It was as if a storm were slowly losing its power and a sea breathed in darkness. He smiled at Farangu and indicated the letter with his eyes, meaning, "See there? Wasn't I right to have waited all this time for an answer?" Events were happening according to precise calculations, as in a mathematical equation. Only he couldn't understand why it had taken more than a month for a single-page letter to arrive from America. At any rate, here it was, crumpled in his fist. He smoothed it and replaced it carefully in the envelope. Whatever he'd believed about Whitehurst College had turned out to be the absolute truth. Everything was just as he'd predicted.

Farangu asked, "Besharat, what was in the letter?"

"Nothing."

"What do you mean, nothing? Why do you look as if you're running a fever? Are you running a fever?"

"I'm not running a fever."

"Why are you so pale, then?"

"It's because of my anemia."

"Shall I get you a drink of water?" She looked toward Ahmad Bayat. "He needs a drink of water."

"I don't want any water," Hadi Besharat said. But Ahmad Bayat had already turned to give the order to someone just outside the door.

Hadi Besharat got up and went over to Ahmad Bayat. He stood on tiptoe to whisper in his ear, "Will you let me take my wife upstairs?"

Ahmad Bayat didn't seem to understand. He looked at Hadi Besharat suspiciously and said, "If you want to go home, nobody's stopping you."

"Ahmad Agha, I want to show her my old classroom."

This was something Ahmad Bayat hadn't counted on. He said, "Will you be long?"

"Just a few minutes."

Ahmad Bayat considered a moment and then nodded. Hadi Besharat went back to Farangu. He said, "Right now I can see Hassan the wheel sitting in his shop. An army blanket hangs in front of his storage room and a straw mat covers the floor. He's on his stool behind the cash register. There's a leather notebook on the counter. When he collects his payments he enters them in that notebook, not in numbers but in words."

A Revolutionary Guard appeared at the door and handed Ahmad Bayat a bowl of water. Ahmad Bayat walked over and gave the bowl to Hadi Besharat. First Hadi Besharat made his eyelids droop in an expression of appreciation and then he said, "Greetings to St. Hosein's thirsty lips." He drank a few sips of water and set the bowl down on the table. "Let me tell you—"

Farangu screamed, "It's enough, Besharat! Let's go home now."

"But I want to show you something."

Ahmad Bayat asked, "Why do you insist on staying here? Take your package and go home."

Hadi Besharat picked up his umbrella, took the package from the table, and walked quietly to the door. But when he reached the hall he didn't go out the main entrance to the street. Instead he started up the stairs. Ahmad Bayat and Farangu were forced to follow him. Farangu said, "Besharat, where are you going?" but Hadi Besharat didn't say a word.

In the waiting area Yar Ommat was sitting at the reception desk. As soon as he saw Hadi Besharat he stood up and said, "Stop. What's in that package?"

Without looking at him, Hadi Besharat held out the package. Yar Ommat said, "You have to open it."

Hadi Besharat untied the string and opened the package in front of everyone. Inside were three sweet oranges, two ironed shirts, and his gray pajamas. Yar Ommat said, "The envelope too. I want to know what's in that."

Ahmad Bayat stepped forward and said, "There's no need to search Professor Besharat's envelope."

Ahmad Bayat retied the package himself, handed it back to Hadi Besharat, and motioned for him to proceed. Hadi Besharat bowed in obedience and limped on. When they reached the hall he turned and told Ahmad Bayat, "This imaginary friend of mine wants to thank you for last night's restful sleep."

"Professor, it's a shame that you kept yourself here like a prisoner."

Hadi Besharat shook his head silently.

Ahmad Bayat said, "I can remember so well. The martyr Mehrdad Razi was committed to nothing. All he knew how to do was drink arak and talk gibberish. But you made a man out of him. You taught him the meaning of sacrifice. The meaning of passionate conversation with death. How to sing an ode to martyrdom, how to open his arms to that rapturous promised moment, how to fly to the sky and make a birth out of death."

Hadi Besharat walked on down the hall without responding. When they reached his old classroom he stopped and motioned for Farangu to go in ahead of him. Then he closed the door in Ahmad Bayat's face. There was a moment of silence, after which they heard Ahmad Bayat's footsteps departing.

Farangu frowned. She was running out of patience. "Tell me why. What did you bring me here for?"

Hadi Besharat pointed to the walls and said, "Look. I used to lecture in this room."

"Why didn't you go to the doctor?"

"What doctor?"

"The Japanese doctor."

"I should go to the Japanese doctor for what?"

Farangu pulled her veil over her head. "I don't say you have a serious problem. It's just that you ought to take better care of yourself. I talked to the Japanese doctor. He said you do these things because of your unusual intelligence. He said you have a strong imagination. You see everything very vividly."

Farangu paused. Hadi Besharat said, "You talked about me to the Japanese doctor?"

"He said there's nothing wrong with you. Whatever you do is because of your high intelligence and your powerful imagination. He's right. Besharat, you are very intelligent and you have a powerful imagination. I'm sure the Japanese doctor will see you, and maybe it won't be necessary for me to act as go-between. He may say that I should leave you alone and not bother you. But at least I know there's nothing wrong with you. It's just that your thinking is unusually clear and powerful."

"Listen! Thirty years ago I lectured in this classroom. Listening to this room is like listening to a revelation. You feel like a prophet."

"You brought me here to be with you. But I can't be with you. You are somewhere else, listening to a revelation."

"Hearing a revelation makes a prophet out of you."

Farangu threw herself on a bench. She stared at the ceiling and moaned, "Oh, dear God."

Hadi Besharat turned to her and said, "You were supposed to go to America. Why didn't you go? What happened to your Sayid-jon?"

"How can I leave you in this condition and take off for America? Do you understand what I'm saying at all?"

"Why shouldn't I understand? I'm not deaf."

Hadi Besharat laid his belongings on a desk and went over to the window. Bright, pleasant sunlight spread everywhere. Heli and Nili were standing on the other side of the street beneath the window. Mr. Abolhassan Hashiyeh was waving his hand behind them. Hadi Besharat felt he was flying at a high altitude. In his mind the cluttered images were growing distant from each other. He wished he could hang his boots around his neck, the way Shah Abbas did when he went for a pilgrimage on foot. He could see the potato fields far, far away. The Allied warning leaflets were circling in the air like snowflakes and landing somewhere behind the avalanche that was blocking the road. He could hear the strains of "La Comparsita" and see the young Tehranians whirling around each other. The girls' skirts puffed in the air and the boys' faces were tipped back.

Down in the street Nili raised her arms and clapped her hands above her head. The sound was confident, measured and regular. As soon as Hadi Besharat opened the window Nili stopped clapping. She turned to Heli and the two of them said something to each other, their mouths moving simultaneously. He remembered the article about the Nehashbat Angel. He ought to finish that chapter discussing the roots of the word "angel." Of course its Sanskrit root was *angriras,* which was changed in Parthian to *angaras* and then to *angireh.* This last version in turn became *angelo,* a word used in almost the same form today in many European languages.

Instead of answering, Hadi Besharat stood up and retrieved his umbrella from the desk. Suddenly the door burst open. Ahmad Bayat entered the room, followed by Haj Ghadam the Koran reciter. Ahmad Bayat asked, "Did you call?"

Hadi Besharat shook his umbrella in Ahmad Bayat's face. "Agha, I want to leave. You can't force me to stay here forever."

He saw Haj Ghadam smiling at him, offering his greetings. Hadi Besharat responded with a small bow. He asked Ahmad Bayat, "Agha, am I free to leave?"

Ahmad Bayat seemed confused. He looked over at Haj Ghadam. Haj Ghadam put his hands inside his wide sleeves and spoke in a reassuring tone. "The road to the front is open to everyone. You can go there like anyone else and no one will stop you."

Farangu asked, "The front? Who's going to the front?"

Hadi Besharat didn't answer. He gave another quick bow to Haj Ghadam and started toward the door. His shoe swung from one hand and his umbrella swung from the other. To ease the pain, he walked down the hall without bending his left ankle. He heard Farangu scurrying after him, and then he heard the footsteps of Ahmad Bayat and Haj Ghadam. Ahmad Bayat called, "Professor, why go barefoot? It's still too cold for that."

Hadi Besharat stopped and turned. He pointed a thumb toward Farangu. "I break ice in the dead of winter and swim in our pool."

Farangu smoothed his coat around his shoulders and pulled at his sleeves until they were straight. She said, "Put your shoe on, Besharat, and then we'll go home."

Hadi Besharat sat down on a bench next to the wall and took his other shoe off. Then he took off his socks as well. He tied the laces of his shoes together. Standing barefoot in the middle of the hall with his shoes slung around his neck, he declared to Farangu, "I'm ready."

Happy and full of enthusiasm, Haj Ghadam wrote in the air with his finger:

The Lord Is the Key, All-Knowing.

He saw the two sisters take hold of each other's hands. Behind them Mr. Hashiyeh removed his glasses and put a palm to his forehead, absorbed in his own thoughts. Hadi Besharat was reminded of the satisfied, receptive face of Adam, lowering his lids in Michelangelo's painting; or the sad solitude of Isis, pressing Horus to her bosom with closed eyes. Everything was a reflection of the moment's eternal flow. It meant that now is always. The motion of time, the motion of the stillness was like a deep vacuum that would never increase or decrease. It had a form and yet it was formless. It was shining through the seams of the day like a thousand bright suns. It was like a thousand carefree pigeons in whose soaring there was silence and yet also speech.

He leaned farther out the window and took a deep breath. The morning air touched his face, melting like a very thin sheet of ice. He motioned for the two sisters to stop worrying about him and leave. But they tucked their veils behind their knees and squatted on the sidewalk. Hadi Besharat closed the window, went over to Farangu, and asked her, "How would you like to spend the New Year holidays in Khezrabad?"

Farangu said, "Let's go home first. Then we'll think about Khezrabad." She sighed. "We haven't done anything about Khosro's troubles."

Hadi Besharat sat on a bench and read Professor Humphrey's letter one more time. Then he put it back in the envelope and slid it into his pocket. He got up, went limping to the door, and opened it. No one was in the hall. "Agha!" he called, and then he closed the door again and walked back over to where Farangu sat watching him. His ankle was paining him considerably now. Maybe he should take his shoe off. He wanted to be able to leave as quickly as possible.

He felt his forehead with his hand and decided he was running a fever. But it wasn't important. He heard the clump, clump of footsteps in the hall, drawing closer to the room. He sat down on the bench next to Farangu and untied his shoe and took it off. Farangu said, "Besharat, what's wrong with your foot?"

Ahmad Bayat asked, "Professor, are you going home bare-foot?"

Hadi Besharat lifted his chin and said, "What's wrong with that? Haven't you ever walked barefoot?"

This time Haj Ghadam wrote in the air:
He Is the Living.

Hadi Besharat was no longer thinking of himself. Distant, unintelligible music came to him. It was like a new movement for that old private symphony, a movement he had never heard before. The dingdong of a bell dragged through space like an iron chain. The metallic, stony sounds kept falling into the deep, one after another. With their descent a whirlpool appeared in the ocean. He couldn't feel the turmoil in the constant swirl of sounds. He could only imagine the blades of a windmill, slicing the air and separating the light from the darkness. With the passing of the wind, the ruffled skirt of a gypsy girl spun on top of the hill.

Hadi Besharat limped barefoot through the waiting area, down the stairs, and out the front door.

Mr. Hashiyeh addressed all present. "He shouldn't walk around with those bare feet."

Across the street Nili was holding Heli's hand and looking at him with a happy smile. She wore that poor boy's military fatigues beneath her veil, and she'd strapped his knapsack to her back. Hadi Besharat imagined the poor boy standing there, sharpening his pencil with a pocketknife. He had his usual indifferent, witty smile, as though pretending that his mind was elsewhere. But he watched everything with cunning eyes. It was as if he wanted to tease them and play one of his old tricks.

Hadi Besharat asked Farangu, "Where is Engineer Gharib? Everybody else seems to be here."

"Didn't you know?"

"Know what?"

"Keep it to yourself. They brought the news that his son Kyumars had an accident in the street and broke his leg."

Hadi Besharat was taken aback. Was she telling him the truth?

Was it really only his leg that was broken? He stood there, wanting to say something. But he only passed the tip of his tongue over his lips. The wind wrapped Nili's veil tightly around her body and fluttered the tail end of it behind her. Hadi Besharat began walking again. Farangu came along, muttering beneath her breath. "Don't make yourself miserable. I'm right here."

Hadi Besharat felt the icy pavement against his bare soles. The blood began to rush through his veins. Nili resumed clapping. "Professor, run! Run and don't mind anything!"

Hadi Besharat walked faster. Nili's clapping increased its tempo. Farangu was having trouble keeping abreast of him now. He heard Ahmad Bayat's voice from far back. "Professor, be careful, a little slower . . ."

Despite the pain in his ankle he increased his speed. He felt in the depths of his heart a sort of innocent happiness that he had all but forgotten. He limped and he ran. He could see Farangu's breath drifting across his face and disappearing behind them like thread from a bobbin. The silk curtains of light, the wrapped spirits of the morning, whirled in the air and settled on the avenue and became absorbed by the buildings' walls as lightly as an angel's breath. Hadi Besharat thought the bygone years were passing rapidly over the walls, over the graffiti and the posters. He could lie down by the stream next to Khezrabad's water mill under the old plane tree. Fakhr Zanjani would come for two weeks' vacation and talk with his father in front of the passion-play theater. The passion players would stream toward Khezrabad with their helmets, their chain mail and silver shields, like the ghosts of Phoenician sailors. Haj Ghadam drew his finger through empty space and wrote:

He Is the Living.
He Is the Dead.

In rhythm with the applause of the passersby on the avenue, the butterflies of Hadi Besharat's imagination began to flutter, reflecting and repeating in themselves the images of the sea. He was listening to a Syriac ode, or perhaps it was Coptic or Soghdian. He thought of Xerxes, his naval and ground forces. He thought of a crowd of soldiers approaching him barefoot. He thought of antiaircraft guns and the soldiers sitting behind them, pivoting to follow the enemy bombers. He thought of a military commander bringing down his hand in a sharp sweep. The gunner pulling the lever with a snapping sound and the gun bursting into grumbles. He thought of burned landscapes with broken walls. He thought of Khezrabad's fields growing brown beneath the drizzling sky. And he ran. He thought of the Angel of Time with her cape on her shoulders. With one foot on the ground and one foot in the water, she walked the banks of Khezrabad's river. She was ascending above the tumbling rapids, rising in the wastes of space, and Hadi Besharat kept running. He recognized the Angel of Time by the shining circlet on her forehead—the circle that spun eternally, without beginning or end. Like life, it was everywhere, and it was nowhere.

ABOUT THE AUTHOR

Born and educated in Teheran, *Taghi Modarressi* is a member of the faculty of the Department of Psychiatry of the University of Maryland School of Medicine, where he is Director of the Center for Infant Study. He lives in Baltimore with his wife, novelist Anne Tyler, and their two daughters.